Cursed with a poor sense of direction and a propensity to read, **Annie Claydon** spent much of her childhood lost in books. A degree in English Literature followed by a career in computing didn't lead directly to her perfect job—writing romance for Mills & Boon—but she has no regrets in taking the scenic route. She lives in London: a city where getting lost can be a joy.

Born and raised on the Wirral Peninsula in England, **Charlotte Hawkes** is mum to two intrepid boys, who love her to play building block games with them and who object loudly to the amount of time she spends on the computer. When she isn't writing—or building with blocks—she is company director for a small Anglo/French construction firm. Charlotte loves to hear from readers, and you can contact her at her website: charlotte-hawkes.com.

Also by Annie Claydon

Firefighter's Christmas Baby
Resisting Her English Doc
Festive Fling with the Single Dad

London Heroes miniseries

Falling for Her Italian Billionaire
Second Chance with the Single Mum

Also by Charlotte Hawkes

A Bride to Redeem Him
The Surgeon's One-Night Baby
Christmas with Her Bodyguard
A Surgeon for the Single Mum
The Army Doc's Baby Secret
Unwrapping the Neurosurgeon's Heart

Discover more at millsandboon.co.uk.

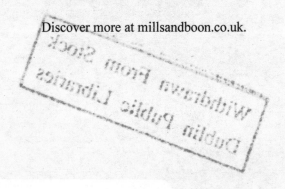

BEST FRIEND TO ROYAL BRIDE

ANNIE CLAYDON

SURPRISE BABY FOR THE BILLIONAIRE

CHARLOTTE HAWKES

MILLS & BOON

First Published in Great Britain 2020
by Mills & Boon, an imprint of HarperCollins*Publishers*
1 London Bridge Street, London, SE1 9GF

Best Friend to Royal Bride © 2020 by Annie Claydon

Surprise Baby for the Billionaire © 2020 by Charlotte Hawkes

ISBN: 978-0-263-27960-3

MIX
Paper from
responsible sources
FSC® C007454

This book is produced from independently certified FSC™ paper
to ensure responsible forest management.
For more information visit www.harpercollins.co.uk/green.

Printed and bound in Spain
by CPI, Barcelona

BEST FRIEND
TO ROYAL BRIDE

ANNIE CLAYDON

MILLS & BOON

CHAPTER ONE

The first Friday in February

THE EVENING OF the first Friday in February had been marked out as *'busy'* in Marie's calendar for the last twelve years. As she looked around the table, stacked with food and wine, twelve people all talking at once, she could only hope that it would be booked for the next twelve years.

During her final year at medical school there had been one class that was special. A tight-knit group who had laughed together and shared the ups and downs of their studies. Since then they'd graduated and gone their separate ways, but one evening every year still belonged to them.

Sunita was passing her phone around so that everyone could see the pictures of her new baby. Will was just back from America, and Rae had stories to tell about Africa. Nate was having relationship problems, and was talking intently to David, who was nodding thoughtfully. When she got the chance, Marie would change seats and offer what support she could.

And Alex…

Marie didn't like to admit it, but she looked forward to seeing him the most. He had been the golden boy of the class, managing to combine a carefree love of life and a wicked sense of fun with academic brilliance. He and

Marie had struck up an especially close friendship and, in truth, if you were looking for anything long-term with Alex, then friendship was the way to go. He was seldom without a girlfriend, but those relationships never lasted very long.

Tonight he looked as if he had things on his mind. He'd flipped through Sunita's photographs, grinning and saying all the right things, but when he'd passed the phone on he'd gone back to playing with his food and staring abstractedly into space.

Marie leaned over, feeling the softness of his cashmere sweater as she brushed her fingers against his arm to get his attention. 'What's going on, Alex?'

'I'm…coasting at the moment. One hand on the driving wheel with the wind in my hair.' He shrugged, smiling suddenly. Those long-lashed grey eyes were still the same, and so was his mop of dark hair, shorter now but still as thick.

The memory was as fresh as if it had been yesterday. Alex pulling up outside her student digs, the soft top of his car pulled back, saying he just wanted to feel the warm breeze on his face and would Marie like to keep him company? It was a world away from the worries that seemed to be lingering behind his smile now.

'And you're still moving mountains?'

Marie laughed. 'I'm still shovelling, if that's what you mean.'

'Moving mountains one shovelful at a time. That's your speciality.'

He made it sound like a good thing. Something that was fine and virtuous, and not just a fact of life. Her life, anyway.

Alex had never had to worry about money, and had received a generous allowance from his family. Marie had gone to medical school knowing that her family needed her help rather than the other way around. Hand to mouth, taking each day as it came. Mostly she'd had enough to eat and cover her rent, but sometimes it had been a struggle. She'd made it through, one shovelful at a time.

On the other side of the restaurant a waiter was bringing a cake, flaming with candles, to a table of six young women. He started to sing 'Happy Birthday' and the tune was taken up around all the tables. Alex was watching, singing quietly, and Marie wondered whether he had any wishes tonight.

The birthday girl stood up, leaning over the cake. And suddenly Alex was moving, ducking adroitly past a couple of waiters and making his way towards her. It wasn't until Marie was on her feet that she saw what the matter was. The girl was waving her arm, which only fanned the flames licking at her sleeve.

Stop, drop and roll. She hadn't done the first, and it looked as if she wasn't going to do the second or the third either. Alex reached her just as she started to panic, grabbing her arm and deftly catching up a pitcher of water from the table.

Suddenly the restaurant was deathly quiet, the girl's keening sobs the only sound. Alex had his arm tightly around her and he flashed Marie a glance, to check that she would stay with the other young women at the table, before hurrying their injured friend towards the ladies' restroom.

'Where are they going? We'll go with her…'

One of the party rose from her seat and Marie motioned to her to sit down again. She knew Alex had this under control, and if he'd needed any help he would have left no one in any doubt about what he wanted them to do.

'It's okay, we're doctors. The burn should be cooled straight away and that's what my colleague has gone to do. It's best that we stay here.'

Alex would be checking for signs of shock, and being surrounded by people wasn't going to help.

'But…is she going to be all right? She was on fire…' Another of the friends spoke up.

Things could have been a lot worse. It had looked as if her blouse was cotton, not a man-made fabric, and the flames had spread relatively slowly. If Alex hadn't acted so quickly precious minutes would have been lost…

'The fire was extinguished very quickly. I'll go and check on her.'

Marie turned towards her own table, where everyone was watchful but still in their seats, trusting that Marie or Alex would call them if they were needed. She beckoned to Sunita, who rose from her seat, weaving her way past the tables towards them, and asked her to stay with the group of friends.

A waiter was standing outside the restroom and let Marie through. Inside, Alex had sat the young woman by a basin and was gently supporting her arm under a stream of lukewarm water. He was smiling, his voice gentle and relaxed as he chatted to her quietly.

'How many candles on that cake, Laura?'

'Eighteen. It's my eighteenth birthday tomorrow. I'm having a party.' Laura turned the corners of her mouth down.

'You'll be fine. This is a first-degree burn, which is the least severe. It's going to hurt for a little while, but it won't leave a scar. You're going to have a great birthday.' He glanced up at Marie. 'This is my friend, Marie. She's a doctor too, so she can't help poking her nose in and making sure I'm doing everything right.'

Alex shot her a delicious smile, the kind that reminded Marie of when they'd been young doctors together in A&E. Laura turned towards Marie, and Alex steadied her arm under the water.

'He's doing pretty well.'

'Glad to hear it. What about you? How are you doing?'

'I'm all right. Where is everyone? Are they eating my cake?'

'They sent me to find out how you were. They're not eating the cake.'

Alex had done a great job of keeping Laura calm if her main concern was cake.

'That's a relief,' Alex broke in. 'Laura's promised me a slice. Not for another ten minutes, though. We need to keep cooling the burn. Then I think we'll send you off home, with a list of instructions.'

'Oh, you're going to write a list of *instructions*?' Marie grinned conspiratorially at Laura. 'Watch out for those.'

Alex chuckled. 'First on the list is to have a very happy birthday…'

Things might have been so different. Laura's eighteenth birthday could have been spent in a burns unit, with a prognosis of skin grafts and a great deal of pain. But she was going home with her friends, a little wet from the pitcher of water that Alex had poured on her arm to extinguish the flames, and with a couple of miraculously minor burns. Whatever future she wanted for herself was still waiting for her.

Alex spent another half an hour making sure she was all right, and advising her on how to care for the burns. Sunita had persuaded Laura's friends to come over and sit with her, and the cake was being divided into portions and wrapped. The low hum of chatter in the restaurant indicated that the incident was already largely forgotten, cleared away along with the debris from Laura's table.

Alex had gone outside to see Laura and her friends into a taxi, and Marie saw him turn, leaning back against the railings that separated the pavement from the front of the restaurant, staring up at the scrap of sky that showed between the tops of the buildings. It appeared that his easy, relaxed air had been all for Laura's sake.

Whatever the last year of medical school had thrown at them, Alex had always bounced back, but now he seemed brooding, almost heartbroken. There was definitely something wrong.

Maybe she could help. Maybe he'd stayed outside hoping she'd join him. It wouldn't be the first time they'd confided in each other, and Marie had always wanted him to feel he could talk to her about anything.

She picked up Alex's jacket from the back of his chair and slipped away from the table.

Alex had been looking forward to seeing Marie again. He'd wondered whether he should confide in her, and now that he'd sent Laura safely on her way the yearning to do so reasserted itself. He knew he wouldn't, though. Marie normally understood everything, but she wouldn't be able to understand how difficult the last few months had been. She'd struggled for everything she had, and it felt somehow wrong to confide his pain and dismay at finding he had much more than enough of everything.

'Aren't you cold?'

When he heard her voice it didn't come as much of a surprise. Maybe that was what he was doing out here, shivering under the street lamps: waiting for Marie to come and find him.

'Not really.' He took his jacket from her, wrapping it around her shoulders. The pleasure he got from the gesture seemed way out of proportion to its true worth.

'That was a bit like old times.'

She turned her gaze on him and suddenly it felt a lot like old times.

'Yes. I'm glad Laura's okay.'

'She has you to thank for that. So, since we seem to be

out here, and your jacket's nice and warm…' Marie gave him an impish smile. 'You can tell me what the matter is.'

It was tempting. Alex had never been able to resist her eyes. Almost violet in the sunlight and deep blue in the shade. She wore her dark hair in a shining pixie cut, and Alex always thought of mischief and magic when he looked at her.

'I'm fine…just tired. You remember tired?' He smiled at her.

She chuckled. 'Remember that time you came round to my place and I'd been up all night working on abstracts?'

'I've never seen anyone actually fall asleep *while* they're drinking coffee before. Particularly since I'd made it so strong…'

Marie had got a job writing abstracts for scientific papers, which had been more lucrative than waitressing and had fitted around their busy study schedule better. Working and studying at the same time had been a struggle for her, but Alex had learned early in their friendship that she never took help from anyone.

Suddenly he was back in that time when he'd first felt completely free. Marie's two shabby rooms, right at the top of a multiple-occupancy house, had been as clean as one pair of hands could scrub them, and full of outrageous low-cost colour.

'Funny thing about that…' Marie gave him a knowing look. 'When I woke up you were gone, but I sat down to review my abstracts and found they were all perfect. Not a spelling or grammar mistake in any of them.'

Alex had reckoned he'd got away with that. He'd tried to make Marie stand up but she'd slumped against him, still asleep, so he'd had to practically carry her into the bedroom. He'd taken off her cardigan and shoes and decided to stop there, covering her up with the brightly patterned quilt. He'd sometimes imagined their two bodies naked together under that quilt. But Marie was far too good a friend, too good a person, to contemplate having a throwaway romance with her.

Alex had glanced at the document that was open on her laptop, meaning to close it down. He'd seen a mistake in the text, and had sat down and worked through everything, correcting the slips that fatigue had forced upon her.

'You must do your best work when you're flying on autopilot.' He tried to maintain a straight face.

'I suppose I must. Apparently I also spell synthesise with a *z*.'

'Really? There must be a study in there somewhere. How fatigue alters your spelling choices.' Alex shrugged guiltily. 'They're both correct, according the dictionary.'

'Yes, they are. Although I imagine that "ize" as a verb ending is considered either an anachronism or an American spelling these days.' She smirked at him.

'You can mock if you want. Just because I went to a school that prided itself on having been the same for the last few hundred years...' Alex had hated school. It had been only slightly less snobby and suffocating than his parents' home.

'I'm not mocking; I thought it was very sweet of you.' She took a step towards him. 'Along with all those expensive textbooks you used to lend me. And dropping round to pick me up so I didn't have to take the bus.'

'Why bring that up all of a sudden? Just to let me know I'm not as tactful as I thought I was?' Alex wondered if he was in for a lecture about how she could have managed perfectly well on her own.

Marie shook her head. 'You were *very* tactful. I hardly even noticed what you were doing most of the time. And you were my friend and you helped me. That's something that goes both ways.'

He knew that. But he couldn't talk to Marie about this. 'I'm fine. Really. And I appreciate your concern.'

'Just as long as you know that I'm always here for you.'

She reached out, touching his arm, and Alex almost flinched. All his senses were crying out for comfort, and yet he just couldn't bring himself to ask. Was this the way she'd felt, despite all her self-sufficiency?

'I know. Thank you.'

He'd meant to give her a basic friendly hug, the kind he'd given her so many times before. But when he felt her body against his he couldn't let her go. Marie seemed to be the one thing in his life that wasn't tainted right now.

He leaned down to kiss her cheek. But she turned her head and his lips brushed hers. Before he could tear himself away her gaze met his, her eyes midnight-blue in the darkness.

What if…?

What if…?

What if he could turn his back on the vision of his parents' unhappy marriage and sustain a relationship for more than a few months? What if he could trust himself to get involved with the one person he cared about the most, even knowing he might break her heart and his? And what if everything he'd sought to escape hadn't just caught him again in its iron clutches?

They were all serious questions that needed to be asked and answered before he took the step of kissing her. But then he felt her lips touch his and he was lost. Or maybe this was exactly what it was like to find himself. Alex wasn't sure.

She was soft and sweet, and when he kissed her again she responded. Maybe it lasted a moment and maybe an hour. All Alex knew was that it was impossible to attach a time frame to something that was complete and perfect.

Even the way she drew away from him was perfect. A little sigh of regret, her eyes masked by her eyelashes.

He'd always supposed that kissing Marie was the one thing he mustn't do. The one thing he wouldn't be able to come back from. But in a sudden moment of clarity he realised that kissing her had only made him more determined that he couldn't do it. Marie wasn't just another pretty face he could walk away from without looking back. She was his friend, and he wanted her for a lifetime, not just a few months.

'Do you want to go back in?' If it meant keeping her then he had to let her go.

She still wouldn't look at him. 'Yes…'

He felt her move in his arms and let her go. Marie looked up at him for a moment, and he almost forgot that this had been a very bad idea that had the power to spoil something that had been good for years. Then suddenly she was gone, back into the restaurant to take her seat at the table again.

Alex waited, knowing the group always swapped places between courses, so everyone got to speak to everyone else. When he went back inside there was a free seat for him at the other end of the table from Marie. Alex sat down without looking at her, and was immediately involved in the heated debate about football which was going on between Emily and Will.

She didn't meet his gaze until the restaurant closed and a waitress pointedly fetched everyone's coats. Then, suddenly, he found himself standing next to her. He automatically helped her on with her coat and Marie smiled up at him.

'I'll see you next year. Be well, Alex.'

'Yes. Next year…'

He'd scarcely got the words out before she was gone. Marie had made her meaning clear. They were friends, and nothing was going to spoil that. Not fire, nor flood, nor even an amazing, heart-shaking kiss. By next year it would be forgotten, and he and Marie would continue the way they always had.

The thought that he wouldn't see her again until next February seemed more heart-rending than any of the other challenges he'd faced in the last six months.

CHAPTER TWO

The first Friday in May

IT WAS ONLY four stops on the Tube from the central London hospital where Marie worked, but shining architecture and trendy bars had given way to high-rise flats, corner shops and families with every kind of problem imaginable.

Marie knew about some of those problems first-hand. She'd grown up fifteen minutes' walk away from the address that Alex had given her. Her father had left when she was ten, and her mother had retreated into a world of her own. Four miserable months in foster care had seen Marie separated from her three younger brothers, and when the family had got back together again she'd resolved that she'd keep it that way.

It had cost Marie her childhood. Looking after her brothers while her mother had worked long hours to keep them afloat financially. She'd learned how to shop and cook, and at the weekends she'd helped out by taking her brothers to the park, reading her schoolbooks while they played.

It had been hard. And lonely. After she'd left home she'd had a few relationships, but knowing exactly what it meant to be abandoned had made her cautious. She'd never found the kind of love that struck like a bolt of lightning, dispelling all doubts and fears, and the continuing need to look after her family didn't give her too much time for regrets.

When she reached the Victorian building it looked just as ominous as she remembered it, its bricks stained with grime and three floors towering above her like a dark shadow in the evening sunshine. The high cast-iron gates creaked as Marie pulled them open, leaving flakes of paint on her hands.

'This had better not be a joke…'

It wasn't a joke. Alex's practical jokes were usually a lot more imaginative than this. And when he'd called her it had sounded important. He'd made a coded reference to their kiss, saying that he wanted her to come as a professional favour to a friend, which told Marie that he'd done exactly as she'd hoped and moved past it. That was both a relief and a disappointment.

She pushed the thought of his touch to the back of her mind and made her way across the cracked asphalt in front of the building. There was a notice taped to the main door that advertised that this was the 'Living Well Clinic'. Marie made a face at the incongruous nature of the name and pressed the buzzer, wondering if it was going to work.

The door creaked open almost immediately.

'Hi. Thanks so much for coming.' Alex was looking unusually tense.

'My pleasure. What's all this about, Alex?'

'Come and see.' He stood back from the doorway and Marie stepped inside, trying not to flinch as the door banged shut behind them.

'Oh! This is a bit different from how I remember it.'

At the other end of the small lobby was an arch, which had been sandblasted back to the original brick, its colour and texture contrasting with the two glass doors that now filled the arch. As Marie approached them they swished back, allowing her into a large bright reception space, which had once been dingy cloakrooms.

And it wasn't finished yet. Cabling hung from the ceiling and the walls had obviously been re-plastered recently, with dark spots showing where they were still drying out. One of the curved-top windows had been replaced, and the many layers of paint on the others had been sanded back, leaving the space ready for new decoration.

'You know this place?'

'Yes, I went to school here.'

'Did you?' He grinned awkwardly. 'I wish I'd known. I would have looked for your name carved on one of the desks.'

'You wouldn't have found it.'

'Too busy studying?'

'Something like that.'

Leaving her name in this place might have signified that she would look back on her schooldays with a measure of nostalgia, when they'd been no more than a means to an end. They'd been something she'd had to do so she could move on and leave them behind. Just like she'd left that kiss behind. The one she couldn't stop thinking about…

'What's going on, Alex? Are you working here now or is this something you're involved with in your spare time?'

'I don't have spare time any more. I'm here full-time; I gave up working with the practice.'

Alex had always said he'd do something like this, and now he'd actually done it. The next logical step from his job as a GP in a leafy London suburb would have been to go into private practice, and Alex had the contacts and the reputation to make the transition easy. But he'd given all that up to come and work here, in a community where his expertise was most sorely needed.

'And you'll be seeing patients here?'

'As soon as we don't have to supply them with hard

hats.' He bent, picking up two safety helmets and handing her one. 'Come and see what's been going on.'

As he showed her around, the scale of the project became obvious. Some of the classrooms had been divided into two to make treatment rooms, with high ceilings and plenty of light from the arched windows. A state-of-the-art exercise suite was planned for the ground floor, which would be staffed by physiotherapists and personal trainers, and the old school hall was being converted into a coffee shop and communal area. Upstairs there was provision for dieticians and other health advisors, along with a counselling suite and rooms for self-help groups of all kinds.

'We'll have facilities for DEXA scanning in here...' He opened the door of one of the old science labs, which had now been reduced to a shell. 'Along with other diagnostic equipment. There's a space for the mobile breast-screening unit to park at the side of the building, and when the clinic's finished it'll be part of its regular route. We'll be able to undertake general health screening as well.'

'It's wonderful, Alex. Everything under one roof.'

The project was ambitious and imaginative, and would be of huge benefit to the local community.

'That's the idea. It's a kind of one-stop shop, and although it'll cater for complex medical needs it's also going to be for people who just want a healthier lifestyle.'

'What's going to happen with the courtyards?'

They were walking along a corridor that looked out onto one of the two central light wells. They were one of the few things that remained unchanged, and the dingy concrete floors were a reminder of what this place had once been like.

Alex shrugged. 'There are no plans for them just yet. Some planting might be nice.'

'And what about the old gym?' The annexe at the back

of the school was enormous, and it seemed a waste not to use it for something.

'We made a discovery. Come and see.'

He led the way to the large double doors that opened onto the gym and Marie gasped. The folding seats had been taken out and light from windows on three sides flooded into the space. Instead of sprung wooden floors there was a large concrete-sided hole.

'That's not...not a swimming pool, is it?'

He nodded. 'When we looked at the plans we found that this annexe was built in the nineteen-thirties as a full-sized swimming pool. Later on it was made into a gym, but when we took up the floors we found that the pool had just been filled in with hardcore and the foundations were still there and solid enough to use. There's room for a hydrotherapy pool, as well as the main pool.'

Alex seemed less excited about this than he should be. Maybe he was about to tell her that they'd run out of money, or had found some catastrophic problem with the building's structure and it was all about to fall down.

'This is marvellous. Are the pool and gym just for patients or are they available to the whole community?'

'There'll be a nominal charge, well below the usual rates. Anyone who's referred by a doctor or one of the medical staff here won't have to pay anything.' Alex was suddenly still, looking at her thoughtfully. 'What about you? Would you be interested in being part of it all?'

That sounded a bit like the stuff that fairy tales were made of. A gloomy old castle brought to life and transformed. Alex would fit in there quite nicely as the handsome Prince. But something about the quiet certainty in his manner stopped Marie from brushing the suggestion off.

'You'd put in a good word with the boss for me?'

'It's more a matter of putting a good word in with you. We'd be lucky to get you.'

Excitement trickled down Marie's spine. This was real. In that case, Marie needed to ask a few real questions.

'What exactly is your role here, Alex?'

He frowned, as if that might be a problem. 'It's rather a long story… Why don't you come to my office and we'll have some coffee?'

Marie followed him to a small suite of offices situated at the front of the building, off the main reception area. From here it would be possible to see all the comings and goings, and Marie guessed that Alex would have had a hand in the location of his office. He always liked to be in the thick of things.

His office was one of the few rooms in the building that was finished, but it didn't seem much like the kind of place the Alex she remembered would like. The cream walls and tall windows lent themselves to minimalism, but Alex didn't.

'How long have you been here, Alex?'

'A couple of months.' He looked around at the sleek wooden desk that stood at one end of the room and the comfortable easy chairs grouped around a coffee table at the other end. 'Why?'

Alex had been here for two months? And he hadn't yet covered the walls with pictures and stamped his own personality on the space? That wasn't like him at all. Perhaps the clinic had some kind of rule about that.

'It just seems a bit…unlived-in.' Marie looked around for something, anything, to comment on, instead of asking whether all that light and clear space hurt his eyes. She nodded towards the stylish chair behind his desk. 'I like your chair.'

'I reckoned I'd be sitting in it for enough hours, so I wanted something that was comfortable. Give it a try.'

He walked over to the wood-framed cupboards that

lined one wall, opening one of the doors to reveal a coffee machine and a small sink unit.

The chair was great—comfortable and supportive—and when Marie leaned back the backrest tipped gently with her movement. She started to work her way around all the levers and knobs under the seat.

'I love this. It's got more controls than my first car.'

She got to her feet as Alex brought the coffee and he motioned her to sit again, smiling as if it hurt his face to do so.

'You've missed a few of the adjustments. The knob on the left lets you tip the seat forward.' He sat down in one of the chairs on the other side of the desk.

'Oh!' Marie tried it, almost skinning her knuckles on the stiff lever. 'Nice one. I'm glad to see the clinic practises what it preaches and looks after its staff.'

She was just talking. Saying things that might fill the space between them and hoping to provoke a reaction. She'd never seen Alex look so worried before.

Not worried…

Burdened.

It was time to grasp the nettle and find out what was going on. She leaned forward, putting her elbows on the desk as if she were about to interview him. 'So what's the story then, Alex? I'm intrigued, so start right at the beginning.'

He paused, staring into his mug, as if that would tell him exactly where the beginning was.

'A hundred and ten years ago…'

'What? Really?'

He gave her a strained smile and Marie regretted the interruption. Whatever had happened a hundred and ten years ago must be more important than it sounded.

'You said start at the beginning.'

'I did. Sorry…' She waved him on and there was silence for a moment. Then he spoke again.

'A hundred and ten years ago the King of Belkraine was deposed and his family fled to London. They brought with them a lot of very valuable jewels, the title deeds to property in this country, and what was literally a king's ransom in investments. His eldest son was my grandfather.'

Marie stared at him.

She'd thought that she and Alex had shared most of their secrets over the years but he'd obviously been holding back. Marie wasn't entirely sure how she felt about that.

'So you're…a prince?'

He gave her a pained look. 'Belkraine no longer exists as a separate country. I'm not sure how you can be a prince of something that doesn't exist.'

He was missing the point. The role of many monarchies had changed in the last hundred years, but privilege and money was something that didn't change.

'A prince in exile, then?'

'Strictly speaking a king…in exile. My father died in June last year.'

'Alex, I'm so sorry.'

'Thank you. But it's… We'd been estranged for some years. Ever since I first went to medical school.'

'But—'

Marie bit her tongue. He'd never spoken much about his family, but she knew that he was an only child and that his parents lived in a big house in the country somewhere. There hadn't ever been any mention of an estrangement, and Marie had always assumed he came from a normal happy family.

Now wasn't the time to mention that this was what Alex had allowed everyone to believe. He had no chance to make things right with his father now.

'That must have hurt you a great deal.'

He shrugged. 'That door closed a long time ago. I came to terms with it.'

There were too many questions, piling up on top of each other like grains of sand in an hourglass. What was Alex doing here? Why had he never said anything about this before?

Maybe she should just stay silent and listen.

Alex glanced at her uncertainly and Marie motioned for him to keep talking.

'I didn't expect that my father would leave me anything, let alone his whole estate. But he did. I find that I have more money than I know what to do with.'

'How much...?'

It wasn't good manners to ask, but money had never bothered Alex all that much. If this was a life-changing amount, then that was both good news and bad. Good, because he could do the things he'd always wanted to. Bad, because he seemed so burdened by it.

'If you include all the assets and property then it runs into something more than two billion. Less than three.'

She stared at him. That was the kind of number that Marie would never get her head around, so it was probably better not to even try.

'And this... *You've* done all this?' She waved her finger in a wild circle.

'My ancestors viewed wealth as a way to gain power and more wealth. I want to spend the money a little more wisely than that.'

It was worthy. Altruistic. Right now it was about all she recognised of the Alex that she knew. The smiling, carefree soul who was in the habit of taking one day at a time had gone.

'Wait a minute...' A thought struck her. Had Alex been hiding all this in plain sight? 'Alex *King*?'

'Dr Alex King is who I really am. But my birth certificate says Rudolf Aloysius Alexander König.'

Suddenly she couldn't bear it. She hadn't even known his *name*? The man she'd thought of as her friend, whom she'd dared to kiss and had loved every minute of it…

Marie sprang from her seat, marching over to the window and staring out at the street. Maybe that would anchor her down, keep her feet firmly on the ground, and then she could begin to address the question of whether this really was Alex any more, or just a stranger who looked like him.

Marie wasn't taking this well. It was almost a relief. The small number of other people he'd had to tell about this had congratulated him on his sudden and immense wealth and started to treat him as if he was suddenly something different. It was typical of Marie that her objection to the whole thing wasn't what he'd expected. She brushed aside the money and his royal status as if they didn't exist. All she cared about was that she hadn't known his name.

'King is a translation of König. Alex is my middle name…' He ventured an explanation.

She shook her head. 'I thought I knew you, Alex…'

There was no point in telling her that a lot of people changed their names, or that a lot of people came from unhappy families. Marie was hurt that he'd never told her about any of it before. Maybe if she'd known his father she would have understood a little better.

'Rudolf König was the name my father gave to me to remind everyone who my family was. I wanted to make my own way in life, Marie, and to be measured by what *I've* done.'

'Yeah. I see that.' She was staring fixedly out of the window and didn't turn to face him.

'Then…?'

'Give me a minute. I'm processing.'

Okay. Processing didn't sound so terrible. If Marie could come to any conclusions then he'd like to hear them, because all he'd felt since he'd heard about his father's will was that he was being dragged back into a life from which he'd previously torn himself. Money and status had soured his parents' lives, and it already felt like it was slowly squeezing all the joy out of his.

She turned slowly, leaning back against the windowsill and regarding him thoughtfully.

'So…it's still Alex, is it?' Not *Your Majesty…?'*

'You don't need to rub it in, Marie. Who the hell else do you think I know how to be?'

Her face softened and she almost smiled. It was one step towards the warmth that he craved.

'Sorry.' She pressed her lips together in thought. 'Who knows about this?'

'A few people that I know from school. No one here. But it's not a secret. I just don't talk about it.'

She turned to face him, her eyes full of violet fire. 'Isn't that what secrets are? Things you keep from your friends?'

'I *never* lied.' He heard himself snap, and took a breath. 'I want the clinic to be about the work and not about me.'

'It *is* about you, though. You built it.'

'I facilitated it. I want people to talk about the things we do here, and talking about who I am is only going to divert attention away from that.'

Alex decided to leave aside the fact that he really didn't want to talk about who he was, because that would be a matter of reopening old wounds.

Marie was nodding slowly. It was time to take a risk.

'If you're not interested in a job here you can always just walk away.'

She pursed her lips. 'I never said I wasn't interested.'

Good. That was a start. He knew she'd seen the possibilities that the clinic offered, and maybe it was a matter of getting her to look at those and not at him. Not at the friend who'd broken the rules and kissed her. The friend who'd never told her about where he came from.

'This is the deal, then. This clinic is a flagship development, which is funded and run entirely by a trust I've set up with part of my inheritance. I don't want it to be the only one of its kind; it's intended that what we do here will be a model for future clinics all over the country. In order to achieve that we'll need to attract extra funding from outside sources.'

'You always did think big, Alex.'

He saw a flicker of excitement in her eyes. That was exactly the way *he* wanted to feel.

'I want you to share that vision with me as my co-director for the whole project. This clinic and future developments as well. You'll be able to dictate policy and do things on your own terms.'

She stared at him. 'Me? You want *me* to do that?'

Marie hadn't said no yet. He resisted the impulse to laugh and tell her that she could do anything she set her mind to doing. He was offering her the job on purely business grounds and he had to treat this conversation in that light.

'Your professional experience in A&E and diagnostic wards makes you ideally suited to the work here, where we're suggesting effective therapies and ways forward for patients. And you're not afraid of a challenge.' Alex allowed himself the smallest of smiles. 'That's one thing I happen to know about you.'

'This would be the first time I've taken on a management role.' Marie gave a little frown, obviously annoyed that she'd betrayed a little too much interest. 'If I decide to take the job, that is.'

'We already have a practice manager on board. She's very experienced and can advise on the practical aspects.

It's your vision that matters, and your knowledge of what this community needs.'

'Is that your way of saying that you don't understand "poor people" and I do?'

She crooked two fingers to indicate quotation marks. There was a touch of defiance in her tone, and it would be very easy for Alex to say that the thought had never occurred to him.

'I think you understand some of the issues that people who live in this neighbourhood face. I want to formulate policies that are appropriate and which are going to work. If you want to boil that down to understanding poor people then be my guest.'

She grinned. He hadn't given her the expected answer, but it had been the right one.

'I think I *could* help…'

'I don't want you to *help*. This is a full partnership and I expect you to tell me what's wrong with my thinking.' He could trust Marie to do that. Their friendship was founded on it.

'It's a big step for me, Alex. I need to think about it.'

'Of course. Take as long as you like.'

Alex knew that Marie wouldn't take too long; she was nothing if not decisive. If she said no then that would be the end of it. But if she said yes then maybe, just maybe, she'd save him from being the man his father had wanted him to be and make him into the one *he* wanted to be.

By the time she got home Alex's email was already in her inbox, with a full job description and a detailed brief of his plans for the clinic appended. It took a while to read through it all, and Marie didn't finish until the early hours. She decided to sleep on it.

But sleeping on it didn't help, and neither did extending her usual running route around the park to almost twice the distance. Neither did staring at the wall or surfing the internet.

She wanted the job—very badly. It would give her a chance to shape policy and to be part of a bold initiative that promised to be a real force in helping people to live fuller and better lives.

But Alex...

Before she'd kissed him, before she'd known that he wasn't who he'd said he was...

That wasn't entirely fair. Thinking back, he'd never actually said anything about who he was. If it hadn't occurred to her to ask if his father was an immeasurably rich king in exile then maybe that was a lapse in imagination on her part.

But it still felt as if she'd kissed a man she didn't really know at all and had let herself fall a little in love with him. A future working closely with Alex seemed fraught with the dangerous unknown.

By Sunday evening she'd distilled it all down. There was no doubt in her mind that this was her dream job, but there were three things she wanted to know from Alex. Could he forget the kiss? Why hadn't he told her who he was? And what did the clinic really mean to him?

They were tricky questions. She had to find a way of asking indirectly, and after an hour of scribbling and crossing out she had three questions that might or might not elicit the information she wanted.

Marie picked up her phone and typed a text.

Are you still awake? I have some questions.

Nothing. Maybe he'd taken the evening off and gone out somewhere. Or maybe he was asleep already. As Marie put her phone down on the bed beside her, it rang.

'Hi, Alex...' She panicked suddenly and her mind went blank.

'Hi. Fire away, then.'

She'd rather hoped that she might ask by text, as that would give her a chance to carefully edit what she intended to say.

'Um...okay. Have you interviewed anyone else for this post?' That was the closest she could get to asking about the kiss.

'Nope.'

Marie rolled her eyes. 'That's not much help, so I'm going for a supplementary question. Why not?'

He chuckled 'You're asking if I offered you the job because we're friends? The answer's no. I need people around me who I trust and who are the best at what they do. If I wanted to meet up with you I'd call and ask if you were free for lunch.'

Okay. That sounded promising. Alex had drawn the line between professional and personal, and if he could take the kiss out of the equation then so could she.

'Next?'

Marie squeezed her eyes closed and recited the next question. 'That Christmas, at medical school, when we all went home for the holidays, what did you do?'

He was silent for so long that Marie began to wonder whether he'd hung up on her. She wondered if he knew how much this mattered, and why.

'Okay. I'll play. I stayed in my flat and watched TV all day.'

Marie caught her breath. He knew, and he'd answered honestly. 'You could have come to ours. You just had to say you were on your own.'

'You're *really* going to take that route, Marie? You'd have been too proud to let me bring as much as a box of mince pies with me. And you're wondering why I was too proud to admit that I was going to be on my own?'

Marie could understand that, even if she was sorry that he'd felt that way.

'Next question. And tell me you're not going to let me down by making this an easy one.'

Marie felt her ears start to burn. But that was Alex all over. He could be confrontational, but there was always that note of self-deprecatory laughter in his tone that made it all right.

'Do you think the clinic's going to save you, Alex?'

He was silent for a moment.

'Nice one. Those aren't the words I'd have used... But the inheritance is a responsibility, and I know from bitter experience that it's the kind of thing that can subsume a person. I want to hold on to who I am. So, yes, I guess I am hoping that the clinic will save me.'

These were the answers she'd wanted. And there was only one thing more to say.

'It's a great project, Alex. And, yes, I'd really like to take the job.'

CHAPTER THREE

THE MONTH'S NOTICE Marie had given at her old job had seemed like an age. She'd received daily email updates about what was going on at the clinic, and she'd spent many evenings and most of her weekends replying to Alex. If their exchanges seemed more businesslike than friendly, then that was all good. They needed to start as they meant to go on, and Marie was ready to begin work in earnest.

She knew what had been done, but that didn't match the effect of seeing it for herself. The facade of the building had been cleaned, exposing the soft yellow of the brick and the red terracotta detailing around the windows and door. The railings had been sanded and painted, and the old Tarmac playground was now a paved area, dotted with saplings that would soften the space as they grew. The main door had been stripped and varnished, and the dents from being kicked a thousand times as pupils had passed this way only added to its character.

The bell was new as well, and when she pressed it Alex appeared at the door, looking far less formal than his emails had been, and suspiciously like the man she'd dared to kiss. Maybe seeing him every day would quash that reaction.

Marie smiled nervously as he led her through the glass lobby doors. 'This is amazing!'

Everything was neat and tidy, with cream-painted walls

and comfortable seating. Marie knew that the large curved barrier between the receptionist and the public space had been designed to protect the staff by stopping anyone from climbing across, but the sloping front looked like a thing of beauty and not a defence mechanism.

'I'm pleased with the way it's turned out.' Alex looked around as if this was the first time he'd seen the space. 'You didn't have to start until Monday, you know. How was your leaving party last night?'

Marie rolled her eyes. 'Long. We had too much cake, and then we went to the pub. I cried. I need something to do today to work off all the calories and the emotion.'

'You're not regretting this, are you?' He frowned.

'No. Looking forward to what's next doesn't mean I can't miss my old job a bit as well.'

He quirked his lips down, as if missing the past was something he'd been struggling with, and then smiled suddenly in an indication that he wasn't about to dwell on that.

'You want to see your new office?'

'Yes, please.'

Alex had suggested that she take the office next to his, but Marie wanted to be close to the two practice nurses and the health visitor who comprised their medical support team, and who would be located on the first floor. The problem had been solved by giving her an office that was directly above his and connected by a narrow private staircase.

'What do you think?'

Cream walls, lots of light and plenty of space. That was standard issue here, but no doubt she could inject a little colour of her own. Marie had chosen a light-framed wooden desk, and behind it was an identical chair to Alex's.

'You got me one of these!' Marie had wanted one, but hadn't wanted to ask.

'Yes. Call it an investment. I don't want you taking any time off sick with a bad back.'

Marie grinned at him and sat down, feeling the chair respond to her weight. 'I'll just take two days off to adjust it, shall I?'

'Mine took a week. The instructions are in your top drawer. Would you like to offer me some coffee?'

'Have I got any?'

Actually, Marie could do with some coffee. The combination of cake and beer last night had left her feeling a little fuzzy this morning.

'Behind you.'

He indicated a door at the far end of the cupboards that lined one wall, and sat down in one of the chairs on the other side of the desk. Marie went to look and found that the door concealed a neat worktop with a coffee machine and supplies. A splash of colour next to the line of cream mugs caught her eye.

'You got me a mug!' She took the bright pink mug down from the shelf and examined it. 'With a flying pig! You remembered!'

'You always used to say that you wanted an office with a sofa, and time to sit and talk with your patients.'

The informal seating area in his office contained four easy chairs, covered in a chocolate-coloured fabric, but for Marie he had chosen a sofa and two chairs in a lighter cappuccino colour.

'And when you said that nothing was impossible, I told you that pigs might fly...' It had been a joke between them. 'Thank you, Alex.'

He seemed pleased with her reaction, but there was still a hint of reticence about his manner. The man Marie knew would have seen only exciting new opportunities, but Alex seemed burdened by his responsibilities.

He'd come round. The clinic would be opening next

week, and as soon as it started to fill with people he'd respond to that. He was going to have to if this place was to reach its full potential. Alex had so much more than money to give, and it needed his creative enthusiasm to thrive.

Marie switched on the coffee machine, running her finger along the selection of different capsules. 'I'm going to have to try all of these, you know. I'll work from left to right.'

'I'd expect nothing less of you.'

When she put his cup down in front of him, he nodded a thank-you and pushed a manila envelope towards her. Marie opened it, tipping the contents out onto her desk.

'These are yours. The credit card is for any purchases you need to make, and the key card opens every door inside the clinic. Those two keys are for the main door, and the other one is the main override for the alarm system. The car keys are for the practice's vehicles.'

Marie laid the keys and cards out in front of her on the desk. This was the start of it all…

'The IT guy will be coming in on Monday to set up your computer. Let me know if there's anything else you need.' Alex got to his feet, picking up his mug. 'I'll leave you to settle in, if that's okay. I have a few things to do.'

Marie had wanted to share all this. Unpacking the bag she'd brought with her and taking a tour of the clinic to see all the work that she and Alex had been discussing for the last month. But Alex was already halfway out of the door.

'Yes, okay. Maybe we can sit down together later today to go through some things?'

'That would be great.' He flashed her a sudden smile. 'You like your office?'

'It's better than I could have imagined. Thank you so much, Alex.'

'My pleasure.' He turned, closing the door behind him.

Marie leaned back in her chair, listening to the silence. There was a lot to do here. A whole community of health professionals to build. There were mountains to move, and the most stubborn of them had just walked downstairs. Alex had built his dream, and although he had a fierce determination to see it thrive, Marie sensed he couldn't love it.

That was going to have to change.

After Saturday's quiet solitude, most of which Alex had spent closeted in his office, the bustle of workmen and staff on Monday morning was a welcome relief. Marie spent two days with Sofia Costa, the practice manager, interviewing the shortlisted candidates for the medical support team, and on Wednesday morning picked up the flowering plant she'd brought from home and went down to Alex's office.

She'd wondered if his subdued manner was a reaction to their kiss, part of some kind of attempt to keep things professional, but he was like that with everyone. Thoughtful, smiling, but without the spark that made him Alex. In one way it was a relief to find that it wasn't just her, but it was clear that the change in Alex's life and the months spent developing this place had taken their toll on him. He normally thrived on hard work, but this was different. It seemed to be draining all the life out of him.

'The interviews went well?' He looked up from the pile of paperwork on his desk.

'Very well. It was difficult to decide, as they were all good candidates. But Sofia and I have chosen three who are excellent. I've emailed their CVs to you so you can take a look at them.'

She put the Busy Lizzie plant down on his desk and Alex picked it up, examining the bright red flowers. 'Is this a subtle hint that my office could do with brightening up?'

'No, I don't do subtle. It's more in the way of a brazen, in-your-face hint.'

Alex smiled, walking over to the windowsill and putting the pot at the centre. He moved it to one side and then the other, finding the place he wanted it.

'I don't suppose you have any more of these, do you?'

Marie hid her smile. The old Alex was still there—he just needed a bit of coaxing out. If he wanted more plants she'd fill his windowsill with colour.

'I've got loads at home. I took some cuttings from my mum's. I'll bring you more tomorrow.'

'Thanks.'

'I've got an idea.' She sat down in one of the chairs on the other side of his desk.

'Fire away.'

His lips curved a little. Alex clearly hadn't lost his penchant for ideas of all shapes and sizes.

'The light wells. They're pretty awful as they are, and I'd like to turn them into gardens. I spoke to Jim Armitage and he says that there are some brick pavers that were taken up from around the gym and he saved because they were still good. He reckons they should be fine on top of the concrete, but he needs to get out there to check everything. The key card lock disengages, but there's an original lock still on the door. Jim was going to climb out of the window, but I persuaded him not to.'

The foreman of works was a portly man approaching retirement, and Marie had feared he'd either get stuck while climbing out or not be able to get back in again. The same thing had obviously occurred to Alex, because one of those flashes of humour that reminded Marie so painfully of the man he'd once been lit his face.

'Good call. I might have the key somewhere...' He opened the bottom drawer of his desk, producing a large cardboard box full of keys of all shapes and sizes.

'So you'll come and have a look with me?'

If Alex was going to tell her that she was quite capable of doing this alone, then she was going to have to argue with him. She was capable, but that wasn't the point.

'I have a few things to do…'

'This is much more important, Alex. As your co-director, I'm telling you that you need to come.'

He grinned suddenly and stood up.

Step one accomplished. Step two might be a bit trickier…

Marie never had been much good at hiding the motives behind her actions. It was something Alex wished he hadn't had to learn how to do. She'd decided to get him out of his office and there was no point in arguing that he had work to do when Marie was determined. And when Alex thought about it, he didn't really want to argue.

He'd missed this. Marie had brought colour to a life that had become suffused by restful cream walls and spaces that were fit for purpose. He followed her along the corridor that ran parallel to one of the light wells, holding the box of keys.

She took her key card from her pocket, swiping it to disengage the main lock, and then started to fish around in the box for keys that looked as if they might fit the older one. It took a few tries to find one that fitted, but finally Alex heard a click as the key turned in the lock.

She rattled the handle of the door. 'It's still stuck…'

Alex tried the door. 'Looks as if it's been painted shut—no one ever goes out there. You want me to open it?'

She gave him a beatific smile. 'Yes, please.'

He put his shoulder to the door, and there was a cracking sound as it opened. Marie picked up a plastic bag, which had been sitting on one of the windowsills, and stepped out into the courtyard.

'Right. We need to check the height of the pavers…'

She produced a brick from the bag, wedging it under the bottom of the doorframe. 'That looks okay to me. And Jim says there's drainage, so we'll be fine there…'

She pulled a folded A2 sheet from the bag, spreading it out on the stained concrete. Marie was nothing if not prepared, and Alex was getting the feeling that he'd been set up. But Marie did it so delightfully.

'I reckon seats there…and planters in groups here and here… Perhaps a small water feature in the centre? What do you think?'

'I think that's great. Do we have the budget for it?'

'Yes, if we don't go overboard with things and we use the resources that we already have. Jim says that one of his guys will take me to the garden centre to get what we need.'

'Fine.' But something told Alex that his agreement to the plan wasn't enough. Marie wanted more.

She turned to him, her eyes dancing with violet shards in the sunlight. 'What do you say, Alex? Do you want to make a garden with me?'

Suddenly the one thing that Alex wanted was to make a garden, but there were more pressing things on his agenda.

'Do you think that's the best use of our time? We're opening in six days.'

'And the clinic's ready. You're not, though. You've been stuck in your office, working seven days a week, for months. You need a break before we open, and since I doubt you'll go home and take one this is a good second-best.'

This. This was why he'd wanted Marie to be his co-director. For moments like now, when she glared at him and told him exactly what he was doing wrong. He'd hoped she might come up with a plan, and that it might not just be for the clinic but for him as well.

'Well?' She put her hands on her hips.

She was unstoppable, and Alex did need a break. Something to refill the well that felt in imminent danger of running dry.

'Okay. I'm in your hands. What do you want me to do?'

'I'll go and get what we need for this courtyard, and we can store it all in the other one and start planting everything up. I'll ask Jim exactly when he can lay the paving; he said he'd probably be able to fit it in this week.'

'Maybe I can help with that. I could do with the exercise.' The waistband of his trousers was slightly tighter than usual, and Alex reckoned that he really needed to get to the gym.

'I wasn't going to mention that.'

Her gaze fell to his stomach, and Alex instinctively sucked in a breath. He hadn't thought he was *that* out of shape.

'It's nothing a little sunshine and activity won't fix.'

'What? You're my personal trainer now?'

'Someone has to do it, Alex. What are friends for?

This was exactly what friends were for. Crashing into your day like a shaft of light, slicing through the cobwebs. Doing something unexpected that turned an average working week into an adventure.

Alex dismissed the thought that it was also what lovers were for. He'd never had a lover who meant as much to him as his friend Marie. He doubted he ever would. He'd seen the way his father had reduced his mother to a sad, silent ghost. Alex had decided a long time ago that he would concentrate on making the best of every other aspect of his life and pass on marriage and a family.

He caught her just as she was leaving the clinic with Eammon, one of Jim Armitage's builders. 'Don't worry about the budget on this. Get whatever you want. I'll cover it.'

Marie shook her head. 'We have the money to buy a few planters and grow things. It's better that way.'

He'd said the wrong thing again. It would mean nothing to him to buy up a whole garden centre. It occurred to Alex that he was becoming used to throwing money at any problem that presented itself, because that meant much less to him than his time. He hadn't realised he'd lost so much of himself.

'Okay, well…' He'd play it her way. 'Let me know when you get back and I'll help unload the van.'

'Great. Thanks.' She gifted him with an irrepressible smile and turned, hurrying across to the front gates, her red dress swirling around her legs.

As she climbed up into the front seat of the builder's van that was parked outside the gates, Alex couldn't help smiling. Marie always looked gorgeous, but somehow she seemed even more so now, rushing towards a future that held only excitement for her and looking oddly pristine in the dusty, battered vehicle.

She'd be a couple of hours at least. Alex turned back to his office, feeling suddenly that those two hours were going to drag a little, with only a desk full of paperwork to amuse him.

When Marie returned, Alex had already found the key to the other courtyard and opened it up, then changed into the jeans and work boots that he kept in the office for inspecting the works in progress with Jim.

The van pulled into the car park, and Marie climbed down from the front seat, cheeks flushed with excitement.

'You got everything?'

'Yes, we've got some small shrubs and loads of seeds, along with planters and growing compost. I came in two pounds under budget.'

'And you didn't buy yourself an ice cream?' Alex

walked to the back of the van, waiting for Eammon to open the doors.

'*I* bought her an ice cream.'

Eammon grinned, and Alex wished suddenly that he'd volunteered to drive. He'd missed his chance to play the gentleman.

He started to haul one of the heavy bags of compost out of the back of the van, finding that it was more effort than he'd expected to throw it over his shoulder. He and Eammon stacked the bags in the courtyard while Marie unloaded the planters from the van.

'What do you think? I was hoping that less might be more.'

She'd arranged some of the planters in a group and was surveying them thoughtfully. There was a mix of colours and styles. Some large clay pots, a few blue-glazed ones, which were obviously the most expensive, and some recycled plant tubs, which were mostly grey but contained random swirls of colour. Each brought out the best in the others.

'They're going to look great.'

Alex picked up two of the heavier clay pots and Eammon took the pot that Marie had picked up, telling her to bring the lighter plastic tubs through.

Another opportunity for gallantry missed. Alex had carefully avoided any such gestures, reckoning that they might be construed as being the result of the kiss that they'd both decided to ignore, but he reckoned if they were okay for Eammon then they were probably permissible for him, too.

Alex was clearly struggling with his role at the clinic. If he'd worked for this then he would have seen it as the re-alisation of a lifetime's ambition, but it had all fallen so easily into his lap. The inheritance had left him without anything to strive for and it was destroying him.

Marie's ambitions had always been small: helping her mother cope with the pressures of four young children and a job, then making a life for herself and keeping an eye on her younger brothers. But at least they were simple and relatively easily fulfilled.

After they'd unloaded the van, carrying everything through to the courtyard and stacking it neatly, Alex seemed in no particular hurry to get back to his office. Marie asked him if he wanted to help and he nodded quietly.

She set out the seed trays, filling them with compost, and Alex sorted through the packets. Then they got to work, sitting on a pair of upturned crates that Alex had fetched.

'So...tell me again what country your great-grandfather was the king of?'

They'd worked in near silence for over an hour, and now that everyone had gone home for the evening they were alone. Marie had been regretting her reaction to Alex's disclosure about his family, and the subject had become a bit of a no-go area between them.

Alex looked up at her questioningly. 'It doesn't matter. It doesn't exist any more.'

'I'm just curious. And... I feel sorry about giving you a hard time when you told me about it.'

'It's nothing.' He puffed out breath and then relented. 'Belkraine. My great-grandfather was Rudolf the Most Excellent and Magnificent, King of Belkraine. Modesty doesn't run in the family.'

'I guess if you've got a few squillion in cash and a palace then you don't need to be modest...' She paused. 'Did he have a palace?'

'Why stop at one when you can have several? The old

Summer Palace still exists; it's near the border between Austria and Italy.'

'Have you ever been there?'

His lip curled slightly. 'It was my father's idea of a summer holiday. We'd go there every year, for a tour of what was supposed to be our birthright. It was excruciating.'

Alex sounded bitter. He wasn't a man who held on to bad feelings, so this must be something that ran deep with him.

'I'd be interested to see where my ancestors lived. Although I can say pretty definitely that it wasn't in a palace.'

'I guess it's an interesting place. It's been restored now, and it's very much the way it was when my great-grandparents lived there. Unfortunately my father used to insist on pointing at everything and telling my mother and me in a very loud voice that all this was really ours and that we'd been exiled to a life of poverty.'

'Ouch.'

Marie pulled a face and his lips twitched into something that resembled a smile.

'Yes, ouch. Even though my great-grandfather brought a fair bit of the family's wealth with him—and we had more than enough—my father used to reckon that he was poor because he didn't have everything he thought he should. He had no idea what real poverty is. It was just… embarrassing.'

'Is that why you never said anything about it?' Marie was beginning to understand that this hadn't been a wish to deceive, but something that had hurt him very badly.

'That and a few hundred other things. Like having to wear a version of the Crown Prince's military uniform at the annual party he gave on the anniversary of our family ascending the throne in 1432. After a particularly bloody series of wars, I might add. My family took the kingdom from someone else, so I never could see how having it taken from us was any cause for complaint.'

He ripped open a seed packet as if he was trying to chop its head off. Seeds scattered all over the concrete and Alex shook his head in frustration, cursing under his breath.

Marie swallowed down the temptation to tell him that it was okay, that they could pick them up again. This wasn't about the seeds, and he'd obviously not had much chance to get it out of his system. The idea that it had been nagging at him for so many years, concealed beneath the carefree face he'd shown to the world, was unbearably sad.

She bent down, picking the seeds up one by one. 'Good thing these aren't begonias. We'd never be able to pick up those tiny seeds.'

He laughed, his resentment seeming to disappear suddenly. Marie would rather he held on to it. His feelings were shut away now, under lock and key, and when he'd tipped the last of the seeds back into the packet, he stood.

'I've a few things that I really need to do. Do you mind if we start again in the morning?'

'Of course not. Anything I can give you a hand with?'

'No, stay here. We really need a garden. It will give people hope.'

Would it give *him* hope? Or just other people?

Marie decided not to ask, because Alex was already opening the door that led back into the building, and she doubted whether he would have answered anyway.

CHAPTER FOUR

WAS THIS REALLY what Marie wanted to know about him? That he was the great-grandson of a tyrant king? Alex decided he was overreacting, and that it was just natural curiosity. *He'd* be curious about the mechanics of the thing if he'd suddenly found out that Marie was a fairy princess. But then that wouldn't come as much of a surprise—he'd always rather suspected that she was.

He waited until he heard the main doors close and then threw down his pen. The table of dependencies he'd been sketching out for Jim Armitage wasn't working anyway, and he should probably just tell him what needed to be finished before the clinic opened, and leave him to work it out. There was such a thing as being too hands-on. And he couldn't leave without taking a look…

Marie had moved some of the planters, obviously having changed her mind on how best to group them. The shrubs were arranged under a makeshift plastic canopy to protect them from the weather, along with the seed trays that they'd filled.

Alex sat down on the upturned crate he'd occupied earlier. It occurred to him that this was the first garden he'd ever really had a hand in. His parents' garden had been designed to be looked at, preferably from a distance, and hadn't really been the kind of place for a child who might disturb its well-ordered beauty. When he'd left home, the indoor plants he'd bought to brighten up his flat had generally died from neglect, and Alex had decided that his contribution to the environment was to leave them in the shop and let them go to someone who would remember to water them.

But this time the idea of creating something from scratch and tending it over time was something he very much wanted to be a part of. And so what if Marie had asked him about the one thing he always shrank from discussing? She wanted to know about the Kings of Belkraine because she wanted to know about him. If she had any questions tomorrow, he'd answer them.

When he arrived at the clinic the next morning, Marie was already sitting on her crate, wearing a T-shirt and jeans. His crate had been left in exactly the same place it had occupied last night, in mute invitation.

Alex opened the door of the courtyard and went to sit opposite her.

'Morning.'

She gave him a bright smile. Her cheeks were still a little red from where the sun had kissed them yesterday.

Alex nodded and sat down, reaching for an empty seed tray from the pile. He filled the tray with compost and opened one of the seed packets, letting the cool quiet of the hour before everyone else arrived for work seep into him for a while before he spoke.

'I argued with my father and he threw me out of the house when I was eighteen.'

She looked up at him, her lip quivering. 'That's a hard thing to have to bear, Alex.'

He shook his head. Marie knew far more about hardship than he did. 'Your father left when you were ten.'

'It's not a competition, Alex. You don't have to keep quiet about what happened to you because you think what happened to me might have been worse—it doesn't work that way. Anyway, my father left because of what happened between my mum and him. She told us that. It's different.'

Alex wondered how different it really was. Marie had worked so hard to help support her brothers, and he'd always had a sense that she felt somehow responsible for her father leaving.

But this wasn't about probing her; Marie had never made any secret of her childhood. He'd hidden his past out of a wish to leave it behind. Now, for the sake of the friendship that was so precious to him, he had to put that right.

'What did you argue about?' Marie had clearly been waiting for him to go on, and finally she asked the question.

'My father was an embittered man. He had everything money could buy, but he considered that our family had been deprived of its birthright. He insisted that we live as if we *were* royal, but I wanted more from life than that. I wanted to make my own choices. I wanted to be a doctor. He told me that if I went to medical school he'd disinherit me, and I told him to go ahead and do it.'

A faint smile hovered at Marie's lips. 'I wouldn't have expected you to do anything else. Didn't he ever see what you'd achieved and come around?'

'No, he never accepted what I wanted to do. The money that took me through medical school was from a trust that my grandfather had set up for me. He knew what my father was like, and he locked the trust in an ironclad agreement so my father couldn't get his hands on it.'

'Would he have tried? It sounds as if he had enough already.' Marie's eyebrows shot up.

'My father didn't care about the money; he thought it a paltry amount. He wanted control over me. I got to do what I wanted when I was eighteen because of that trust.'

'So being disinherited…that was a good thing in a way. Your father couldn't force you into his mould.'

'I felt as if I was free.'

She chuckled, picking up another seed tray. 'Free was how you seemed then. I used to envy you for it, but I didn't know what you'd had to go through to get your freedom. Did you never reconcile with your father?'

'I didn't want to. He was never a good husband; he hurt my mother very badly. I couldn't forgive him for that.'

There was nothing like telling a story to find out which parts of it really hurt. Alex could feel his chest tightening from the pain.

'Alex…?'

Marie was leaning forward now, concern registering on her face. Maybe she knew that this was what he really needed to say.

'He had mistresses. Lots of them. He used to spend a couple of nights a week in London, and my mother always seemed so sad. When I was little I thought she must miss him, but by the time I was fifteen I knew what was going on. He didn't go to much trouble to hide it.'

Marie's hand flew to her mouth. 'Your poor mother…'

'She just accepted it. That was the thing that hurt the most. She grew thinner and sadder every year, until finally she just seemed to fade away. She died five years ago.'

'And you never got to see her?'

'I used to visit her all the time. I'd call her, and she'd tell me when my father would be out of the house and I could come. It was the only thing she ever defied him over and she used to love hearing about what I was doing as a doctor. She knew that she always had a home with me, but she'd never leave him.'

'People…they make their own decisions. Parents included.' Marie shot him a wry smile.

'Yeah.'

Alex had made his decision too. However much the idea of a wife and a family might appeal to him in theory, his parents' unhappy marriage had always made him balk at the prospect of commitment. His father's money and title were new reasons to make him wary. Alex didn't know how he was going to cope with that yet, and the last thing he wanted to do was inflict his own struggle on anyone else.

'I did try to speak to my father once—at my mother's funeral. It was a very lavish affair, and after the way he'd treated her it made me feel sick. But I decided that it was what she would have wanted, and so I went up to him to shake his hand. He turned his back on me. I'll never know why he changed his mind about leaving me his money and I wish he hadn't.'

Marie frowned at him suddenly. 'It sounds as if he did the right thing, for once.'

'What? You think I'm *better* as a billionaire king in exile?'

'No, I think you're pretty rubbish at it, actually.'

The tension in his shoulders began to dissolve and Alex grinned at her. 'That's one of the things I like about you. That you don't think it's a good thing.'

'I didn't say it wasn't a good thing. I said you were rubbish at it. Look around you and tell me it's not a good thing.'

'Point taken. So the clinic's a good thing and I'm a rubbish king. Is that right?'

She nodded. 'You can write your own script, Alex. If you let the money and the title define you then maybe that's what your father wanted. But if you define it, then you can do anything. Things ordinary people only dream of.'

As usual, Marie was right. He'd been letting the money and the title define him a little too much recently, and the idea that he could become anything he wanted lifted a weight from his shoulders. And right now he wanted to be a gardener.

Marie had finished planting three seed trays and they were lined up on one side of her. He hadn't completed any yet. Alex picked up his tray.

'I was wondering if you'd cover for me in the office. Today and tomorrow.' He finished planting the tray and laid it down next to hers.

'Yes, of course. You're going out?'

'No, I spoke with Jim Armitage and he's given me the go-ahead to lay the pavers. I've never done anything like that before, but...' He shrugged.

'You can learn. I don't think it's that difficult.' Marie's sudden smile told him what she thought of the idea.

'You don't mind, then?'

It had been Marie's idea for him to get involved with the garden, and now he was going one better.

'Mind?' Marie laughed, a clear happy sound that echoed slightly against the walls that surrounded them. 'Do I mind you getting covered in brick dust and sand while I sit in a nice comfortable office? Nah, I don't mind that at all.'

Marie had spent most of the morning in her office, trying to find things to do. When three-thirty came around and the stream of mothers walking past the clinic from the school began to start she fetched the printed leaflets which detailed the services the clinic had to offer from the stockroom, along with one of the chairs from the café, and went to sit out in the sun by the main gates.

It would be one thing if Alex had changed over a few years—everyone changed. But he'd always carried this burden. The pressure of inheriting the money after his father's death had just made him less adept at hiding it.

And she'd never noticed. Caught up in her own work

and looking after her family, she'd seen Alex as someone she wished she could be. A golden dream that she'd held on to, wanting to believe that work and responsibility weren't the only things in life. But now she'd seen a new Alex, challenging and complicated, and she couldn't help loving him better for it.

The stream of parents and kids had lessened now, and she'd given away almost all her leaflets. She'd catch the two young mums who were dawdling down the road towards her, plastic bags hanging from the arms of their pushchairs, and then she'd call it a day.

'Hi. May I give you a leaflet, please? About what we're doing here…'

One of them nodded, taking the leaflet and stuffing it into one of her shopping bags. The other took hers, and started to read it.

'I was wondering what was happening with this place. I used to go to school here…'

'Me too.' Marie grinned. 'Looks a lot better now.'

'Tell me about it. It was a real dump when I came here. We transferred over to the new school after a year.'

'We're opening next week. You're welcome to come and have a look around, see how it's changed.'

'I don't know…' The woman shook her head.

'You don't have to sign up for anything. Just look. There's a café.' Marie fished in her pocket for one of the printed vouchers. 'And this is for a free coffee.'

The woman took the voucher, stowing it away in her purse. 'Okay, thanks. What do you think, Nisha?'

Marie offered a second voucher and Nisha took it. Now that she had a conversation going, Marie decided that she should capitalise on it.

'I don't suppose you'd like a few extra leaflets, would you? To give to your friends? We have a range of services.' Marie pointed to the list on the leaflet. 'There's going to be a gym and a swimming pool, and they'll be open seven days a week. There's a nominal charge for those, but we've tried to keep it affordable.'

'I used to like swimming. The pool over on Stratton Road closed down, you know.'

Two pairs of eyes suddenly focussed away from her and over her left shoulder. Marie turned and saw Alex, wheeling a barrow full of bricks around the side of the building.

'That's the director of the clinic.'

Nisha's eyebrows shot up and the other woman choked with laughter. 'Really? Doesn't mind getting his hands dirty, then?'

'When he's not laying bricks he's a doctor. But we don't just tackle specific medical problems—it's all about living well.'

'And what do you do here?'

'I'm a doctor too.'

'Neesh…?'

The other woman nudged her companion, but Nisha shook her head. A sixth sense pricked at the back of Marie's neck. This was just the kind of thing the clinic was here for—the problems that people didn't want to talk about.

'Take my card.' Marie offered one of the cards that had been printed with her name. 'If there's ever anything I can help with, just ask for me.'

Nisha nodded, taking the card. She looked at it, glanced at Marie, and then unzipped her handbag, putting the card inside. Maybe she'd take the offer up, but Marie knew from experience that she needed to let her think about it. Pushing now would only elicit a *no*.

'My name's Marie.' She turned to the other woman.

'Carol. Do you do mother-and-toddler swimming classes?'

'Yes—you can sign up for them next week, when the clinic opens.'

'I'll definitely do that. We come past here every day. We might get another eyeful of that director of yours...' Carol laughed as Nisha raised her eyebrows. 'Only joking, Neesh.'

The toddler in Carol's pushchair started to fret. 'Yeah, all right, Georgie. We'll be home soon, and then we're going to the park. It was nice to meet you, Marie.'

'You too. Hope I'll see you again soon.'

The two women started to walk again, chatting companionably. Marie heard footsteps behind her and turned to see Alex, holding two glasses of lemonade. He handed her one.

'Thanks, I could do with that. I've talked my head off, given out a whole handful of leaflets and also some free coffee vouchers. How are you doing?'

Alex grinned, leaning towards her as if he was about to impart something highly confidential. 'Rather well, I think.'

'Can I see it?'

'No. The courtyards are my territory for the next couple of days. You can have the offices and the front gates. I'll water the seeds for you.'

'You won't forget? You know how bad you are at watering plants.' Marie shot him an imploring look.

'That's reassuring. I'm expecting people to put their lives in my hands, and you can't trust me with a few seed trays.'

It was nice to see Alex teasing again. Marie had missed that, and it seemed that a little practical work had lifted some of the weight from his shoulders. He was looking a lot more like the relaxed and cheerful Alex that she'd known before all this had happened.

Alex nodded at the pavement behind her and Marie

saw Carol hurrying towards them. It looked as if she had something on her mind.

'Hey, Carol. This is Alex, our director.'

'Pleased to meet you.'

Alex wiped his hand on his jeans and held it out. Carol shook it, nodding at him quickly, and then turned to Marie.

'Did you mean what you said? To Nisha?'

'About coming to see me? Of course. Is there something wrong?'

Carol nodded, tight-lipped.

'Do you want to come inside and talk?'

Perhaps it was something Carol didn't want to say in front of Alex.

'No. No, that's all right. I've got to get home—this one's going to start playing up in a minute.' She gestured down at Georgie, who was wriggling in the pushchair, clearly cross that the park was on hold for the moment.

Alex squatted down on his heels and poked his tongue out at the toddler. Their game of pulling faces seemed to be keeping them both occupied for a moment, which left Carol free to talk with Marie.

'Is there something Nisha needs? Something we can help with?'

'Yeah. Look, I can't really talk about it…'

Carol was almost whispering now, and Marie lowered her voice too.

'That's okay. Has she been to see her GP?'

'No, she won't. This place looks…' Carol shrugged. 'She might come here. I could get her to come. But you will see her, won't you? I don't know that it's a strictly medical thing.'

'If it's not a medical problem I'll refer her to someone who can help her. The whole point of this place is to find whatever answer is appropriate.'

'Right. Thanks. When are you opening? For…um… whatever… Appointments?'

'Next week. But Nisha doesn't need an appointment—she can come at any time. All you need to do is get her here and I'll make time to see her.'

'Great. Thanks.' Carol looked down at Georgie, who was laughing and trying to reproduce the faces Alex was making. 'I'd better get back. I told Nisha I was just popping back for something at the shops and I'd meet her in the park.'

'All right. But, Carol…' Marie caught Carol's arm before she could leave. 'This is important. If you think Nisha's in danger in any way you must get her to call someone. Or bring her here.'

'No, it's nothing like that. Her husband's a good man. It's just…embarrassing. You know?'

'Okay. I can do embarrassing. Get her to come and see me—you can come with her if that helps.' She glanced down at Alex, raising her voice to catch his attention. 'I don't think Alex's quite used up his stock of funny faces.'

Alex grinned up at Carol, getting to his feet. 'He's a great little chap.'

'Thanks. He can be a bit of a handful.' Carol was smiling now. 'I'll see you, then…?'

'I hope so.' Alex gave her a smile and Carol turned and hurried away.

'What was all that about?'

Marie shrugged. 'I don't know. Something about the friend she was with a moment ago. She wouldn't say.'

'You think she's in any danger?' Alex's first question was the same as Marie's had been. It was always their first question.

'No, Carol says it's embarrassing.'

He nodded, tipping his glass towards hers. 'Here's to

your first patient, then. Congratulations, you've pipped me to the post. I haven't got any yet.'

'Thank you. I dare say that'll change, but I'm quietly triumphant over having beaten my excellent and glorious co-director.'

Marie took a sip of her lemonade and saw the corners of Alex's mouth quirk downwards. Maybe the joke was a little too close to the mark for him.

'All right. Never say that again.' His face was serious for a moment, and then he smiled, knowing he'd fooled her. 'I might consign you to the dungeons.'

'How about Your Majesty? I suppose that's out as well?'

He chuckled. 'Definitely. That's a throwing-from-the-battlements thing…'

'Get back to work, Alex.' Marie drained her glass, handing it back to him.

CHAPTER FIVE

MARIE HAD MADE no secret of the fact that staying away from the courtyards was driving her insane with curiosity. Alex had escorted her off the premises at five o'clock and gone back to work, sorting out the best of the bricks and discarding those that were damaged.

The second day of Alex's practical introduction to laying pavers had involved an early start and a concentrated burst of work, but by the afternoon he was surveying the newly swept paving with Charlie, the lad Jim Armitage had sent to help him. Alex suspected Charlie had also been instructed to report back to Jim if it looked as if he was about to make a complete mess of things, and it was a matter of some pride to him that Charlie hadn't gone to seek out his boss at any point.

'What do you think, Charlie?'

Charlie nodded sagely. 'Nice job. Are we going to lay out the planters now?'

'Yes, I think so. Then we can show it to Marie.'

'She can put her flowers in. She'll like that.'

Charlie spoke with the certainty of all his nineteen years, and Alex smiled. The warm colours of the brick had made all the difference to the space.

'Yes, I think she will. Thanks for all your hard work.'

Charlie nodded, obviously pleased.

They set out the planters from the chart Marie had given them, and Alex left Charlie to bring some of the shrubs through from the other courtyard while he went to find Marie.

She was sitting in the reception area, where she could keep an eye out for anyone whose curiosity had brought them to the door, staring at the screen of her laptop.

As soon as she saw him she jumped to her feet. 'Is it finished?'

'Yes. You want to come and see it?'

'There are a few things I have to do, but I'll have a look later on...' Alex's face must have shown his dismay and she laughed. 'Of *course* I want to come and see it!'

'Okay.' From his pocket he produced the extra-large handkerchief he'd brought from home that morning, brushing a speck of brick dust from it. 'Stand still for a moment.'

'You're going to blindfold me? Seriously?'

'Charlie's worked hard on this. I think it deserves a little bit of a ceremony, don't you?'

The blindfold was nothing to do with Charlie. Alex just wanted to see the look on Marie's face when she saw the paved courtyard.

'Yes, okay, then. Hurry up!'

He tied the blindfold carefully over her eyes, trying not to breathe in the scent of her hair. Then, just for good measure, he turned her around a couple of times. Marie flung out her hand, her fingers brushing his chest, before they found a secure hold on the sleeve of his T-shirt. Alex shivered as tingles pulsed down his spine. They were almost in an embrace.

'Enough, Alex! Take me there or else!'

'Okay. Hold my arm.'

She clung on to him as he walked her slowly along the corridor. When the idea of blindfolding her had occurred to him this morning Alex hadn't taken into consideration how good it would feel to have her walking so close, hanging on to him. He was glad he hadn't foreseen it, because if he had he might have thought better of the idea. And it would have been a shame to miss this moment.

Charlie opened the door for them, standing back with a huge grin on his face.

'The step's right in front of you...' Alex held her arm firmly so she couldn't fall, and Marie extended her foot. 'That's it. A little further.'

When her foot hit the surface of the bricks she gave a shiver of anticipation, her fingers tightening around his arm. Alex's knees almost gave way, and then suddenly his body was taut and strong again, ready to catch her if she fell.

Marie stepped out into the courtyard carefully, letting him lead her into its centre.

'You can take the blindfold off now.' He heard his voice catch on the lump in his throat and knew he dared not do it for her. If he touched her hair again he might forget himself.

Marie reached up, fumbling a little with the knot. She was silent for a moment, her hand to her mouth as she looked around.

'Herringbone! I didn't expect that!'

Alex and Charlie exchanged smug looks. The herringbone pattern meant that there had been extra work in cutting the bricks at the edges, but they'd both agreed it would be worth it. Now, it was definitely worth it.

'This is *beautiful*. It's perfect. Charlie, you must have worked so hard...'

It was just like Marie to praise the younger member of the team first. Charlie had worked hard, he'd made sure everything was exactly right, and he deserved it. Alex smiled as Charlie's cheeks began to redden.

'And you've set out all my planters as well. Thank you so much.'

Charlie nodded. 'Would you like to see the drainage gulley?'

'Yes, please.'

Alex watched as Charlie led her to one corner of the courtyard, showing her where excess rainfall would drain away from the surface and into a waste pipe.

'You've made such a good job of it. When we put some flowers and seating out here it's going to be a lovely place for people to sit.'

Charlie was grinning from ear to ear, and had obviously taken about as much praise as one young man could stand from a beautiful woman. He muttered something about having to report back to Jim, and made his escape. Then Marie turned her gaze onto Alex.

No words. Just a smile. But Alex felt just as pleased with her reaction as Charlie had obviously been.

'You like it?'

'You really need to ask, Alex? I love it.'

Alex nodded. This was everything he needed. It was well worth the hard manual labour, the aching muscles and the scraped fingers.

'Our garden…' Marie turned around as if she could see it right now. Flowers and seating—everything as it would be when it was finished.

'Yes. I like the sound of that.'

'Me too. I could really, really hug you. If you weren't so dirty.'

He could really, really hug her too, and love every second of it. It was just as well that he was covered in grime, with streaks of adhesive all over his jeans.

'I think I'll go and give the showers in the gym changing rooms a trial run. Then I'll go to my office.'

'This has been keeping you from your other work…'
Marie shot him a guilty look.

'There's nothing so urgent that it won't wait until tomorrow. I just really need to sit down.'

'Then come out here. I'll fetch you a chair and a cold drink, and you can sit and watch me work.'

The idea was much more enchanting than it should be. He could survey his handiwork with a sense of pride at something started and finished amongst a list of tasks that never seemed to end. Better still, he could watch Marie. Her dress brought a splash of colour to the monotonous pale walls of the clinic, and the way she moved injected life and fluidity. He loved the way the light glinted in her hair and—

Enough. He should confine himself to appreciating the colours of the brick. He might even allow himself a moment of self-congratulation that all that tapping with a mallet had borne fruit and they were perfectly level.

'I'll be back in ten minutes.'

He grinned at her, leaving her standing in the middle of the courtyard, still looking around, while he headed for the shower.

Marie couldn't wait to get started. By the time Alex had returned she'd brought the rest of the pots and seed trays through from the other courtyard and was shifting the planters around into different configurations.

'Stop!' Alex was leaning back in his seat, drinking lemonade. 'That's the one I like.'

Marie stood back. 'Yes, me too. Then there's space for some seating.'

Alex nodded. 'Where are you thinking of getting that from?'

Now or never… The idea had occurred to her yesterday, and since then Marie hadn't been able to stop thinking about it. 'I had my eye on some old garden benches I saw in a junk shop. They'd scrub up nicely. But…'

Suddenly she felt as if it was too much to ask. As if this little garden with its recycled pots and bedding plants grown from seed wasn't really good enough.

'But what?'

Marie must have shown her embarrassment, because Alex was suddenly still, looking at her thoughtfully. There was no way out now…

'I thought… Did your mother like flowers?'

He raised his eyebrows in surprise. The question had come so much out of the blue.

'She loved her garden. She was always out there, planting things and helping the gardener. Whenever my father wasn't around, that is. He reckoned she shouldn't get involved with any actual work.'

'I thought… Well, I know this garden's never going to make the Chelsea Flower Show, but you made it… And you know how they have seats in the park with people's names on them…?'

She couldn't quite say it, but Alex had caught her meaning and was nodding slowly. Marie held her breath, hoping Alex wouldn't take offence at the suggestion.

'My mother would have loved this garden. And I'd like to buy something for it in memory of her.'

Marie let out a sigh of relief. 'You're sure, Alex? I know it can't do your feelings for her justice.'

He shook his head. 'My father thought cut flowers and ostentatious wreaths did her justice. I hated her funeral and I wanted to go away and do something simple for her on my own, but I never could find the right thing. *This* is the right thing. You said you wanted a water feature?'

'Yes? Do you think that would be better than seating?'

'Much better. She liked the sound of water; she used to

say it was soothing.' Alex thought for a moment. 'No brass plates with her name, though. I don't want that.'

His obvious approval for the idea gave Marie the courage to suggest another. 'What was her name?'

Hopefully it wasn't something too long…

'Elise.'

Perfect. 'If you wanted we might spell her name out? With the plants we choose to put around the water feature?'

He smiled suddenly. 'I'd love that. Thank you for thinking of her, Marie. She'd be so pleased to be part of this garden.'

'Good.' Marie's heart was beginning to return to something that resembled a normal pace. She felt almost light-headed.

'As this is Friday, and we'll be opening on Monday, I'll have to go to the garden centre this weekend. I don't suppose you could spare a couple of hours to help me choose?'

Marie rolled her eyes. 'Where else did you think I was going to be this weekend? Yes, of course I'll help you.'

They'd worked hard at the weekend. Alex had chosen an old millstone, with water bubbling from the centre of it, which was a great deal heavier and more expensive than Marie had envisaged. Jim was going to have to construct a base for it, and install the motor and drainage tank, but Alex and Marie had heaved the millstone into the place reserved for it in the courtyard, and it already looked stunning.

She hadn't stopped Alex from buying plants, some more planters for them, and four wooden benches. This was a labour of love, and the look in his eyes when they'd hauled the first of the planters through into the garden, filled it with compost and arranged echinacea and lavender in it had told her that it meant a great deal more to him than anything money could buy.

On Monday morning everything was ready. Tina, the receptionist, was at her post, and Alex and Marie were sitting in the chairs at the far end of the reception area, along with one of the counsellors, a physiotherapist, and therapists from the pool and the gym. Tina would welcome visitors and summon the relevant person to talk to them.

'You're sure we shouldn't be next to Tina? She looks a bit on her own.' Alex waved across to Tina, who waved cheerily back.

'No. We don't want to frighten anyone away with a horde of therapists waiting to pounce.'

'But I *want* to pounce. Actually, I want to go out onto the street and kidnap anyone who walks by.' Alex was looking a little like a caged lion at the moment.

'Well you can't. We're supposed to be friendly and non-intimidating. We wait, Alex. We've got some groups coming soon. Before you know it you'll have more people than you can cope with.'

'I hope so...' He caught his breath, stiffening suddenly as a shadow fell across the entrance. 'Aren't they the women you were talking to the other day?'

Carol and Nisha had manoeuvred their pushchairs into the lobby and were standing by the door, looking around. They moved forward to let a group of young mums past, who had obviously just dropped their children off at school.

'Yes.' Marie smirked at him. 'They're mine, Alex. You can wait here until Tina calls you...'

He grinned at her, obviously relieved that the reception area was beginning to fill up. 'No one likes an overachiever, Marie.'

'Too bad. I'm still first.'

She stood up, walking across to where Carol and Nisha were standing.

'Hi, Marie.' Carol saw her first, and gave her a wave. 'We've come to check out the mum-and-baby swimming classes.'

'That's great. I'll get you signed up... Would you like to come and see the pool first? It's in the old gym.'

'The gym?' Carol rolled her eyes. 'That I'd love to see.'

Marie led the way. Both women had been to school here, and by the time they got to the swimming pool the three of them were swapping memories of their years spent here.

'You've worked wonders with it all, that's for sure.' Carol nodded her head in approval of the changing rooms and showers, and then stopped short when Marie opened the door that led through to the pool area. 'Wow! This is a bit different!'

The aqua blues and greens of the tiles and the light playing across the water made this one of Marie's favourite parts of the clinic. 'This is the main exercise pool. The hydrotherapy pool is where we're holding the mum-and-baby classes.'

'Does it matter if I can't swim?' Nisha was looking uncertainly at the pool.

'No, the hydrotherapy pool is much shallower than this one. You'll be able to stand up in it. It's kept at a warmer temperature, which makes it more suitable for babies and children.'

Marie led the way through to the smaller pool, where the same blue-and-green tones lent a more restful, intimate atmosphere. Georgie whooped with joy and started to wriggle in his pushchair, obviously keen to try it out straight away.

'I think that's one taker!' Carol grinned, taking him out of the pushchair and keeping a tight hold on him in case he decided to try and jump in. 'What do you think, Nisha?'

'Yes, definitely.'

The matter was settled. Marie had filled two places on the mother-and-baby swimming course, and maybe she'd get a chance to talk a bit more to Nisha.

'Would you like to come to the cafeteria for some coffee?'

'That would be nice. There was something I wanted to ask…' Nisha smiled hesitantly.

'Oh. Yes—good idea. I'll leave you to it, then. See you tomorrow, Nisha. Thanks for the tour, Marie.'

Georgie's protests went unheard as Carol put him back into the pushchair and hurried away, giving them both a wave.

Marie turned to Nisha, who was grinning broadly at her friend's receding figure. 'If there's something you want to talk about we could have coffee in my office.'

'It might not be anything at all. I'm probably just being silly…' Nisha twisted her mouth into a grimace.

'If it matters to you then it's something. The one thing I'm *not* going to do is tell you that you're being silly. You're the one who tells me what's important.'

Nisha nodded. 'It *is* important to me. I wish you could help me…'

Half an hour later Marie walked Nisha through to the reception area, which was now buzzing with activity. Nisha was grinning, clutching the information pack and the appointment card Marie had given her. Alex was nowhere to be seen, and it was another half hour before he appeared again.

'Everything okay with Nisha and Carol?'

'Yes, it's all good.'

She nodded towards his office, and by silent agreement they walked away from the bustle of people. Alex closed the door.

'I had a talk with Nisha; she says she hasn't felt right about sex since having her baby. She's worried about her relationship with her husband.'

He nodded. 'So what did you both decide?'

'Nisha's coming back to see me tomorrow. I'll examine her, and she's given me permission to write to her doctor so he can send her for some tests. Once we've ruled anything physical out we can discuss relationship therapy here.'

'She looked as if she was happy about that?'

'Yes—she said she'd get her husband to come with her tomorrow. He's tried to talk to her about it, but she says she panics and shuts him down.'

'Just talking about it helps.' He threw himself into his chair, staring at the ceiling. 'Of course, I'm a proven expert on talking about things.'

The heavy irony in his tone set off an alarm bell. Something was up with Alex. His hand was shaking, and it didn't seem that hopeful nerves about their opening day was the cause.

'What's up?' She sat down.

'It's…' He waved his hand dismissively. 'Telling you it's nothing and that we should be getting back isn't going to wash, is it?'

'No. There are plenty of people out there to greet visitors, and we're confident the staff here can manage without us for ten minutes. Aren't we, Alex?'

'Yes. Absolutely.' He puffed out a breath. 'In that case… I had a boy who came in to ask about bodybuilding classes. He's only ten. I talked to him a bit, and told him that he'd have to bring one of his parents with him before he could sign up for any kind of exercise class with us.'

'Why did he want to do bodybuilding?' she asked, knowing Alex must have had the same instinct she did.

'It turned out that he'd skipped off school, so I got Tina

to phone the school and they sent a teacher down to fetch him. He's being bullied.'

'Poor kid. And he wants to be able to fight back?'

'Yes. His teacher's going to talk to the parents, and I told her we would enrol him in our anti-bullying programme. He's a little overweight, so if he wants to do exercises then I'll get Mike to devise an exercise programme that suits his age and build.'

'That makes sense.'

'Yeah… But when he realised I wasn't just going to sign him up for bodybuilding he threw a tantrum and then… started to cry—' Alex's voice broke, suddenly.

'That's good, Alex. You got through to him. He must have a lot of negative emotion bottled up.'

Alex was committed to setting up a programme for both kids and adults who were being bullied. He'd applied his customary insight and thoroughness and then left it to a specialist.

Marie had supposed that someone with Alex's charm and natural leadership ability couldn't possibly have first-hand knowledge of being bullied, so he'd left the finer points to the experts he'd recruited. But she'd based her supposition on what she'd thought she knew about Alex. The happy childhood she'd imagined for him.

'You know, I always wanted you to have been happy as a child.'

He looked up at her. 'Yeah? That's nice.'

'Not really. I just wanted to know someone who'd grown up normally. It made me feel better—as if that was something I could shoot for.'

'Ah. Sorry to disappoint you, then.' He turned the corners of his mouth down.

'But, thinking about it, I guess it might have been a bit difficult to make friends when you were little.'

He was gazing at his desk, as if something there might

provide an answer. 'My father didn't think I should play with any of the kids who lived nearby because I was a prince. I was taught at home until it came time for me to be packed off to an exclusive boarding school. I was a shy kid, with a name that invited a thousand jokes. Of course I got bullied.'

And so he'd become the student who everyone liked. He'd listened to what people said and charmed them all. Marie had never looked past that.

'I wasn't much of a friend, was I?'

His eyebrows shot up. 'What? You were kind and honest. You brought me colour, and you showed me that however hard things are there's always time to celebrate the good things. I wanted...'

He fell silent suddenly, and in the warmth of his gaze Marie knew what he'd wanted. He'd wanted *her*. She'd wanted him too. Honesty was good—but this was one place they couldn't go.

'I wanted to be like you.'

His smooth refusal to face that particular fact was a relief, because Marie couldn't face it either. She'd never really moved on from wanting Alex.

'Will you do me a favour?' she asked.

'Anything.'

The look in his eyes told her he meant it.

'You've got a lot you can give to the anti-bullying programme. All those feelings and the things no one ever said. I want you to get more involved with it.'

He laughed suddenly. 'Don't underestimate me by giving me the easy option, will you.'

'You *want* me to underestimate you?'

'No, not really. Keeping me honest is what you do best.' He held his hands up in a gesture of smiling surrender. 'Yes, I'll do it. And now we really should be getting back to our visitors.'

CHAPTER SIX

YESTERDAY HAD BEEN a success. The flood of people who'd wanted to be first to explore the new clinic had subsided into a steady but satisfying trickle. Alex had received a couple of calls from local doctors, enquiring about referring patients to the clinic, and he'd shown a consultant from the nearby hospital around. She had a young patient whose family were currently travelling an hour each way to get to a hydrotherapy pool, and was pleased to find a closer facility that would meet the girl's needs.

Today there was a new challenge.

Alex assumed his best trust-me-I'm-a-doctor smile, and when he looked down at Marie he saw a similar one plastered uneasily across her face.

'Oh, really, Alex.' Sonya Graham-Hall flapped her hand at the photographer from the local paper, indicating that he was to stand down while she gave her clients a good talking-to. 'Can you try not to look as if you've eaten something that doesn't agree with you? You're supposed to be welcoming. And stand a little closer to Marie. You're a team…'

Marie was looking a little overawed by Sonya. Alex took a step towards her, feeling the inevitable thrill as her shoulder touched his arm. He bent towards her, whispering an old joke from medical school, and she suppressed a laugh. He couldn't help smiling, and heard the camera click rapidly.

'Wonderful!'

Sonya beamed at everyone, and Alex stepped forward to shake the photographer's hand and thank him. Then Sonya marched across the reception area to where the local reporter was standing, leading him towards the front doors.

'What's she doing?' Marie looked up at him. 'Can't he find his own way?'

'It's Sonya's modus operandi. She's making sure he knows what he's meant to write. Although he probably won't realise that's what she's done until after he's filed his story.'

Alex knew Sonya's husband from school, and knew she was the best PR representative in London. She was so much in demand that it was usual for her to interview clients, rather than the other way round. Alex had been lucky, though, and a phone call had not only managed to secure Sonya's services, but they were on a pro bono basis, because she loved the idea of the clinic. There was something to be said for the public school network.

'She's formidable, isn't she?' Marie's smile indicated that she thought formidable was a really good thing. 'I'm a little scared of her.'

Alex couldn't fathom what Marie would have to be scared about. If he'd been asked to define 'formidable', the first person who would have come to mind was Marie. But not quite in the same way as Sonya, who relied on killer heels, designer jackets and an upper-class accent that would have sliced through concrete.

'She knows so many important people...'

'It's her job to know people. Anyway, don't we prefer to think of *everyone* as important?'

Marie frowned, nudging him with her elbow. 'Of course we do. You know what I mean.'

Alex knew. Marie had already told him that she felt like a fish out of water with the great and the good, but they were exactly the kind of people who had the money and influence to help them make this project grow into a whole chain of clinics in different parts of the country. He wished Marie would stop thinking of them as somehow out of her league, because she was just as good as any of them.

'Right, then.' Sonya returned, beaming. 'I think he's on track. While I'm here, perhaps we can review where we are with everything else.'

'Thanks, Sonya. My office?'

Alex led the way, hearing Sonya chatting brightly to Marie, and Marie's awkward, awestruck replies.

Sonya plumped herself into one of the easy chairs, drawing a slim tablet out of her handbag. In Sonya's eyes, paper was messy, and she didn't do mess.

'Ooh, look. I love these. Such lovely colours. Can I have one?'

She leaned forward towards the coffee table, catching up the sheet of brightly coloured stickers that Marie had presented him with this morning. They had the name of the clinic on them, along with the main telephone number and website address, but Alex suspected that their real intent was to bring yet another much-needed shot of colour into his office.

'Help yourself. Marie has had a few printed. Shall we get some more?' Marie was already squirming in her seat, and Alex decided to embarrass her a little more.

'Definitely. This is just the kind of fun thing we want. Something to get away from the boring medical image.'

Alex felt his eyebrows shoot up.

'You know what I mean, Alex. Of course the medical part is the most important, but we want people to feel that you're approachable and not a stuffy old doctor.'

'Yes, we do.' Marie spoke up, reddening slightly at her audacity, and Sonya nodded.

'Now. I have the local radio interview set up—you're on your own with that one, Alex.'

'I can handle it.' Alex reckoned he could talk for ten minutes about the clinic easily enough.

'I'm sure you can. But I'm sending you a list of key-words and I want you to memorise them.'

Sonya swiped her finger across her tablet, and Alex heard a ding from the other side of the room as his desktop computer signalled that he had mail.

'Really? Keywords?'

'Yes, of course, darling. Think of it as like…' Sonya waved her hand in the air, groping for the right words.

'Like talking to a patient? Sometimes you have to em-phasise what's important without confusing them with a load of irrelevant detail,' Marie ventured.

'Yes, exactly.'

Sonya gave Marie a conspiratorial smile, indicating she was pleased to see that at least one of them was on track, and Marie reddened again.

'I'm still working on the TV appearance, and there are a couple of functions that I'd like you to go to if I can get you an invitation.' Sonya leaned forward in her seat. 'You still have reservations about promoting the royal aspect in the media?'

Alex felt the side of his jaw twitch. 'If by *reservations* you mean that I'm absolutely sure that I don't want any of that in the media, then, yes, I'm still absolutely sure.'

'But it's such a good story, Alex. It would catch people's imaginations. It doesn't get much hotter than this—you're a doctor, very rich, royal, and to top it off a handsome bachelor.'

Alex shook his head, and then Marie spoke. Like an angel coming to rescue him.

'We've agreed a policy about this.'

'Ah… Yes?'

Sonya turned to Marie, clearly wanting her to elaborate. And Alex wanted to know what policy he'd agreed, as well.

'The compelling nature of Alex's story is the problem—it could quite easily prompt a media circus. Our values are that the clinic is the one and only important thing. Once it's a bit more established we could look at it again, but now's not the right time.'

Nicely said. Alex shot Marie a thankful look and she received it with the quiet graciousness of a queen.

Sonya nodded. 'Yes, that makes sense. Why didn't you say that before, Alex?'

'Marie sums it up a great deal better than I can.'

Sonya flashed him a look that told him she agreed entirely with the sentiment, and then moved on. 'Now, I'm rather hoping you have something presentable to wear, Alex.'

'I have a suit…' Just the one. It was the suit he wore for job interviews, and he hoped it still fitted.

'All right. I'll send you the names of a few good tailors, just in case.'

Alex's computer dinged again and Sonya swiped her finger across her screen, in clear indication that she'd ticked that particular item off her list.

'I'm very pleased with the website—are you getting anything via the enquiries page?'

'Yes, quite a few things. Sofia's coordinating that.'

'Good. She seems very efficient. And the mural for your reception area? There are lots of possibilities there. How ever did you find these people? I've had a look at their previous work and it's stunning. Inspirational, even.'

'That was Marie's idea.'

'Of course…' Sonya's questioning gaze swept towards Marie.

'Oh. Yes, well… They're a group of artists who do wall

art for charities and public spaces like hospitals and libraries. They choose the organisations they want to be involved with and work for free—we just pay for their materials.'

'And who's in charge?' Sonya enquired.

'Corinne Riley's their coordinator. She's about as much in charge as anyone is. She's an artist, and works part-time as an art therapist. Her husband, Tom, is head of Paediatrics at the hospital where I used to work.'

'And would they consider a magazine article, or even a short TV piece featuring their work here?'

Marie shrugged. 'I could ask. I know Corinne's very interested in spreading the word about how art can change spaces and involve people.'

'It's fascinating…' Sonya's mind was obviously hard at work on the possibilities. 'Yes, please. And I'd love an introduction if you feel that's appropriate?'

Alex smirked, wondering if Marie was taking notice of the fact that Sonya had just asked her for an introduction. It seemed she was, because she smiled suddenly.

'I'll email Corinne today and get back to you. Do you have any particular time in mind?'

'If she sends me a couple of dates which suit her I'll fit in with them.'

Sonya swiped again, and Alex braced himself for the next item on her agenda.

'You do have a suit, don't you?'

Now that Sonya had left, Alex's office seemed a little quiet. Marie had waited to ask the awkward question.

'Somewhere. Unless I left it at the dry cleaner's…'

Marie frowned at him. 'It's not that suit you bought for your job interviews, is it?'

'What's wrong with that one?'

'It's not going to fit you any more.'

Alex put his hand on his stomach, sucking it in, and Marie laughed.

'I meant across the shoulders. You've lost those few extra pounds you were carrying.'

So she'd noticed. Alex couldn't help smirking. 'You think I've lost a bit of weight?'

She made a thing of eying him up and down. She was teasing, but her gaze made his stomach tighten with apprehension. When she grinned, it felt as if a warm wave was washing over him.

'You're in good shape, Alex. But you'll probably need a proper suit for these functions that Sonya was talking about.'

Alex sighed. 'Yes. Probably.'

'How many suits did you have when you were a child?' Marie homed in unerringly on the exact reason why Alex never wore a suit.

'Oh, about a dozen, all told. New ones each year.'

'That sounds excruciating.'

'It was.'

But he was doing things on his own terms now. Marie had told him that, and she wasn't going to underestimate him by reminding him again. In the silence he could feel her presence pushing the memories back and turning his gaze forward.

'You're right. I'll order two new suits; that old one probably doesn't fit me any more.'

She nodded. 'You'll be your own kind of excellent and glorious. What about some striped socks to match?'

Alex chuckled. His father would have blown a gasket at the thought of his wearing striped socks with a suit. Or with anything else, for that matter. Having to be excellent and glorious suddenly didn't seem so bad.

'Okay. Striped socks it is. You can choose them.'

* * *

The clinic's first week was reassuringly busy. Marie and Alex had agreed on a 'walking around' approach, to see how things were going and to iron out any teething problems, and they took turns with it. One dealt with patients and any urgent paperwork, and the other simply walked around the clinic, visiting all the different departments and talking to people.

It was working well—the staff were encouraged to talk about any difficulties they had, and the clinic's clients were beginning to know that either Marie or Alex would always be somewhere in the building if they wanted to chat.

'Hi, Terri. How are things going?' Marie saw a young mother with whom Alex had been working approaching her.

Terri's older child had been born with spina bifida, and although surgery had closed the opening in her spine, the little girl had been left with weakness in her legs and needed a specialist exercise regime.

'Good, thanks. This place is an absolute godsend.' Terri beamed at her. 'All that travelling we used to do to get to a hydrotherapy pool for Amy, and now we can just walk around the corner.'

'You're enjoying your swimming?' Marie grinned down at Terri's eight-year-old daughter and Amy nodded.

'*I'm* going to swim too.' Five-year-old Sam had been walking next to his sister's wheelchair, hanging obediently onto the side of it. 'I'm going to be a really good swimmer, and then I can help Amy.'

Terri grinned. 'It's great for both of them. We couldn't afford the time to take Sam to a class as well, but the hydrotherapist says she'll book Amy's sessions at the same time as the junior swim class, so Sam can swim too. Usually he just has to sit with me by the pool.'

'That's great.'

It was exactly what the clinic was for. Helping whole families to cope. Terri was looking less tired than she had when Marie had first met her.

'What's that?' Sam had left his sister's side and was standing on his toes, peering through the window into the courtyard.

'It's our garden. If you've got time, you can come and have a look.'

Marie shot a questioning look at Terri and she nodded. Opening the door, Marie let Sam into the courtyard and he started to run around, stopping in front of each planter to look at the flowers.

Terri parked Amy's wheelchair next to the water feature, so she could reach out to touch the plants around it. Then she sank down onto a nearby bench.

'This is lovely. I could stay here all day.'

Sam and Amy were amusing each other, and Terri gave a satisfied smile.

'Hello, Amy.' A woman stopped in the corridor by the open door. 'How are you, dear?'

'Very well, thank you, Miss Fletcher.' Amy sat a little straighter in her wheelchair and Marie suppressed a smile.

Jennifer Fletcher had been one of the first people through the doors when the clinic had opened. A retired primary school teacher, she seemed to know every child in the district, and had taught a number of their parents as well.

'This is lovely.' Jennifer craned her neck to see the garden, obviously hesitant to inspect it more closely without being asked.

'Come and join us, Miss Fletcher.' Terri grinned at her.

'It's about time you called me Jennifer.'

Miss Fletcher walked slowly across to the bench and Marie moved to make room for her.

'What brings you here...um...Jennifer?' Terri was

clearly reticent about calling her old schoolteacher by her first name.

'I've been having a few aches and pains since I retired last spring, so I decided to come along and see if I could join an exercise class. I had a full physical, and the doctors have found I have an inflammation in my right hip.'

Jennifer beamed at Marie. She'd had the distinction of being the first patient to try out the new MRI scanner, and it had shown that, instead of a touch of arthritis, the bursa in her right hip was inflamed. Jennifer had professed delight at the thought that this could be rectified, and was already seeing the clinic's physiotherapist.

'I've got a full exercise programme and I think I'm doing rather well. It's early days, of course, but the physiotherapist here says that core strength is important as you enter your seventies.' Jennifer looked around the garden. 'You'll be adding a few bedding plants?'

'It's a work in progress. We've planted some seeds, and we have some cuttings over there in the corner.' Marie pointed to the yoghurt pots, full of water, where the cuttings were beginning to grow roots.

She saw Amy's head turn, and the little girl leaned over to see. 'I don't suppose you'd like to help us plant some, would you, Amy?'

'Mum...?' Amy turned to Terri.

'Of course. But we mustn't take up Dr Davies's time.' Terri flashed Marie an apologetic look.

'That's all right. If Amy would like to help with the garden—'

'Well, I would, too...' Jennifer spoke up.

It seemed that the garden had just acquired its first few volunteers.

Marie brought some of the pots over, moving a table so that Jennifer and Amy could work together, planting the

Busy Lizzies. Sam had taken a couple of action figures from his mother's handbag, and he was playing with them.

'Would you like a drink? I'll pop over to the café.'

Everyone else was occupied and Terri deserved a break.

'You know what…?' Terri gave her a wry smile. 'I'd like to just stroll over there and get something. On my own. If you or Jennifer don't mind staying here with the kids, that is…?'

Marie knew the feeling well. Terri craved a moment to herself, so she could do something ordinary. She'd felt like that when she was a teenager. Wanting just five minutes that she could call her own, without one or other of her brothers wanting something.

'Of course. We'll be another half an hour with this, if you want to sit in the café?'

'No, that's okay. Can I get you something?' Terri pulled her purse out of her bag. 'My treat.'

If Marie wanted coffee, she had the lovely machine in her office. But that wasn't the point. It was clearly important to Terri that she get it, and she should accept the offer.

'A cup of tea would be nice. Thank you.'

Terri grinned, turning to Jennifer. 'Would you like a drink?'

Fifteen minutes later she saw Terri strolling back towards them, chatting to Alex. He was carrying a tray with four cups and a couple of child-sized boxes of juice, and when he'd handed the drinks around and stopped to find out how Jennifer and Amy were he strolled over to Sam to deliver his drink.

'They never quite grow up, do they?' Terri was drinking her coffee, watching Alex and Sam. The little boy had shown Alex his action figures, and the two were now busily engaged in making them jump from one planter to another. Sam jumped his onto the water feature with a splash and Alex followed with his, and the two figures started to fight in the swirling water.

By the time Terri said that they should go home, Alex's shirt was dappled with water. The pots were gathered up and labelled as Amy's, so that she could watch her plants grow and transfer them to the planters when they were big enough. Sam said goodbye to Alex, promising that they would continue their fight the next time he was here, and Alex thanked him gravely.

'I'm hoping your mother wouldn't have minded too much…' Marie nodded towards the water feature.

'Mind? She'd have loved it.' Alex grinned at her, coming to sit down on the bench.

'Good. And of course all that splashing about was entirely for Sam's benefit?'

It had occurred to Marie that Alex's love of silly games was because he'd never got the chance to play them when he was a child.

'Of course.' Alex brushed at his shirt, as if he'd only just noticed the water. 'I have absolutely no idea why you should think otherwise. Ooh—I had a call from Sonya.'

'What does she want us to do now?'

Sonya's calls generally meant smiling for one camera or another, but every time they did it Sofia Costa received a fresh wave of enquiries.

'It's an evening do at the Institute of Business. They throw a very select party once in a while, so their members can meet people who are doing groundbreaking work in various charitable and medical fields. Most big businesses like to have their names associated with a few good causes, and making those contacts now will help us in the future.'

Even the scale of Alex's wealth wasn't going to finance his dreams of creating and running a chain of clinics all over the country. This was about the future—one that Alex was going to build for himself.

'That sounds great. Does Sonya know someone at the Institute?'

'No, but it turns out that a couple of the Institute's board of directors went to my school and they vaguely remember me. Sonya's managed to swing a couple of invitations.'

'So Sonya's going with you?' That would be good. She'd keep Alex in line and on message.

'No, she's going with her husband. The second invitation is for you.'

'What?' All the quiet peace of the garden suddenly evaporated. 'Tell me you're joking, Alex.'

'Why would I be? You have as much to say about the clinic as me.'

He leaned forward, his eyes betraying the touch of mischief that Marie loved so much. At any other time than this.

'And the whole point of a man's dinner suit is to show off a woman's dress.'

Suddenly she felt sick. 'I can't hobnob with the rich and famous, Alex. I don't know how to talk with these people, or how to act.'

'How about just the same as you always do?'

There was a trace of hurt in his voice. *He* was rich. And it was only a matter of time before he'd be famous. She knew Alex was under no illusions that he could keep his royal status under wraps indefinitely—he just wanted to put the moment off for as long as he could.

'I can't, Alex. I just…can't.'

He thought for a moment, his face grave. 'Okay. If you can't do it, then you can't. I'm not going to tell you that the clinic needs you, or that I need you, because that wouldn't give you any choice. You're always there for the people who need you.'

'What do you mean?' The lump in Marie's throat betrayed her. She knew exactly what he meant.

'You've always been there for your mother and brothers.

Don't get me wrong—that's a fine thing, and I envy you it. I'd have done anything for my mother to need me a bit more. But I know it's not been easy for you; it never is for people who care for the people they love.'

She'd been thinking the same about Terri, just moments ago. He was right, but Marie dismissed the thought. It was too awkward.

'So you're telling me I don't have to go?'

'Of course. You don't *have* to do anything. I'd really like you to go, because I think you're selling yourself short. And because a very wise person once told me that I needed to accept who I am and write my own script. I'd like you to accept who I am and come with me, as my friend.'

Dammit. Saying he needed her would have been easy compared to this. Alex was reaching out, asking her to step out of her comfort zone and meet him halfway.

'So when is this reception?'

'Next month. I could go dress-shopping with you…?'

He looked as if he'd enjoy that far too much.

'No, that's fine. I can handle that.'

'Then you're coming?'

'Yes, all right. I'll come.'

At least it would serve as a reminder to her that she and Alex came from different worlds. That they could be friends, but anything more was unthinkable. It had always been unthinkable, but it was doubly so now that they were working together.

He grinned. 'Great. I'll let Sonya know. Should I quit while I'm winning?'

She could never resist his smile. 'Yes. Please do that, Alex.'

CHAPTER SEVEN

MARIE HAD BOUGHT Alex an action figure. She reckoned it was what every boy needed, in case someone turned up in his office needing to play, and Alex had arranged the jointed arms and legs so that the figure leant nonchalantly against one of the plant pots on his windowsill.

She tried to repress a yawn, failing miserably. Jennifer Fletcher had expressed enthusiasm over an idea for a carers' support group for mums like Terri, and said that she had another couple of friends who might be interested in helping. They were having to sort out all the relevant statutory checks for the volunteers who were going to be working with children, and assess the needs of the kids so that the clinic could provide the professional staff that would be required. It was going to take a couple of hours.

'Why don't we finish for the evening? This can wait,' said Alex.

'It can't, Alex. We've both got a full day tomorrow.'

And Marie had left work at five o'clock sharp for the last couple of evenings. She was feeling guilty about having left Alex alone working, but her mother was having one of her crises and Marie had been up late, talking her down.

He opened his mouth, obviously about to protest, but the sound of the front gates rattling silenced him.

Alex went to the window, and then turned. 'Nisha's outside. You don't have an appointment with her, do you?'

'No, all her medical tests came back okay, so I referred her to our relationship counsellor…'

Marie followed Alex outside and saw that Nisha was walking away from the gates now. He hurried to unlock them.

'I'm sorry…' Nisha turned back to him, tears streaming down her face. 'I shouldn't have come…'

'That's all right. Come inside and tell us what the matter is.'

Alex's question provoked more tears. 'When I spoke to Anita at the clinic she said that we didn't have to have sex…we could just spend time together. But one thing led to another…'

It was a measure of her distress that Nisha had forgotten all her reticence in talking about the problem.

'Okay, well, come inside.'

Alex glanced at Marie. He had no hesitation in talking to patients about sexual matters, but he was clearly wondering if Nisha wouldn't feel more comfortable discussing this with Marie.

'We had such a lovely time. But now it hurts to pee, and I'm passing blood. Carol says it's cystitis. What am I going to tell my husband?'

Alex frowned, clearly wondering whether Nisha wanted him to respond or not.

Marie decided to put him out of his misery. 'Let's go inside, eh? Alex, why don't you take the pushchair?'

'I'm so sorry. It's later than I thought—you must be closed by now…'

'That's okay. I'm glad you came.'

That was almost the truth. Marie *was* glad Nisha had asked for help—she just wished she'd needed it on another evening, when she wasn't so tired. But when she took Nisha's hand she felt it warm and trembling in hers and forgot all about that.

Nisha was running a fever, and clearly not at all well. After Marie had tested a sample of her urine, to confirm Carol's diagnosis, she curled up on the examination couch, shivering and crying.

'Can we call your husband? I think it would be best if he came and picked you up.'

Nisha nodded. 'I'm so disappointed. I thought we were doing everything right, at last…'

'I know it's easy to feel it is, but this is not your fault. Recovery isn't always a straight line; it's sometimes two steps forward and one step back. But this is an infection and we can deal with it. You'll feel a lot better when the antibiotics start to take effect.'

'Sorry…'

Marie smiled at Nisha. 'And stop apologising, will you? This is what we're here for.'

'I'm so glad you *are* here. Thank you.'

Nisha's husband arrived—a quiet, smiling man, who made sure that the first thing he did was hug his wife.

Prompted by Marie, Nisha told him what had happened and he nodded. 'I'll stay home from work tomorrow to look after you.'

'No. You don't need to…'

But Nisha obviously wanted him to, and Marie guessed it wouldn't take much before she gave in and accepted his offer.

'Give us a call if there's anything we can help with.' She handed Nisha's husband her card. 'If the clinic's closed, you can use the out-of-hours number; there will be someone on hand to advise you.'

'Thank you—for everything. I'll take good care of her.' Nisha's husband helped her down from the couch, putting his arm around her protectively.

Alex opened the gates and bade the couple goodbye, reserving a special smile for the child in the pushchair, who had slept soundly through the whole thing.

Then he turned, walking back to his office, where Marie was waiting for him. He picked up her laptop and papers, tucking them under his arm. 'We're going back to mine. We'll get a takeaway.'

Just like the old days. When he'd brook none of her arguments about needing to work and insist she take a break for just one evening. That had usually involved food, as well, and the tradition had persisted. His flat was on her way home, and after a day spent at the clinic it would be nice to talk over a meal.

'It's my turn to get the takeaway, isn't it? Shall we go for Thai this time?' Marie's resources stretched to taking her turn in paying for the food now.

He shrugged, picking up his car keys. 'That sounds great.'

Alex's flat was on the top floor of a mansion block in Hampstead. Quiet and secluded, but just moments away from a parade of artisan food shops and cafés, and little boutiques that sold clothes with hefty price tags.

Inside, it reeked of quiet quality. Large rooms with high ceilings, and a hallway that was built to accommodate cupboards and storage and still give more than enough space. Alex might have rejected his father's lifestyle, but he'd absorbed an appreciation for nice things, and he always bought the best he could afford. The sofas were the same ones he'd had in medical school, but they were still as comfortable and looked as good. If you could afford it, there was economy in that.

'You order. I'll put some music on. What do you fancy? A little late-night jazz?'

The sitting room was lined with cabinets that housed Alex's extensive books and music collection. Marie had never hesitated in sharing his music with him—it was one of those things that cost nothing and brought them both joy.

But it wasn't late-night yet, even though Marie felt tired enough. 'Late-night jazz is going to send me to sleep.'

'Right. Driving music?'

'No, that's a bit too wakey-uppy. Have you got a soul mix?'

It was a rhetorical question. Alex chuckled. There was a pause while he decided which soul mix fitted the occasion best, and then a muted beat began to fill the room.

They began to work, spreading their papers out on the large glass-topped coffee table. When the food came they added a couple of plates and a jumble of takeaway cartons. Ideas came more easily in this setting, and by the time they were ready for coffee they were finished.

He stood, stretching his limbs with satisfaction. Marie leant forward to gather up the plates and he batted her hand away.

'Leave it, will you? Try relaxing for a few minutes.'

It was impossible not to, in the heat of his smile and the rhythm of the music.

'I'll take a hot towel for my face while you're there...' she called after him as he made his way to the kitchen, laden down with the remnants of their meal.

'Sorry, ma'am, we're fresh out of hot towels. Coffee will have to do.'

Marie rolled her eyes, teasing him. 'No hot towels? What kind of service is this? I'm not coming back here again!'

'I've got a dark roast arabica...' he shouted through from the kitchen, and Marie chuckled. Alex always served good coffee.

'You're almost forgiven,' she shouted back.

He returned with two cups of black coffee, with a thick foamy crema on top. Even the smell of it was gorgeous.

'That's it. This is definitely a five-star establishment.'

'It can't possibly be. I'm not done yet.' He grinned at her, catching her hand. 'I've got moves.'

Another one of those old jokes that had stood the test of time. They both loved to dance, and Alex's grinning query as to whether *she* had moves, and his promise that he had a few of his own, would often prompt them to dance until they were exhausted. Marie had often wondered whether it was a substitute for sex, but had decided not to think too deeply on the question.

'My moves are already asleep. I will be too, as soon as I get home.'

Alex was far too tempting at the moment. Too delicious and complicated. She'd never wanted to be one of those women who went out with Alex for a few months only to see him walk away without looking back.

'Are you sure? You're tapping your foot.'

He turned the music up, trying to tempt her, but when Marie laughed and shook her head, he turned it back down again.

'Okay, your loss. It means you'll just have to tell me what the matter is.'

'Nothing. I'm just tired…'

How many times had Alex heard Marie say that nothing was the matter? How many times had he asked and felt shut out when she wouldn't talk about it? He'd accepted it once, but it was becoming more and more difficult to take what she said at face value and turn away from her.

'I can wait you out.' He sat down, taking a sip of his coffee.

Marie smiled. How she managed to do that, when she was so tired she could hardly keep her eyes open and clearly worried about something, was beyond him.

'Great coffee.'

'Yes, it's a good blend.' Alex decided that Marie's diversionary tactics weren't going to work on him any more. 'I'm still waiting.'

She puffed out a breath. 'It's nothing, really. I just… I was up a bit late last night, talking to my mum. She's worried about my youngest brother.'

'What about you? Are you worried about him?'

She gave a frustrated shrug. 'I'm *always* worried about Zack.'

This was something new. Alex knew Marie had always supported her younger brothers, but she'd never really said much about the day-to-day process of that. Just that her mum often found that three boys could be hard to handle on her own and needed a bit of help. Alex had assumed that Marie helped out financially, but it seemed there was more to it than that.

'What's the problem?'

Perhaps he'd remind her that they'd been friends for a long time. Maybe he'd even mention that Marie had given him a hard time over the secrets he'd kept.

'You know… He's twenty…'

'He's having difficulty finding time to study and check out all the bands he needs to see?'

She laughed suddenly. 'No, Alex. He's not like *you* when you were twenty. Anyway, you never seemed to have much difficulty keeping up.'

'Yeah. It was easy. You managed your studies, as many jobs as you could find, *and* about five minutes per day for recreation. So what's Zack not managing to do?'

She shrugged, reaching for her coffee cup. That was a sure signal that she was done talking.

They'd been through a lot together over the years. Studying, dancing, working until they were too tired even to speak. He'd carried her into her bedroom once and then turned his back, walking away, because the one thing Alex had always known for sure was that he couldn't take things any further with Marie.

He'd rejected the idea that he'd always loved her and instead he'd asked her to help him build a clinic. But he *had* always loved her, and when she turned her gaze on him, her eyes dark in the approaching dusk, he knew he wasn't going to flinch from this.

'What is Zack not managing to do?' he repeated. He heard the quiet demand in his tone and saw surprise on Marie's face.

For a moment he thought she would get up and leave, but then she spoke.

'At the moment he's not managing to do anything very much. He did well with his A levels, but decided he wanted to take a year out before university. I think it was just that he couldn't get motivated to choose a course. I got all the prospectuses and sat down with him, but he wasn't very enthusiastic about it.'

'So he's working?'

'No. He had a few jobs, but couldn't stick at any of them. He's been unemployed for the last six months, and increasingly he's staying up all night and sleeping all day. Mum doesn't know what to do with him. A few days ago he took money from her purse and went out. He came back the following afternoon, went straight upstairs and slept for fourteen hours. She's worried he might have been taking drugs, but I took a look at him and didn't see any signs of it.'

'How much money did he take?' Alex felt a cold weight settle in his chest. This wasn't fair…

'Two hundred pounds. She'd just gone to the bank to get the money for her main monthly food shop. She can't afford that; she's already keeping him in food and clothes.'

'So you gave her the money?'

Marie rolled her eyes. 'What else was I supposed to

do? I told Zack this was absolutely the last time, and that I wasn't going to bale him out again.'

'Did he listen?'

'Yes, he listened. Listening's not the problem with Zack. He'll hear what you have to say, and tell you all the things he thinks you want to hear. Then he'll ignore it all and do exactly as he likes. Mum knows he's got to change, but she makes excuses for him. About how he's never had a strong father figure, and how she's not been able to give him enough time because she's at work.'

The words came out in a rush of frustration. Then Marie reddened a little, as if she'd made a faux pas by admitting that there was something she couldn't manage on her own. He wasn't going to give up on her now.

'What about your other brothers?' He knew that both of Marie's other brothers had been to university and had good jobs.

'Dan's washed his hands of him completely—he says Zack needs to pull himself together. And Pete lives up in Sunderland. He tried talking to him last time he was down on a visit, but Zack just gave him that lovely smile of his and told him everything will work out.'

'And your mother?'

'She's…she does her best. Mum's fragile. She had a breakdown when my dad left, and we were all put into foster homes for a while. It was awful.'

Alex nodded. Marie had told him, years ago, how all she'd wanted when she was a kid was to have her family back together and to keep it that way. At the time he'd almost envied her for having something she cared about so much.

'It never was your fault, Marie. You didn't have to be the one to put things right.'

A single tear rolled down her cheek. Suddenly the room was far too big and the distance between them too great.

He couldn't reach for her and comfort her, and if he moved she'd only shoo him away and tell him that she was okay.

'In a way, it was my fault. My dad left because a wife and four children was too much for him. He couldn't deal with it. My mum broke down over it…'

'You were ten years old.' The impulse to hold her and comfort her was wearing him down fast. 'You were trying to clear up a mess that adults had made.'

'Families, huh? Who'd have them?' She brushed away the tears and gave him a smile.

Was he supposed to empathise with that? Alex reckoned so. And Marie was only telling him what he already knew. He couldn't contemplate having a family of his own because he'd lived with the consequences of failure and seen what they had done to his mother. Marie had lived with the consequences of failure as well, and she needed someone who would be there for her.

Maybe that was why he'd always maintained his distance. He'd helped her as much as she would let him in practical terms, but always shied away from the emotional. It was time to redraw the boundaries.

'What do you need?'

She shrugged, shaking her head. 'I've had a takeaway and some music. Now an early night.'

She obviously wasn't going to discuss the matter any further, and Alex needed a plan. Something with no loose ends, that she wouldn't be able to argue with or reject out of hand. Something that was going to work and maybe change things in the long term.

'I'll take you home, then.'

'That's okay. It's early enough to take the Tube.'

Alex got to his feet. 'You can take the Tube, then, and I'll drive over to your place. I'll see you there.'

The expected smile almost tore his heart in two.

'Since you're going my way, I suppose I *could* ask you to drop me off, then.'

He walked through into the hall, picking up his car keys and waiting for her there. Marie appeared, her bag slung across her shoulder, but before he could reach for the latch on the front door she suddenly flung her arms around his waist.

'Uh!' He allowed his hands to move slowly towards her back, returning her hug as impersonally as he could. 'What was that for?'

'For being my best friend. And for listening to me blather on.'

She hugged him tight, and then let him go, stepping back. Alex's knees almost gave way.

'This is just between you and me, right?'

She saw everyone else's needs and yet treated her own as weakness. And she was clearly regretting saying as much as she had.

'Of course. What are friends for?'

The look on her face seemed a lot like relief that he'd decided to drop the subject. For once, Marie had misread him. Alex wasn't going to back off and if she put up a fight then so be it.

He'd fight her back.

A good night's sleep had applied some perspective to the matter. Marie would deal with Zack, and she'd deal with her mum the way she always had. Alex couldn't help her with this.

She retreated to her office, and then spent most of the day showing a few local GPs and hospital doctors around the clinic while Alex saw patients. Working together with other health professionals, becoming one of their options when they thought about what their patients needed, was a must if the clinic was going to reach its full potential for helping the community.

When Alex appeared in the doorway she couldn't help starting. Last night had lit a slow-burning fuse, which had been fizzling all day. Sometimes it seemed to go out, but that was just an illusion. The spark never quite died.

'How was your day?'

His question was much the same as it usually was when they'd been working on separate things and hadn't seen much of each other.

'Good, thanks. They all seemed impressed with what we had to offer, and a couple of them have said that they already have patients on their books they'd like to refer.'

'That sounds great.'

He dipped his hand into his pocket and put a small box on her desk. Marie looked inside, finding a tangle of pink paper clips, and when she tipped some of them out she saw that they were in different animal shapes.

'They're wonderful—thank you. Where do you get all this crazy stuff?' Marie already had a collection of unusually shaped, brightly coloured things on her desk, which Alex had bought for her.

'That's my secret. If you knew, you wouldn't need me to feed your stationery habit. And, by the way, I saw Anita just now. She popped in to see Nisha today.'

'Yes? How is she?'

Alex had clearly decided to forget her show of emotion last night, and they were back to business as usual. If he could do it, then so could she.

'Feeling much better.' He grinned. 'I'm going to stick with that blanket assurance and leave the details to you and Anita. I imagine that Nisha will be more comfortable with that.'

'Good move.'

Marie bit her tongue. She didn't need to be thinking about Alex's moves—or hers. Last night was last night.

Alex seemed to be loitering, neither sitting down to talk nor about to leave. Suddenly he planted his hands on her desk, leaning forward towards her.

'I want Zack.'

'You...want Zack?'

Marie felt her jaw harden. Alex obviously thought he could solve this problem, but he didn't know Zack.

'What for? There's nothing you can do, Alex.'

'Why on earth not? We're friends, Marie. Heaven forbid we'd actually try to help each other with our problems.'

All right. He had her there.

'I can deal with it. I appreciate the offer, but—'

'It's not an offer. You can't deal with this on your own, and I can help. You told me I had to accept what I've been given and do the right thing with it. I'm just following your advice.'

'Well...what are you going to do with him?'

Alex was clearly on a mission. If she wasn't so cross with her brother for treating their mum so badly Marie might have felt sorry for Zack.

Alex straightened up. He suddenly seemed very tall, his determination filling the room. 'He's going to work here. I've had a word with Sofia, and there are a lot of things she can get him to do, so he'll be working hard. He'll need to, because he's going to have to pay you back the two hundred pounds he took.'

'That doesn't matter, Alex. It's done now.'

'It matters. This isn't about the money. It's about how he treats people. I need you to take the two hundred pounds and for your mother to accept something from him for his bed and board. Everything else I'll deal with. He'll work a full day and he'll pull his weight. If he turns up here with a hangover I'll find a job for him that'll make a cracking headache even worse. And if I see any evidence of drug-taking I'll test him myself and put him into our drug rehab programme.'

It was exactly what Zack needed. But Alex shouldn't have to do this.

'The clinic can't afford it, Alex. We have budgets and that money could be spent elsewhere.'

'Yes, but it appears that I have a small inheritance on my hands, and my income is embarrassing enough to be able to pay Zack without even noticing the difference. My real problem is *you*. Which I guess makes you Zack's real problem as well.'

Marie felt herself redden. Alex was right—she was standing between Zack and an amazing opportunity.

'He does need something like this. Zack's just so charming that he thinks that everyone will forgive him anything. He's right, and I'm just as much at fault as anyone in falling for his promises…'

Alex chuckled, finally sitting down. '*I* can be charming, can't I? You never have any problem resisting that.'

'That's different. I respect you.'

'Okay. I'm not sure how that works, but I'll take it. Can you get your mother on board?' Alex finally sat down.

'Yes. That won't be a problem.'

Alex had come up with a plan that would make a real difference for Zack. Marie had to acknowledge that with good grace.

'Thank you, Alex. It would do him a lot of good, and I really appreciate your help. If you're willing to take him on for a couple of weeks, that would be great.'

He smiled. If he was about to make some comment about how that hadn't been so difficult to agree to, then she was going to throw him out of her office.

'I want him for more than a couple of weeks. I reckon it'll take him a little while to earn enough to pay you, and he's going to have to do all the boring jobs that no one else wants. When he's earned it, he'll get the chance to choose something that interests him. I'll be reviewing things with him every month, and if he decides on a study path then we'll support him in that. If he wants to look for employment then he'll get the experience he needs, and I'll write him a great reference.'

'This is too much, Alex.' Marie couldn't think of a reason why it was too much, just knew that it was.

'That's what I'm offering. Take it or leave it, Marie. But know this—I'll think less of you if you turn down an opportunity for Zack just because of your own pride.'

She felt herself redden. Alex had just stripped her of all her excuses, and the loss of that armour made her want to shiver. If it had been anyone else she wouldn't have been able to countenance it.

'I'll take it. Thank you, Alex.'

'It's my pleasure. Is tomorrow too early for an interview? Or do you need a bit more time to convince your mother and Zack?'

'Tomorrow's great.' Marie frowned. 'He won't be wearing a suit, though…'

Alex chuckled. 'Good—neither will I. Will nine o'clock suit him?'

'He'll be there.'

'Right, then.' Alex looked at his watch. 'It's nearly five o'clock now and I guess you'll be needing to go.'

It would have been nice to stay a little longer. Zack was difficult to contend with at the moment, and Marie wanted Alex's company. She loved the give and take that had developed between them, which made her feel that it was possible to step into new territory.

But she did need to speak to her mother, and to Zack. If he was going to make the best of this opportunity she needed to prepare him, convince him that this was an opportunity and not a punishment.

'Yes, thanks. I'll…um…see you tomorrow, then. With Zack.'

'You will.' He got to his feet, a satisfied smile on his face. 'You're doing the right thing, Marie.'

'Yes, I know…'

She wanted to hug him again. For caring and for being the tower of strength that had given her a way to really help her brother. Alex had been a true friend.

'You were right. Thank you.'

He narrowed his eyes. 'I think we'll never mention that again.'

Alex's dry humour always made her laugh. 'Yes, okay. It'll be our secret.'

CHAPTER EIGHT

MARIE HAD DONE her part. She'd convinced her mother that this was exactly what Zack needed, and then the two of them had hauled him out of his room and given him little choice but to accept the plan. Zack, as always, had been accommodating and cheerful at the prospect of working for his keep and paying back the money he'd taken. Whether he would stick with it for more than a week would be the real test.

She'd called round to her mother's house at seven-thirty the next morning and found Zack sorting through shirts, throwing them onto the bed. Marie gathered them up, putting them back onto their hangers.

'Mum's ironed all these.'

Sometimes she felt like a broken record, nagging Zack about everything. Like the grumpy big sister who squeezed all the joy out of his life.

'Sorry, sis.' Zack gave her a winning smile. 'I just want to make a good impression. I don't want to let you down.'

'I'm not your problem.' Zack knew she loved him, even though he did make her want to scream at times. 'This is about not letting yourself down.'

'Okay…' Zack frowned at the line of shirts that Marie had put back into the wardrobe and then whipped out a checked shirt with a plain tie that matched one of the colours. 'What about this?'

'Perfect. My handsome little brother.'

'I don't want to look handsome. I want to look…contrite. Hard-working. That kind of thing.' He pulled a face that indicated deep sorrow.

Marie rolled her eyes. 'Don't pull that one with me, Zack. I'm not Mum. You're going to look nice because this is an interview, but just turning up and saying the right things isn't going to get you off the hook. Afterwards is when you get to prove whether or not you're contrite and hard-working.'

She got yet another of Zack's dazzling smiles. That was his trouble; he never took anything too seriously. She was going to have to keep a close watch on him if he came to work at the clinic.

'All right. Half an hour to get washed and dressed and have a shave. Then we're leaving.'

Getting Zack to the clinic was a bit like getting a recalcitrant six-year-old to school. But at least he straightened up a bit and smiled cheerfully when Alex came out of his office and greeted him.

Alex whisked Zack and Sofia into his office, shutting the door firmly behind them. It wouldn't do to listen at the door, so Marie returned to her office and frowned at the wall, fiddling with a pink paper clip.

After an hour, she called down to Reception, asking Tina to give her a buzz as soon as Alex was free. Zack might be blissfully free from interview nerves, but Marie couldn't help worrying about him.

Zack was a graceful, engaging youth, with a ready smile. He declared himself ready for all kinds of hard work, and was excited at the prospect of earning the opportunities that Alex and Sofia outlined. Yes, he wanted to study. And, yes, he wanted to take responsibility for all the jobs in the clinic that no one else wanted to do. He wanted to show that he could take on the outreach tasks that Sonya had outlined as well. But if he could manage to do all that, he'd be working for more hours than Marie had at his age, and that wasn't really possible.

Despite himself, Alex liked the kid. He was charming and intelligent and he reminded him of Marie. And there was something in those heavy-lashed blue eyes that made Alex feel the boy might just have the same grit as his sister, if it were only possible to bring it out in him.

After they'd shown Zack around Alex left him in Sofia's care. Then he returned to his office and waited.

He didn't have to wait long. Marie appeared in the doorway, clearly trying to give the impression that she'd just happened to walk past on her way somewhere else. She put a large piece of card face down on his desk and sat down. They'd fallen into the habit of bringing things for each other's offices—unusual stationery or pictures for the walls—and he turned the card over, wondering what she'd found this time.

'Oh! That's wonderful. Where shall I put it?'

His wall was filling up now, and he'd brought some pictures and vintage record covers from home to go with the various prints Marie had given him. This one was an old photograph she'd got from somewhere, which reeked of late nights and the blues, showing a drink propped on top of a piano and one of his favourite artists, shirtsleeves rolled up and eyes closed as he played.

'You're beginning to run out of space.' Marie surveyed the wall.

'Not for this one.'

It was clearly something Marie had gone out of her way to get, and an image that Alex hadn't seen before. He took one of the framed pictures off its hook, and started to prise open the back of it, so he could replace it with the photograph and put it in pride of place.

Marie obviously wasn't going to ask, so he told her anyway. 'Zack seems…unrealistically enthusiastic.'

Marie laughed. 'Yes, that's him all over.'

'Maybe an eight-hour day will slake his zeal a little.'

'He'll be here before nine o'clock tomorrow morning. I promise.'

Marie flashed him that intent look that he'd seen so many times before. When she took on the troubles of the world and tried to work her way through them. She usually succeeded, but Alex had seen the toll it had taken.

'Will you do me a favour? Don't go round to your mother's every morning and chivvy him.'

'He told you about that?' Marie looked a little as if she'd been found out.

'No, I guessed. You have enough to do here, without running around after Zack.'

Alex could see that this wasn't reason enough for Marie and decided she needed a bit more persuasion.

'I've told him that he'll work eight hours, with an hour's lunch break every day. If he's late then he can work an extra hour in the evening, but he's not to stay here after six o'clock. If he gets here after ten in the morning I'll dock his pay.'

'That's very generous. He really should be here at nine every day.'

'Flexible hours work for us. But he needs to take responsibility for himself. I'm hoping your mother won't decide to give him spending money for the weekend if he finds his pay has been docked at the end of the week.'

Marie shook her head. 'No, she'll do whatever you ask; she's really grateful that you're taking Zack on. I'll mention it to her, though.'

She seemed a little unhappy with the arrangement, and Alex answered the question that she hadn't asked but which was clearly bothering her.

'You won't be helping him, Marie. Let him suffer the consequences if he can't get here on time. If he needs to be told to buck his ideas up, let Sofia and me do it.'

She saw the sense in it and nodded.

'I rather wish I had brothers or sisters.' Alex leaned back in his chair. It would have been nice to have someone to care about so ferociously. Someone for whom he'd do anything.

'Sometimes they're a pain in the neck.'

'You wouldn't be without them, though.'

'No. I wouldn't. Even Zack.'

She loved her little brother. He was driving her to distraction at the moment, but she loved him all the same. And she'd given him to Alex, trusting that he'd do the right thing. Alex felt a little unequal to the prospect, but it warmed him all the same.

'So...' All that was better left unsaid. 'Anything you want to discuss?'

'I've got the ideas for the mural in Reception back. Would you like to see them?'

'Not really.'

Marie's eyebrows shot up.

'Surprise me.'

She did that all the time, and it was always fantastic. Alex wondered vaguely what he'd do if Marie ever left the clinic. Left *him*.

But that wasn't going to happen. He wouldn't let it.

Alex had stayed out of the way while the artists took over the reception area. He had a final fitting for his dinner suit, and a few other errands to run, and although he'd spent most of the day itching to see what Marie was doing he'd decided that this was her project and she should be allowed to enjoy it alone.

Zack had expressed a fervent desire to come in on Saturday and help, and since he'd managed to turn up on time for nine of the last ten working days Sofia had allowed it.

When he'd arrived at two in the afternoon one day he'd been abject in his apologies. Alex had smilingly shrugged them off and simply docked his pay. After that, Zack had made sure he wasn't late again.

Alex arrived at the clinic at four o'clock and saw a dark-haired man walking across the courtyard, pushing a buggy and talking to the small boy who walked beside it. Alex caught him up. He introduced himself and they shook hands.

'I'm Tom Riley—Corinne's husband. That's Matthew, and this is Chloe...' He bent down to the pushchair, taking the little girl out of it and letting her stagger uncertainly towards her brother.

'We really appreciate this, Tom. I know your wife has a waiting list for this kind of thing.'

Tom chuckled. 'I get to spend a day with the kids, and Cori gets to cover herself with paint. What's not to like about that—particularly when it's for a project as exciting as this one? Although I'm still cross with you for poaching Marie away from the hospital.'

'I needed someone who's the best at what they do.'

Alex shot Tom an apologetic look and he laughed.

'Then you made the right choice. I'm interested to see what you're doing here; some of my patients' families live in this borough.' Tom swung round, calling to Matthew. 'Leave the tree alone, son. I don't think digging around it is going to do it any good.'

'I'll give you the tour. And if Matthew would like to plant something we have a garden. There are some bedding plants that need to be put into planters.'

'Thank you.' Tom grinned down at his son. 'Hear that, Matthew? We can help with the garden.'

The pushchair was manoeuvred up the ramp and into

the reception area. Tom was greeted with an excited cry from a woman in dungarees spattered with paint, some of which had made its way into her red curls. As she hurried towards him Tom backed away, a look of mock horror on his face, and she laughed, leaning forward to kiss him without allowing any of her paint-spattered clothes to touch his. She greeted Matthew and Chloe similarly, making a show of not getting any paint on them.

It was the picture of a happy, relaxed family. Secure in each other and the obvious love that bound them together. Alex felt a pang of loss. It was all that he hadn't had, and probably never would have. He couldn't imagine ever trusting himself enough to believe that his were a safe pair of hands which could hold such precious gifts as Tom had.

The reception area was full. Artists were working with people from the clinic, who'd come in to help. Sonya was deep in conversation with one of the film crew who were packing up in one corner. From her paint-spattered hands, and the marks on her designer jeans, she'd obviously been tempted into ruining her manicure by picking up a paint brush.

Zack had obviously torn himself away from painting duties and was working his way round with a large tray, distributing cups of tea. A sudden warmth at his side told him that Marie had seen him and come over to greet him.

No kiss. However much it would have made the moment complete. But Marie was grinning from ear to ear, and that was a very good second-best. She had a smudge of paint on her nose and wore a baggy T-shirt and a pair of frayed jeans. Diamonds couldn't have outshone her.

'What do you think?'

Alex tore his eyes away from her, scanning the mural. A black-and-white line-drawn representation of the clinic building was in the middle, surrounded by colour. There was a blue sky, a sparkling rainbow and, at the bottom in freehand writing, the words *Living well at our clinic*, followed by a list of all the clinic's services. When he looked more closely, the cloud that floated across the otherwise clear sky was made up of the word *Welcome* in many different languages.

'It's fantastic. Way beyond anything I could have dreamed of.'

The mural brought life and colour into the otherwise bland reception space.

'Those are mine...' Marie pointed to a group of people depicted outside the clinic doors. 'I didn't draw them; Cori did the outlines and I filled them in. I like people best...'

Of course she did. And Marie was right—the people made the picture. Doctors and nurses, a fitness instructor in gym wear, mothers with babies, old people, young people, people of different colours, sizes and cultures, talking together in groups or walking past. There were animals as well. A family of foxes trekked in a line at one side of the building, and birds flew in the sky, eyed by a lazy cat curled up on the roof of one of the clinic's cars.

'It's breathtaking. It'll take me a few hours just to look at it all. I think your people are the best, though.'

She gave a little snort of laughter, but was obviously pleased. 'Cori suggested that we have some extra seating over there, all in different colours.' She waved her hand towards the space opposite the mural. 'Just to balance things up a bit.'

'Good idea. And were you talking about painting in some of the other areas, as well?'

'We were, and Cori's offered to do something for the children's areas. But she's got some stencils and pictures to work from, so I said we could give that a go ourselves. I said that we were looking for paintings from local artists to hang in the café and communal areas, and she's given me the names of a few people.'

'That's perfect.'

'You're happy with it all?'

His opinion seemed to mean a lot to Marie.

'More than I can say. It's fabulous.'

He'd planned and built this place, but it had been bland and devoid of any personality. Marie had brought life to it in a way he never could have done alone. She'd made him bring a little of himself as well, and now he felt at home here.

'There's still lots to do. Would you like to help?'

He'd resolved to step back and let Marie see this through on her own, but that was all forgotten now.

'Try and stop me…'

CHAPTER NINE

LAST WEEK HAD been all about getting paint in his hair and under his fingernails. After work every day Alex had donned a pair of overalls and laboriously filled one of the walls in the children's playroom, using the stencils Cori had given them. Zack had been allowed to help too, on account of being on time each day, and doing every job that Sofia gave him cheerfully and well. He was showing real artistic flair, bringing life to Alex's rather flat representations with a just a few extra brushstrokes.

This weekend was entirely different. Alex had picked up his evening suit from the tailor and gone to the bank to open his safety deposit box. He'd scrubbed every trace of paint off under the shower, and while he towelled himself dry he regarded the suit that was hanging on the door of the wardrobe.

He sat down on the bed. He'd actually rather go naked tonight than pull that dark jacket on over a crisp white shirt. And the bow tie? He had a step-by-step diagram, downloaded from the internet, but he'd never tied a bow tie himself. His mother had always done that for him, brushing specks of dust from his jacket and telling him he looked every inch a prince.

Suddenly he missed her very much. Planting the flowers that spelt out her name and switching on the water feature in the garden had felt like his own very personal goodbye. It had awakened feelings that Alex had tried hard to repress.

Would his mother have loved the clinic the way he did, and allowed it to bring some colour into her life? Or would she have stubbornly clung to his father, fading into his shadow?

But thinking about that now would only make it harder to put the suit on, and there was no way he could answer the door to Marie in this state of undress. Alex pulled the white shirt across his shoulders, looking at the full-length mirror in the corner of the room as he did so. He'd lost all the extra weight he'd put on and felt better for it.

He picked up the pair of striped socks Marie had added to his ensemble and smiled. He was ready for anything now.

Almost anything.

When the doorbell rang he wasn't ready for Marie.

She smiled at him, stepping into the hallway. 'Where's your tie?'

'Uh?'

She was wearing a pair of high-heeled black court shoes, which made her legs look even longer than usual. She had a dark green brocade coat on, fitted at the waist, and her hair was sleek and shining. She looked stunning.

'Alex!' She snapped her fingers in front of his face. 'Earth to Alex!'

'Yes. Nearly ready.'

That was about all he could manage in the way of communication at that moment. He just wanted to drink her in.

She put a small black clutch bag down on the hall table and started to unbutton her coat.

Where were his manners?

Alex helped her out of the coat, admiring the shape of her arms and the silky softness of her skin. The plain, sleeveless green dress was perfect, because it didn't draw any attention away from her beauty. It was flattering, slim at the waist to show the curve of her hips and breasts.

Alex decided not to think the word 'breasts' again tonight; it would be sure to get him in trouble.

'Please tell me you didn't forget to get a tie.' She was looking at him quizzically. 'I'm not sure I can manage a late-night mercy dash to your tailor in these heels.'

'I've got a tie. And some instructions.'

She turned the corner of her mouth down in a look of resigned humour. 'You want me to give it a go?'

'Yes. Please.'

He went to retrieve the tie and found her sitting in the lounge, perched on the edge of a chair, her legs folded neatly in front of her. He was beginning to revise his opinion of formal dress.

'Let's give it a go, then.' She took the instructions from his hand and studied them carefully. 'I haven't done this before, but it doesn't look so difficult…'

She got to her feet again, reaching up to button his collar. The touch of her fingers against his neck made him feel a little dizzy.

Consulting the diagram every now and then, she went through each step carefully. She was concentrating too hard on getting the tie right to be as aware as he was of how close they were.

'That's okay.' He glanced at his reflection in the mirror over the fireplace. The tie was slightly crooked, but it was a big improvement on any of his efforts.

'No, it isn't—it's lopsided. Come here, I'll give it another go.'

Marie untied the bowtie and Alex stared at the ceiling, glad that he didn't have to look her in the eye. He could feel the brush of her body against his, and reminded himself yet again that breasts were a forbidden thought.

'I think that's it.' She stood back to survey her handiwork and gave a little nod. Alex looked in the mirror.

'That's perfect. Thanks.'

'Okay, now the jacket.'

They'd said they would stick together tonight, and Marie was making his dislike of dressing up much easier to bear. Alex fetched his jacket, and handed her the pocket handkerchief. She folded it carefully and brushed a speck of dust from his shoulder. Then she tucked the handkerchief into his top pocket and Alex buttoned his jacket.

'Let me look at you.' She stepped back for a moment, looking him up and down. 'That's great, Alex. You've scrubbed up *very* nicely.'

'You…' Alex realised suddenly that he hadn't told her how wonderful she looked, and that he really should make some effort to do her justice. 'You've scrubbed up really well too.'

It was a paltry kind of compliment, but Marie was still pleased with it. 'Are we ready to go, then?'

Not quite.

He went to his bedroom to fetch the velvet-covered box he'd taken from the bank that morning. 'I thought… I mean, I'd be very honoured if you would wear this.'

She stared at him. Maybe this hadn't been such a good idea after all. Alex knew Marie was nervous about tonight, and he'd reckoned this would maybe give her confidence. It was a bauble that would outshine anything that any of the society women might wear.

He'd committed himself now, though. He opened the box, taking out the exquisitely crafted platinum-and-gold chain, the delicate filigree strands of which were deceptively strong. They had to be, to support the large diamond that hung from it.

Marie backed away from him. 'That must be… That's… How big is it?'

'Um…around twenty carats, I think.' Thirty-one, actually.

'It's got to be worth an absolute fortune. Alex, I can't wear this. We're going to be asking people for money.'

'That's not really how it works. I couldn't sell the Crown Jewels to raise funds for the clinic even if I wanted to. They're held in trust.'

Marie shook her head, tears welling in her eyes. She blinked them away furiously, trying not to spoil her make-up, and Alex regretted his gesture immediately.

'Marie, I'm sorry…'

His apology seemed to upset her even more, and a tear rolled down her cheek, leaving a thin trail of mascara.

'You don't have to be sorry, Alex. I just… I can't wear this. It's too good for me.'

'Oh, no. I'm not having that. Nothing's too good for you, Marie.'

She sniffed and he handed her his handkerchief. She dabbed at her eyes, trying to smile.

'Alex, I really appreciate this; it's a generous and kind gesture. But I'm not someone who wears diamonds. I can't meet the people who are going to be there tonight on their terms, and you told me it was okay to meet them on mine.'

That was the crux of it all. Marie saw them as being stranded on opposite ends of a spectrum—so much so that she couldn't even accept the loan of a necklace for the evening. Maybe she was right. Maybe asking her to fit in with the kind of people he'd known all his life made him just as bad as his father, demanding that Alex's mother fit in with his grand aspirations.

'Let's forget about all this, eh? Go to the bathroom and fix your make-up and we'll start again, shall we?'

She nodded, blowing her nose and then frowning at the handkerchief.

'Don't worry about that. They come in packs of two. I have another one.'

He propelled her out into the hallway, where she grabbed her bag and made for the bathroom.

She was back in less time than he'd thought, her make-up reapplied and flawless. Alex was standing in front of the mirror, trying to retie his bow tie after he'd pulled at it to loosen his collar a little.

'Let me do that. I think I have the knack now.'

She got the bow tie right first time, and folded the new handkerchief, putting it into his top pocket. A second chance to do things right. Alex picked up the velvet box, ready to put it back in the safe in his bedroom.

'Alex, would you mind…? Would you be able to perhaps lend me just the chain to wear? It's so pretty.'

She was meeting him halfway. Alex decided this wasn't the time to tell her that the workmanship on the chain was of such quality that it was considered a work of art just by itself.

'I'd like that very much. I think it's the better choice with that dress.'

He could go halfway too. Maybe that would be enough to breach the gaping chasm that seemed to have opened up between them.

He unclipped the fabulous stone from its place on the necklace, and then carefully fastened the chain around Marie's neck. 'There. What do you think?'

She walked over to the mirror. In Alex's experience, women didn't usually look this grave when trying on jewellery.

'I really like it. I'd love to wear it…just for tonight…'

Marie turned to him, smiling. And suddenly all Alex had wanted in having her wear the diamond was turning out better than expected. In choosing just to wear the chain Marie had made a powerful statement. She could take or leave one of the best-known stones in the world, but she still wanted to wear something of his.

'Tonight's going to be a little weird for both of us. We'll stick together, eh?'

She nodded. Alex stepped forward, catching her hand in his and pressing it to his lips. Not actually a kiss, it was the kind of thing his father had taught him that a gentleman would do. A royal kiss for the hand of a beautiful woman. But the sudden warmth in her eyes made the hollow gesture into something that lived and breathed.

'You look gorgeous.'

Finally Alex got to deliver the compliment he should have given when he'd first laid eyes on her. And, better still, she accepted it.

'Thank you. Shall we go?'

Marie was *very* nervous. But Alex seemed determined to get her through this one way or another. The diamond had been too much of a gesture, and the panic she'd felt when she saw it had only driven home the sinking feeling that she could never fit into his world. The kind of woman who should be on Alex's arm would have accepted the loan and given him the pleasure of seeing her wear it.

But they'd worked it out. The chain was delicate and very pretty, with silver-and-gold tendrils that made it seem as if it were almost floating around her neck. And when Alex relaxed into the back seat of the taxi and started to talk about the everyday matters that took their attention in the clinic she felt a little calmer.

The taxi took them right to the door, stopping outside the wide portico that stretched out to touch the gravel drive. The mansion was in one of the many secluded streets in central London, just moments away from the noise and bustle but surprisingly quiet. This was the territory of the rich, living cheek by jowl with everyone else, but separated by privilege and heavy closed doors.

This door was open, though. Perfume from the flowering shrubs that bordered the portico lay heavy in the air. And when she took Alex's arm, walking into the spacious lobby, the scent of wealth was all around her: beautifully waxed wooden panelling, and the smell of the fuel for the flares burning at the doorway, in the heat of the early evening.

He solved the question of when exactly she should take her coat off by stopping and helping her out of it himself, handing it to a porter. Then he made an almost imperceptible gesture and a waiter materialised with two glasses of champagne.

'Ah. There's Sonya…'

He shepherded Marie across the crowded ballroom, smiling and nodding as he went, without allowing himself to be diverted from his intended trajectory.

When Sonya saw them she waved wildly.

As always, Sonya looked as if she'd just stepped out of the fashion pages of a magazine. She wore a bright red look-at-me dress that Marie would have loved to have had the confidence to wear, with just one heavy diamond bracelet. She flung her arms around Alex's neck, air-kissing his cheeks, and then it was Marie's turn.

'You look *wonderful*!' Sonya loudly confided this information to Marie. 'I see you've managed to shoehorn Alex into looking respectable too.'

He didn't look at all respectable to Marie. She'd heard the adage that women had the same reaction to a man in a really good suit as men did to a woman in fine lingerie, and she hadn't given it much credit before now. But that exact reaction had been fizzling away inside her for a while now. Alex looked meltingly gorgeous, and the feelings that he engendered in her were anything *but* respectable.

'I'm always respectable,' Alex protested, and Sonya laughed.

'Yes, I know you are, darling, but sometimes running

around saving people's lives leaves you dishevelled. You know that as well as I do.'

She turned to Marie, rolling her eyes, and Marie grinned, feeling some of the tension slip away.

Sonya took her arm. 'I suppose we'd better get to work, then. I have some very interesting people I'd like you both to meet...'

Sonya had oiled the wheels and she was making things easy. But Marie couldn't have got through it without Alex. His glances that were just for her. The way he steered the conversation, always asking first about the other person's interests without indulging his own. And when anyone asked why he was there, he spoke about the clinic, effortlessly including Marie in the conversation.

Chandeliers glinted above their heads as Marie talked about the issues that ordinary people faced, and how the clinic was being set up to address them. Under the stern eye of the lords and ladies looking down from the oil paintings on the wall, she spoke of inclusivity and the modern art that adorned the wall of the reception area, feeling the words flow naturally from her lips. And when someone who knew Alex's family asked about his plans, now that he had inherited his father's title, he said that he was taking his family traditions into new and exciting areas and left it at that.

'Did you see Sir Richard's face?' Sonya whispered in her ear as they returned together from the ladies' restroom. 'He was so impressed with everything you said, and I'd be very surprised if he doesn't want to know more. He's very influential, you know... Oh, no! You just have to leave them alone for one minute!'

Sonya came to a sudden halt, staring across the room. When Marie followed the line of her gaze she saw Alex approaching a dark-haired man in an impeccable dinner suit.

'What's the matter?'

'I didn't know Mark was going to be here. Where's Andrew?' Sonya stood on her toes, looking around for her husband.

'I can't see him. What's going on?'

Sonya puffed out an exasperated breath. 'Mark was at school with Andrew and Alex. You know that Alex was bullied?'

Marie nodded. 'Are you saying that man was the bully?'

'Yes—him and some of the other boys. Andrew told me some of the things they used to do to him and it made my toes curl. Oh, dear… I hope Alex doesn't hit him or something…'

Alex was the taller and broader of the two. One blow from him would fell the other man.

'No. It's okay, Sonya. He's not going to hit him.'

It was almost as if he'd heard her. The two men exchanged a few words, and then Alex held his hand out to Mark.

'Oh, thank goodness.' Sonya whispered the words as the two men shook hands.

Marie felt her head begin to swim. Alex must have known that this man might be here, and he'd never said a word. He was making his way back across the ballroom now, and as soon as he got within touching distance she took his arm, holding on tight.

She looked for Sonya, but she'd melted away into the crowd. She could let this go but… No. Actually, she couldn't let this go. She needed to tell Alex how proud she was of him.

'Sonya told me that man was one of those who bullied you at school.' She stretched up onto her toes, murmuring into his ear.

Alex nodded, guiding her towards the back of the ballroom, where large doors opened out onto a terrace edged by stone balustrades. As they walked down the shallow steps to one side, into a secluded garden, she clung tight to his arm.

'You did just shake his hand, right? That wasn't some kind of death grip and he's going to fall over any minute now and need urgent resuscitation?'

Alex chuckled. 'No, it wasn't a death grip. I shook his hand.'

'It was a generous act. Sonya was afraid you were going to hit him.'

'And you?'

'For a moment, maybe, but then I realised you're a lot braver than that.'

The lights of the city were beginning to brighten in the growing dusk. Here, in the quiet darkness, it felt as if they were all for her. Marie could be a queen tonight but, like Cinderella, it was only for one night. Tomorrow she'd have to give up the glass slippers and get back to work.

He let out a sigh. 'It didn't feel... When I saw him, and decided what I was going to do, I thought it might be one of those cathartic moments that changes everything. But it was a bit of an anticlimax. He seems like just an ordinary guy now.'

'Perhaps that's the whole point.'

Marie reached up, brushing her fingertips against his cheek. He wrapped his fingers around hers, pressing her hand to his chest. Everything else seemed to take a step back, the chatter of the city and the noise of the party diplomatically turning their backs on them to give them one moment alone.

'I'm so proud of you, Alex.'

The extra height her heels gave her meant that Marie didn't have to stand on her toes to kiss his cheek.

'I'm proud of you, too. I know it wasn't easy for you to come here.'

Marie shivered as she felt his lips brush her cheek in return.

Slowly he propelled her away from the path and into the dark shade of an enormous spreading tree. Marie could feel the rise and fall of his chest against hers, and as her eyes adjusted to the darkness she saw tenderness in his face.

Marie couldn't help herself. She heard his sharp intake of breath as she moved against him, brushing her lips against his. He put his arms around her, steadying her on the uneven ground, and then he kissed her.

Careful and tentative turned to demanding as a ferocious wave of pent-up desire washed over her. And Alex was already there, holding her tightly against his body as if somehow they could melt into each other and become one being.

His kiss was one that wanted it all. Everything that Marie wanted to give him.

This couldn't last. Maybe that was why it was so exciting. They both knew that these moments were stolen, and that real life would take them back soon enough.

He held her tenderly, his breath caressing her ear as he murmured words she couldn't help wanting to hear. That she was beautiful. How much he adored kissing her on a moonlit summer's night.

'So a tent in Siberia doesn't push any of your buttons?' She smiled up at him.

'You can organise the tent and I'll get the plane tickets. We'll find out.'

He obviously found the thought as interesting as she did, but she knew they could talk this way because they both knew they'd never do it. They had something that was much too important to both of them to contemplate anything more than a forbidden fantasy.

'Or we could go to Egypt. Ride out into the desert on camels… Or to Paris and climb the Eiffel Tower…'

'We could. And there's always Camden. Hoxton. Maida Vale…'

The familiar names sounded suddenly exotic on his lips. Alex would make anywhere exciting, and his kiss would be equally intoxicating.

'Or we could go back inside. Finish off the job we came to do.'

'That would be good, too. In a completely different way.'

Alex's arms loosened around her waist. They both knew this had to end, and that they'd never go to Siberia or Egypt or Paris together. That Camden, Hoxton and Maida Vale would seem perfectly ordinary in the morning.

He was the one who had the strength to move, to take the first step back. Marie had his arm, but when they emerged from the shadows she stopped.

'Lipstick.' She pointed to her own mouth, to indicate where the smear was on his, and then pulled the handkerchief from his pocket, shaking out the folds and giving him the end that would be hidden when it was refolded.

'Did I get it all?'

'Bit more.' Marie took the handkerchief and wiped tiny smudge from the side of his mouth.

'Thanks. You've got some…er…' He waved his finger in a circle, pointing at his own face.

That wasn't a lot of help. Marie was sure she didn't have lipstick in her eyebrows. She wiped her lips, deciding she would go straight to the ladies' room and repair the rest of the damage.

'Okay?'

He nodded, offering his arm again. Marie took it and they walked together back up the steps to the terrace. They had a job to do, and it didn't involve kissing.

CHAPTER TEN

LAST NIGHT HAD been a mixture of emotions: wanting to protect Marie and the horrible suspicion that one of the things he needed to protect her against was him; meeting Mark and finding that he was an ordinary man and not an ogre; the feeling that if Sonya made any more introductions he was going to go out onto the terrace and yell for mercy.

And also sheer, unthinking delight.

Alex had tried to convince himself that their kiss was something that happened between friends. Out of curiosity. Like the way that, as boys, he and Andrew had kissed the backs of their own hands, to practise what it might be like to kiss a girl.

But kissing Marie had been nothing like kissing the back of his hand.

He felt a little less awkward at seeing Marie again than he might have done. She'd made it easy—going back to the party with him, slipping her hand into the crook of his arm just as she had before. They'd talked about the evening in the taxi together without mentioning the kissing part. And then they'd said their goodnights and he'd watched her to her door.

It was over. Done. And even if it couldn't be forgotten they'd both put it behind them because it was impossible to do anything different.

He saw Marie strolling across the front courtyard now,

chatting to Zack. She seemed happy, smiling in the late-morning sunshine.

Alex quickly got the papers he was supposed to be working on out of his briefcase and laid them on his desk to make it look as if he had actually been doing something. He heard a knock on his door and then Zack entered, leaving a respectful distance between himself and the desk.

'Is it okay if I help Marie, please? She's going to do some more wall-painting.'

'Yes, of course, Zack. Thank you very much.'

Alex wondered whether Marie would decide to do all her communicating with him via her brother today. It was a possibility.

But as Zack turned to go Marie popped into the doorway. 'Charlie and a couple of the other guys are here. They've come to help for a few hours.'

'That's nice of them. Tell Charlie I'll be along soon.'

'I'm sure he could do with a hand from his number one apprentice.' Marie grinned.

'Yep. As soon as I've checked the accounts I'll be there.'

Alex could almost manage to look at her without thinking about last night. The softness of her lips…

'Here…'

She had something in her hand, and she tossed it towards him. Alex caught it, opening his fist to see what it was.

'That's exactly what I need. Thank you.' She'd brought him an eraser in the shape of a dinosaur.

Then she was gone. Alex congratulated himself on not embarrassing either her or himself, and turned his attention to the papers in front of him.

Half an hour later, he scribbled his signature on the last page, and was about to write a note to the accounts manager, when Zack came bursting into his office.

'Come and help… Marie…'

Panic and breathlessness had rendered Zack capable of alarming Alex, but not able to tell him where he needed to be.

'Zack!' Alex stood up taking him by the shoulders. 'What's happened? Where's Marie?'

'Over the road—at the site office. Charlie went over there for something and didn't come back. Marie and I went to find him...'

That was enough for the time being.

Jim knew the letting agent for the small row of shops across the road, and he'd negotiated the use of an empty one as office space and storage while the works at the clinic were being carried out.

'We called him but he didn't answer...we looked through the front window and his hat was there...we banged on the door... Marie broke in...'

Zack was breathlessly recounting the story, running behind him as Alex crossed the road. He didn't need to know any of that. Just that Marie and Charlie were all right.

The door of the shop was open, and there was a bent piece of wire that Marie must have shoved through the let-terbox to flip the lock. Alex cursed under his breath. Why hadn't she come to fetch him?

Because she could do it herself.

The warm, pliable woman who had clung to his arm last night, to balance herself over the uneven ground in her high heels, was more than capable of doing what needed to be done this morning. That was what he loved about Marie...

There was no time to consider his use of the word *love*. Alex noticed Charlie's bright red baseball cap, propped on one of the drawing boards by the window, and hurried past the desks and storage boxes to the open door at the back, which led to the stairs. He could hear sounds of effort, fol-lowed by a loud crack, and then a clatter.

He ran headlong down the stairs. At the bottom he saw Marie's face, shining up at him.

'Alex. Thank goodness!'

He resisted the impulse to hug her. 'Are you all right? Where's Charlie?'

'Inside. I heard him.' She gestured towards the door that led into the basement. 'But I can't get the door open—there's a pile of stuff behind it.'

She'd made a good start. The door stood open a few inches, and the light was on inside. Alex could see a mess of plaster from a broken sack and pieces of wood piled against the other side of the door, which stopped it from opening any further. Marie had found a crowbar from somewhere, and had managed to lever the bottom hinge away from the doorframe.

She wasn't tall enough to get good leverage on the top hinge, and nor was she strong enough to move the heavy door, which was now hanging on just one hinge. Alex took the crowbar, inserting it as far as it would go between the door and the jamb.

'Hold that in place.'

Marie stretched up to grip the crowbar, and Alex felt Zack jostling at his back.

'Zack, get out of the way, will you?'

Zack jumped back, giving them some room. Alex jerked the door closed, bracing his foot against the door, and holding on to the handle.

'A bit further...'

When he pushed the door open again he could see that the hinge had given a little. Marie slid the crowbar further into the gap and he pulled again. This time it gave, and he grabbed the other side of the door before it fell forward.

'Zack, mind out.'

Marie stepped back, taking Zack with her as Alex tipped the door forward, turning it slightly so that it would fit through the frame and then backing with it into the lobby.

Before he could stop her Marie had slipped past him and into the basement, climbing over the sacks of concrete mix that had slipped from a pile further inside the room and blocked the door. Dust hung heavy in the air, and there was a mess of spilt paint cans, brushes and other supplies, which had come from the heavy timber shelves that had once lined the wall. The shelves must have collapsed, because there was splintered wood everywhere.

'Charlie!'

She picked her way across the debris to where Alex could see Charlie's red T-shirt and fell to her knees.

'He's hurt, Alex. We're going to need an ambulance.'

Zack was ready to pile into the room and help, but Alex pulled him back. 'Go upstairs, Zack. Call an ambulance and tell them there's been an accident and to hurry. When you've done that, I want you to fetch the medical kit from the urgent care room in the clinic and bring it down to us.'

'But… Marie…' Zack's eyes were full of frantic tears for his sister.

'Do you want me to stand here arguing with you, or shall I go and help her?'

Zack nodded, pulling himself together suddenly. 'Look after them, Alex.' He threw the order over his shoulder as he ran up the stairs.

He would. Both Marie and Charlie.

Marie was vaguely aware that Alex was making his way across the piles of debris towards her. She'd heard Charlie crying out when she'd first reached the door that led into the basement, but now he was still and unresponsive, the lower half of his body pinned down under a pile of rubble.

'Airway?' Alex was there beside her.

'He's breathing and his airways are clear. I don't see any

major bleeding...' She leaned forward, finding Charlie's wrist. 'And his pulse is surprisingly steady.'

'Okay, stay with him, and I'll move some of this wood away from his legs.'

Marie nodded. She'd known that she couldn't get the door open by herself and had hoped that Zack would find Alex quickly. Together they would be able to help Charlie, and now they'd fallen automatically back into the habit of depending on each other to get the job done.

'Glad you're here.'

'Yeah. Glad *you're* here.'

Alex set to work, clearing the mess of paint cans and smaller pieces of wood from around Charlie's legs. Charlie was alive. All they had to do now was keep him that way.

Marie bent over him, smoothing his hair from his brow and tapping his cheek with her finger. 'Charlie! Charlie, can you hear me?'

Charlie moaned, moving his arms as if to push whatever was holding him down away. Marie caught his hand, holding it tightly in hers.

'Charlie. It's Marie. Look at me.'

As Charlie opened his eyes he let out a long, keening cry of distress.

'Charlie, I want you to stay still, if you can. Just look at me.' Marie clung to his hand, trying to calm him.

'I can see his legs,' said Alex. 'The right one looks okay...'

Which meant that the left one didn't. But Alex would tell her if he needed her, and Marie concentrated on Charlie's pulse, beating beneath her fingers.

'It hurts...'

'I know. We'll have you out of here soon, Charlie. You're doing really well—just hold my hand.'

'Yeah. Hold on.' Charlie groaned as Alex carefully lifted the piece of wood that was lying across his leg.

One more piece to go, and then Alex would be able to see better. It was a big piece, though—one of the shelves that had fallen from the wall. Marie glanced up at Alex and he nodded.

'Charlie, Alex is going to move the last piece of wood. It's going to hurt, so hang on to me.' She bent over Charlie, so he wouldn't see what Alex was doing.

Alex positioned himself in order to take the strain, and carefully lifted the heavy shelf. Charlie howled in pain, his fingers digging into Marie's arms.

'Okay. Okay, we're done. That's the worst bit over, Charlie.'

She could see his left leg now, twisted and certainly broken. Blood was pluming out over his jeans and dripping onto the concrete beneath him.

Alex leaned forward, gripping the top of Charlie's leg, putting pressure on the main artery to stanch the flow. His other hand found Charlie's, gripping it just as tight.

'Where's the medical kit?' Alex muttered the words, looking up as movement in the doorway indicated that Zack was back.

Marie broke free from Charlie and picked her way across to Zack. He was standing staring at Charlie's leg, and looked as if he was about to faint.

Marie grabbed the medical bag from his hand. 'Is the ambulance on its way? Zack!'

'Yes… I told them to hurry.'

'Good. Well done. Now, go back upstairs and wait for them outside. Got it?'

'Yes. Yes, I can do that.'

Zack straightened suddenly, and Marie turned him around, pushing him towards the door. Her little brother had been thrown in at the deep end, but he was doing fine.

She opened the medical kit, sorting through the contents of the bag to find a pair of surgical gloves and scissors. Alex was talking to Charlie, trying to reassure him while he did what he could to slow the bleeding. Carefully cutting Charlie's jeans, Marie exposed the wound on his lower leg.

The broken bone was sticking through his flesh, blood pumping out around it. There was no way that Alex could put any pressure on the wound to stop the bleeding.

'Tourniquet?'

Alex nodded. Marie took the tourniquet from the bag, looking at her watch and writing the time on the tab.

'Let go of Alex, Charlie. Hold *my* hand.'

As soon as Alex was free to work he wrapped the tourniquet around Charlie's leg. The bleeding slowed and then stopped, and Alex turned his attention to check that there was no other bleeding.

By the time the ambulance crew arrived they were ready to move their patient. Alex helped them to carry Charlie through to the small goods lift at the back of the building, and he was transferred into the ambulance.

'I'll go with him.' Alex moved towards the back of the ambulance.

Marie caught his arm. 'You're sure?' She knew the ambulance paramedics could be trusted to look after Charlie.

'He's my responsibility.' Alex's jaw was set firm.

It was a bit of a stretch to feel that any of this was Alex's responsibility, but there was no talking him out of it. He and Charlie had struck up an unlikely friendship, and Alex wouldn't let him go to the hospital alone.

'Okay. I'll call Jim and get him to contact Charlie's family. When you're done, give me a call; you can't walk back looking like that.' She nodded towards the blood on Alex's jeans.

He looked down, seeming to see it for the first time. 'Yeah, okay. Thanks. Zack did well. Don't forget to tell him that.'

'I won't.'

Zack had been frightened, but he'd done everything he'd been asked. Marie wondered whether her little brother would have been able to do that before he'd come to work here, and was proud of how far he'd come.

She watched as Alex spoke to the paramedic and then got into the back of the vehicle. The doors closed and the driver climbed into her seat. There was a short pause, and then the ambulance drew away from the kerb.

Jim had arrived at the hospital with Charlie's parents. About ten minutes later Charlie's older brother and his wife had come bursting through the doors of the waiting room.

Alex had sat them all down and explained what had happened, and the surgeon's prognosis. Charlie would need an operation to set his leg, and he'd be in hospital for a few days, but he had no other major injuries. The bruise on his face looked distressing, but it would heal.

When Charlie's mother saw her son her hand flew to her mouth, but she steadied herself and walked over to his bed, kissing him. Charlie's father shook his hand and thanked him, and Alex knew that it was time for him to leave.

He called Marie and then sat on a bench outside the A&E department, adrenaline and concern for Charlie still thrumming in his veins. All he wanted to do was hug Marie—but he saw Zack walking towards him from the direction of the car park.

'I said I'd come. Marie needed to wrap things up at the clinic.' Zack settled himself down on the bench next to him, asking the obvious question. 'How's Charlie?'

'They'll need to set the leg, and that means—'

'An operation and he'll be here for a few days. Yeah, Marie told me. They didn't find anything else?'

'No. He's got lots of cuts and bruises, but he'll be fine.'

Alex grinned. Marie had obviously talked everything

through with Zack and he seemed to be taking it all in his stride.

'When can we go and see him?' Zack peered at the doors of the A&E unit, obviously wondering if he might go in and see Charlie now.

'His family are with him, and we shouldn't interrupt. I'll call tomorrow, and you can take some time off in the afternoon if he's up to having visitors.'

'Great. Thanks. I'll make the time up.'

'That's okay. I think it counts as official clinic business. Charlie's one of ours.'

Zack nodded, his face suddenly thoughtful.

'What, Zack?' Alex leaned back on the bench, ready to listen to whatever Zack had to say.

'It's nothing really. I just…' Zack turned the corners of his mouth down. 'I didn't know what to do.'

'Your sister's a doctor. She's been trained to know what to do.'

Zack nodded. 'Yeah, I know. But… I was afraid. I said we should phone someone to come and let us in. If we'd done that Charlie might have bled to death. She was so brave the whole time, and nothing stopped her. I didn't know she knew about breaking and entering.'

'The coat hanger trick?' Alex grinned again. Marie hadn't actually used a coat hanger, but she'd found a piece of wire that had done just as well. 'I taught her that years ago.'

'Really?' Zack gave him a searching look. 'It was *you* that led her astray, then?'

Not really. Getting Marie into her student flat—when he could have asked her back to his place for the night—could be construed as *not* leading either of them astray. But Zack didn't need to know that.

'You did well, Zack. You did what we needed you to do and let us work.' Alex held out his hand, reckoning that

Zack needed something a little more definite than words. 'I'm proud of you.'

'Thanks.' Zack brightened suddenly, shaking Alex's hand. 'You know, Marie's always looked after me… Mum too. A bit too much sometimes.'

That was Alex's opinion, too. But he had no business saying it.

'I'm going to take more responsibility for things. I'll pay her back every penny of the money I took. I want to make a difference, the way she does.'

Alex laid his hand on Zack's shoulder. 'You made me proud today, Zack, and I'm sure your sister feels the same way. And, yes, you *are* going to keep working until you pay her back.'

Zack nodded, getting to his feet. 'She'll be wondering where we are. I'll drive.'

Marie's jeans were still spattered with blood, but she'd washed the grime from her face and hair, and cheered up considerably when Alex gave her the exact details of Charlie's condition.

'He was lucky. How on earth do you think it happened? Everything coming down on top of him like that?'

'Jim told me that he caught him climbing up those shelves the other day, to get something at the top. He gave him a dressing down—told him it was dangerous and said he should use the stepladder. But I guess Charlie didn't listen.'

Marie quirked her lips. She knew as well as Alex did that there was no saving people from themselves. 'What about the mess? Should we go and clear up a bit?'

'That's okay. Jim's been on the phone to a couple of his guys and they'll take care of it. I think we're done for today.'

Neither Marie nor Zack argued. Alex claimed the car

keys from Zack, saying that they'd drop him home, and Marie directed him to a neat two-up, two-down terraced house with a riot of colourful plants in the front garden.

'I'll come in with you…' Marie went to get out of the car but Zack reached forward from the back seat, grabbing her.

'I'll deal with Mum.'

Marie frowned. 'Are you sure? You can't just tell her about it and then disappear up into your bedroom. You know she worries.'

'I'll make her a cup of tea and talk to her. You're not the only one who knows how to do that, you know.'

'No, I know.' Marie grinned suddenly. 'Okay, then, Zack. See you tomorrow?'

'Yep. Bright and early.'

Zack shot Alex a grin and then got out of the car, loping up the front path and turning to give them his characteristically ebullient wave.

Alex put the car into Drive and accelerated away before Marie could change her mind.

'He did well today.'

Marie didn't ask where they were going, and Alex decided to head for his flat. Maybe he could make her lunch.

'Yes. He told me he wanted to make the kind of difference that you make.'

'That's nice.' She smiled. 'Mum tells me that he's got a severe case of hero-worship. "Dr King says this…" "Dr King did that…"'

She was twisting her fingers in her lap, clearly thinking about something. Alex wondered if it was the kiss, and hoped not. In between dealing with Charlie, he'd been thinking about it enough for both of them.

'I was wrong.'

'Were you?' In his view Marie was perfect. 'What about?'

'I thought that if I worked hard enough then I could fix

things. I could pay Mum back myself and persuade Zack to buck his ideas up. But I couldn't. I had to stand back.'

'That's the most difficult thing sometimes. Not that I'd know—I don't have a great deal of experience with families…'

Marie was so involved with her family. That might have its difficulties, but she felt a part of them. Indissolubly linked. Alex had worked for most of his life to distance himself from his family.

'You know people, though.' She reached forward, pulling her phone out of her handbag. 'Mum hasn't called me yet. I suppose that's a good sign…'

'Put it away, Marie. Give Zack a chance to deal with things. I know you've always been there for him, ever since he was little, but maybe it's time to let go now.' Alex ventured it as a suggestion.

'What? And have a life of my own?'

She made it sound like a joke, but Alex knew she'd got his point, and that she was thinking about it.

He shrugged. 'Funnier things have happened.'

'Yes, they have.' She gave a little sigh. 'I couldn't do what you did, Alex—taking Zack on like that and giving him direction. Thank you.'

A warm feeling spread through Alex's veins, making his hand shake a little on the wheel. He felt as if he'd been part of something good, and in his experience good things didn't happen in families.

Suddenly the idea of driving Marie home and leaving her there seemed impossible.

'It's Sunday afternoon. Would you like to go for a late lunch somewhere?'

'Like we used to?' Marie smiled.

'Yes.'

Driving out into the country would be good. He'd lost something from those days and he wanted it back.

'I can't go anywhere like this.' She pointed to the grime and blood on her jeans.

'We could drop in to your place.' Or, better still, he could avoid Marie's flat entirely so she didn't get a chance to change her mind. 'Or I could lend you a pair...?'

Apparently they called the style 'boyfriend jeans'—rolled up at the bottom and cinched tight at the waist. But Alex decided that he didn't need to be her boyfriend to lend Marie a pair of jeans, and that plenty of women wore the manufactured version.

'You've got diamond-encrusted jeans?'

Marie giggled suddenly, and Alex realised she was teasing him. 'Yeah. It was all the rage in eighteenth-century Belkraine.'

'This I have to see...'

CHAPTER ELEVEN

THE NEEDLESSNESS OF Charlie's accident, the repeated wish that he'd applied a bit of common sense, or a least listened to what Jim had told him, was beginning to be set aside now, along with her worry about Zack and her mother. This afternoon there was just Alex—and he was irresistible.

There had been a bit of awkwardness about who should go where to get changed, which Alex had solved by laying out a pair of jeans for her in his bedroom and then going to get changed and take a shower in the bathroom.

She could hear the sound of water running, and tried not to think about the inevitable consequence of that. Alex... soaking wet and naked.

Resisting Alex had always been hard, but she'd grown used to it. Now that she'd felt his touch it was a whole new ball game. And now that some of the responsibility for Zack and her mum had been lifted from her shoulders there might be time to indulge her fantasies.

But it was too risky. They were friends and colleagues and they were both at turning points in their lives. Anything could happen and they would smash all that they'd built together.

She rolled up the legs of the jeans, cinching the waist tight. They didn't look so bad with her flat canvas shoes, which had thankfully escaped any specks of blood. Her lace-edged sleeveless shirt was fine on its own, and now that the sun had burned away the early-morning cloud she didn't need the zipped hoodie she'd been wearing.

She walked back into the sitting room. Perhaps Alex had always looked her up and down like that but she'd never noticed, and it made her heart jump. His smile was even better.

'Diamonds really suit you.'

She laughed, and the joke loosened the tension between them. Alex picked up his car keys, hooking his sunglasses onto the front of his shirt, and Marie put her purse in her pocket. They were ready to go, travelling light the way they'd used to do. Just the open road and what they could carry in their pockets.

He left the clinic's car to charge in the basement garage under the flats and they took his car. With the top rolled back, raw power purring from the engine and a warm breeze caressing her skin, this felt a lot like sex. Although she reckoned that sex with Alex would be a lot better.

After a drive that was enough to blow the most stubborn of cobwebs away they found a picturesque pub in a picturesque village and ordered lunch to eat in the garden. The artisan burgers weren't quite as nice as they'd looked on the menu, but it didn't matter. They were taking the world as it came.

'Careful…' said Alex.

Marie had slipped off her shoes, putting her feet up on one of the plastic chairs, and luxuriating in the sun. 'Careful of what?' She opened one of her eyes, shading her face so she could see him.

'You'll catch the sun. Might even look as if you've been on holiday…' He smirked at her.

The last holiday she'd been on had been the summer before her father had left. Since then, the only thing that had seemed remotely like getting away from it all had been the times when Alex had persuaded her away from her books and out into the sunshine.

'We can't have that, can we?' She wrinkled her nose at him.

He chuckled. 'Too late. I think I see a touch of pink on your shoulder.'

'Oh, no!' Marie pretended to brush it off and Alex laughed.

'Do you want to tell me about your plans for the open day? It's only two weeks away.'

'Not right now.' Marie stifled a yawn. 'This is our afternoon off. We can go through them tomorrow.'

'I never thought I'd hear you say that. *Mañana* has never been your thing.'

Marie let the idea roll for a moment. *Mañana* never *had* been her thing, but that was because there'd always seemed to be so much to do.

'I might take it up. Take a break once every month or so.'

'Yeah… I wouldn't overdo it—you might find it becomes a habit. *Then* where would you be?'

If all her breaks were like this one she would be… happy. Marie dismissed the thought. However alluring it was, it was a fantasy.

They spent another hour in the sun together, and then Alex suggested that a film might fill the evening nicely. But after they'd driven back to his place and consulted the listings they found there was nothing that either of them particularly wanted to see.

'Shall we download something to watch?'

'That would mean making a decision, wouldn't it?' Marie was too relaxed to move.

'Yep. Good point.' He grinned, reaching for the remote for the sound system and switching it on. 'Random will do…'

'Random' did very nicely. Some soul, some rock and roll—a bit of everything.

Marie's foot started to tap against the leg of the coffee table and suddenly Alex was on his feet, catching her hand.

'You want to dance?'

She hesitated, and he shot her an imploring look. He picked up the remote and suddenly the sound swelled and the beat became irresistible.

Alex was irresistible.

Marie stood up and he swung her round, away from the sofas and towards the clear space to one side.

Alex was a great dancer. He had always moved well, and he danced without any of the tense awkwardness that made sitting it out the best choice with some partners. They seemed to fit together, anticipating each other's next steps, and by the time the rock and roll track was finished she was out of breath, falling laughingly into his arms.

There was a moment of silence in which she looked up at him, felt his body against hers, her chest rising and falling with excitement. And then the next track started.

'I love this one…'

'Me too.'

He wrapped his arms around her and they started to sway slowly to the music. Each movement was perfect. There was nothing more that she needed.

Then she felt his lips brush the side of her forehead, and realised there *was* something more she needed. She tipped her face up towards his, stretching her arms around his neck.

This was better than last night. They were truly alone, without having to worry about lipstick or someone strolling into the garden and discovering them. She could feel his body, hard against hers, still swaying to the music. But now there was another, more insistent rhythm, which gradually began to take over.

'Alex…'

He moved from her mouth to her neck, and she felt herself shudder with pleasure. Pulling at the buttons of his shirt, she slid her hand across his chest, feeling muscle move under soft skin.

They were breathing together now. He gasped as she tucked one finger under the buckle of his belt, knowing that this was a statement of intent. She intended to make him feel everything that she did.

Suddenly he lifted her off her feet. Marie wrapped her legs around his waist, feeling the hot surge of desire suddenly let loose after far too long spent denying it. He took a step and she felt her back against the wall, his hand curling protectively around her head.

'Alex…' She fumbled for the heavy belt around her jeans, trying to pull it off. 'Now. Please…*now*.'

It had to be now. While she was still lost in the powerful force of trembling expectation.

Suddenly he stilled. And as he let her gently down onto her feet he planted a tender kiss on her brow.

It was gone. The moment was gone.

'We can't, Marie. Not like this.'

One of his arms was braced against the wall above her shoulder. He seemed to be pushing himself back, away from her.

What did he mean? Not like *how*? Marie stared up at him, frustrated longing bringing tears to her eyes. She was too scared to say anything.

He picked up her hand, pressing it to his lips. 'I want to make love to you, Marie. But if we rush at it before we have a chance to think and change our minds… I need to know that you're not going to regret this when you do get a chance to think about it.'

He'd known her haste was borne of uncertainty. That

they had a lot to lose. A friendship that had lasted for years. Their work together.

He turned away from her suddenly and flipped the remote. Silence. Picking up the keys of the clinic's electric car from the coffee table and then putting them into her hand, he closed her fingers around them.

Alex wouldn't tell her to go. He didn't want her to go—she could see that in his eyes. But if she stayed, it had to be a real decision. They couldn't just let themselves be carried away by insistent desire.

They could go back now. Pick up on Monday morning and keep working together. Working together was their strength and anything else was a weakness. They could stick with what they were good at or...

They could want more.

Suddenly, she knew. Marie put the car keys down onto the coffee table. 'Alex, you're my friend, right?'

'Always. You know that, Marie...'

'We both have regrets about the past. You wish your mother had left, and I wish my father had stayed. And although we're so different we've always talked about things. I feel that whatever happens we can work it out.'

He didn't move. 'Is that a yes?'

'I trust you, Alex. It's a yes.'

The heat of his gaze was more exciting than the heavy beat of the music had been. More arousing even than his touch.

'I trust you too. My answer's yes.'

Marie stepped forward, undoing the buttons of his shirt that she hadn't already torn open. He didn't move, letting her slip it from his shoulders. When she ran her fingers across his chest he caught his breath, stifling a groan.

He reached for her, pulling her vest over her head in one swift movement that made her gasp. He traced the edge of her bra with his finger, bending to kiss her neck, and Marie felt her knees start to shake.

'Alex…?'

Just moments ago this had been unthinking desire, but now it was a true connection. If he severed it now she didn't know how she would survive.

'I've got you.'

He understood everything. He understood all her fears. And she understood his, and they'd face them together.

Alex picked her up in his arms, carrying her along the hallway and kicking the bedroom door open.

They undressed each other. Alex had thought about this so many times before, but never dared go there. He wasn't in the habit of sleeping with girlfriends on a first date, but he'd never known someone so well. The challenge was so much greater, and yet the rewards might be equally so.

It would be all right. He'd dreamed his dreams, and now that Marie held them in her hands he knew that they were safe there.

'I never imagined you'd be so exquisite.'

He'd lingered over taking off her underwear and they were both trembling now. She flushed with pleasure. Her fingertips were exploring his body, her gaze fixed on his. This was the first time he'd made love to a woman who really knew him.

'You're the only one, Marie, who knows who I am.'

'I'm not going to call you Rudolf.' She whispered the words. 'I prefer Alex.'

'So do I.'

He lifted her up, feeling the friction of their bodies healing him. He knew exactly what to do now. When he tipped her back onto the bed she gave a little cry of joy that made him feel like a king. A *real* one.

She was reaching back, her hand feeling behind her to

the curved wooden headboard. Alex grinned, warming to the task of making it as hard as possible for her to concentrate on anything but him, and she moaned, her body arching beneath his.

Long minutes of teasing ensued, but finally she managed to do what she'd set her mind on. Marie knew that about him too. She hadn't forgotten that late-night conversation between five young doctors during which Alex had declared that the best place to keep condoms was taped to the back of the headboard. Always handy to reach, and never in the way.

She pressed the packet into his hand. He wouldn't normally reach for them so soon, but he knew they were both ready now. They'd waited for this for years, and there was no denying it any more.

'I can't wait any longer, Alex. We've waited too long already...'

CHAPTER TWELVE

ALEX WAS THE kind of guy who liked to talk. Marie liked that, because he knew what to say and he also knew exactly when to stop talking.

The first time, he'd been as careful and tender as any new lover should be. It might have lasted hours if it hadn't been for the groundswell of emotion making every gesture into something that had taken them both to the very edge. When he'd pushed gently inside her they'd both known there was no going back. And when the moment had come it had gripped them both with the same splintering, tearing pleasure, ripping the world as they'd known it apart. Marie could pretend all she wanted, but things were never, ever going to be the same again.

He'd held her in much the same way as he was holding her now—curling his body around her as if she were finally truly his. They should have drifted off to sleep, but it had still been early, and light had been streaming in through the windows. Marie had felt more awake than she'd ever felt, and Alex had murmured comfortable words until shared jokes and whispered tenderness had become spiked again with longing.

That seemed like a very long time ago now. They'd made love and slept in equal measure for hours, and now it felt as if his body and hers belonged together.

'You're awake?' Marie shifted slightly in his arms as he spoke.

'I'm too comfortable to open my eyes. What's the time?'

She heard him chuckle and felt the brush of his lips against her cheek. 'Four o'clock. We don't have to get up yet.'

'Hmm… Good.' They'd been in bed for ten hours already, but Marie didn't want to move. Not yet.

'I really liked ten o'clock…'

Marie opened one eye. 'You were looking at the time?'

'You're not going to tell me that you didn't hear the clock chiming in the other room, are you?'

'Yes, I heard it. Was that ten?'

'I counted ten. Did you lose count?'

The innocence in his tone made her smile. As the clock had chimed ten she'd been astride him, and he'd taken hold of her hips, moving suddenly in the same rhythm as the sound. Marie had got to three and then lost count. A couple more thrusts and she'd started to come so hard that ten hadn't even existed.

Alex knew how to break her, and he knew how to be broken. Marie had always felt that was what sex must be all about, but this was the first time she'd allowed it to happen with anyone. He knew how to make her beg, but he had no hesitation in putting himself at the mercy of her touch.

'So what's four o'clock going to be?'

She snuggled against him, dropping a kiss onto his lips. They really shouldn't be doing this. They should both be considering the benefits of an IV drip to combat exhaustion by now.

'I can't imagine.'

The glint in Alex's eye told her that he probably could imagine and that he was doing so right now.

Marie closed her eyes again. 'Surprise me.'

His arms tightened around her and he pulled her back

against his chest. Already desire was beginning to make her tremble.

'You like this…?'

One of his hands had covered her breast and the other was moving downward, nudging her legs apart. He held her tight, dropping kisses onto her neck.

'Yes, Alex!'

She wriggled, trying to make his fingers move a little faster, and heard his low chuckle.

'Four o'clock is all for you…'

At six in the morning there was the smell of coffee. Alex had left two cups on the table beside the bed, and was gently kissing her awake. They wished each other a drowsy good morning, and Marie reached for a cup.

'Mmm. That's better.' Neither of them spoke again until the caffeine began to kick in. Then she said, 'I should be going soon.'

Alex turned the corners of his mouth down. His expression of regret was just what Marie wanted to see.

'I've got to go home for a change of clothes and a shower.'

She didn't want to go either, but the idea of turning up to work in Alex's jeans was impossible. The dress code at the clinic was relaxed, but that was a little too relaxed, and someone was sure to notice.

'You won't shower with me?'

Tempting. 'We could try to leave *one* thing for next time.'

Voicing that fantasy had prompted a slip of the tongue and turned into a suggestion that there *would* be a next time. Neither of them had broached the subject; last night had been an exercise in the here and now, and no forward planning had seemed necessary.

He grinned suddenly. 'I'm hoping that means you're not

going to break my heart and tell me that this is the first and last time this is going to happen.'

Break his heart? Marie left the thought where it belonged, along with all the other professions of love spoken in the heat of the moment.

'I want a next time, Alex.'

'Me too.' He gathered the scattered pillows and leaned back against them, putting his arm around her. 'It's not going to be easy to keep everyone from noticing at work today.'

'We could just stay in our offices.'

Marie didn't really care if everyone knew, but it was common sense not to advertise the fact when you were sleeping with someone you worked with—especially not until you knew exactly where the relationship was going.

'Nah. That's not going to work. When two people suddenly start avoiding each other at work, the first thing everyone thinks is that they're sleeping together.'

'Hmm. True. How about being so busy that we don't have time to think too much about it?'

'Might work.'

He thought for the moment. 'Although I'm not sure I can sustain that level of busy for more than a couple of hours. I guess we'll just have to wing it.'

He took the cup from her hand, putting it down on the table.

'Alex! Not again!'

'We have time. You could be half an hour late for work, couldn't you?'

'No, I couldn't. And neither could you. What kind of example is that?'

He chuckled. 'It's a dreadful example. We shouldn't do it…' His eyes flashed with boyish mischief as he raised her hand to his lips.

'There you go, then.'

She really wanted to stay…just for another fifteen minutes. But temptation was there to be resisted.

Marie pushed him away, and he flopped back onto the pillows, laughing.

'Can I at least watch you dress? Crumbs to a starving man…?' She was picking her clothes up from the floor.

'You are *not* starving, Alex.'

He couldn't possibly be—not after last night. She pulled on her underwear, and then his jeans, belting them tight around her waist. Then she crawled onto the bed, keeping the crumpled duvet between his body and hers.

'One kiss.'

'Just a kiss?' He grinned at her.

'Yes. No cheating, Alex…'

He held his hands up in a gesture of surrender. Those hands were his most potent weapon. She dipped down, planting one kiss on his lips, thrilling at his sigh of disappointment as she left him, hurrying into the sitting room to find her top and shoes.

She drove home in the clinic's electric car, with the radio playing and Alex's scent still on her body. Even after she'd showered it felt like she was still his. He'd claimed her, and she couldn't escape by merely being apart from him.

She dressed, drying her hair in front of the mirror. There was something different…something she couldn't quite put her finger on. Her expression made her look like the cat that had got the cream, and try as she might she couldn't persuade her face to assume her usual smile.

But Marie need not have worried. When she saw Alex at the clinic, he smiled his usual greeting. He made the Monday morning meeting easy, not seeking out her gaze but not afraid to meet it. He acted as if last night had never happened. If anyone should divine that something earth-shaking had happened to her over the weekend, they never would have connected Alex with it.

It was slightly unnerving. Marie didn't want anyone to know any more than he did, but her vanity felt he might have made this appear a little more difficult.

But it was just the way Alex was. He was protecting his privacy and hers. He'd grown up learning to maintain a face for the world that didn't show any of his true feelings, and it had become a matter of habit for him. She shouldn't confuse that with the real Alex. The one who'd made love to her last night, who'd listened to her heart calling him, and whose heart had replied so eloquently.

Alex had phoned the hospital and the news was good. Charlie's leg had been operated on yesterday afternoon and he was recovering well. Zack was eager to visit him, and Alex had said he'd go too. Marie had decided that three around his bed might be a little too much for Charlie, so she contented herself with packing a bag full of things he might need, along with a few treats, and had given it to Zack to take in.

'So how is he?' When Alex walked into her office later, she breathed a sigh of relief that she no longer had to pretend to work while she waited for them to get back.

'He's okay.' Alex closed the door behind him and sat down. 'He's pretty sore and he's got a real shiner. But I spoke to his surgeon and he'll mend.'

'Great. That's good.'

Marie wondered if she was supposed to keep the pretence up now that they were alone. Perhaps the rule was that they only referred to last night when they were off clinic premises.

'I saw his mother as well. I told her we'll provide whatever Charlie needs in the way of rehab and that either you or I will personally oversee his case.'

'Good. Thanks. She's happy with that?'

Knowing what to do with her hands was a problem. She'd known exactly what to do with them last night, but that wasn't appropriate here.

'She asked me to thank you for everything you did yesterday. Charlie might well have bled to death if it hadn't been for your decisive action.'

Marie's heart was beating even faster than it had been. Rolling a pencil round and round in her fingers took the edge off the tension a little. 'It's…you know…'

He grinned. 'Yes, I know. All in a day's work.'

So far there was nothing. Not even any of the in-jokes that they cracked all the time. Marie could do this. She just wished that there was one hint from Alex that he hadn't already left last night behind. That he didn't regret it.

'I've sent Zack out to get an MP3 player and a decent pair of headphones. Charlie's phone got smashed in the accident and the hospital radio doesn't play his kind of thing.'

Marie frowned. 'What is his kind of thing?'

'I'm not completely sure. Zack's going to help me with that; we'll download some music for him after work. You want to join us?'

Something sparked in his eyes. Maybe it was just the mention of music, and the prospect of exploring a few new artists. But even if it was just that, the thought of spending a few hours with two of her favourite people was incredibly tempting.

'I can't—sorry. I'd like to, but I promised I'd call round and see Mum after work. She wants a chat.'

A crease formed on Alex's brow. 'Okay.'

It wasn't okay with Marie. She wished now that she'd asked her mother whether it really needed to be tonight, instead of just automatically acquiescing. But that was what she'd always done before.

'We'll miss you.'

What would have happened if he'd said that before? All

the times when their friends at medical school had gone to play softball in the park, or gone to the pub to talk out a long day's work.

Marie dismissed the idea. She'd always tried not to think about the things she was missing out on, and concentrate on the things she needed to do instead.

Suddenly he got to his feet, leaning across the desk towards her. Meeting Alex's gaze was hard, because his grey eyes held all of the promise of last night. It wasn't over between them.

'Could I persuade you to come back to mine after you've seen your mother?'

The pencil snapped suddenly in her fingers. Marie jumped, dropping it onto the desk, and saw the edge of Alex's mouth curve.

'Yes. That was what I had in mind, too.'

'You want to snap pencils with me?'

'All night.'

'I might be late... I won't get away from Mum's before about nine.'

'I'll wait. I have a spare door key downstairs; you can let yourself in. And take one of the clinic cars—you'll get back to me sooner...'

'It's an emergency?'

'Yes.'

He brushed a kiss on her lips and her whole body went into overdrive. Definitely an emergency...

It was ten o'clock before Alex heard the key turning in the door of his flat. He'd decided to go to bed and allow himself to doze a little before Marie arrived. She'd know where he was.

She did. He heard her footsteps in the hallway and the light outside being flipped off. The warm glow of the lamp in the corner of the bedroom threw shadows across the floor.

Alex watched as she took her clothes off. No words. She knew he couldn't take his eyes off her, and it seemed that her movements were slower and more deliberate than usual. She took the time to hang her dress carefully across the back of the easy chair that stood next to the lamp, and he devoured the shadows that played across her body.

When she was naked, she walked over to the bed. She hesitated, as if she'd forgotten something, and then ran her fingers across one breast and down towards her stomach. The sudden urgent wish to take her now crashed over him, but he resisted it. Waiting would make the having so much better.

'Get into bed…'

His words sounded suspiciously like an order, which made Marie smile. Her movements seemed to slow even more and Alex grinned. She knew exactly how to tease him.

When she slipped under the duvet he moved towards her, wrapping his arms around her but keeping thick layers of down between them. He could tease too.

Alex leaned forward, planting a kiss on her mouth, and she let out a gasp.

'Everything okay?' He smiled innocently at her.

'Yes. Mum just wanted to say how pleased she was about Zack.' She turned the corners of her mouth down. 'She could have said that when she called me.'

Alex resisted the temptation to agree. He loved the way that Marie was so close to her family, and wished he could have had a measure of that himself. It was hypocritical to say that he wished they'd give her a bit more time to herself. Because what he really meant was that *he* wanted her time.

'We've got a few hours to catch up on…' she said, disentangling her arm from the duvet, caressing the side of his face.

'Hey... You know I don't mind if you've got something else to do.' Tearing Marie in two wasn't going to solve the problem—it would only make things worse.

'I know you don't. But *I* mind.'

The thought shattered the last of his self-control—that Marie had wanted to give up the responsibilities that she clung to so ferociously in favour of this.

He pulled the duvet away from them and rolled her over onto her back, covering her body with his. She could see and feel how much he wanted her.

'Where do you most want to be now?'

He wanted to hear it. If she screamed it out, then all the better. He wanted every moment she spent with him to be time that she didn't want to be anywhere else.

Her eyes darkened suddenly, the light playing that trick he loved so much and turning them to midnight blue. Marie reached behind her, giving an impatient huff when she remembered that they'd used all the condoms taped to his headboard last night. Her fingers searched the surface of the bedside table until she found the packet he'd bought on his way home.

He gritted his teeth, waiting while she fumbled with the wrappings. Then she reached down, and he felt his blood begin to boil as she carefully rolled the condom into place.

When she took him inside her it felt as if he was coming home after a long journey. He stared into her eyes, watching every small movement, listening to the way her breathing started to quicken and match his as he pushed deeper.

One moment of stillness.

They spent it wisely, feeling the warm sensations of being together at last.

Then Marie's lips parted. 'Here, Alex. I want to be right here.'

CHAPTER THIRTEEN

ALEX HAD ENVISAGED a rather sedate affair for the clinic's open day—a Saturday afternoon spent coaxing people in with the promise of free coffee and then showing them around to give them an idea of what the clinic could offer to the community.

Marie had dismissed that idea with a wave of her hand and started to search the internet for someone who could supply bunting.

Alex knew that Marie thrived on organising this kind of thing and he'd passed the preparations to her, taking over her clinic caseload for a week while she appeared and disappeared, off on various missions to secure the things that they simply couldn't do without. When they were alone at night he got her undivided attention. Alex had always reckoned that sex was a pleasant addition to a relationship, but when he had Marie in his arms it was more important than breathing.

He arrived at eight in the morning the day of the open day, six hours before the doors were due to open, and found that a bouncy castle was already being set up on the grassy area at the back of the clinic. When he walked into the café, he found Marie supervising a couple of Jim Armitage's men, who were manoeuvring a piano into place.

'Where did you get this?' Alex ran his finger over the

wooden frame. It was a good one, and had clearly been polished recently.

'I found it in the outhouse where Jim puts all the things you ask him to get rid of.' She tapped her nose, in the way that Jim did when he was about to impart a pearl of wisdom. 'You never know what might come in handy.'

'I thought it was just old pieces of wood. What else is in there?'

'Loads of stuff. I found one of those old-style blackboards, with a wooden stand. You should go and take a look sometime. This was from the school music room.' She opened the lid that covered the keyboard. 'I had it tuned.'

Alex hadn't seen or heard the coming or the going of a piano tuner. Marie's innocent look indicated that she'd probably kept that activity well away from his notice.

'What are you going to do with it?'

Alex supposed it might make a nice piece of furniture for the café. Marie had added a few things in there to make the clean lines into a more welcoming area.

'Well, we could always play it. We've got some people coming to sing this afternoon; I thought it might help break down a few barriers.'

'So that's where you and Zack disappeared off to the other evening. Auditions?'

Marie nodded. 'I've got an a capella group. A few of them are backing singers for other bands, and they look and sound marvellous.'

'Great.' Alex had no doubt he'd approve of her choice.

'Why don't you try it out?'

She opened the lid that covered the piano keys and Alex reluctantly jabbed a couple of notes with his finger.

'Sounds as if it has a good tone.'

Marie rolled her eyes. 'Come on, Alex, I know you can play.'

Long hours at the piano when he was a child had seen

to that. But Alex didn't play any more. Apart from just that one time…

'I don't think Christmas carols are going to be appropriate for today.'

She rolled her eyes. 'I don't know all that much about music, but I know that anyone who can play Christmas carols with the kind of tempo that gets a whole ward full of kids singing along can play pretty much anything.'

That had been a good evening. A Father Christmas had turned up from a local charity, but no one had admitted to being able to play the piano that had stood in the corner of the family room on the children's ward. Alex had sat down, and the kids' faces had made him forget for a while that all the piano meant to him was rapped knuckles.

'I haven't played for years.'

She flashed him an imploring smile. 'It's like riding a bike, isn't it? Do you know this one?'

She started to sing, her voice wavering up and down, somehow managing to hit every note but the right one. He grinned. Marie had never been able to carry a tune, and it was yet another thing that was perfect about her. But he could recognise which song she meant from the words and he picked it out with one finger.

'That's the one.' She gave him a thumbs-up.

He'd do anything to make Marie happy—even this. So Alex sat down, trying a few chords and then moving down a key. That was better. He was rusty, but he could still play.

Alex operated the volume pedal and added a little oomph to the tune, gratified at the way she smiled, moving to the music. He improvised, adding a few extra choruses. He was enjoying watching her.

When he'd finished, a muffled round of applause came from the kitchen.

Marie shot him an I-told-you-so look. 'That's great. I wish you'd play more.'

Alex was almost tempted. But in a world where everything seemed to be changing he had to hang on to a few of the rules he'd made for himself when he'd left home.

'I don't have good memories of playing the piano. You wouldn't either if you'd been at one of my father's music evenings. Twenty adults, all staring at you, just waiting for you to make a slip.'

'It sounds awful, Alex. But you love music—you always have. You have a talent, and you can't let anything take that away from you. And...well, the a capella band did tell me they have a couple of numbers that they usually sing with backing tracks...'

'Even if I wanted to, I can't just sit down and play for them. There's such a thing as rehearsal.'

Marie shrugged awkwardly. 'They'll be here soon to set up their equipment. There's plenty of time before we open the gates to the public.'

Alex sighed. 'Have I just been set up?'

She capitulated so suddenly that he almost hugged her. Marie was the one person he couldn't resist, and her transparency made her all the more seductive.

'No. Well...yes. But not really. The band have a recorded backing track they can use.'

'So that's not quite a yes. But it's not a no, either.'

She gave him an agonised look. 'I always wondered why you didn't play—you're so good. When you told me about your father I put two and two together. But this is...it's *your* place. You should fill it with your sound. Of course, if you really don't want to...'

He held up his hand and Marie fell silent. 'Send them through when they arrive. I'll help them set up their equipment.'

'So that's a yes?'

'Not quite. But it's not a no, either.'

'Okay. Good.'

She gave him a ravishing smile and hurried away.

Marie could have made more of a mess of that, but she wasn't sure how. Although Alex hadn't seemed too cross, and he was at least going to talk to the a capella band.

There was plenty left to do. She had to make sure all the examination rooms were locked, and call Sonya to check that she had their special guests in hand. Then rescue Zack before he got himself completely buried under piles of bunting, and make sure the cafeteria staff had everything they needed...

The bouncy castle was inflating nicely, and when the band arrived she sent them through to the cafeteria. Zack appeared, red-faced and grinning, declaring that the bunting was finally all under control.

'Who's playing the piano?'

Soft strains of music were floating through into the reception area. A few chords, and then a woman's voice, singing a few bars and then stopping as player and singer began to adjust to each other.

'Um... Alex, probably.'

'He plays?' Zack took a few steps in the direction of the music. 'I've got to see this.'

'No, I need you here.' Marie frowned at her brother.

'But...'

'Help me get these display boards up.'

This was something Alex needed to do on his own for a while. The woman's voice had begun to swell, more powerful now, and she could hear Alex beginning to follow her lead. They didn't need any interruptions.

Zack pulled a face. 'Okay, where do you want them...'

The countdown seemed to fly by. Sonya arrived, along

with the special guests she'd promised to bring—a foot-baller and a runner—who ceremonially opened the gates at two o'clock to let the small crowd that had gathered in.

The sun shone, and more people came. The sound of voices and music echoed through from the cafeteria, and the two celebrities set up shop in the reception area to sign autographs and smile for an endless number of pho-tographs.

The clinic staff were all busy showing small groups around and answering questions, the café was packed, and the bouncy castle was a big hit with the children. People were sitting out on the grass at the back of the clinic, just enjoying the sun. Sonya had the reception area well under control, and Alex was nowhere to be seen.

When she heard the singers stop for a break, and the strains of the piano drifted through from the cafeteria, Marie smiled. Finally she felt that she might join him.

The lead singer of the a capella group, a shy woman who suddenly became a force of nature when she opened her mouth to sing, was standing by the piano, tapping her foot and drinking a glass of lemonade. When she put her glass down and nodded to Alex, he smiled, working the music around to what seemed to be an agreed point, when the woman started to sing.

It was breathtaking. Full of energy and soul. And both of them were clearly enjoying themselves.

Marie sat down in the corner of the cafeteria and Zack hurried up, putting a cappuccino down on the table in front of her before turning to help the serving staff. Everything was under control.

This was what the clinic was all about. A community helping each other. It was about Alex too. She'd asked him if he thought that the clinic would save him. Watching him here, it seemed that it just might.

* * *

Saturday had been great. Sunday had been delicious and lazy. Monday was nerve-racking.

'Are you nervous?' she asked.

Alex didn't look a bit nervous; he looked handsome and dapper in his dark blue suit.

'Terrified. You?' He shot her a smile across the bedroom.

'I don't think this dress is right. And my jacket's far too bright…' Her make-up was probably wrong as well, for a TV appearance, and Marie hoped that part of the reason they had to be at the studio hours before their scheduled appearance was because they would fix that.

'You look gorgeous. Anyway, the whole purpose of a dark suit is to show off the woman next to you.'

Marie wasn't sure that made her feel any better. She'd rather fade into the background and have Alex take the glare of the attention they were hoping to generate.

'I'm a doctor, Alex. Not a mannequin.'

'Who says you can't be a stunningly beautiful doctor? The two aren't mutually exclusive.'

'Stop.' She held her hand up. 'I know you mean well, but you're not making this any easier.'

'Does this?'

He walked around the bed, enveloping her in the kind of careful hug that was designed not to crease their jackets, but still felt warm and reassuring.

'What happened to being able to do anything together?'

'It's live TV, Alex!'

'We've built a clinic and we can do this.'

Marie nodded, disentangling herself from his arms and smoothing the front of his jacket. He was steady and secure, like a rock. She just had to remember not to hang on to him too much in public, however much she might want to. She knew Alex wasn't ready to let that mask of his slip yet. He guarded his private life fiercely.

The car arrived to take them to the TV studio and they drove through clear streets, bathed in early-morning light. She slipped her hand into his, knowing that this was breaking all their rules about keeping their relationship strictly behind closed doors, but not really caring. Alex's touch might be subtle, and he didn't kiss her fingers the way he had before they'd left his flat, but it was enough to keep her from panicking and trying to jump out of the car when it stopped at a red light.

A cheery make-up girl applied lipstick in a shade that seemed too bold for Marie, explaining that it would look much the same as her normal colour under the lights of the studio. They were shuffled from one place to another by various production assistants, and finally they walked onto the set.

Alex was standing to one side, to let her go first, but still keeping protectively close. The presenters of the morning show beamed at them, murmuring a few words of encouragement. They were clearly used to dealing with nervous guests.

First there was a short film about the clinic that had been made earlier in the week. Sonya had picked out all the elements which were most important in the accompanying press release, and the questions were easy enough. Alex answered his with exactly the kind of friendly approachability that they wanted to be the hallmark of the clinic, and Marie managed to get through hers without stumbling.

It was going well. She kept her gaze on the two presenters, trying not to look at Alex. She knew he was there with her, and that gave her courage.

Then the female presenter leaned forward, smiling at Alex. 'I believe that it's your inheritance that has made the clinic possible, Alex?'

Too close for comfort. But Alex's face didn't show any of the dismay that Marie felt.

'I count myself fortunate in having been able to use it to do so.'

'And as you've also inherited a royal title...' the presenter paused for effect '...I think we can all agree that you're one of London's most eligible bachelors now. Is there any chance that we have a royal wedding to look forward to?'

The woman was being deliberately challenging. Marie wondered whether strangling her on live TV would be considered an appropriate response, and glanced up at Alex.

His smile didn't change. 'I'd far rather everyone saw me as a doctor. One who's working a little too hard to contemplate romance at the moment.'

'You're sure...?'

The male presenter shot a pointed look at Marie, and she wondered whether her body language had given her away. She'd been so frightened that maybe she'd unconsciously sat a little too close to Alex on the sofa.

'I'd love to think that there's a woman out there who could put up with me.' Alex's tone took on an appropriately rueful note. 'But I'm still waiting to find her.'

The female presenter laughed, looking quickly at the overhead screen. 'Well, I think we have a few offers coming in already on our social media feeds. Thank you, Alex and Marie, for being with us this morning.'

A new topic was started, and the programme cut to a filmed report. The two presenters thanked them again, and they were hurried off the set. Marie's heart was beating so fast she could hardly breathe.

As soon as they left the glare of the cameras Alex's face turned ashen. Marie grabbed his arm. 'Not a word...' she said. Not until they could talk privately.

He nodded down at her. The kind of decision-making that had seen them through so many medical emergencies would get them through this one.

They walked back to the small dressing room where they'd left their things, and quietly managed to elude anyone who might stop them. The receptionist called after them, asking if they were going to wait for their taxi there, and Marie gave a smiling shake of her head while Alex kept walking. As soon as they were on the pavement he hailed a taxi, and to Marie's relief the driver saw him and stopped to pick them up.

'I suppose it was going to happen sooner or later. I'll speak to Sonya,' Alex said. His whole body was tense, as if he was waiting for some new blow to appear from somewhere. 'It can't hurt the clinic so much now. We've started to establish ourselves in the community and people know what we're about. We just have to hold on to our values and try to keep the press away.'

Clinic first. Always. But this had to hurt Alex. He'd spent so much time leaving his past behind, and now it had come back to haunt him in the most public way possible.

'My father would have *loved* this.' There was a trace of bitterness in his voice. 'Just think—all he had to do was one good deed and the press would have come snapping at his heels.'

'He missed a trick there.' Marie tried to lighten the mood between them, and Alex smiled grimly.

They both knew that with a little careful management this wouldn't compromise their work at the clinic, but it had raised a question that neither of them wanted to answer just yet. If Alex was going to be caught in the media's spotlight, what would happen to their relationship?

Alex fell silent, his face clouded with worry. When the cab drew up outside his mansion block he paid the cabbie and wished him a good day. He didn't say another word until they were inside his front door.

'I'll protect you. I'll make sure none of this touches you,' he said.

Marie suppressed the urge to shake him. 'What if I don't want you to protect me?'

'This isn't the time, Marie. I know you can do everything by yourself, but things would be a lot easier if you'd let me help.'

Her face was itching from the heavy make-up and suddenly all Marie wanted was to be alone. 'I'm going to wash my face...'

He nodded, and she escaped to the bathroom, washing her face and splashing it with cold water.

Sonya had been right. Alex's royal heritage and his determination to do something good with it was a great story. He was one of the most eligible bachelors in London, and of course there would be interest in his love life. What had she been thinking when she'd got involved with him?

She'd been thinking about his touch. About how they got each other, as best friends *and* as lovers. She hadn't been thinking about the practicalities, about how when the news became public she'd be standing with him in the glare. About how she'd cope with navigating his world when she had no compass.

She wanted to get out of these clothes. She went to the bedroom, changed into a pair of comfortable trousers and a shirt. She heard the phone ring and the low resonance of his voice.

'No. No comment... You can speak to Sonya Graham-Hall about any publicity matters to do with the clinic. You have her number... No, I really don't have anything else to say...'

When she went back into the sitting room the jack for

the landline lay unplugged on the floor and he was holding his mobile against his ear.

One minute...

He mouthed the words, holding up his finger to indicate that the call wouldn't last long, and then spoke into the phone.

'Hi, Sonya. Did you see it?'

Suddenly Marie didn't want to listen to this. She went into the kitchen and set the kettle to boil, making two mugs of tea. When she heard Alex stop talking, she walked back into the sitting room.

'Thanks.' Alex was in full damage-control mode now. He took the tea, putting it down on the coffee table in front of him. 'I've spoken to Sonya, and she's going to field all the press enquiries for now. We don't answer any questions from anyone.'

'Okay.' That sounded sensible enough. 'So what do you think we should do?'

He pressed his lips together. 'I don't see that we have much choice. We don't see each other for a while—until this all blows over.'

'I have a choice. I can stand by you.'

'You don't want this, Marie. You've told me yourself that you're not comfortable with my royal status, and it's about to get a whole lot worse.'

'I never said that!' Marie reddened. She'd demonstrated it, though, by refusing to wear the diamond. Actions spoke louder than words.

'Are you going to tell me you'd be happy with that kind of notoriety?'

'No. But I don't have to be happy with it, Alex. If it's who you are then that's what I'll be.'

'That's...'

His gaze softened for a moment, and Marie though he was about to relent. Then steel showed in his eyes again.

'I've seen the damage that can do, and I won't let you do it, Marie.'

'But I *want* to do it. I don't want to be the kind of person who thinks the best thing to do when things get tough is to walk away. My father did that, and I've been dealing with the consequences ever since.'

That was the difference between them. It wasn't just a matter of lifestyle—although it terrified Marie to think she might be catapulted into a world where she felt like a fish out of water. They'd both lived through different versions of an unhappy childhood, and they'd always have different solutions for life's problems.

Tears suddenly blurred her vision, burning like acid. Maybe the answer to this was that there *was* no answer. That there was nothing either of them could do to make it right.

He got to his feet. 'Perhaps we should talk about this later. I have to go over to see Sonya, to work up a press release. Just the basic facts; she reckons that'll give us some breathing space.'

That was probably wise. It would give them both a little time to cool off. Although in truth Alex looked perfectly cool now. He'd switched off, retreating behind the mask he'd worn all his life—the one he'd hidden behind as a child, which had protected him from his past ever since.

'Yes, okay. You'll go back to the clinic?'

'Yes, I'll see you there.'

He turned away. When Marie heard the front door close it sounded just the same as it always did. She'd almost prefer that he'd slammed it—at least it would have given some hint of what was going on in his head.

She should go to work. By the time Alex returned to the clinic she'd be calm. And when they came back here they'd go to the bedroom and forget all about their differences.

Maybe.

Marie picked up the overnight bag into which she'd folded her dress and jacket, collecting up the other odds and ends that had found their way here and putting them into it too. A comb and a tub of moisturiser. A book that she was only halfway through, which lay on the kitchen table. The pages were creased at one corner from where it had been dropped on the floor, discarded when Alex had leaned over to kiss her and passion had made her forget everything else. Tears pricked at the corners of her eyes and she stuffed it quickly into her bag.

She didn't need to do this. Gathering up her things seemed so final…as if a decision had been made. People argued all the time…

But Marie couldn't see the way back from this. As she closed his front door behind her the click of the latch seemed to mark an ending.

Alex's meeting with Sonya lasted half an hour. She'd seen that he couldn't concentrate, and had kept it short and simple. 'Just tell me what you want and I'll handle it,' had just about covered it.

He took a taxi back to his flat, but Marie was already gone. That at least gave him some time alone, to think. He just wanted to take shelter from a world that wanted to know nothing about *him* and everything about his royal connections.

Running to the comfort of Marie's arms would ease his pain, but it was the same as hiding inside the walls of the clinic. If he was going to protect them—Marie and the clinic—he had to distance himself from them both for a little while.

Sonya would manage things, and a few well-chosen media releases and interviews would draw the press away from the gates of the clinic, so their patients didn't have to run the gauntlet of photographers. It would draw them away from Marie, as well, so she didn't have to face the bright glare of publicity.

Marie would never forgive him if he walked away. She'd told him already that she would stand by him, but he'd never forgive himself if her commitment to the job, to the clinic, to his dream, meant she had to change in an attempt to fit in with what she thought was expected of her.

If he stayed he'd lose her completely, but if he left there was a chance that their friendship might survive.

For the last few weeks he'd been beyond happy, and he'd allowed himself to think that maybe he did know how to make a relationship different from his parents' marriage. But he'd fallen at the first hurdle.

When he finally made a move, changing out of his crumpled suit and making his way back to the clinic, he knew what he had to do. Marie was in a staff meeting that was due to last for the rest of the afternoon, and he waited until Tina, the receptionist, popped her head around his office door.

'Everyone's gone for the evening. It's just you and Marie.'

'Thanks, Tina. Have a good evening.'

'You too. Are you okay…?'

Tina shot him a puzzled look, and Alex nodded and smiled back at her. The last thing he wanted was to make his relationship troubles the talk of the clinic.

He heard the front doors open and then slam shut again. He had to do it now. Before his courage failed him and wanting Marie took over, driving everything else from his mind.

Alex walked upstairs, feeling his burden increase with every step. Marie's office door was open and he stopped in the doorway, afraid that if he went in and sat down he wouldn't be able to do this.

She looked up from the papers in front of her and her

eyes seemed suddenly hollow, as if she hadn't slept for a week. 'You're back.'

'Yes.'

No invitation to come in and sit down. It seemed Marie had nothing to say to him—which was fair enough because he had nothing to say to her. They'd always understood each other, and they understood this as well.

He took a breath. 'I think we should stop. For good. We'll tear each other to pieces if we don't.'

She nodded. 'Yes. I think so too.'

That was the most difficult part and it had been achieved in a matter of a few words. Alex bit back the temptation to fall on his knees and beg her to fight him. That would just prolong the agony, because he and Marie had never been meant to be together.

'I'm going to bring forward my trip,' he said.

The trip had been planned for him to scout out sites for new clinics around the country. It was an ideal excuse to get him away from London for a couple of weeks.

'After that I'll be concentrating on development, so I'll be working from home most of the time.'

'But... No... I'll clear out my things. There are plenty of jobs for qualified doctors in London. I'll just call an agency and I'll have another job by the weekend.'

She was regarding him steadily, her lip trembling and her eyes filling with tears. This wasn't what he'd meant to happen at all.

'What? No, Marie. We always kept our private lives separate from our work before. You can't leave.'

He knew he was in no position to tell her what she could or couldn't do. Thankfully Marie overlooked that.

'I'm not sure I can stay, either.'

Alex thought fast. It was beyond unfair that a broken relationship meant Marie felt she had to walk away from her job. If she decided to leave he'd make sure she was paid until the end of the year, but that wasn't the point. She'd put her heart into this place and given it life. It was as much hers as it was his, and she'd see that once the initial shock of their parting had subsided.

'Stay for a couple of weeks at least. I need you to be here while I'm away. We can talk again when I get back.'

She nodded. 'All right. Just until then, Alex.'

It was almost a relief to walk away from her, so he could no longer see the pain in her beautiful eyes. He'd never wanted to hurt Marie, but all he'd brought her was sorrow. He'd come to love this place, but he'd give it up a thousand times over if it meant she would stay.

He needed her in his life, and he hoped desperately that in time they'd learn to be friends again, but he was beginning to doubt that. There was no coming back from this.

CHAPTER FOURTEEN

IT HAD BEEN ten days since she'd seen Alex. He'd walked out of the clinic that evening and Marie had been able to hold back her tears only just long enough to hear the main doors close downstairs. Then she'd got unsteadily out of her chair and walked over to the corner of her office. Sliding down the wall, she'd curled up on the floor, sobbing.

But they'd done the right thing. They needed completely different things from a relationship, and it never could have worked. That didn't mean it hurt any less.

The emails had started the following day. Alex's first one had been short and polite, and Marie had replied in the same vein. They'd loosened up a little as the days went by and his itinerary took him further and further away from London. Maybe after a year or so one of them might crack a joke.

She missed him so much. Her head wanted him and her body ached for him. Sofia Costa had asked if she was coming down with something, and Zack had noticed too.

'What's up, sis?' He wandered into her office now, carrying a packet of sandwiches, and plumped himself down, offering her one.

Marie took it, wondering whether he'd made extra this morning just for the purpose of sharing.

'What's this?' She peeled one of the slices of bread up. 'Ah…cream cheese and cucumber. Thanks.'

Zack nodded. He knew that was one of her favourites. 'I've made egg and bacon as well.'

Zack was definitely on a mission to spoil her. Marie smiled at him, grateful for both the sandwiches and his concern. Her little brother had come a long way in the last few months.

'Is something going on? Between you and Alex?' he asked.

'What...?' Marie almost choked on her sandwich. 'What makes you think that?'

'Well, he's never around any more. You know that's always a sign there's something going on...when two people start avoiding each other at work.' Zack nodded sagely.

'Where did you get that from?' Clearly not from his own experience; Zack hadn't managed to hold a job down for more than a week before he came here. Marie wondered if people at the clinic were talking.

'It was in a film on TV. Two people started an affair and all the people at work knew because they suddenly started being really horrible to each other.'

'Well, I'm not having an affair with Alex.' That was strictly true—she wasn't having one with him any more. And she wouldn't be having one with him in the future, either. 'And he's not been around because he's in Edinburgh at the moment, talking to people about possible sites for a new clinic.'

'Only half an hour away by air... You were looking pretty tired on Monday—'

'Stop!' Marie brought her hand down onto her desk and Zack jumped. 'I haven't been sleeping so well recently.'

Zack frowned. 'So what is it, then?'

'Nothing. Really.' Marie decided this was as good a time as any to tell Zack. 'I'm going to be leaving the clinic.'

Zack's eyes widened in shock. 'But why? You love it here.'

'It's…not what I thought it would be. I'm not with the patients as much as when I was working at the hospital.'

'I thought you liked it? You know…developing stuff. Finding solutions.'

She did. But it was the only reason that Marie had been able to think of which didn't involve talking about her split with Alex. She wasn't able to do that just yet without dissolving into tears.

'It's a lot of paperwork. But, Zack, this won't affect your job here. That's between you and Alex, and my going won't make any difference.' Marie knew Alex would honour his agreement with Zack, whatever happened.

Zack thought for a moment. 'I want to stay. I like it here.'

And Zack had been more than pulling his weight. He'd turned into an asset for the clinic, and people were beginning to depend on him.

'Like I said, my leaving doesn't make any difference to your position here.'

'Okay. Thanks.' Zack was obviously a little unhappy with this, but he'd run out of questions to ask. Instead he offered her another sandwich. 'Bacon and egg?'

'Thanks. I'll keep it for later, if you don't mind.'

Their email conversation hadn't been an easy one, but Marie had been determined. She couldn't stay at the clinic. Even when Alex wasn't there everything about it reminded her of him. She had to make a clean break. And it wasn't fair that he was staying away, because she knew he loved the place. He'd built it and she wanted him to have it.

He'd protested, but she'd stood firm, because she knew it was the best thing for both of them. They'd agreed that she should stay on for another week, until he was back, and that he'd take on her current medical and management duties after that.

It was where he was supposed to be. It was where he'd always intended to be, and Marie was just making things right.

She cleared out her office, trying not to cry over the box of pink paper clips and the lava lamp that Alex had given her. Then she said her goodbyes to everyone and left. Alex would be coming to the clinic tomorrow, and she wouldn't even lay eyes on him.

The next two weeks were hard. She missed Alex every day. She missed the clinic every day. But she kept going, cleaning her flat from top to bottom and applying for jobs. Running in the park, with the express purpose of exhausting herself so that she'd sleep. Sometimes it worked and sometimes it didn't.

But today was a good day. There were two emails asking her to job interviews. The sun was shining. She still missed Alex, but even that was beginning to subside from a sharp, insistent pain to a dull ache. Her life would never be the same without him, but it could still mean something. She could still make a difference.

She replied to both the emails, saying she'd be there at the times stated, and sorted through her wardrobe to find a suitable outfit. Her red jacket might go nicely with a plain dress, but that was still in her overnight bag, creased and crumpled. Marie hadn't been able to bear opening it to go through all the things that had once been at Alex's flat.

The doorbell rang and she pressed the Entryphone. That would be Zack. She opened the front door of her flat and went into the kitchen to put the kettle on. She heard footsteps on the stairs, and then a quiet knock on the door.

'Come *in*, Zack.' Why was he messing around knocking at the door?

'It's not Zack.'

Marie froze. Alex's voice. When she looked out into the hallway she could see him, standing outside the open door.

He looked tall, tired and handsome. Marie swallowed down the lump in her throat, willing her heart to slow down, but it ignored her.

'Alex… I'm sorry, I was expecting Zack.'

Polite was the way to go. They'd been ruthlessly polite in their emails and that had worked. Perhaps it would work in person, too.

'I wanted to talk to you. I asked Zack if he knew whether you'd be at home this morning.'

Light suddenly dawned. Zack had called her, asking if she'd be in, because he had something for her. It was Alex. Seeing Alex again was what Zack had for her. She was going to kill him.

'Well, come in.' She switched on a smile that didn't feel even vaguely natural. 'I dare say I've got things mixed up.'

He was holding the soft leather briefcase that he used for his laptop and papers. Perhaps he needed to speak to her about something to do with the clinic, in which case she was going to be professional. She wouldn't cry, and she wouldn't hold on to him, begging him to stay.

'Thanks.' He stepped into her hallway, closing the door behind him. They were standing twenty feet away from each other, but suddenly he seemed very close.

'I'll make coffee. Go and sit down.'

She motioned him towards the sitting room and he nodded a thank-you. Good. Two minutes to breathe deeply and try to recover her composure.

By the time she carried the coffee into the sitting room she was feeling a little giddy. Maybe the deep breathing had been a bad idea.

'What can I do for you?' She didn't dare say his name. Not after she'd whispered it so many times to herself in the dark hours of the night. 'Something to do with the clinic?'

'No.'

He opened his briefcase, reaching inside and producing a large thick book, bound with an elastic closure. He put it down on the coffee table, laying his hand on it as if he were about to swear an oath on it. Whatever the oath was, it seemed to be a matter of some importance to him; he was looking unbearably tense.

'This is my life. Everything about me. It's for you.'

She stared at him. Perhaps he'd been in therapy and this was his homework. If that was the case, she wished it hadn't brought him here to seek closure.

'The final pages are blank…'

'Alex, I'm not sure this is a good idea.' Closure was going to take a little longer than this for her. Her whole life, if the last few weeks were anything to go by.

'They're blank because I want you to write them with me. We both want the same things, but we've both struggled with a way to find those things. I love you, and I believe we can find a way together.'

It was as if the sun had just emerged from behind a cloud. Light streamed into a very dark place.

'You love me?'

'Yes, I do. Tell me now if you don't feel—'

'I love you too, Alex.' Now wasn't the time to listen to him work his way through any of the other options. 'I always have.'

He leaned forward, stretching out his hand. Reaching for her across the chasm that divided them.

'I've always loved you too, Marie. I couldn't put the past behind me, and that broke us apart. But I want to make this work and I'll do anything to be the man you want. I'll stick by you always, whatever happens.'

Marie reached for him, putting her hand in his. 'And I'll never give in to you. You'll never make me into someone that I'm not.'

He grinned suddenly. 'I know. I shouldn't have underestimated you.'

She could feel herself trembling. All she had to do was give herself to him, and it was the only thing she wanted to do. She and Alex could do anything they wanted…

'I only want you, Alex. Just as you are.'

The urgency of her need to be close to him took him by surprise. Marie bolted across the top of the coffee table and fell into his arms, kissing him. He caught his breath and then kissed her back with the same hunger that she felt.

'Just as I am? Crown and all?' His lips curved into a delicious smile. 'You're sure about that, now?'

'I'm sure.'

When he kissed her again, it all seemed wonderfully simple.

It was the best day of Alex's life. They were both finally free.

Marie had reached for the book he'd been labouring over for the past couple of weeks, pulling it onto her lap, but they hadn't been able to stop kissing each other. It had slipped unnoticed to the floor when he lifted her up to carry her to her bedroom. She'd practically torn off his clothes, and he'd been just as eager. If this was what commitment was like, then he was its new biggest fan.

'What do you want to do? Apart from spending the rest of your life with me…?' he asked. Marie had told him that already, and he'd voiced his own pledge. He belonged to her, and he always would.

'Mmm…' She stretched in his arms. 'I want to shower with you and then look at my book.'

Her book. It was her book now. His memories, his life, were all hers.

Alex loved it that Marie found it important enough to choose a bright summer dress from her wardrobe and apply a little make-up, just to look at it. It gave it a sense of occasion.

She laid the book on the small dining table at one end

of her sitting room, along with a couple of photograph albums from her own shelves. Then she sat down, opening the first page of the book.

'Oh! I think you might just be the cutest baby I've ever seen!' Marie reached forward, flipping over the cover of one of her own albums. 'That's me.'

'So you were born adorable, then...?'

It took hours to go through everything. But it felt as if they were slowly taking possession of each other. As if Marie was saving him, and he could save her.

'Are you hungry?' By the time they finished it was late in the afternoon.

She nodded. 'Why don't we go out somewhere and eat? Anywhere. Then we could go to the seaside.'

'We'll drive down to the coast and find somewhere to stay for the night.' Alex grinned. Just the two of them. No baggage, just his car keys and his credit card, and maybe a change of clothes. 'There's something I want to do first, though.'

He went to fetch the velvet-covered box from his briefcase, putting it in front of her on the table. She recognised it immediately, and raised her eyebrows quizzically.

'I didn't tell you all you should know about this.'

He opened the box and the large diamond glinted in the sunshine that filtered through the window.

'Go on.'

'This diamond is called Amour de Coeur.'

'It has a name?'

'Most large and well-known diamonds do. It was given by one of the more enlightened Kings of Belkraine to his wife, a few hundred years ago. They were very famously in love, at a time when a king's marriage wasn't really about love. And although she had her pick of all the other royal jewels, she only ever wore this one.'

'It's a beautiful story.'

'Will you dare to wear it, Marie?'

Alex could hear his own heart beating. She caught her breath, and then she smiled.

'I'd be proud to. It's a part of your heritage so it's a part of me, now.'

She reached forward, running one finger over the large diamond and the beautiful filigree chain. Suddenly the jewels of Belkraine and Marie's smile—which outshone them all—seemed to go naturally together.

'I have one more diamond for you.'

He got up from his seat, falling to his knees before her and taking her hand in his.

She let out a gasp, knowing exactly what this was.

'Alex!' Tears began to roll down her cheeks.

'Will you marry me, Marie?'

'Yes!' She flung her arms around his neck, forgetting all about the diamonds.

The ring had been burning a hole in his pocket, but it wasn't the thing that sealed their loving covenant. It was Marie's kiss.

'Will you let me go?' He finally managed to tear his lips away from hers.

'No. Never.'

He chuckled. 'Just long enough for me to do this properly…'

Alex took the ring from his pocket. It wasn't the biggest diamond in his inheritance by a very long way, but it had been carefully chosen and was one of the best in quality, flawless and slightly blue in colour.

'I'm starting a new tradition.'

Her eyes widened. 'What? Tell me!'

'My tradition is that when the King of Belkraine wants to marry he takes one diamond from the royal diadem, replacing it with another gem.'

'That's…from a crown?' She pointed at the diamond

ring. It was modern and simply fashioned, made to Alex's exact specifications.

'Will you make it yours? We'll take our inheritance and mould it into something that we're proud to pass on to our children.'

She held out her hand and Alex slipped the ring onto her finger. Suddenly everything fell into place. Their love... his inheritance. All that they wanted to do with their lives. It was all one.

She laid her hand on the book filled with pictures of him as a child. 'I want a baby that looks just like you.'

Alex chuckled. 'And I'd like one that looks like you. We can work on that.'

She hugged him close. 'Can we run away together now? To the seaside.'

Alex kissed her. 'There's nothing I'd like better.'

Alex took Marie to the old manor house in Sussex a few weeks after their engagement. She recognised the carefully laid out gardens and the brickwork around the massive doorway from the photographs in the book he'd made for her. She held on to his hand tightly as he showed her around.

'What do you think?' His brow creased a little as he asked the question.

'It's...okay...'

She loved the Victorian knot garden, the Elizabethan rooms with their nooks and crannies and large, deep fireplaces, the massive banqueting hall which had been turned into a sitting room, big enough to hold a beautiful grand piano at one end. The decor left a lot to be desired—it was far too ostentatious for Marie's taste—but the house was a pure delight.

'You love it, don't you?' He shot her a knowing look.

'A house with a maze in the garden? I'm sure there'll be lots of interest when you put it up for sale.'

It was a wonderful, magical place. But Alex had been so unhappy here when he was a child.

'What if *we* live in it? The location's perfect—it's only an hour out of London by train. We can keep the flat for when we're working late and make this our home.'

'But…you don't want this, do you?' Marie looked around the large sitting room. She could almost see their children playing here. 'The decor…'

'The decor can be changed. You could make this into a wonderful room. We could keep the piano.'

That would be nice…

'And there would be loads of space here to set up an office. We could convert the west wing and run the main charity from here.'

This place could be a wonderful family home. The kind Alex had always wanted and Marie had always dreamed of.

'What do you say to this? We'll bring some of our things down and camp out here for a while. It'll give us time to go through everything, and then you can decide how you feel about living here.'

He wrapped his arms around her, holding her close. 'That would be perfect. Where do you want to camp first?'

'The summer house?'

They should start with the place he liked the best. Alex had written about the summer house as the one place where he had been able to get away from the stifling hold of his family.

He chuckled. 'That sounds wonderful. I'll wake up and make love to you in the morning sunshine.'

'How do you feel about a trial run now?' Marie smiled up at him. 'The afternoon sunshine might do just as well?'

He grabbed the richly upholstered cushions from an ugly sofa, loading half of them into her arms.

'I'll race you there…'

EPILOGUE

The first weekend in February

FOR THE FIRST time in twelve years the plan had changed.
Only half the group had arrived at Alex and Marie's home
on Friday afternoon; the rest were due the following day.
They'd spent a relaxed evening around a roaring fire in the
sitting room, celebrating the eve of a wedding.

In the morning Alex had walked to the old church in
the village, surrounded by family and friends and with
Marie's mother on his arm. After Zack had left home to
go to art college she'd moved to be near her other son in
Sunderland, and she loved village life there and the cot-
tage Alex had bought for her.

He sat nervously in the front pew, waiting for Marie.
'Have you got the ring, Zack?'

Marie's three brothers had fought over who was to give
her away, and in the end her two elder brothers had been
given the task, and would both accompany her up the aisle.
Alex had claimed Zack as his best man.

'No.'

'What?'

'You've already asked me a hundred times. I thought
I'd try a different answer and see how that went.' Zack
patted the pocket of his morning suit. 'I've got the ring.'

'Don't do that to me, Zack.' Alex tried to frown, but

today wasn't the day for it. 'You're supposed to be a calming influence, not frightening me to death.'

Zack's laughing reply was lost in the swelling sound of the organ as it struck up the 'Wedding March'. Alex turned and saw Marie and his heart leapt into his throat. He was marrying the most beautiful woman in the world.

Her dress was the simplest part of her attire, the soft lines complementing the riot of flowers in her bouquet. The Amour de Coeur hung at her throat, its sparkle dimmed by her smile.

'You're sure about this?' Zack leaned over, whispering in his ear. 'You've still got time to run…'

'Be quiet, Zack. Of course I'm sure.'

The day had been wonderful—one delight after another: the warmth of family and friends, the way Marie had looked at him as they said their vows… Marie was the most precious thing in his life, and he knew she felt the same about him.

Their reception had taken place back at the home Alex had thought he would never return to, which Marie had made into the place he loved most in the world. Zack had come up with a surprisingly short but touching speech, blushing wildly as he'd sat down to a round of hearty applause.

'I'm so happy, Alex. I love you so much.' Marie whispered in his ear now, as they danced together.

'I love you too.'

That was all he needed to say. It made everything complete. His life and hers were woven together now, and it was a bond that couldn't be broken.

He led her over to the table where their ten oldest friends were sitting with their families. Hugs and kisses were exchanged, and Sunita whispered in Marie's ear.

She laughed, her fingers moving to the Amour de Coeur. 'Yes, it's real.'

Sunita's eyes widened, and Will laughed. 'It's your own fault, Sunita. If you *will* insist on marrying a farmer and burying yourself in the countryside, then you're going to miss some of the gossip. Don't you read the papers? We're in the presence of royalty.'

'You're joking! I *knew* I should have come last night and not this morning. Which one of you is it?'

Alex chuckled. 'Well, technically speaking, it's both of us now. But actually I'm just Marie's loyal and faithful servant.'

'Stop it.' Marie's elbow found his ribs. 'Let's drink a toast, and then Alex will tell the story.'

There were two toasts—the usual one *'to us all'*, and one to the bride and groom. Then Marie sat down next to him.

'Start at the beginning.'

He rolled his eyes. 'Again?'

The story had already been told more than once.

'That's okay. I'll hear it again.'

Will settled himself in his chair and Alex realised that everyone around the table was looking at him.

Marie took his hand, squeezing it. This was no longer his story, it was theirs, and he loved it more each day. They'd rewritten it as a tale of hope—one which would endure in the bricks and mortar of the clinics they planned to build and run, and in the family they'd raise here.

'A hundred and ten years ago...'

* * * * *

SURPRISE BABY FOR THE BILLIONAIRE

CHARLOTTE HAWKES

MILLS & BOON

To my boys.

Even as I write this dedication you are running up and down the decking, arguing over who has had a pop-up ice cream and who has only had an ice-pop.

But I hang on to every moment of it, because I can't stop time and this won't last forever. At 7yrs and 5yrs, you are both growing up far too fast!

xox   I love you   xox

CHAPTER ONE

She couldn't hide away in here for ever.

Forcing herself to open her eyes, Saskia glanced gingerly around the stark, pristine hospital bathroom, relieved to find it was no longer spinning. She'd spent more time in one of these than she cared to remember over the past three months, but for once she wasn't here experiencing morning, afternoon, and evening sickness.

No, this time she'd ducked in here because she'd caught a glimpse of Malachi Gunn—looking as solid, as indomitable, and as smouldering as ever—stepping out of the stairwell to her paediatric ward. Apparently her body's fight-or-flight response had got its wires crossed and so she—the girl who was renowned for her fearless attitude and for never backing away from anything—had made a dash for the relative safety of the nearest ladies' room.

Not that it did any good, of course; in the end she was going to have to tell him. She had to, no matter how terrifying the idea of doing so might be. Besides, she *wanted* to tell him; she'd wanted to for the last few months. Desperately. She'd just been too afraid, and had no idea exactly what to say.

Because, really, how on earth was she to tell the only one-night stand she'd ever had in her entire life that he was the father of her unborn child?

In truth, she had been prepared to tell him both times

she'd made her monthly pro bono visit to Care to Play, the centre he had set up where young carers could forget their responsibilities and burdens and simply be kids, if only for a few hours each week. But Malachi hadn't been there since their weekend together, which in itself had set off alarm bells in her head.

Admittedly she hadn't been coming to the centre for long—and only once or twice each month, and only since her engagement to Andy had unravelled so spectacularly—but as far as she'd been able to tell Malachi was *always* there, and the kids loved him. And they weren't the only ones—it hadn't been long before she'd started counting down the days to her next visit.

The fact that since their one-weekend stand he hadn't once been at the centre at the same time she had could surely mean only one thing—he'd been deliberately avoiding her.

It hurt more than she cared to admit.

Even now her hand went subconsciously to her belly, where the tiniest bump was just beginning to make itself known. As though the gesture could somehow protect her precious cargo from the idea that Malachi wouldn't want to know. And from other people who might judge her or cast aspersions.

It shouldn't matter, of course. Saskia knew that. But you didn't grow up the daughter of a Tinseltown starlet without having people judging your every move. And she'd never really had as thick a skin as she'd pretended.

Not that anyone else could even tell that she was pregnant, of course. Not even Anouk, who had been Saskia's best friend since kindergarten and hanging out on a movie set where their rival Hollywood actress mothers had battled to out-diva each other.

Saskia felt a fresh pang of guilt about keeping silent

with the one person she had always trusted most in the world, but somehow it seemed wrong to tell other people before Malachi. It was ludicrous, really, since she wasn't even sure he would want to know.

Besides, work had been so busy lately, and she'd already brought enough drama into her quiet friend's life by landing on Anouk's doorstep, suitcases at her feet, after she'd walked out on Andy.

Not that Anouk had ever uttered a word of complaint, of course. No, her friend had merely hugged her and then gone out and found a stunning two-bedroom apartment more suitable for them to share. Anouk had simply made it feel like an exciting new stage in the adventure on which they'd embarked over a decade earlier, when they'd boarded a plane out of the States in order to go to medical school in the UK and track down the father Anouk had never known.

It was bizarre, the way people always seemed to consider her to be dynamic and fun whilst they viewed Anouk as reserved, even a little cold. To Saskia, Anouk was focused, loyal, gentle—all the qualities that Saskia, who hated the way she herself seemed continually to find herself in the middle of some new, unwanted drama, envied most.

Gripping the moulded plastic sink top as she glowered at herself in the mirror, Saskia berated herself. *Anouk* wouldn't be hiding out in a bathroom on the paediatric floor whilst she worked out what the heck to say to Malachi out there. Then again, wise, pragmatic Anouk would never be pregnant from a one-night stand in the first place.

'Well,' she grumbled at her reflection, '*you* are. So you're just going to have to face the man and get on with it.'

With a satisfied nod, Saskia pushed herself off the cold

plastic and marched across the bathroom floor. Then she hesitated. Carefully, slowly, she opened the door a crack.

And nearly fell backwards as a face loomed in the tiny gap.

'Oh, Saskia…' the voice cooed. 'You're not squirreling yourself away in the bathroom to avoid *me*, are you, babe?'

Gritting her teeth, Saskia opened the door firmly and forced herself to step outside. Babette was one of the paediatric nurses on Saskia's ward, and there was no way she could ever avoid the woman, however much she might want to.

'No, Babette, I am most certainly not trying to avoid you.'

Babette's laugh was more grating than tinkling, Saskia thought, and then chided herself for being so uncharitable.

'Are you sure? Only, I don't know how I'd get myself out of bed if I were you…'

Okay, maybe she wasn't being uncharitable after all.

'Indeed. But I'm lucky enough to have an ejector button built in under my mattress.'

'Really?'

Babette's eyes went large and round, and it was all Saskia could do to shake her head.

'No, Babette, not really. I was just joking.'

'Oh…' Babette narrowed her eyes in a calculating manner. 'Well, it's good that you still have a sense of humour. Especially now.'

Don't rise to the bait. Don't rise to the bait.

'What do you mean, "especially now"?' Saskia couldn't help herself, even as her skin prickled in warning.

'Oh, I *really* didn't want to be the one to have to tell you, babe…' Clearly the other woman could barely supress her glee. 'But I didn't want you to have to hear it from someone else. I feel…*responsible*.'

Yeah. Right.

'Tell me what?' Saskia managed, her heart now hammering around her chest so hard that it would surely leave bruises.

Lifting her hand, Babette waved it so close to Saskia's nose that she had to take a step back. But not before she'd noticed the huge, glistening stone.

'Andy and I are engaged.'

Her heart stopped in an instant. She was going to be sick. *Again.* She wanted to grab the wall behind her just to stop herself from plummeting to the cold vinyl floor, but she didn't want to give Babette the satisfaction.

Most days the shame of her ex-fiancé's betrayal didn't get to Saskia at all. But occasionally it felt as raw as it had ten months ago, when she'd walked in on him and his... mistress *in flagrante* in that on-call room, barely half an hour after she had been in bed with him herself in their own home.

Today was one of those raw days, Saskia thought with another sickening lurch—although, mercifully, this lurch was a little less intense. Not even when his new fiancée was standing opposite her and smiling superciliously.

'Isn't it stunning?' Babette cooed. 'Thank goodness! I was afraid he might get me something like a tiny quarter-carat thing that I'd need a magnifying glass to even see.'

'Perish the thought,' Saskia managed dryly.

Babette's eyes widened in feigned innocence.

'Oh, I didn't mean any offence about the ring he bought *you*, of course. I'm sure you must have been perfectly happy with it. I guess being the daughter of a Hollywood diva doesn't guarantee good taste.'

'Of course you don't mean any offence,' Saskia murmured quietly, ignoring the jibe.

She might have come to terms with her parents' death years ago, but it didn't mean she wanted someone like Babette dismissing it as though it meant nothing. Besides which, she was still fighting to quell the nausea as she thought of the tiny solitaire Andy had bought for her, on the premise that he was saving money for a decent house.

What a naïve idiot she'd been.

Then again, had she *really* been completely oblivious?

Sucking in a steadying breath, Saskia considered— not for the first time—whether she had always known, on some level, that Andy was wrong for her. He had been more interested in using her name and perceived connections to further his ambition of becoming a plastic surgeon to the stars.

Was that why, from the very first moment she had stood on Anouk's doorstep, surrounded by her worldly possessions, a strange tangle of emotions had tumbled inside her? Sorrow, humiliation, and rage, of course. But then also fleeting lightning bolts of something she had only been able to categorise as…*relief.*

'Anyway, I just wanted to tell you personally. I always pride myself on being honourable, babe. And Andy agrees.'

Saskia's jaws ached from being clamped shut. But it was better than saying that neither Babette nor Andy would recognise honour if it danced a jig in front of them. The woman would only take it as jealousy, and Saskia couldn't bear for Babette to think that. Or to acknowledge that was her motivation.

But that had been before Andy. And before she'd fallen pregnant with Malachi Gunn's baby.

How many times had she tortured herself over the last couple of months by scouring the local papers to see if there were any photos of local events where Malachi might be seen with some new, impossibly beautiful date on his arm?

Not that she'd seen any. But it didn't mean he was pining for her the way she seemed to be for him.

Saskia faltered, then caught herself. *No.* She'd be

damned if catching her ex-fiancé cheating on her with the abominable Babette was going to change who she was deep down. Malachi was supposed to have been her rebound. Up until that night Andy had been the only man Saskia had slept with—*ever*—and Malachi was to have been her long overdue one-night stand.

Although if a one-night stand stretched into three glorious days and four nights of a long weekend could it still be called a one-night stand?

What was the etiquette?

Who knew?

Either way, despite the sick feeling she had now, the last thing Saskia felt was *jealous*. Certainly not of Babette or Andy, anyway.

But she really did feel ill. Another wave of nausea threatened to engulf her and Saskia pressed her hand to her stomach. The other woman didn't miss a trick.

'Oh, babe,' Babette crowed. 'I never expected you to take it this badly. I *told* Andy it was too soon. I hope it isn't going to be too much for you, seeing us together at the charity ball on Saturday night?'

Saskia fought it, but the darkness was closing in. Fast.

'It's not about you or Andy, Babette,' she muttered, as her mind fought to battle that little bit longer. 'I need you to get a doctor.'

'You don't need to pretend with me. I understand, babe. Perhaps it's better that you don't come…'

Through her blurring eyes Saskia could see that the woman was practically beside herself with joy at the idea that her engagement was causing Saskia such pain.

'No, Babette,' Saskia managed. 'You really don't understand. I need you to get a doctor. I'm pregnant.'

She just about heard Babette's shocked intake of breath as her head spun again.

And was that the floor coming up to meet her?

Abruptly, two strong hands grabbed her shoulders. Heat from a body was behind her back. An unmistakably citrusy, woodsy male scent filled her nostrils. And then she was being swept up into the oddly familiar arms of a hulk of a man, and nestled against his shoulder as he carried her down the corridor.

Malachi.

Her mind railed even as her body slumped against him, and by the time she came round fully they were in an on-call room and Malachi was sitting on the edge of the bed, cradling her head, a plastic cup of water in his other hand.

Saskia groaned inwardly.

'Stop squirming, *zvyozdochka*,' he commanded gruffly. 'You'll hit your head if you fall backwards.'

Reluctantly, she obeyed, taking another sip of the proffered water, then another, letting her mind stop whirling and twirling like the teacups ride at a theme park. As if water could somehow dampen all that heat and desire which she was sure still swirled around them even now.

At least he had the grace to stand up and move to the chair next to her, instead of being so close on the bed that it felt as though her entire left side was on fire.

It seemed like an age before she could shift position again, moving her legs to swing them carefully over the edge.

'Better?' he asked.

'Better.' She bobbed her head tentatively. Then, when it felt okay, she nodded a little more confidently. 'Thanks.'

But he didn't move. Neither of them did.

How much had he heard?

For several long moments a kind of tenseness swirled around them. Saskia waited for him to mention her pregnancy, but he didn't. Clearly he hadn't caught her last comment to Babette.

An odd sense of deflation rolled through her. She should

probably be happy he hadn't overheard—that would have been no way for him to find out. But at least it would have taken the decision out of her hands; it would have meant she didn't have to sit here frantically trying to work out what to say and how to phrase it. Or even *when* to say it.

Her brain whirred. Whatever she said, though, dropping such a bombshell right now, in an on-call room during a busy shift, wasn't the way to do it. And that wasn't just an excuse. She *would* do it. Just not here, not now, and not like this.

'Anyway, I can't lie around here all day. I have patients to see,' Saskia began, forcing out an attempt at a jolly little laugh and placing her fists on the hard mattress to push herself to a standing position. Suddenly a tiny rod of hope punched through her. 'Although…you didn't come here to see me, did you?'

He didn't answer immediately, and it felt as though the air had suddenly been sucked from the room. Something dense and heavy was threatening to close over her, and before she could stop herself she began to babble.

'It's just…well, with not seeing you at Care to Play these last few months, I was beginning to wonder if you've been avoiding me. You know…after that weekend. What we did. Together.'

She tried for another jolly laugh, but it sounded as stilted and awkward as she felt.

Malachi hesitated. It was only the briefest of moments, but Saskia caught it nonetheless. Her heart launched itself at her ribs, slamming against her with painful force. It had been one thing to suspect it, but having it confirmed scraped at her much more deeply and painfully than it had any right to do.

And still she stood, rooted to the spot as he stared at her with a closed expression that said far more than any words could have.

The silence pressed on until she couldn't bear it any longer. 'I should go. Forget I said anything. I didn't intend to make things…'

'There's a patient called Izzy here.' His voice was clipped. Distant. 'She came in today after falling off a climbing frame. I just brought her mother in.'

Saskia snapped her head up.

'That's my patient.'

The seven-year-old girl had been brought into Resus several hours ago, where she'd been seen by Malachi's neurosurgeon brother, Sol, and Anouk, after she'd fallen from a rope climbing apparatus in the local park. Sol had told her that someone would be bringing Izzy's mother— who was an MS sufferer—in as soon as possible. She just hadn't realised that someone would be Malachi.

'So Izzy is a young carer from Care to Play? I didn't realise…' She faltered under the intensity of his gaze. 'I mean, I haven't seen her there before.'

'You haven't been going that long.'

'No…true. But Sol never told me it would be you bringing her mother in.'

'He has no reason to think you and I know each other.' Malachi shrugged.

He couldn't know how much that dismissive gesture cut her.

'How is Izzy, anyway?' he asked abruptly, his concern evident.

Saskia felt another stab of something she didn't care to identify. She forced it aside and made herself focus. In all her years as a doctor she'd never felt so torn before.

The young girl had landed on her face and her head and suffered loss of consciousness. Along with a laceration over one eye, and the loss of a couple of teeth, their main concern had been internal bleeds, so she'd been sent for a head and neck scan, with the possibility of a broken jaw. Fortunately the CT scan had come back as clear as they could have hoped, along with all the other tests they had run.

But she couldn't tell Malachi any of that. Not when he wasn't technically anything more than her patient's mum's lift in.

'I'm sorry, I can't discuss this with you,' she apologised. 'I need to speak to Izzy's mum.'

'Of course,' he confirmed instantly. 'I left Michelle with Sol before. She forgot some things in the car.'

For the first time Saskia noticed the small pink rucksack Malachi was carrying. Despite everything she couldn't stop a little smile from playing at her lips; his evident concern for Izzy and her family was touching. Not that it surprised her. Malachi was as dedicated to his role as co-founder of Care to Play as he was to his multibillion-pound investment empire, MIG International.

The fact that he seemed so utterly committed to helping those kids had been part of what had attracted her in the first place. So different from her self-serving ex.

'I should go and see Izzy's mum. Bring her up to date.'

'Don't worry. Sol's with her.'

She tried to skirt past Malachi without looking pointed.

Not because she didn't want to touch him. More because if she did she was certain she would self-combust. Her mouth was insanely dry. Her body throbbed mercilessly. It was all she could do to keep her brain functioning.

'The little girl is my patient.'

'And Sol saw her, too,' he countered.

'I'm perfectly aware that your brother is a doctor. One of the top neurosurgeons in this place, in fact. But he isn't my patient's doctor now. *I* am. And, as such, I should be the one to talk to her mother.'

Saskia only realised she'd drifted forward when her hands made contact with his unforgettable granite chest.

She leapt back like a scalded cat, and fought valiantly to drag her mind back to the present.

They'd had a gloriously wild, wanton time together, but she couldn't afford to rehash it in her mind. She had no claim on Malachi Gunn, and she still hadn't even told him her life-changing news.

And could she really drop her pregnancy bombshell on him? He had a right to know—but would he prefer not to? Her mind was spinning, and it didn't help that he was still standing there, scrutinising her.

'I really should go,' she said.

'I'd rather you rested a little more.' He frowned, looking irritated.

She shifted from one foot to the other, reaching out to place her hand on the door handle. But she didn't open the door and she didn't walk out. Instead she shuffled some more and wrinkled her nose.

'I'm fine.'

He didn't look impressed.

'Have you eaten?'

'I'm *fine*, Malachi,' she repeated, more firmly this time.

He lifted his arm past her, holding the door closed with his hand, and for a moment she thought he was going to say something else. Then, without warning, he dropped his arm.

She told herself she wasn't disappointed, yet it was all she could do to tug at the handle and make herself walk through the door, overcompensating a little by hustling fast to the unit where Izzy was being treated.

With every step she was conscious of the fact that Malachi was following her. It was all too easy to imagine his long, effortless stride as she schooled herself not to sashay her hips or appear in any way as though she was being provocative. No mean feat when her whole body was so hyper-aware of him, her belly clenching. If the baby had given a good, strong kick in response to Malachi's presence she doubted she would have been surprised, even though logically she knew it was far too soon for that.

It was as though the man was somehow imprinted on her. On both of them. She'd be glad when this moment was over and she could get away from him and back to her patients.

At least, that was what she told herself.

The truth was that she wasn't entirely convinced she was buying it.

CHAPTER TWO

WAS SASKIA PREGNANT?

Malachi sat on one of the plastic seats in the hospital corridor. Saskia was still in the room, telling Michelle about her daughter, and he was out here…uncharacteristically rattled.

His brain fought to focus; his body felt supercharged. He rolled the idea around his head as if testing it, seeing if it might fit.

Pregnant?

The problem was that he couldn't be sure. Certainly he *thought* that was the last thing she'd said to that godawful nurse with the irritating voice, but then he hadn't been thinking straight from the moment he'd stepped around that corner and caught sight of Saskia—the woman who had haunted his dreams for the last three months.

The blood roared through Malachi's ears.

And elsewhere, if he was being honest.

When he'd heard her mutter—*thought* he'd heard her mutter—that word *pregnant* as he'd approached, he hadn't really thought a lot about it. After all, she might have been talking about any one of her patients. Or colleagues. But then they'd sat in that on-call room together and she'd been so…*odd*…that slowly things had started slotting themselves into different places and suddenly he'd found himself wondering if she'd actually been talking about herself.

In that moment everything had…*shifted*. Kids. Family. Two things he'd thought could never be in his future. Two things he'd sworn never *would* be in his future. Not after the childhood he and Sol had endured. Not after becoming responsible and providing for his drug-addled mother and kid brother when he'd been a mere ten years old. He'd endured enough responsibility and commitment to last a lifetime, and he'd sworn to himself he would never put himself through any more as an adult.

Nor would he put any kid through the trauma of having someone as detached and emotionally damaged as he was for a father.

Instead he had dedicated himself to his work, his business, his charity. Partly because he lived for those things, but also because it ensured he'd never have time in his life for anything—or anyone—else.

And now this.

Maybe.

Possibly not.

Yet some sixth sense—the one he had trusted his entire life, the one which had allowed his eight-year-old self to keep his brother and mother together and a roof over their heads, the one which had helped him make his first six-figure sum by the age of fifteen, his first million by the age of eighteen, the one which had ensured he could send his brother to medical school and make MIG International a global business—told him it was true.

No wonder his entire world was teetering so precariously on the edge of some black abyss.

How was it that in the blink of an eye everything he'd worked for could suddenly be hovering over some unknown precipice? Everything that made him…*him* gone in one word.

Pregnant.

His body went cold. His brain fought to process this

new information and make some kind of sense out of it. But the only thing it could come up with was that any baby couldn't be his. They'd used protection.

He always used protection.

Except that first time, when all his usual rules had splintered and shattered one by one. Not least any thought to the notion of protection.

Which meant that he had no one else to blame for the fact that a baby wasn't wholly out of the question.

So how the hell was any kid to cope with him as a father?

Malachi's mind hurtled along like a car with no brakes. He was usually controlled, intuitive—effective when it came to dealing with business problems put in front of him—but right now he felt as if the ground beneath his feet was opening up. Instead of focusing on the issue all he could picture was her lush naked body, spread out before him like some kind of personal offering. He could still practically feel the heat from her mouth, as wild as it was sweet.

He couldn't say she'd been experienced, or skilled, and yet he'd never replayed sex with any other woman the way he'd replayed those nights with Saskia.

Why?

Maybe because he'd been lusting after her from the moment she'd walked into Care to Play as a medical liaison volunteer a few months earlier. Somehow during the so-called interview she'd ended up telling him about her failed engagement and her cheating fiancé, and she'd been so refreshingly open with him that he'd found himself captivated, wondering what kind of an idiot man would let a woman like Saskia slip through his fingers.

He'd had no intention of acting on the attraction, of course. Even as it had sizzled between them for months he'd been determined not to go there. Firstly, she was bound to be rebounding, and secondly she was a volunteer at the centre that he'd set up, and he'd told himself that was tantamount to making him her boss.

He'd even said those very words to her that evening at the nightclub, several months later, when Saskia, Sol, and a group of their Moorlands General colleagues had been letting loose for once, and she'd laughed in his face. Confident, sassy and oh-so-sexy, she'd told him in no uncertain terms that he was nothing like her boss. She'd also told him that maybe a rebound fling was exactly what she needed, given that she'd never had a one-night stand in her life before.

And he'd believed her. More than that, he had *wanted* to believe her. Because she'd spoken to something utterly primal deep within him...and what was the harm of a one-night stand?

Only he hadn't been able to let her go that night. Or the next night. Or the next.

It had been the most indulgent, incredible long weekend Malachi could ever have imagined, and when she'd finally left he hadn't been prepared for how quiet—how empty—his luxury bachelor pad would suddenly feel. As ridiculous as that was.

He'd fantasised about her returning with a sharpness that punctured him. Whether because he knew he was nothing more to Saskia than a rebound fling, or because he knew that he didn't have the time or inclination for a relationship, he couldn't be sure. Either way, what choice had he had other than to put a little distance between them and avoid Care to Play every single time he'd known she was due there, in the hope of letting that sharpness dull?

Only it hadn't dulled. It hadn't faded at all.

If anything, this latest encounter had only proved that he wanted Saskia more than ever—pregnant or not.

His baby.

It was enough to bring his head round a full three-sixty.

Surely he was the last person in the world who should ever have a kid? He wouldn't love it. That quality wasn't in him—not any more. It was gone. Spent. Used up all those years ago when he should have been the one being loved and cared for—not the other way around.

A baby?

He could provide for it, but he couldn't be the all-attentive father figure it would need.

Worse—and he was ashamed of this more than anything— he would end up resenting it, and the time and attention it demanded, the way he'd resented his own mother. The way he'd once resented even Sol.

He still hated himself for those feelings. Even now.

The responsibility he'd had for his younger brother since they'd been little kids had made him so angry back then. And even now, over two and a half decades later, he still felt it. Especially as Sol looked a million miles away now, a plastic cup of vending machine coffee in his hands.

'What's the story, *bratik*?'

Sol frowned before parroting out information in a way that only confirmed that he was sidestepping the real answer.

'The scan revealed no evidence of any bleed on the brain, and Izzy didn't damage her neck or break her jaw in the fall, which we suspected—hence why she's been transferred to Paediatric Intensive Care. Maxillofacial are on their way, to deal with the teeth in Izzy's mouth that are still loose. We have the two that came out in a plastic lunchbox someone gave to Izzy, but I think they're baby teeth, so that shouldn't be too much of an issue. We won't know for sure until some of the swelling goes down.'

'I know all that. I was there when the paediatric doctor told Michelle.'

The paediatric doctor.

As though simply saying Saskia's name would allow his brother to read the truth all over his face.

As though he didn't know how every inch of how her body felt and tasted.

As though she wasn't carrying his baby.

Possibly.

Probably?

Shaking it off, he tried for levity.

'I was asking what the story was with *you*, numbnuts.'

Not exactly his most convincing attempt at humour, but it was all he had in him. Fortunately Sol seemed too caught up in his own issues to pick up on it.

'Don't know what you're talking about,' he mumbled, a sure-fire giveaway that he was lying.

Malachi snorted. 'You know exactly what I mean. You forget I've practically raised you since we were kids. You can't fool me.'

Sol opened his mouth and Malachi waited for the usual witty comeback. But for once it didn't come. Instead his younger brother glowered into his coffee. Strangely, he was avoiding Malachi's stare. And when Sol spoke his voice was unusually quiet, his words coming out of the blue.

'I haven't forgotten anything. I remember everything you went through to raise us, Mal. I know you sold your soul to the devil just to get enough money to buy food for our bellies.'

The words—the previously unspoken gratitude—slid unexpectedly into Malachi's chest. Like a dagger heading straight to the heart and mercifully stopping just a hair's breadth short.

How was it that the very moment he was ready to doubt himself his brother seemed to say the words that made him think again? As if Sol had known just what to say when he couldn't possibly have guessed about Saskia being pregnant, let alone that it might be Malachi's.

Or was it just that he was reading into it what he wanted to read? Trying to convince himself that perhaps Saskia and her baby—*their* baby—wouldn't be better off without him?

Which made no sense—because he didn't *want* a family.

Did he?

Savagely, he tore his mind back to the present once more.

'Bit melodramatic, aren't you, *bratik*?' he gritted out. 'Is this about Izzy?'

'I guess.'

Sol was lying again, and Malachi couldn't say why he wasn't calling his kid brother out over it.

'Yeah. Well...no need to get soppy about it.'

'Right.'

Downing the last of the cold coffee and grimacing, Sol crushed the plastic cup and lobbed it into the bin across the hallway. The perfect drop shot.

Then, without warning, Sol spoke again.

'You ever wonder what might have happened if we'd had a different life? Not had a drug addict for a mother? Not had to take care of her and keep her away from her dealer every spare minute?'

It was as though the tiniest, lightest butterfly had landed on that invisible dagger in his chest, beaten its wings, and plunged the blade in that final hair's breadth deeper. Driving to the heart of the questions which had started circling around his brain ever since he'd heard Saskia utter those words to that nurse, creeping so slowly at first that he hadn't seen them over the chaos of the fear.

If he'd had a different childhood, would he be greeting this news differently now?

He didn't know. He never *could* know.

It wasn't worth his time or his headspace.

'No,' Malachi ground out, not sure if he was trying to convince Sol or himself. 'I don't. I don't ever think about it. It's in the past. Done. Gone.'

'What the hell kind of childhood was that for us?' Sol continued regardless. 'Our biggest concern should have been whether we wanted an Action Man or Starship LEGO for Christmas—not keeping her junkie dealer away from her.'

'Well, it wasn't. I wouldn't have asked if I'd known you were going to get maudlin on me.'

'You were *eight*, Mal. I was five.'

'I know how old we were,' Malachi growled, not sure whether he welcomed the reminder or not. 'What's got into you, Sol?'

Their shameful past—their horrendous childhoods—they were the reason why he'd always sworn to himself that he would never have a child. Whenever he looked back—which he never usually did—all he could feel was age-old bitterness and anger tainting his soul.

How could he ever be a good father?

Yet if Saskia's baby really was his—and he still needed to hear her say the words to him, not to some stranger—how could he turn his back on them?

He couldn't. It was that simple. And Sol raking up wretched memories wasn't helping.

'It's history.' Censure splintered from Malachi's mouth. 'Just leave it alone.'

'Right.'

His brother pressed his lips into a grim line and they each lapsed back into their respective silences.

He didn't want Sol's gratitude. He didn't deserve it. He hadn't taken care of their little family out of love, or a desire to be a unit. He'd done it because he'd been terrified of where they would all go if they were split up.

But he'd begrudged every moment of it. Resented the

fact that at eight years old he'd had to effectively become a father to a five-year-old—had had no choice but to become the man of the house and earn money to put food on the table. At eight he had felt like a failure every time the electricity cut out and he had no money left to put anything on the card.

He'd sworn to himself that his adult life would be about himself, the way his childhood had never been. He'd been adamant that when he grew up he would never marry or have kids. His life would be his own. Finally. He had been determined that his business—which had made him a billionaire against all the odds—would be his only drive. As selfish as that might have sounded to anyone else—anyone who didn't know what his life had been like.

And it had been. Nothing had stood in his way. Not his lack of experience, nor the competition, nor any relationship.

He'd been ruthless.

All too often he wondered if the only reason he had founded Care to Play—the centre he'd set up with Sol, where young carers from the age of five to sixteen could just unwind and be kids instead of feeling responsible for a parent or a sibling—had been to make himself feel good about his ability to shake other people off so easily.

He'd believed that he wanted to make a positive difference to other kids' lives—if something like Care to Play had existed when he and Sol had been kids, then maybe it could have made a difference. He'd even convinced himself it was true.

But now, suddenly, he wondered if it had been just another selfish act on his part. If helping kids like Izzy, who clearly adored her genuinely struggling mother, was less about them and more about making himself feel better for the way he'd hated his own drug-addicted mother.

So now there was Saskia. Pregnant. With his child. And

he couldn't shake the idea that he had to *do* something about it. He was going to be a father, and fathers weren't meant to be selfish. They were meant to be selfless.

Malachi was just about to open his mouth and confide in his brother, for possibly the first time in for ever, when Sol lurched abruptly to his feet, shoving his hands in his pockets the way he'd always done when his mind was racing, ever since he'd been a kid.

It was so painfully familiar that Malachi almost smiled. *Almost.*

'I'm going to check on some of my patients upstairs, then I'll be back to see Izzy.'

Malachi dipped his head in acknowledgement, but Sol didn't even bother to wait. He simply strode up the corridor and through the fire door onto the stairwell, leaving Malachi alone with unwelcome questions.

'You can go back in now.'

Malachi jerked his neck around, and the sight of Saskia standing there brought a thousand questions tumbling to his lips.

'Is there anything you'd like to tell me?' he rasped, before he could swallow the words back.

She blanched, her eyes widening for just a fraction of a second before she pulled a smooth veneer into place.

'If you want to know about Izzy then you'll have to ask her mother. As you aren't a direct family member, it isn't my place to tell you.'

Was she playing a game? He couldn't tell.

'Tell me, do you always faint like that?'

Two high spots of colour suffused her cheeks. 'Of course not.'

'Then perhaps you'd like to explain what this morning's little episode was all about.'

For a moment he thought she looked panicked.

'That was a one-off.'

'Is that so?'

'It is.'

He arched his eyebrows. 'And why do you think this "one-off" episode happened?'

She shook her head back, straightening her shoulders. It shocked Malachi to realise that he knew her well enough to know it was a stalling tactic.

Or, more pertinently, it *should* have shocked him.

'I don't know,' she asserted. 'Like you said, I probably hadn't eaten properly, so I was running on empty. I didn't have a proper breakfast and it's been a long shift.'

He didn't know whether to be impressed or insulted that she lied so easily. Straight to his face. And then, without warning, anger surged through him—whether at the way she wanted to exclude him or at the fact she thought he was *that* blind, he couldn't be sure—but he quashed it, quickly and effectively.

Never let anyone see they can get to you.

Another life lesson he'd been forced to learn from an early age.

So this was the game she wished to play?

Well, he was just going to have to find a way to play against her.

Not here, not now. Not with Izzy injured in that room. Her mother and sister would need his support more than ever right now. They had no one else, which was what made the centre so vital.

Right now he was here for Michelle and her daughters. Saskia and her lies would have to wait.

But if that was her game, then fine; he would play her at it and he would win. He just needed to take a step back and regroup so he could work out his next move.

CHAPTER THREE

'THIS PLACE IS STUNNING...' Anouk breathed as she took in the huge sandstone arches reaching up as though in exultation to a breathtaking stone-carved vaulted ceiling.

'Isn't it?' Saskia demurred, following her friend's gaze, trying to quell the kaleidoscope of butterflies which seemed to have taken up residence in her stomach ever since Anouk had told her she had two tickets to a gala evening and asked Saskia to join her.

A gala evening for a local young carers' charity.

Saskia had known instantly whose charity it was. Anouk had mentioned something about Sol giving them to her, and something about a patient... Izzy? To her shame, Saskia hadn't really been listening—she'd been too caught up in her own head.

Tickets to a charity event for Care to Play. As though fate itself was intervening.

Saskia hadn't even asked how her friend had got the tickets, or why. She just knew that Malachi would be there and that this was her chance to do what she should have done two months ago. She had to tell him about the baby. Whatever he chose to do after that was his business.

'I feel positively shabby by comparison.'

Anouk was still gazing at the architecture and Saskia laughed, grateful for the momentary distraction.

'Well, you don't look it,' she told her friend. 'You look

like you're sparkling, and it isn't just the new dress. Although I'm glad you let me talk you into buying it.'

'I'm glad I let you talk me into buying it, too,' admitted Anouk, smoothing her hands over her dress as though she was nervous.

'You look totally Hollywood,' Saskia assured her wryly, knowing that it would break whatever tension her friend appeared to be feeling.

'Don't.' Anouk shuddered on cue. 'I think I've had enough of Hollywood to last me a lifetime.'

'Me, too.' More than anyone else could ever possibly know, thought Saskia. 'But still, the look is good.'

'Maybe I should be in a more festive colour.'

Anouk glanced at Saskia's own dress enviously— another much-needed boost to Saskia's uncharacteristically wavering confidence.

In fact, her friend had already waxed lyrical about the 'stunning' emerald dress, claiming that it might have looked gorgeous on the rack but 'on your voluptuously feminine body it looks entirely bespoke'.

For a moment Saskia had been worried that it had been code for, *I can tell you're pregnant and it's beginning to show.* Even though Saskia knew she wasn't showing at all. There wasn't a hint of any swell over her abdomen yet, and she couldn't help wondering if it was this lack of physical manifestation of her pregnancy which had stalled her in seeking Malachi out at MIG International when he hadn't shown up at Care to Play.

As if a part of her believed he might doubt what she was saying if he couldn't see it for himself.

'I think I look like a Christmas tree.' Saskia made herself laugh again, with a wave of her hand towards the glorious eighteen-foot work of art which dominated the entrance of the venue. 'Although if I looked *that* amazing I'd be happy.'

'You look even better and you know it.' Anouk replied instantly. 'You've only just walked in and you've turned a dozen heads.'

And yet there was only one head she wanted to turn. Supposed rebound or not.

'They're probably looking at you—and, either way, I don't care. Tonight, Anouk, we're going to relax and enjoy ourselves.'

'We are?'

'We are,' Saskia said firmly, hoping she was convincing her friend even if she wasn't convincing herself.

She snagged a champagne flute from the tray of a passing waiter, for something to do with her hands, before realising she couldn't drink it and passing it straight to Anouk. 'Starting with this.'

'You still feeling sick?' Anouk frowned, eying her with a little too much intensity.

'Yeah,' she lied, and another stab of guilt shot through her as she tried to suppress the heat flooding her cheeks.

Anouk didn't look convinced. If anything, her friend seemed to tense, as though she knew.

The guilt pressed in harder. They'd never deceived each other in over twenty-five years. As soon as she'd told Malachi she would tell Anouk. Why hadn't she told her before? Was it because she'd always known that, much as her best friend had never encouraged her to leave her ex-fiancé, Anouk had never really taken to Andy?

Ironically, Anouk had even apologised on the one occasion when Saskia had pressed her for an opinion, only for her friend to tell her that whenever she looked at Andy all she saw was another playboy—just like Anouk's mother's lovers.

'Relax.' Saskia nudged her gently now. 'Enjoy your drink.'

'I don't really like…' Anouk began, but her friend shushed her.

'You do tonight.'

Anouk balked, and Saskia knew that all Anouk could see was her mother, downing glasses of wine and popping pills.

'One glass doesn't make you your mother.' Saskia linked her arm through Anouk's, reading her mind.

It was Anouk's turn to offer a rueful smile. 'That obvious, huh?'

'Only to me. Now, come on, forget about your mother and enjoy this evening. You and I both deserve a bit of time off—and, anyway, we're supporting a good cause.'

'We are, aren't we?' Anouk nodded, dipping her head and taking a tentative sip.

Saskia told herself to stop scanning the room for Malachi, like some meerkat on watch duty. If it was meant to happen tonight, then it would. Otherwise she would go to his offices in the morning and she would finally tell him.

He had a right to know. And he had a right not to want to be involved.

She wouldn't force him.

He would have to want her. And their child.

'A word.'

Every inch of her skin prickled into goosebumps at the rich, deep sound of Malachi's voice in her ear. As lethally silky as the hand sliding around her elbow even now.

And something about the tone sent a warning whisper coiling its way through her body.

He couldn't know about the baby, could he?

Unless he'd spoken to Babette.

Saskia cursed inwardly. She was an idiot for letting that woman get to her enough to tell her a single thing, let alone for Babette to be the first person to find out that she was pregnant.

She couldn't shake the idea that Malachi knew and,

worse, that he'd found out from her ex-fiancé's new fiancée instead of straight from her. It was little wonder that the air between them positively hummed with barely restrained tension.

Saskia wasn't sure why she allowed him to lead her across the ballroom at the charity gala without even a word of objection.

She'd only managed to slip away from Anouk by taking advantage of Sol's unexpected appearance to pretend she was going to check the seating plan. Just so that she could see if she could find Malachi.

And now he'd found her.

If he'd come to say what she feared then she had only herself to blame. She should have told him herself. The unspoken accusations already bombarding her were her own fault for being such a coward. And the longer the silence the more forcefully they hurtled into her, leaving her edgy and agitated and full of apprehension—and something else which she didn't care to examine too closely at all.

As if Malachi knew that the uncertainty was unsettling her, he seemed to be prolonging it, by not speaking another word until they were near the now deserted entrance, well away from the beautiful, well-heeled crowd bustling inside the ballroom, each jostling to set themselves ahead of the pack. Too many of them would be competing with each other to write the biggest cheques just to prove who was higher up the food chain.

It was disheartening to see just how few of them were actually there because they cared about the charity. About the kids.

Like Malachi does?

Abruptly Saskia pulled her head back to the present just as Malachi stopped, turning her to face him before he released her. The fierce, furious expression on his face was one she hadn't ever seen before, but she feared she could read it in an instant.

'It's mine.'

So that answered *that* question, at least.

Malachi knew she was pregnant, and whether Babette had told him, or someone else had, it hardly seemed to matter now.

Saskia fought to breathe. It was as though someone was sitting on her chest, squashing her lungs, stealing her air. Perhaps it was at the sight of the utterly masculine, foreboding figure in front of her. Or maybe it was because he was suddenly watching her with a cold, hostile expression in those eyes, when up until now she'd only ever known them to be kind and friendly—the colour of the richest, warmest cognac in his enviable drinks cabinet.

Every thought fell from her head, and everything tumbled around her. Her heart accelerated so fast she could barely even feel it. Or maybe it simply stopped.

And then suddenly a sense of calm overtook her and she knew she couldn't deny it. There was only one thing she could say.

'Yes.'

He tilted his head sharply.

'I suppose I should be grateful you didn't make this any more complicated than it already is by lying.'

Then, taking her elbow again, he steered her outside, neither of them speaking a word, and into the back of his waiting car. When he slid in beside her, filling up every last bit of space, Saskia was sure she was going to suffocate from the sheer pressure of the moment.

And all the heat she remembered from their time together—the heat which had been simmering again the other day at the hospital—flooded around her, almost drowning her in its intensity.

Lord, how was she to survive being in such proximity to him when a traitorous part of her wanted to revisit every inch of that hewn, addictive body which the tuxedo did nothing to temper?

'May I ask where we are going?' she asked primly, surprised at how even her voice sounded when she might have expected it to be shaking.

The unexpected truth was that it was almost a relief.

'My place.'

His tone was grim but he didn't even look at her. His gaze was trained out of the window, as if he couldn't bear to.

It hurt. More than it had any right to.

'Why?'

Her voice was sharper than she'd intended, but the idea of being back in his penthouse was daunting. Every room would surely trigger X-rated memories of their weekend together—and she already had enough of them in her own brain, without returning to the scene of the crime.

His head swivelled slowly to face her and abruptly she decided she preferred him staring out of the window after all.

'To discuss how we proceed from here.'

His low, controlled voice didn't fool Saskia for a second. And there was a carefully restrained fury in the cognac depths of his eyes—though whether that was because she was pregnant or because she had concealed it from him, she couldn't quite be certain.

Either way, he sounded ominous. Especially when she already knew what kind of a force of will Malachi Gunn was.

There was something else in those depths, too—and it was infinitely more dangerous than his anger.

Desire.

Still.

She could feel it rolling over her body as sure as if it were his hands themselves.

A low ache began building *right there*. Right between her legs, deep and insistent, and only Malachi had ever made her feel it.

Good grief, she couldn't trust herself around him for a moment.

The realisation was like a blow to the gut. If she went back to his apartment it would only amplify her haywire emotions that much more. Until they were completely out of control. Until *she* was.

Panic clutched at Saskia.

'Stop the car,' she muttered abruptly.

'Sorry?'

'I said, *stop the car*.' She raised her voice, tapping on the glass between them and the driver. 'I need some air.'

She was vaguely aware of Malachi dipping his head in confirmation before the car slowed. Stopped.

Saskia was out in an instant—but not fast enough to beat Malachi, who had materialised right by her side. He took their coats from his driver, who must have retrieved them from the cloakroom before they'd left the gala.

Why was she even surprised? Of *course* Malachi hadn't left the event on a whim. The man never did anything on a whim. Except that long weekend with her, that was.

And now this baby.

Taking her arm, Malachi steered her to the riverside. The bracing air walloped her, mercifully knocking her out of her panic.

'Not exactly the balmiest evening for a walk along the promenade.' His tone was clipped. 'But at least the wind has dropped.'

'It's invigorating,' she lied, turning away from him and beginning to walk.

Anything was better than being pressed up to him

within the confines of that car. Remembering the feel of his hands as they had explored every last millimetre of her body with such reverence. The heat from his breath as he had tracked down the column of her neck, leaving her shivering with desire and desperate for more. And the way he had moved between her legs, holding himself up and locking his eyes with hers before he surged into her, making her whole world explode in a riot of colours she'd never known before.

Had that first time been the moment the die had been cast? The moment her journey to pregnancy had begun? Or had that been later, in his apartment? On the couch or on the rug? In the swimming pool or in the bedroom? In his shower or in his bed?

He had claimed her over and over and over again, as if she were his.

She had actually felt like she was. For that one incredible weekend.

And then it had been over.

She'd made herself leave, sneaking out when he hadn't been able to postpone a conference call for a fourth time, because she'd been afraid she wouldn't be able to walk out through the door if he was watching her.

Over the last three months she'd told herself that she'd imagined the way it had been between them. That her memories had been blown out of proportion to all reality.

Now, with her body reacting in ways it had no business doing, Saskia was beginning to fear that her memories hadn't even done reality justice.

'Is this really where you want to talk?'

Malachi's rich voice cut through her thoughts. She toyed with telling him that a part of her didn't want to talk at all. But she knew that would be unwise. Either way, it was better here…where her body wasn't so assaulted by memories.

'There's no one around.' She shrugged, even as a faint shiver entered her voice.

She wouldn't last long in this cold, wearing only what she had on. He would use that to his advantage.

'So be it.'

They managed about fifty metres in silence, but if she'd been hoping the location might put him off then clearly she'd been mistaken.

'Were you planning on telling me?' he demanded, without preamble.

When she didn't answer it appeared that he couldn't stop himself from goading her—just a little.

'Or was there some doubt in your head that it was mine?'

She lifted her eyes up to his dark, blazing ones. A sense of belated dignity was apparently struggling to make itself known.

'*Is* yours.'

'Sorry?'

'Is,' she repeated clearly. 'Not *was*.'

'My apologies.' He didn't look in the slightest bit apologetic.

'And, for the record, I don't make a habit of one-night stands,' she managed stiffly, compelled to make the point even though it didn't remotely answer his actual question. 'I've slept with two people in my life. Andy was my first. You were my second.'

Another flash she couldn't recognise went through his eyes, and another thread of taut silence wove its way around them, as if binding them tighter together even in the expanse of the promenade.

'Is that so?'

She licked her lips.

'It is. And I know I told you that already. Three months ago.'

He still didn't answer, and she had to wonder whether her pedantry made her more of an idiot in his eyes or less. Either way, his intense glower did funny things to her insides. The way it had three months ago. And the way it had every time she'd thought of him since then.

Except that *this* was so much more…real. So much more potent.

'You should have told me,' he growled.

Yes, she should have. No matter how she ran events through her head, that simple fact was unmistakable.

Saskia paused. She wasn't used to feeling so cautious, as though she was on the back foot. She prided herself on being confident, strong and bold. Ordinarily she would have brazened it out. But then ordinarily she wouldn't have been facing off against Malachi.

Still, she tilted her head up boldly.

'I know that it was a one-night stand. I understand that. And that this is an unforeseen consequence. But I want to keep my baby, and that's my choice. It doesn't have to be yours. Right here, right now, I'm officially releasing you from any responsibility.'

'Is that so?'

His eyes glittered furiously, and it was all Saskia could do to hold her ground.

Not that she thought she was in any danger from Malachi—at least not physically. But *emotionally*…? That was a whole different concept.

It made her choose her next words very, very carefully. 'I'm trying to be reasonable here,' she offered at last, trying surreptitiously to take a step back.

He took a step closer to her. Just one, single step. But his stride was longer than hers anyway, and it was enough to force her to tip her head back to look up at him.

Enough for her entire traitorous body to leap in thrilled anticipation. Her hands actually itched to reach up and grab the material of his dark wool coat which had no business clinging to every ridge and muscle which she already knew lay beneath.

'Reasonable?' he echoed quietly. Too quietly. 'Is that what you call it, *zvyozdochka*?'

'It is.'

Her voice was altogether too raspy for her own liking. And the name he'd called her that first night coursed through her as though it somehow made her his.

She took another step back before she realised how it might look to him. 'You don't agree?'

'Damned right I don't,' he growled, taking them both another step backwards, until she felt the cold sea wall against her back and realised she had no further to go, and his arms locked down either side of her, effectively to cage her.

What was wrong with her that she found the whole thing so utterly arousing?

He wasn't some knight, claiming her. And she certainly wasn't a damsel in distress.

'That's *my* baby you're carrying. You don't have the right to "release" me from it as though I have no say in the matter. As though the baby has no right to a father.'

'That wasn't…' She shook her head. 'That isn't what I'm doing.'

'That's exactly what you're doing.'

'No. I was just…' She took a breath, trying to get her thoughts straight in her head before attempting to articulate them. 'You said that I should have told you, and you're right—I should have. I was all geared up for it the first couple of times I went to Care to Play, only you weren't there.'

She stopped, giving him a chance to respond. Almost hoping that he would say something to explain it, but he didn't. Yet his expression had altered and her heart tumbled.

She was right. He had been avoiding her.

'You were always there before we had that weekend together,' Saskia whispered, with no idea how she managed to stay upright, to seem confident, when inside she was crumbling like a sandcastle on the beach under the onslaught of the incoming tide. 'But after that weekend you were never there. At least not when you knew I would be. As though you were avoiding me...'

And still he didn't answer. He didn't even move. If she hadn't known better she might have thought he'd turned to stone.

She didn't want to hear the answer—she didn't *need* to hear it. She already knew the truth. Still, she couldn't stop the question from slipping off her lips.

'*Were* you avoiding me, Malachi? Were you so concerned that if I saw you at the centre again I'd take it as some sort of sign that we were in a relationship?'

CHAPTER FOUR

MALACHI COULD BARELY remember getting Saskia back into the car, or telling his driver to continue. His mind was too full of emotions so tightly entangled that he couldn't hope to begin to unravel them.

But suddenly he was tapping in the code to let them into his penthouse suite, and the moment Saskia stepped over the threshold he was assailed with images of the last time she'd been there.

He hadn't felt this out of control, this blindsided, since he'd been a kid.

It had been one thing to suspect that Saskia was pregnant, but quite another to actually hear her confirm it. His worst fear.

At least that was what he'd always thought it would be. That was why he'd always been so fastidious about using protection with all his other women.

Only now it wasn't fear he was feeling. It was guilt. Because Saskia was right—ever since their weekend together he *had* been avoiding her. Not because he was afraid, as she'd suggested, that if she saw him again she'd take it as some sign that he wanted more, but rather because a foolish, traitorous part of himself *did* want exactly that, and he was afraid she saw him as nothing more than a much-needed rebound. A fling to be dismissed and forgotten.

Which was why it made no sense at all.

He should have welcomed that—the lack of complication. He might not have the playboy reputation his brother did, but he'd had his fair share of women seeking a relationship with him when he could offer them nothing more than the physical.

Yet, as much as he'd kept telling himself that the weekend with Saskia had just been about sex, deep down he suspected there had been more to it than that. Some deeper, inexplicable connection had drawn him to her from the moment she'd walked into his centre and volunteered her skills as a paediatric doctor.

At a time when other people might have focused on themselves, on what they were personally going through—in Saskia's case, the breakdown of her engagement—Saskia's instinct had been to reach out and try to help others. It said more about the kind of person she was, about her generosity of spirit and her selflessness, than anything she could have told him.

Malachi busied himself trying to get his head around this new, unwanted revelation. This wasn't the time for overanalysing what he did or didn't feel. Or for reading something into nothing. This was the time for taking a problem, looking at it logically and dispassionately, and finding the best response.

Something he usually excelled at.

But he was failing today.

'So, what now?' Saskia managed, in an impressive show of confidence.

Especially after the way she'd halted so abruptly, not allowing herself to progress much further into his apartment before she spun back to face him. And the way her eyes slid away from the room to focus on some point just over his left shoulder, where the front door now closed slickly behind him.

Almost, he considered, as if she couldn't bear to look at

the room where he'd stripped her naked the moment they'd tumbled through the door—it felt like a lifetime ago—and knelt at her feet to bury his face in all that glorious heat.

It was certainly the first image which had raced into his own head the moment they'd stepped into his apartment.

It didn't help that she'd been dressed to kill that night, too. In a dress which had been infinitely sexy, if not quite as stunning as the creation she was wearing now. An emerald green thing, which complemented her dark skin tones to perfection.

Before he could stop himself, his mind leapt to the question of whether she was wearing the same delicate bra and thong set. And were those infinitely long legs encased in the same style of sexy lace-top hold-ups?

God, what was the matter with him?

Malachi fought to drag his mind back to the present and failed, almost despairing of himself—until he saw the quickening, jerky pulse thud at the base of her elegant neck and realised that his wasn't the only mind that had wandered.

Good! Satisfaction pounded through him. *Maybe he could use that to his advantage.*

'We should have this conversation somewhere a little more comfortable than standing in the entrance hall, don't you think, Saskia?' he murmured, moving to usher her through to the main lounge.

'I seriously doubt this is going to be a comfortable discussion wherever we have it,' she shot back crisply.

He had to force himself to keep sauntering into the living area without glancing around, as though he felt as casual and self-contained as he miraculously appeared.

'Surely all the more reason not to exacerbate things, then?'

Moving around the space, he busied himself with a drink he didn't even want for himself, and a bottle of the mineral water he recalled she favoured, then threw himself into a soft leather chair and deliberately stretched out, as if he was at ease. Her eyes widened, even as she drew her lips into a thin line and lifted her nose ever so slightly in the air.

Malachi didn't realise he'd been holding his breath until she finally, stiffly, followed him into the room.

She eyed the leather sofa—where even now he could remember laying her out almost reverently, before finally burying his face in her sweet, intense heat—and she perched, rather awkwardly, on its arm. The mineral water was left untouched on the table between them.

'What now?' she repeated sharply, but he didn't miss the glimmer of nervousness.

The problem was that he didn't really know the answer. She was pregnant with his baby and she'd been so afraid that he wouldn't want to know that firstly she hadn't even told him, and secondly she'd tried to absolve him of all responsibility.

Fresh anger surged through him, and suddenly Malachi found himself talking without even realising what he was saying.

'*Now*, Saskia,' he bit out, 'you will move in with me and I will provide for you and for our baby.'

'I'm sorry…what did you just say?'

She looked utterly stupefied. Exactly the way *he* ought to feel. He could hardly believe the words that had come out of his mouth—*move in with him*—where had that even come from? It was ludicrous. Sheer folly.

And yet there wasn't an atom of him that wanted to take it back.

He ought to feel numb.

Detached.

Instead he suspected that what he was feeling—for the first time in a long, long time—was alive.

And that made no sense either.

Even now, after everything she'd said, it was taking more self-control than he felt it ought to not to reach out and haul her to him. He wanted her with a ferociousness he didn't recognise in himself.

A yearning.

And he didn't yearn. He wasn't desperate. Not ever.

At least not any more. He'd left that nonsense behind along with his childhood. Yearning for a better life, a kinder childhood, a fairer world—all of which he'd quickly learned wouldn't simply come to him. If he wanted them, he'd have to take them. Claim them. Seize them. In business and in his personal life. Fighting with every fibre of his body—even as an eight-year-old—to keep himself and Sol off the Social Services radar.

He hadn't stopped fighting since.

Conquering. Annexing. Discarding.

And people thanked him for it.

Companies were all the better for it even when he stripped them down and walked away from them.

Yes, it suited him just fine.

But *his baby*? That was one thing on which he could never turn his back. He knew that now with a certainty that rocked him to his core. In an instant all the fears which had crowded his head—his heart—had simply...*vanished.*

He didn't feel resentment, or fear, or bitterness when he thought of the two of them in his life. He felt...*odd.*

But not a *bad* odd.

Malachi shoved the unfamiliar sensations aside roughly. They only brought with them a sense of confusion, and that was the last thing he wanted.

'I don't think you're thinking straight, Malachi,' she managed defiantly.

'On the contrary. I'm thinking perfectly straight.'

'You can't really expect me to move in with you as though…as though…we're going to be some kind of… happy family,' she stuttered, flailing her arms around a little too much for someone who was trying to sound in control.

'I don't see why not,' he drawled, as though there *wasn't* a pounding so loud in his chest that it might as well have been a roll of thunder right overhead. 'We've made a baby together, Saskia. In my book that makes us some kind of family—so why not make it a happy one?'

'That's…ludicrous.'

'More ludicrous than you thinking you could cut me out of my own baby's life?'

She stopped, swallowed hard, but then looked him in the eye. 'I apologise for that but, like I said, I intended to tell you until I realised you were avoiding me and I lost my nerve. But this…moving in together…it won't work.'

'I disagree.'

'I want my child to have stability in its life—people who will always be there, come what may. Not someone who decides after a few months or years that it isn't for them after all.'

'I beg your pardon?'

He could see her skin prickle at the unmistakably dangerous edge to his tone, but she continued anyway.

'I want my baby to feel loved, and happy, and secure. Always. I know I can provide all of that for my child. I will never walk away or abandon it.'

'And you believe I will?' Barely restrained fury arced between them, virtually scorching her with its intensity. 'I can assure you that will never happen.'

'You say that now…'

There was no rancour in her voice, and he could tell she

was trying to project a quiet inner strength, but he could hear the faint quiver and see the slight tremor of her hands.

'But however good your intentions are at this moment in time, Malachi, you never wanted any of this—you're happy being a bachelor. What happens when you decide that being a father isn't for you after all?'

'That won't happen,' he gritted out.

But she continued as though he hadn't even spoken. 'You'll leave. Maybe it will happen slowly, maybe overnight, but either way my child will feel abandoned.'

'*Our* child,' he growled. 'And I will not do that to our baby. I do not simply walk away from my commitments or my responsibilities.'

'I'm sure you don't. You don't build a business empire like MIG International unless you're dedicated, single-minded. But this is a baby—not a business. It's a very different prospect.'

'Be very careful, Saskia, about what you think I do and don't understand.' His tone was well moderated, but he could feel the restrained emotion in every syllable.

'Then tell me!' she exploded unexpectedly. 'Tell me something about Malachi Gunn that I don't know. Because you never told me a single thing that weekend.'

His jaw was locked so tight it was almost painful, but he couldn't seem to loosen it however hard he tried. A storm was building inside him, silent but nonetheless lethal. And still Saskia pressed on.

'Tell me something that isn't some morsel of PR carefully crafted for the world at large.' Her voice rose despite her obvious attempts to be calm. 'I challenge you.'

It was all so close to the bone that Malachi was sure she was scraping him, fracturing him, splintering him. Worse, he was almost tempted to answer her. To tell her something about his godawful childhood that no one but he and Sol knew. To make her understand this sudden, driving need to ensure that his child had the kind of family life he had never enjoyed.

Only he wasn't quite sure he entirely understood it himself.

He struggled to maintain his composure. 'The way you told me something personal about yourself?' he countered. 'We both have our reasons for keeping people at arm's length. I recommend you don't ask me questions you yourself wouldn't be prepared to answer.'

'That's precisely my point, though…' She lifted her hand, then dropped it. Confusion flooded through her gaze, as though she knew the tension was escalating but had no idea how to stop it. 'We both like our privacy. How do you see us raising a child together? There's nothing real between us.'

He opened his mouth to reply and then his eyes caught sight of her hands, moving subconsciously to cradle her belly, her baby. *Their* baby. And they were sitting here arguing.

How had things degenerated like this?

Abruptly Malachi reached forward and poured out her water. The sound of it pouring from the bottle into her glass filled the room, and he concentrated on the noise the ice cubes made as they clinked and tinkled together. Anything to distract himself for even a moment.

Then he reached out to hand her the glass and their fingers brushed. It was like a shot of pure adrenaline. He might as well have been dancing out of his own skin. And judging by the expression clouding Saskia's face he wasn't the only one.

So much for *nothing real* between them.

He moved back to his seat, took a moment to compose himself. When he spoke again his voice was low, firm. 'I didn't bring you here to row with you, Saskia. I brought you because I wanted somewhere private for us to discuss what happens next.'

'Discuss?' she asked.

But he noted that her tone was softer now. His attempt to defuse the situation had clearly worked. At least to some degree.

'Or for you to command and for me to listen?' she went on.

'That will very much depend on whether you accept what I say, *zvyozdochka*, or decide to argue against it.'

Zvyozdochka. The endearment he had used that week-end slipped out before he could stop himself, causing Saskia to snap her head up.

He cursed himself for giving too much away.

'I didn't think you accepted people arguing with you?' she challenged softly.

'I don't,' he bit out. 'So allow me to tell you exactly what is going to happen, Saskia.'

He watched her swallow. Hard. Then she folded her arms over her chest. Nonetheless, he didn't miss the tremor that rippled through her body. Just as he noticed that she didn't say anything to stop him.

'You are carrying my child. *Mine.* Whatever you might think that idiot ex-fiancé of yours would have done, or wanted to do, is of no consequence to me. I don't care about him, or the life you thought you were building with him. I don't care about your broken heart or lack of trust. I care that my baby won't suffer because of your hang-ups.'

Or his own, if he were honest.

Though Malachi chose not to voice that.

'Good to know,' she choked out. 'Anything else?'

'Yes, as it happens…' He had no idea what he was say-ing, just knew that words were flowing from him as though they'd been there all along. 'Forget just moving in with me. You will be my wife.'

It hung there between them in the shocked silence. For how long, he had no idea.

And then Saskia gave an indelicate snort. 'That's even more preposterous than your first suggestion.'

An hour ago he might have agreed. Half an hour ago. But now he'd begun to get used to the idea.

Far more quickly than he might have expected to.

'I disagree.'

'We're not living in the last century. I don't have to be married to have a child,' she declared vehemently. And then, almost as an afterthought, added less emphatically, 'Besides, I don't want to be your wife.'

As if she had belatedly realized that was something she *ought* to have thought, rather than something she actually *had* thought.

'Marriage is not an institution that I thought I would ever enter,' was all he could answer. 'But for the sake of your baby, this *will* happen. Our child will know only a close family unit.'

She sucked in a shocked breath. 'You can't be serious.'

'Do I look like I am joking?'

She opened her mouth, closed it again, then shot back at him. 'And in this ridiculous scenario of yours, do you imagine we will be sleeping together, like we're really a couple?'

He could tell she regretted the words as soon as they came out of her mouth, and he knew precisely why.

'How interesting that that's where your mind went, Saskia,' he purred. 'Though I assume *sleeping together* is a euphemism for having sex, since I'll remind you that we didn't actually do much of the former.'

She shifted in her seat and then glowered at him.

She didn't answer. She didn't need to. She was moving restlessly again, clearly jumpy, and he knew in that moment that she was remembering how incredible it had been between them—because he was remembering it, too.

It hummed and whispered through the air around them. The way her body had fitted to his as if she'd been crafted just for him. The way she'd responded to his touch. The way he'd burned with a fire which had never seemed to die down.

'You're mad if you think that's going to happen again...' The words finally tumbled out, sharp and jerky, as if even she didn't quite believe what she was saying.

'You protest too much, Saskia. Especially when your body betrays you. Or did you think I hadn't noticed the way it reacts to me? *Still.*'

He relished the expression which poured out of those rich nut-brown eyes, that tongue flicking over her lips, reminding him of the way it had slid over almost every inch of him a few months ago.

Even the memory made him tighten as surely as if she'd been raking his body with her fingers, and he grabbed hold of it. Because if he held on to their physical attraction, their undeniable chemistry, then he wouldn't have to consider that there might be more to the way he felt about her than merely the superficial.

He was so caught up in his thoughts that it took a moment for him to realise she was still addressing him.

'I won't sleep with you again, Malachi.' She punched her chin out for emphasis. 'You can't make me just because you're insisting we marry as though we're back in the fifties.'

'I have no intention of *making* you do anything,' he commented dryly. 'You will *want* to, Saskia. More than that, you will beg me to take you.'

'Because you know my body better than I do, I suppose?' She lifted one nonchalant shoulder and shook her hair out.

He felt it like a caress against the hardest part of himself.

'I think we both know that your body *longs* right now,' he growled. 'Why you should go on denying it is a mystery.'

'Because you're such a prize, of course,' Saskia bit back, a little of her former feistiness returning.

His grin widened that little bit more, and she shivered as though she could actually *feel* those bared teeth against her skin. He found he rather liked the notion.

'So I've been told.'

'I imagine there are several million things informing that opinion,' she managed pointedly.

'No doubt,' he agreed readily enough. 'It's the way of the world, is it not? Although I think we both know that it isn't simply my multimillion-pound fortune alone which attracts women. It wasn't what attracted you, after all. So, what *did* attract you, Saskia?'

She shivered—a deep ripple of anticipation which he could read like other people could read a book. Despite her attempts to remain at arm's length, she couldn't deny their mutual attraction any more than he could.

'You were just my rebound,' she managed weakly. 'I told you that the first night and you agreed.'

'Indeed.' He dipped his head. 'Except now you're carrying my baby, and I don't intend to be kept out of its life.'

Her gaze simmered. And yet somehow he knew that he was sliding under Saskia's skin all the deeper, and that she was tempted. Just as he was. He felt her everywhere, and it didn't help that he could see she was teetering over the precipice of agreeing.

'So you've said. But…'

'But…?' he encouraged, when she didn't continue.

'But that doesn't mean marriage is the solution. As though I'm just a problem for you to solve like one of your business deals. And marriage certainly shouldn't be a business deal with benefits, as you're suggesting.'

'All right—so what, in your opinion, *should* marriage be, *zvyozdochka*?'

'Forget it.' She shook her head.

'I don't think I will,' he told her lazily. 'I find I'm almost on tenterhooks to hear your answer.'

'You're impossible.'

'Quite probably. So, tell me what marriage should be.'

It was insane. No one else could spar with him the way she could. Or, more to the point, no one else made him feel the way she did when she sparred with him, even when she wasn't even trying. She made him feel almost...*predatory*.

'You realise that the more you evade the question the more fascinated I become?'

'Then you're only setting yourself up for disappointment. I have no great revelation for you. Just my rather ordinary opinion.'

'I would hardly call you *rather ordinary*,' he countered, his gaze sweeping over her as though she'd laid down a fresh challenge.

'For pity's sake...' She exhaled, but then she ducked her eyes from his and he knew he had her.

He pressed his advantage home. 'What is marriage to you, Saskia?'

'Marriage is... Well, it's love. *True* love.'

'Like you had with that cheating ex-fiancé of yours?'

It occurred to him, a fraction too late, that some part of him was jealous.

Ridiculous. He didn't do jealous. And yet...

'No, not like Andy,' Saskia refuted hotly. 'He was an idiot for treating me the way he did, and I was even more of one for letting him.'

It shouldn't, yet her admission buoyed Malachi.

'Then what?'

'I...I don't know.'

'Something Hollywood, perhaps? Glittery and perfect?

I hate to burst your bubble, Saskia, but that's just for the movies—it doesn't really exist.'

'I'm well aware of that,' she managed hotly. 'My mother was big screen royalty, so I've lived it, remember?'

'Then what?' he pushed again. 'Perhaps something more akin to the passionate, heady thing your parents had? That well-documented great romance?'

He was deliberately needling her, but still Malachi wasn't prepared for the bleak look which suddenly pierced her gaze. A split second of pain which he could read only too acutely, could recognise only too easily. It sliced through him, too, spiked and merciless, before Saskia yanked her features into a semblance of equilibrium.

Malachi faltered. It was widely known that Saskia's parents had been madly in love—the Hollywood dream. Even their deaths had been considered the embodiment of romance: dying in each other's arms at the side of a road.

But it wouldn't have been romantic for the young Saskia. What the hell had he been thinking, raking up memories which must be hurtful? And there was something about the expression in her eyes which warned him that the pain he'd seen ran even deeper than losing her parents.

He'd experienced enough to know that there was something else. Something more. Something the rest of the world didn't seem to know.

He sought something to say, but nothing seemed right.

'Passion is overrated,' she managed, breaking the silence for herself. 'We had passion, but it doesn't mean anything. It was a one-night stand. It's over. I don't want you like that any more.'

Something kicked hard in his chest. 'I think we both know that's a lie.'

And then he was right there in front of her, unable to stop himself from reaching out and sliding one hand into those thick, glossy black curls that he imagined he could feel sweeping over his chest as they'd done every time she'd raked that wicked mouth of hers over his chest—and lower.

He tilted his head to look up into her eyes. Their rich, expressive depths were spilling over with unspoken longing, confirming all his suspicions. And still he had to force the next words out.

Testing her? Or himself?

He couldn't quite tell.

'One word, Saskia,' he rasped. 'One word from you and I'll let you go and never speak of it again. So I'd advise you to be sure that's what you really want.'

'I...'

The sound was low, halting. It vibrated around his chest and echoed off the walls, affording him some sense of victory. Clearly she could no longer pretend that she didn't ache for him, just as he wanted her with such intensity that he almost couldn't think straight.

His mind raced ahead before he could rein it in. Perhaps if they indulged this one last time it might sate the hunger which had been eating away inside him ever since this incomparable woman had left his bed three months ago.

Perhaps.

'I didn't quite catch that, Saskia. Was that another failed attempt at denial?'

He lifted his hand and brushed her cheek—the faintest of contacts and yet it ripped through him.

Saskia sucked in a sharp breath as if to echo it. 'Malachi...'

'Repeat it, if you will,' he enjoined, all too aware that his leaden voice betrayed him but not even caring any more.

And then her eyes flashed. They locked with his in unmistakable defiance, just as they had for a moment back on that promenade. A kick of that spirited, feisty Saskia he recognised only too well. It was like a shot of pure lust straight through to his sex.

'Fine,' she gritted out. 'I still want you. I know I shouldn't, but I do. Is that what you wanted to hear?'

'It's a start.' He lowered his head slowly towards her, pulled by some invisible thread which seemed to be as delicate and as strong as spider's silk.

'We can't…' She shook her head weakly. 'This isn't about another roll in the hay. There's a baby now—*our* baby. The fact of whether we still have chemistry or not is irrelevant.'

'I beg to differ,' Malachi growled.

And he was unable to stop himself from closing the gap and finally covering her mouth with his, revelling in the way Saskia surrendered to him in an instant. Her lithe body moulded to his, and her arms snaked around his neck as if they knew her mind better than her brain did.

And Malachi indulged. Deepening the kiss and giving in to the savage, raw ache that roared inside him. The inconceivable *need* he felt to be with her—inside her—over and over again.

She was his.

It thundered through his veins even as he struggled to comprehend what it meant. She was carrying his baby. Never again would another man touch her the way that he did. Be with her the way he was.

She was *his*.

Even if he didn't fully grasp what that meant.

Even if a part of him knew—*knew*—that he was about to complicate things in a way that he had been avoiding his entire adult life.

CHAPTER FIVE

IT WAS ELECTRIC. *He* was electric. Just as it had been three months ago.

Better.

Saskia melted into him in an instant, all her tentative resolve gone, and the painful memory of her parents' death was dissipated the moment Malachi's lips touched hers.

She wanted him with an intensity that should have terrified her. On some level, it did. And yet she couldn't stop—couldn't drag her mouth from the thrilling slide of his; couldn't unwind her arms from around his neck, where they'd slid almost of their own volition.

She didn't *want* to stop.

He gathered her to him, lifting her up and pulling her legs around his waist, running one big, callused hand along the length of her exposed thigh as the long side slit of her dress fell away. And when she locked her heels together, drawing herself that bit tighter to him, he made a low rumble of approval deep in his throat, and it rolled through her like the most delicious storm.

Supporting her with one hand, the other hand brushing the hair gently from her cheek as his mouth still plundered hers, Malachi carried her through his loft-style apartment. Everything in her jolted in anticipation of the intimate reunion she'd imagined over and over in her head, but had never believed would actually happen.

'Last chance, Saskia,' he muttered, his voice hard and dark as he shouldered his way into the plush master suite and carried her to the bed.

She wondered what it had cost him to drag his mouth from hers and stand there now, so still and unmoving.

Could she have stopped like that?

She doubted it. Every inch of her was on fire. She *ached* between her legs. Even her lips tingled, as though objecting to the loss of his mouth on hers.

'I don't want you to stop,' she managed, and the sense of relief was almost overwhelming as he offered barely a grunt of confirmation before lowering her onto the bed.

And then he was pushing the long skirt of her gown up to her hips, deliberately slowly, his hands grazing her thighs, higher and higher. His lips followed—languid, indulgent kisses, all stopping just short of where she yearned for his touch the most.

Again and again he repeated the motion. Up one side, then down the other, so close she could feel his breath brush over her molten heat through her lacy underwear, but never touching her. When she thought she could take it no longer she arched up slightly, only for Malachi to slide his hands under her backside and hold her in place.

'Malachi…'

'Patience, *zvyozdochka*…'

She could hear the amused smile even without seeing it. 'All in good time.'

'This *is* in so-called *good* time,' she grumbled.

'On the contrary. I find I want more time to get reacquainted with every millimetre of you.' Backing off the bed, he ran his tongue down from her thigh to her knee, making her tremble all over. 'Especially these long, incredibly sexy legs of yours, which you wrapped so tightly right around me when I drove deep inside you.'

She remembered. Lord, how she remembered.

But before she could answer Malachi was moving back up again, his lips, his tongue, his teeth, trailing a fiery blaze to the apex of her legs. Only this time he didn't stop short. And he didn't skirt over her core.

This time he bent his head and licked his way straight into her molten heat.

Saskia cried out instantly, helpless to stop her body from writhing under his expert touch. He was chasing her to the edge far faster than she could have imagined—but then she'd been dreaming of being back here in Malachi's bed ever since she'd left it, three months ago.

She was dimly aware that in her dreams it hadn't been just about her. In her dreams Malachi had been just as close to spiralling as she felt now. But then he lifted her backside with his hands, his tongue working a kind of magic inside her, and every thought went out of her head. There was only the pure sensation of what he was doing to her *right now*.

She had no idea how long they remained there. How long he played with her, toyed with her. Only knew that her body was revelling in every minute of it. There would never be anyone else for her like Malachi—she'd known that truth even before she'd realised she was pregnant—so if this was to be their one and only revisiting of history, she intended to enjoy every last second of it.

All too soon a delicious tremor began to work its way through Saskia's body, rippling out from her core to the tips of her toes, her fingers, her head. And Malachi responded accordingly, increasing his wicked rhythm and changing angles until she was grasping at the bedding for purchase, the wildest little sounds escaping from her.

And then he closed his lips over the very centre of her need and sucked. *Hard.*

Saskia exploded.

A detonation of sensations coursed through her entire

body and she shamelessly rode them out. Soaring on every last one of them. It might as well have been a lifetime before she came back down to earth, exhausted, boneless, and not even able to draw a steady breath.

By the time she finally came to and sat up, gingerly, Malachi was watching her. She recognised his dark, intense expression—*desire*—and it sent a thrill of pleasure down her spine.

'Now, I rather think I should return the compliment...' she managed hoarsely, reaching for his hands, which he duly extended, and allowing him to draw her to her feet, before turning her back to him and pulling her hair over her shoulder to expose the pearl buttons at the back of her gown. 'If you wouldn't mind?'

'If you insist.'

His gravelly voice was distinctively loaded and intent, and she knew she wasn't imagining the faint shake in his hands as he began to release one tiny button after another.

It gave her a sense of elation...almost of *power*...that a man with the kind of formidable, controlled reputation in business that Malachi had should be so close to the edge with her.

It felt like an age before the buttons were all undone, but as Saskia felt the halterneck fall, she turned slowly, allowing the dress to puddle at her feet before stepping elegantly out, and Malachi's eyes went almost black as he reached for her, his hands cupping the faintest swell of her abdomen.

'Actually, I rather think...' she licked her lips, her eyes locking with his as she sank to her knees '...that it's my turn.'

It took him a moment to register what she was doing. Long enough for her to unsnap his belt and for him to hear the sinful sound of her undoing his zip before he moved his hands to cover hers and still them.

'No…' He barely recognised his hoarse voice. 'You can't.'

'Why not?' she murmured, and the heat from her breath rushed over his sex, making him tighten and ache desperately.

He could scarcely form the words. 'You're pregnant, *zvyozdochka*.'

'Ah…' she murmured, twisting her hands from under his and releasing him from the confines of his boxers before he could even react. 'And somehow that makes me fragile and innocent in your book?'

'Saskia…' he warned, trailing off as she coiled her fingers around his sex and stroked all that velvet and steel.

'Let me assure you, Malachi, that there is nothing fragile about being pregnant. If anything, it makes me bolder than ever.'

Then, before he could answer, she tipped her head forward and took him straight into her mouth. Hot, and deep, and positively indecent.

When he looked down she was looking right back at him, his sex in her mouth and the naughtiest of smirks curving her lips.

He meant to stop her. To pull her to her feet. Instead he found himself lacing his fingers through her curls and holding on as though he might topple if he didn't.

He thought he was going to explode right there.

Again and again she tasted him, licked him, sucked him. Her tongue, her teeth and her wicked little fingers were all working in perfect lazy synchronicity to stoke that fire in him, hotter and higher.

It was incredible. *She* was incredible.

Malachi had never felt so wholly at someone's mercy and he found, with Saskia, he rather liked it.

And then suddenly it wasn't lazy any more. He was catapulting towards the edge. Closer and closer. Her mouth was so damned wet and hot.

'No,' he ground out, pulling himself out of her mouth although it was delicious agony to do so. 'Not like this.'

Scooping her up, he carried her to the bed and threw her down, shedding his clothes as fast as he could.

Finally—*at last*—he was covering her body with his, skin to skin, as he dropped his head to her jawline and trailed kisses all the way along it and down that glorious neckline, with deliberate care and attention. And then he turned his attention to her collarbone, and the sensitive hollow at the base of her neck. First one side and then the other.

Malachi could feel her nipples, hard and proud, chafing against his chest. He revelled in the way her breath hitched in her throat with every slide of his tongue. And still he took his time.

By the time he'd worked his way down her chest, to draw one exquisite nipple into his mouth, Saskia was gasping and locking her arms around him, trying to pull him down onto her properly.

It took all he had to resist her.

This was her moment, and he wanted it to be perfect.

He drew whorls around her nipples with his tongue. First one, then the other. Then he propped himself over her and let his hands take over.

He was so damned hard it was almost painful, but still he didn't let her touch him, however much she arched and writhed beneath him.

And then he was reaching down between them. Letting his fingers dance over her belly, over the softest of curves where his baby lay within her, over her hip and down her thigh.

His. All his.

'Malachi...' she groaned. 'Touch me...'

'Patience, *zvyozdochka*,' he rasped. 'All in good time.'

The truth was, if he touched her too early he feared he wouldn't hold out.

It had never, *never* been like this before. Only that first time with Saskia, and he'd been fantasising about this moment ever since.

He built up the rhythm in her. Higher and faster. Until eventually he reached down between her legs and let his fingers sink into all that sweet, molten heat.

She sighed and shuddered instantly. 'More,' she moaned. 'I need more.'

And, God help him, he needed to hear it.

'Tell me exactly what you need, *zvyozdochka*,' he commanded. 'I want to hear you say it.'

She groaned again, a low, needy sound which ripped right through him. He couldn't help it. Nestling between her legs, he flexed himself against her wet core.

'You, Malachi,' she muttered, opening her legs and arching as his tip slipped inside. 'Inside me.'

He couldn't stand it any longer. He thrust inside her. Slick, hard, deep. Just as Saskia wrapped her legs around him and clung on.

In and out, and she lifted up and met him stroke for stroke. The only sound was their ragged breathing, and every so often a deep, sensual groan. And then she lifted her legs higher, locking them tightly around his waist and twisting, so he plunged in that little bit further, and Malachi knew he was lost.

Just as he reached down between them, playing with the centre of her need, he heard her cry out his name. Her entire body shuddered, then tensed, then stilled, and he flicked his fingers expertly.

Saskia screamed, calling his name and toppling over the edge. And still he kept going, flinging her straight back over every time she thought she was done, until the final time, when she slid her hands down his back and cupped his buttocks, pulling him into her with such force he couldn't tell where he ended and she began.

This time when she shattered around him his name was on her lips. He drove himself home and followed her into oblivion.

CHAPTER SIX

MALACHI CURSED UNDER his breath. A filthy Russian curse he remembered his mother using—if not in the beginning, then certainly a lot towards the end.

Saskia was carrying his child.

His baby.

And he'd forgotten. All he'd been thinking about was getting inside her again, just like three months ago.

But this wasn't then—this was *now*. She was the mother of his unborn child and everything had changed. He was going to look after them. That was his responsibility. But responsibility and personal life were different things, and that meant there had to be boundaries. He couldn't go blurring the lines by being intimate with Saskia. There had to be rules.

He ignored the voice in the back of his brain asking *Why?* Needling him. Whispering that if there weren't rules, he wouldn't have to keep his hands off the woman who was even now still naked in his master suite.

And, God, how a part of him ached to spin around, go back in there and take her. Over and over again.

'Weakness!' he muttered, slamming his fist on the countertop as he marched into the kitchen to get himself a long, cold glass of water, when what he really needed was a very long, very icy-cold shower.

Though privately he doubted even that would do the

trick. Saskia had got under his skin the first time they'd met and he'd been trying to eject her ever since.

In some ways the appalling misstep he'd made tonight had been inevitable. And if he didn't have those rules in place it could just as easily happen again. He couldn't allow it.

He *wouldn't* allow it.

Being out of control was something he would never accept. And there was nothing controlled about this dark, needy thing which swirled inside him whenever he was with Saskia. Hell, whenever he even thought about her.

It felt altogether too much like powerlessness. And he'd sworn, back when he was eight years old, that when he grew up he would never allow anything to make him feel powerless again. Which meant showing no emotion.

Emotions were a bad thing. They were what made things start to unravel. His parents had loved each other— and hated each other, for that matter—with such intense passion that their relationship had been an emotional rollercoaster. And not just for them, but for him and his brother, too.

Malachi didn't know how much his brother, Sol, remembered about those very early years, if he remembered anything, but for him it had been draining. He'd never known whether their parents were going to be there at any given time, to remember to cook a meal, or give them a bath, or even just tuck them in to bed at a decent hour.

But that had been nothing compared to the powerlessness he'd felt when their father had died. Their mother had been unable to cope with the loss, and spiralling into drug addiction had been the only means of escape she could see.

It had fallen to Malachi to keep things together. From looking after the house to taking care of his baby brother. By the time he'd turned eight he'd been doing whatever it took to survive, to put food on the table for him and his brother, and to keep the local dealers away from his junkie mother.

Something ugly twisted and flipped deep inside him—something which a lesser man might have taken to be regret, maybe sadness, possibly even grief—but Malachi slammed it down in an instant.

God, why was he even thinking of this now?

It belonged in the past.

This was Sol's fault, for raking it all up the other day at the hospital. Stirring up old memories both of them were better off forgetting.

There was no point in *what ifs*. He'd learned that as a kid, the moment he'd taken up the reins as the adult of the house. He'd had rules, and he'd taken control of everything. His single-mindedness had enabled him to drag himself and Sol out of the gutter. He'd built MIG International after learning investment strategies from the internet, and he'd sent Sol to medical school.

Saskia threatened all of that. Or, more to the point, his lack of focus when it came to this one woman threatened all of that.

He forgot himself around her.

And that couldn't happen.

Things had changed; she was carrying his baby and he couldn't let his desire for her make him forget his responsibility as a father. He absolutely would *not* put this child through anything like what his parents had put him and Sol through.

He would not give in to that primal part of him which seemed to crave her so very greatly. He was better than that. And any child of his deserved more than that.

'Malachi…? Why did you leave like that?'

He didn't realise she'd followed him out, hadn't heard her footsteps coming down the hall until he heard her quiet, shaky voice. Despite all his internal cautioning his chest tightened at the mere sound of her near him. And if he hadn't known better he might have actually believed his heart gave a kick of delight.

What the hell was he playing at?

Malachi jabbed his finger on the countertop. 'That should never have happened.'

He could spout about honour and legitimacy and protection all he liked, but he suspected that the real truth of it was far less altruistic. He was being led by something far baser, far more primal. He was being led by his unextinguished desire for Saskia. She was like the worst kind of drug. One taste of her and he'd been hungering for her ever since, craving her in a way which was entirely too much out of his control for Malachi's liking.

And he was *never* out of control.

Yet here he was, desperate to keep her here before she remembered her own mind and walked away from him, just like she had at the end of that weekend.

'I won't marry you,' she said belligerently.

Malachi bared his teeth in what he hoped would pass for a grim smile. 'Yes, Saskia, you will.'

Because his child would *never* have anyone look at him as though he was *less* than anyone else.

'You think that just because you have money you can order people to do whatever you see fit?'

He hadn't anticipated this show of temper.

'It won't work on me. You're not the only one to have come from money. To be used to getting your own way. I can be just as obstinate, too.'

He wanted to tell her that he hadn't come from money. That he had scraped and struggled for every penny he had ever made. But he didn't. Because he knew it mattered to his brother—more than it ever had to himself—not to reveal the true depths of their childhood.

It took him a moment to realise he had hit a nerve.

Interesting.

'We've been through this, Saskia, have we not? I understand that you're the daughter of Hollywood royalty and that your childhood must have been a fairy tale. You had two parents who loved each other right up until the last. But this isn't a perfect movie story. This is real life.'

And he told himself that he didn't covet any of it—because if he hadn't experienced the hell of his own childhood he wouldn't be where he was today.

'Of course,' she managed tightly, her face shutting down just as it had a matter of hours ago.

And Malachi resolved in that instant to uncover just what it was that Saskia was hiding.

He knew he should put a stop to it immediately, but found he couldn't. What was it he'd just been saying about rules and control? Yet in reality he was so far out of his comfort zone he scarcely recognised himself.

Worse. A part of him didn't even seem to care.

He shoved his hands in his pockets, balling them into fists, as though that might somehow help him hold on to his own sanity. He had to do something to recover his equilibrium.

'I think it would be best if I take you home whilst I decide how best to handle this situation.'

'I am not a *situation* that needs to be handled,' she hissed incredulously.

'I would beg to differ.'

People didn't challenge you when you were the boss of a multinational organisation. They certainly didn't talk back or banter. But Saskia bit back with whatever was on her mind—rather like Sol did—and Malachi had to admit it was refreshing.

'And now, as much as this conversation is diverting, I think it's best if I take you home.'

Even though every fibre in his body was screaming for him not to let her leave.

Or maybe *because* every fibre in him was screaming for him not to let her leave.

'And then what?' she demanded.

He didn't have the answer to that. He only knew that whilst she was here he couldn't think straight. He needed time—and a little space—to come up with a workable solution. One that didn't put him straight in temptation's path.

'I'll let you know.' He shrugged, moving towards the door. 'When I'm ready.'

'Hi, I'm Saskia, the doctor who has taken over Caleb's case.' Saskia smiled gently at the frightened-looking woman with her five-month-old baby. 'This must be Caleb, and you're Mum?'

The woman nodded jerkily.

Saskia could only empathise. The woman had brought her baby in the previous night and he had been diagnosed with bronchiolitis, moderate in severity. But, according to the handover team, less than hour ago he'd begun to show signs of deterioration.

'So, the previous doctor told you that my colleague, Maria, is going to start this little man on high oxygen flow?'

'Yes. Will that cure him?' the woman choked out.

'It should help Caleb to breathe a little easier,' explained Saskia. 'Are you here on your own? Is there anyone who can be with you?'

The woman shook her head.

'No one. It's just the two of us. Caleb wasn't planned, and when I found out I was pregnant, Tom—Caleb's dad—didn't want to know. We'd been together for a year. I didn't expect him to propose or anything. But I didn't think he'd leave us without a word.'

'I'm so sorry,' Saskia offered, not sure what else to say. 'Well, we're here for you and your son. Try not to worry—the oxygen should help. I'll check on him in about an hour or so to make sure that it is, okay?'

'Okay.'

Saskia pulled the curtain out of the way and stepped out, confirming her intentions with Maria before moving on to check the next priority on her ward round.

But her head was spinning.

She'd spent the past week since she'd left Malachi's apartment throwing herself into work. Doing everything she could to keep her mind off the man who was the father of her unborn baby.

She'd convinced herself that she'd made the right decision in rejecting his marriage proposal, but now, after that revelation from her young patient's mother, she was seriously doubting herself.

Whatever else she could say about her and Malachi, she couldn't say that he didn't want to know about their baby. They weren't even a couple, yet he'd instantly expected to be part of their life. Had practically insisted on it.

Had she been thinking of *her* best interests or her unborn baby's when she'd dismissed Malachi's marriage proposal so scornfully? It wasn't as though they couldn't stand each other. In fact, quite the opposite.

Without warning, images of Malachi touching her—his hands, his mouth—flashed into her head, leaving her body searing. Feeling as though it might combust at any moment. The way it had been doing every time she'd thought of him over the past few months.

Only this time it was much, much worse. Because with each week that had gone by she'd managed to persuade herself that she was exaggerating quite how good he'd been. Quite how skilled.

But that repeat performance last week had offered her

a whole host of new experiences and, even more galling, had only proved to her that her imagination *hadn't* been overselling Malachi's talent in playing her body. If anything, her memories had seriously underplayed his artistry and the devastating effect he had on her.

And, for all her posturing, the simple truth was that she longed for more. She *craved* it. And that couldn't be a good thing to want with the man who was supposed to have been her rebound one-night stand.

What if marriage to Malachi wasn't so bad after all?

You're just having a wobble, she told herself firmly, heading for the nurses' station, which was mercifully deserted, and gripping hold of the melamine surface so hard that her knuckles went white.

She was having a scan this afternoon. No doubt that was why seeing Caleb's mother had frightened her when she thought about having the baby alone.

As much as she might like to pretend otherwise, she was already watching the door for Malachi, and it didn't matter that it was at least four hours too early. He'd told her it was *'all or nothing'*, but she didn't know whether to believe him. A part of her hoped he would be there. But now she'd seen Caleb and his mother and she'd realised that it was foolish of her to assume Malachi would come after she'd told him he didn't have to.

And yet it had frightened her to think that he might not.

What she ought to focus on was the fact that she wasn't Caleb's mother, and Malachi wasn't this Tom. There was no reason for her to panic and rush into a marriage neither of them would have even considered if she hadn't been pregnant, as though this was last century.

She ignored the tiny voice needling her, telling her that any woman who didn't consider marriage to a man as successful and stunning and all-round masculine as Malachi Gunn had to be a little bit mad.

'Saskia?'

The shrill sound of Babette had Saskia squeezing her eyes shut. Was there no shift she could work in this hospital without that woman seeming to dog her?

'Are you all right? You aren't going to faint again, are you?'

Plastering a bright smile on her face, Saskia squared her shoulders and spun around.

'No, Babette, I'm quite all right.'

The woman didn't even have the decency to disguise her disappointment.

'Your concern is really quite touching, though.'

And she strode off to her next patient before Babette could answer.

Mercifully, the rest of the morning passed quickly. Between rounds and routine jobs she also saw several chest infections, some minor injuries, an undescended testicle and a hip misalignment. Just the kind of busy morning to keep her brain perfectly occupied.

So by the time she'd made sure everything was handed over for the next half hour or so, there were a mere ten minutes until her scan.

And no sign of Malachi.

Her heart beat out a frenetic rhythm in her chest and her stomach dipped, but she told herself that she was fine, and rubbed her hand gently over her abdomen. It was startling how, despite her pregnancy not starting to show yet, she felt attached to her baby. He or she wasn't even planned, and yet she already couldn't imagine not being pregnant.

And in less than an hour she would be meeting her baby for the first time, as it were.

Alone? Or would Malachi come even after everything she'd said?

She wondered what he was thinking. How he might feel.

She'd had three months to get her head around it. And it was growing inside *her* body—she could feel the changes even if she couldn't see them. But Malachi had barely had a week to get used to the idea.

It should have taken her less than ninety seconds to get to the ultrasound unit, yet she dawdled, her eyes darting over every face, the back of every head, as she made her way along the corridor.

The wave of nausea which began to swell inside her had nothing to do with morning sickness.

He really wasn't coming, and it was all her own fault.

Gripping the handrail, Saskia stopped in a glass hallway and fought to draw a breath. She'd thought she didn't know what she wanted. Apparently she knew more than she'd realised.

She wanted her baby to have its father.

Not necessarily marriage, as Malachi had put forward, but…*something*. She'd been lying when she'd told him she could do it alone. Lying to him or to herself, she couldn't be sure. Either way, she should have bent a little more. She should have compromised.

But then she'd never been very good at that. It had been one of the many criticisms that Andy had levelled at her which he'd been right about. Of course there was also an argument to say that if Andy had been a fairer, more honest, more loyal fiancé, then perhaps she would have actually *wanted* to compromise more.

Well, it was too late now. She'd made her bed, as they said. Now she had to go and get scanned on it.

Maybe afterwards, if she was feeling brave, she would take a detour past Malachi's apartment. Perhaps even apologise for her curtness last week.

Lifting her head, Saskia focused on moving forward, one step at a time, until she finally reached the end of the corridor and went through the double doors to the booking-in desk.

* * *

'Cutting it a bit fine, aren't you?'

His dry voice in her ear had Saskia spinning in an instant.

'You came!'

She actually seemed pleased to see him there, and for a moment Malachi was thrown.

He'd half expected her to tell him he was not wanted at the scan. He'd even been prepared for it.

Saskia had laid her position out all too clearly the other night, when she'd turned down his marriage proposal without even a hint of a qualm. She didn't need him and she didn't really even want him—at least not outside the bedroom.

But he was the father of her unborn baby, and he had no intention of letting the child grow up thinking he didn't want to be a part of its life. That he didn't care.

He'd gone through the whole gamut of emotions after Saskia had left his apartment a week ago, yet he still didn't know exactly how he felt. He only knew that he was this baby's father and as such he had a responsibility both to it and to Saskia. Whatever she might wish.

And now she was smiling at him as though she was glad he was here. As though she hadn't told him that she could do it alone. As though she hadn't spelled out that he was nothing more than a rebound to her, and that it made no difference to her whether he was part of their lives or not. As though she hadn't turned on him, dismissing his relevance in her life the way his mother had done to him— and to Sol—all those years ago.

He'd let his guard down with Saskia.

He wouldn't make that mistake again.

'Don't worry. I'm only here for the baby—not for you,' he murmured, as he accompanied her to the chairs, carrying her file in his hand.

She blinked at him, and something he couldn't identify flashed through those rich chocolate depths. Then it was gone.

'Glad to hear it. I wouldn't want to have to turn down yet another hollow marriage proposal.'

'Trust me, I have no intention of repeating that.'

There had to be something wrong with him, because every single word burned in his throat, acrid and bitter, whilst Saskia offered him a curt bob of the head as though finally—barely—she was satisfied.

Malachi gritted his teeth and waited for her name to be called, unable to stop himself from placing his hand at the small of her back as they walked in, helpless to control this protective instinct that surged inside him when he looked at her.

It made no sense. He'd vowed to himself long ago that a wife, children, weren't for him. Hadn't he sacrificed so much of his childhood to playing the part of a parent? It was why he'd set up Care to Play with his brother. In order to help young carers have some semblance of a childhood in a way that he had never enjoyed. But he never wanted to bear that responsibility himself again.

And yet here he was. In a consultation room with a woman who was little more than a stranger and an unborn baby he would never have chosen to have.

But it was what it was, and he would deal with it the best way he could. The way he dealt with everything in his life…

Malachi didn't know the exact moment he went from detached to awestruck.

Perhaps it was when he saw the image come into focus on the sonographer's screen. Or when he saw the distinct outline of the baby's head. Or maybe it was when he heard the strong, rapid beat of his baby's heart.

He didn't know. And yet in that instant everything… *shifted*. His world began to tilt, slowly at first, then faster. It started to rotate, and spin, and he felt himself toppling, then falling.

His baby.

And Saskia's.

And he knew he would go to the ends of the earth to protect it.

'We should talk…' Saskia bit her lip as they stepped out of the consultation room together.

'We should,' he agreed smoothly. 'I think we need to start again.'

She smiled, almost shyly. 'I'd like that.'

Whatever he'd expected her to say, it hadn't been that. But why object when she was only voicing the thoughts in his own head.

'A late lunch?' he suggested, glancing at his watch.

It was the kind of timepiece that cost more than some people's cars. He'd prided himself on that purchase. A reward for his first half a million.

Suddenly it seemed empty.

'I can't.'

Saskia shook her head, and he might even have thought she sounded genuinely disappointed.

'I have to get back to the ward. Technically, I'm in the middle of a full weekend shift.'

'A full weekend?'

Was this her way of giving him the brush-off?

After the scan he'd thought they'd turned a corner.

Had that just been in his head?

'Friday to Monday,' she confirmed. 'We don't get them that often, but when we do it's pretty full-on.'

'Fine. Lunch Tuesday, then. That will give you a day to recover.' It wasn't a question. 'Look after yourself and the baby, and I'll pick you up at midday. I'll take you for lunch.'

'Tuesday.' She nodded, and then she flashed him a smile which seemed to send light cascading right through him.

He really was in trouble.

* * *

'Yep, small bowel atresia.' The paediatric surgeon eyed the X-ray with Saskia. 'Good call.'

Good call—crappy outcome, Saskia thought as she considered the newborn baby at the other end of that X-ray.

She had practically floated back to the ward after her scan—and after talking to Malachi—but now everything had crashed back in. Hard. Painful.

The tiny girl they were discussing had only come into the world days before—a little premature, but apparently healthy, if a touch jaundiced, and passing a little meconium. Within hours it had become clear that she was vomiting every time she tried to feed, and the green colour, along with an examination, had revealed a swollen abdomen, leading Saskia to consider a bowel blockage.

She dealt with sick babies and children on a daily basis, but today it was really getting to her.

She fought to pull her head back into the game. 'No contrast scan?' she verified with the surgeon. 'Enema?'

'Not this time. The image is clear enough.'

'Okay...well, she's on a fluid drip now because she was dehydrated,' Saskia confirmed.

'Fine. I'll go and have a chat with the parents. What are they like?'

'Young. Terrified.' Not that she could blame them.

'Right, leave it with me. I'll give them a brief outline now, and once Rosie is stable I'll take them through the operation in more detail.'

'That's great, thanks,' nodded Saskia as her colleague jerked her head to the end of the ward, where children's A&E lay beyond.

'Looks bad out there.'

'Yeah well, typical winter, even more hectic than usual.' Saskia blew out a breath. 'Lots of respiratory—colds, flu—

and more kids than we have room for, but I can't possibly send them home.'

'You're under pressure to clear out?'

'All the time.' Saskia grimaced as they headed out of the door, her mind still threatening to wander.

'Well, good luck with it.'

'Yeah, thanks.' She bared her teeth in a semblance of a smile as she passed the board again to check anything new.

That little girl could probably go home.

This guy was waiting for bloods.

That boy could go home.

Still, it barely even scratched the surface.

And now she would have to set up a nasogastric tube to drain off Rosie's stomach and bowel contents, as well as any gas build-up. It wasn't the first time she'd had to prep for an operation on a newborn—not by any stretch—but suddenly the enormity of it hit her.

Being pregnant with her own baby had suddenly brought the reality of the situation home to her. As well as how fragile and precious life was. Maybe marrying Malachi and making sure her child had the best possible start wasn't such a bad plan after all.

She would have security. Support. Someone with whom to share the burden—and the joy. Not to mention the fact that she couldn't do any worse than commit her life to a cheat and liar, which she'd nearly done with Andy.

Somehow she didn't think Malachi was the type to cheat or lie.

And sexual attraction has absolutely nothing to do with it, she concluded, somewhat redundantly.

It was a logical decision. One which had absolutely nothing to do with her libido. All that was left to do now was to tell him.

Suddenly Tuesday lunch with Malachi couldn't come around soon enough.

CHAPTER SEVEN

ELEVEN FORTY-FIVE, SASKIA THOUGHT, checking her watch as she exited her apartment block, her stomach in knots as it had been all weekend, when even the avalanche of a caseload hadn't taken her mind off the scan. And Malachi Gunn.

She probably should have waited upstairs, for fear of looking overkeen for this non-date with Malachi, but she'd been wearing a trench in the living room floor as it was. Better to be out here, waiting in the winter evening, than up there getting cabin fever.

And suddenly there he was. Languishing against the side of a sleek black car which looked as though it belonged on a waiting list as long as the A&E department's patient list on New Year's Eve. And he looked as though he belonged in some designer aftershave advert.

Her heart clattered against her ribs, and it was easier to concentrate on the muscular lines of the car than the muscular lines of the man himself. Confident, self-possessed, and altogether too tempting for words.

He shifted, and this time it was her stomach's turn to give a little lurch.

Hunger pangs, she reprimanded herself sharply.

If only they were.

'You're early,' she managed, instantly cringing at such a less-than-stellar opening line.

'I might point out the same,' he replied dryly, opening the passenger door and waiting for her to get in. 'I would have preferred to come up to your apartment rather than hover out here like some adolescent waiting for his girlfriend to sneak out of her parents' house.'

Girlfriend? Was that what she was? She tried not to let her body do funny things at his use of the term.

'Funny,' she threw back, as lightly as she could manage, not quite able to move. 'But I'm telling you, my nosy neighbour is worse than any overbearing parents. The grapevine would have been positively shaking before we'd even left the building.'

'Then I suppose it's good that you came down at all.'

There was something in his voice which made her snap her head up. 'Did you think I wouldn't?'

He shot her a masked look which she couldn't quite read. 'I wondered.'

Her curiosity was piqued. 'What would you have done?'

'I'd probably have come up to your door and thrown you over my shoulder and made a scene in front of all your gossiping neighbours.'

'Oh.'

There had to be something wrong with her, she thought, that the idea should appeal so much to some perverse part of her.

'Or perhaps you might have enjoyed that,' Malachi continued quietly, the gleam in his eyes spearing through her right to her core.

She tilted her chin up. 'I most certainly would not.'

He grinned, a devastating smile that she could feel blooming though every inch of her body.

'Then get in the car, or we'll both find out how false that statement is.'

It was as if he had some kind of hold on her. The way

her body was moving towards him—*obeying* him—even though her brain was bellowing its objections.

He closed her door and strode around the front of the car, powerful yet graceful, making it impossible for her not to gawk. When he slid into the seat beside her, his thigh too close to hers, and the heat from his body radiated over her, she pretended that a delicious shiver *didn't* dance all the way up her spine. That her chest *didn't* tighten as though he'd sucked all the air from the confined space.

Saskia could feel the pulse at her throat, her wrist, her groin, beating out a frantic SOS. Or perhaps it was tapping out a joyous jig.

If he'd suggested ditching the meal and going straight back to his apartment she knew she wouldn't have objected. Heat suffused her, making her dress feel too scratchy on her skin, her body too tight for itself, her breasts too heavy.

God, she really did need to get a grip.

'You also mentioned that you didn't want your friend to see me.'

His voice dragged her back to the present, getting closer to the heart of the matter. Unease washed through her.

'Yet,' she clarified. 'I don't want her to see you *yet*.'

'Because…?'

'Because I haven't told her I'm pregnant.'

'Maybe you don't think it's any of her business?'

Saskia shook her head slowly. Uncertainly. 'No, we tell each other everything.' *Usually.* 'We've been best friends since we were kids, when our mothers were rivals in the same prime-time American soap opera. We've done everything together—including coming to the UK to become doctors.'

'Yet she doesn't know about the baby? About us?'

'And what do I say about "us"?' Saskia asked, before she could stop herself.

It wasn't exactly the way she'd intended to get to the

subject of accepting his marriage proposal, but she supposed it would achieve the same thing.

Instead of replying, however, Malachi simply started the engine, the power of the vehicle humming all around them whilst they pulled away, leaving her fighting to unglue her tongue from the roof of her mouth.

They were speeding along the motorway before she succeeded. He was a good driver, but then, why wouldn't he be? She got the impression that Malachi Gunn was the best at everything he chose to do.

And maybe that wasn't such a bad thing, she considered, since she'd been feeling a little lost ever since she'd found out she was pregnant. Maybe now was the perfect time to tell him everything she'd been reconsidering. Everything she'd spent the past few days practising how to say.

She opened her mouth to speak.

'I apologise for the caveman routine the other week,' he announced unexpectedly.

Her well-rehearsed speech flew out of the window. 'Pardon?'

Something hitched inside Saskia. She couldn't remember Andy apologising for anything, *ever*. Even when he'd been cheating on her. He'd always claimed apologising was a sign of weakness, and she, to her shame, had come to believe him.

Now she realised just how foolish she'd been believing that, too.

It didn't make Malachi look weak at all. Quite the opposite. He looked utterly secure in his own skin. Plus, as she didn't imagine he was a man who often had to apologise, the very fact that he even had made her feel valued. Respected.

'Insisting on marriage,' he was saying as she yanked

herself back to the present. 'Being a couple. That was...
ill-thought-out.'

Saskia's mouth went dry.

Just as she had decided that it was a good idea.

She should have kept her distance after all—emotionally
and physically.

Every fear she'd ever had crashed over her at once. This
had to be how it felt to drown.

Saskia tried to rearrange her thoughts, but they jumbled
together like a tangle of wires that she couldn't even begin
to find the ends of.

'You don't want to be part of our lives after all?' She
barely recognised her own voice. It sounded so detached
and...*alien.*

'No—there's no question that I will be a part of your
lives,' he corrected. 'But you were right to argue that marriage would overcomplicate things. It isn't the solution.'

'I see,' she managed, even though she didn't see at all.
'So what now?'

His momentary silence caught her off guard, and she
swivelled her head to find him looking at her. Gauging.
Assessing. She tried to relax, for fear of him reading every
emotion etched clearly on her face, but she wasn't sure she
had succeeded.

Finally he turned back, to concentrate on the road, and
she exhaled silently. Hopefully she hadn't given herself
away completely, but at least he didn't look entirely at ease
himself. If she hadn't known better, she might have thought
his set jaw meant he felt as at sea as she did.

She tossed the idea over and over in her mind. On the
one hand Malachi wasn't the kind of man she could imagine second-guessing himself. On the other... Well, her
gut was telling her he was playing his cards close to his

chest. That he still wanted her every bit as much as she wanted him.

'Now,' he echoed firmly, 'we find a solution that works all round. Now we talk.'

'And by *talk* you mean we won't end up in bed this time?'

She was hectoring him. Trying to get a rise out of him. The thing was, she couldn't figure out why. Or, more accurately, she was pretending she couldn't. Either way, Malachi didn't look amused. If anything, he seemed to grimace.

'That won't be happening again, believe me.'

'Right.' She told herself she shouldn't feel hurt by his wintry tone. 'Good to know.'

Was he trying to convince her, or himself? Could he turn off his attraction just like that? Because there was no way she was able to do it.

They lapsed into another edgy silence.

Saskia tried to concentrate on the drive, but all she could think about was the fact that only a few months ago Malachi had given her the most intimate, passionate weekend of her life—which was vaguely sad in itself, given how many years she'd been engaged to Andy—and there hadn't been one single uncomfortable moment between the two of them. Yet now they were walking on eggshells around each other.

Eventually, she couldn't stand it any longer. 'So where are we going, then?'

'I thought I might take you somewhere civilised.'

'Civilised?'

She feared she liked the sound of that far more than she should.

'A restaurant.'

'Like…a date?' It was out before she could stop it.

He cast her another impenetrable look. 'More like somewhere we can talk. Somewhere neutral.'

'Out of the city?' she noted.

And not at his apartment.

Who was it he didn't trust? Her? Or himself? She suspected it was sadly the former.

He didn't answer immediately. Instead he pulled off the road and onto a small Tarmac clearing.

A helicopter stood a hundred or so metres away.

'You could say it's out of the city...'

'That's for us?' Saskia schooled her features, ignoring the goosebumps that travelled up her arms.

'It is.'

'And that's the pilot?' She glanced at the man sitting in a car on the other side of the Tarmac.

'No, that's Bill. He's just been looking after the heli for me.'

Her stomach flip-flopped in anticipation.

'Let me guess—you're the pilot.'

Malachi lifted one easy shoulder, then set about helping her up into the passenger seat.

'Trust me...' he murmured.

The startling thing was that she did.

She couldn't help but thrill at it all, even as she knew she was being ridiculous. And part of her whispered that he seemed to be going to a lot of effort for someone he no longer wanted to marry.

The smarting she'd felt earlier eased a little.

Which only served to panic her all the more.

Frantically, she tried to remind herself that Malachi was all about practicality. She told herself that he'd probably chosen the helicopter so she couldn't keep wittering in his ear, the way she had in the car. She instructed herself that there was nothing romantic about this moment.

Nothing at all.

It was a shame her body—and her soaring heart—didn't want to agree. All they wanted to do was revel in the fact that he wasn't walking away from her and their baby after all.

'When I said "out of the city" you didn't tell me you meant out of the country!'

Saskia savoured another delicious mouthful of the sumptuous winterberry soufflé—the final course of her two-Michelin-star meal.

The day had been surprisingly pleasant, given their conversation a few hours earlier in the car. At some point over the English Channel, they had clearly decided that the frosty atmosphere wasn't going to help the situation, so by the time Malachi had landed the helicopter they'd both been trying hard to lighten the mood.

She had to admit that the incredible venue had significantly helped matters.

'I've dreamed of visiting France, and this restaurant, for years.'

'I remember,' he told her, his eyes holding hers without wavering. 'You saw it in a magazine that weekend we were together, and told me you'd heard of this place when you first moved to the UK. You said that you and Anouk had always talked about visiting it.'

'You remember that?' She stared at him.

'I do.'

She cocked her head to one side. 'Well, I also remember reading that it's always booked up months and months in advance.'

'An opening became available.'

He shrugged it off but she wasn't fooled.

He'd done all this for her. This definitely wasn't a way

of brushing her or the baby off. Relief, and another emotion, uncoiled within her.

'I thought it would be nice for us to talk somewhere like this. Besides, you seem to be enjoying the menu.'

Saskia smoothed the frown from her face before it could take hold properly.

'Is that a backhanded compliment?' She forced a lightness into her tone, as if the words didn't really bother her. 'I suppose I could pretend to be one of those people who push lettuce leaves around their plate and claim not to be hungry, but I'm afraid that has never been me.'

'I can't imagine you ever pretending to be anything you aren't.'

He'd surprised her by saying that. And it sent a warm glow through her even as she schooled herself not to react.

'But, for the record, it was a straightforward compliment.'

The glow intensified. 'Good to know…' She had no idea how she managed to sound nonchalant.

'Still, I didn't bring you here to bandy about compliments. I brought you because I want to start over. Talk about our baby.'

'And you want to be part of our lives?' she asked carefully, not wanting him to realise she needed more reassurance right now.

'I believe I said that earlier.' He frowned. 'I'm trying to be understanding here. To bend a little. And believe me, *zvyozdochka*, I am not a man accustomed to having to bend. I suggest you don't take it as a sign that you can try to exclude me from any decisions pertaining to our baby.'

Relief punched through her. And a little bit of her old fighting spirit.

Andy had crushed it by his betrayal, but it appeared as though her each and every encounter with Malachi went some way to restoring it. As if he was somehow…*good* for her.

'I wasn't going to exclude you from anything,' she managed haughtily, in an effort not to let him see what she was really feeling. 'But if you're no longer insisting on marriage, how exactly do you envisage things between us working out?'

How indeed? Malachi wondered, and not for the first time.

In truth, he hadn't got that far in his plan. For a man who usually approached business ventures like a chess game, always making sure he was several moves ahead, he was astonishingly poorly prepared when it came to Saskia and his baby.

It was as though the moment she entered into any thought process he couldn't even see straight, let alone plan straight.

It was frustrating, thrilling, and terrifying all at the same time.

Moreover, her haughty tone seemed to work its way through him like a stormproof match in a state-of-the-art survival kit. Even if she submerged him in the coldest hauteur he was afraid he would still blaze brightly for her.

Which was exactly why marriage to her had been a reckless idea.

He was altogether too afraid that having her under his roof, that sinful body of hers within arm's reach, and knowing exactly how wickedly she melted into him, he wouldn't be able to stay on task.

Even now he wanted to touch her, taste her again. It was one of the reasons he'd chosen to fly her out of the country, well away from the temptation of taking her back to his apartment.

His one priority right now had to be their baby, and

after the scan the other day he knew it wasn't going to be as impossible as he'd feared.

Even at the memory of that ultrasound Malachi felt his chest tighten. His heart stopped, then restarted with a lurch.

His baby. *Their* baby.

So impossibly, exquisitely perfect.

Seeing his baby moving on that screen and hearing its heartbeat hadn't just unlocked the cage on his long-restrained heart—it had smashed it apart and splintered it into a million worthless pieces.

His entire chest felt full. Bursting. And the baby wasn't even born yet. How the hell was he going to cope when it was cradled in his arms?

He had known in that moment that he would protect it with his life. And Saskia, too, of course, as the mother of his child. But marrying her wasn't the way to do that. Not least because being around her made him feel wholly and completely out of control.

It all led to a conundrum he was more than happy not to answer. For Saskia, however, it seemed to be the only question she wanted answered.

'Do you intend for me to live out of a suitcase—some nights of the week at your apartment and some nights at my own?' she asked. 'Or perhaps you propose to come and spend some nights at the apartment Anouk and I share?'

'There is an apartment available in my building. I thought you could move in there. That way we would still have our own space, but our baby would have both its parents around all the time.'

It might not exactly be a stroke of genius, but Malachi was more than happy that it was a fair halfway meeting.

Saskia looked disgruntled. 'Are you serious?'

'You have an objection?' he managed mildly.

'Well...yes!' she seethed. 'You're talking about installing me in an apartment in your building like some kind of mistress you're moving in for your convenience.'

'I was thinking about what makes sense for you and the baby.' He narrowed his gaze. 'But I find it interesting that you should use the term *mistress*. Are you making me a proposition?'

'I most certainly am not,' she returned.

But he noted the dark colour staining her cheeks and her long, elegant neck, and could only imagine just how far it spread down her lush body.

'Your body language might suggest otherwise.'

'Then learn to read it better,' she snapped.

He tried to suppress the urge to grin, but it was too strong. It was this damn spell that Saskia kept putting him under. The idea was that he was supposed to be taking control of this situation, not falling for her charms like some little lapdog.

'That sounds like another invitation,' he drawled. 'A pity that I have to decline.'

'It wasn't an invitation.' She jutted her chin out obstinately. 'And even if it was, I don't believe you would decline. I remember how your body responds to me, Malachi. I know I'm not the only one who was lost in the moment the other night.'

'You're remembering what you want to remember, *zvyozdochka*. My advice to you is to stop fighting me and to remember that we're on the same team.'

'Yes—because it's so easy to feel that way when you're commanding me to upend my life and move away from my support system just to make things easier for you.'

He hated it that her dismissal of his role in her life stung as it did.

'Do I have to remind you, yet again, that you are carrying *my* child? I am your support system. From now on we are one unit.'

'One unit even though you no longer wish to marry me?' she threw back at him. 'One unit even though you don't even want to share your home with me?'

The problem with that, of course, was that he *did* want to share his home with her. And his bed. Possibly far too much.

'Careful, *zvyozdochka*, or I might believe that you're actually pining for that option. That you were anticipating sharing your life with me with pleasure, despite all your earlier objections.'

'You can't really believe that!' She laughed.

It was a brittle little sound that revealed things he imagined she had never wanted him to know. Not least that he was right.

Lust fired through him like a slingshot, right around his sex.

'I've told you how things are going to be. For both you and our child,' he growled.

The temptation to take her hand and lead her from this restaurant to an exclusive hotel he knew was right around the corner was almost overwhelming.

'And you've said it—ergo that is how it will be?' she retorted.

He made an approving click of his tongue, which was guaranteed to get her back up all the more.

It was either that or stir an altogether different emotion in her.

In both of them.

'And now, *zvyozdochka*, I suggest we get back to the helicopter. We have a long flight home.'

'Good,' she muttered. 'Because I'm sure I could do with the thinking time.'

CHAPTER EIGHT

'WHAT'S HAPPENED?' SASKIA yelled over the rotor blades as she raced across Moorlands General's helipad.

The call had come in just as they'd been twenty minutes out. A major incident in the area—some kind of explosion, from what Saskia could gather—meant that all available staff were being called in to the hospital.

Malachi hadn't even needed to ask her. He'd instinctively turned his helicopter, calling in a new flight plan and instructing his PA to check that there were no air ambulances in the area before getting permission for him to land at the hospital with Saskia.

'Some kind of gas explosion on Beechmoor Street!' her colleague shouted. 'Near the junction with King's Boulevard. There are multiple casualties and they're splitting them between us and the Royal.'

'Where do you want me?'

'There's a designated area for incident victims in paediatric A&E. Fortunately because of the time of day, there weren't too many kids around, and those that were appear to have been caught more by the shockwaves than in the blast itself.'

'Thank goodness. Listen, do you know if Anouk—Dr Hart—is okay?'

'I don't know, sorry. Apparently the area has been evacuated.'

Biting her lip, Saskia hurried down the ramp and into

the hospital. Behind her she could hear Malachi's helicopter leaving, but she didn't turn around. There wasn't time.

'Come on, then. Let's go.'

Saskia glanced at the screen as her colleague ran her through the latest admissions.

'First up is five-year-old Molly, who was knocked into a wall during the explosion and suffered a head injury. She was Emily's patient, but Em's now tied up with someone else. Molly has already been to CT and everything is clear—she just needs stitches.'

'Okay, great.' Saskia nodded. 'Let me go and see her and check the injury, and then I'll get some kit together.'

The place was heaving, and her colleagues were triaging new admissions as fast as they came in. The beds were filling up fast. The sooner they could clear the non-urgent patients out, the better.

'Hi, I'm Saskia.' She smiled as she stepped around the curtain. 'I'll be the doctor looking after you. You must be Molly.'

'I am,' the little girl said proudly, returning her smile with a happy, confident one of her own. 'And this is my mummy.'

'Hello, Mummy,' Saskia said dutifully.

'Hi.' The young woman shot her a relieved smile, the hint of tension around her eyes belying her calm exterior.

'Right, I know you've been through this with the other doctor—'

'Dr Emily,' the girl interjected.

'Right…'

'She's nice.'

'Yes, she is,' Saskia agreed.

Clearly there was no impairment in Molly's speech or understanding, which was a good sign. But although the little girl had already been checked over, another set of eyes never hurt.

'I think you seem nice, too.'

'Thank you.' Saskia laughed. 'I'm glad you think so. Anyway, I know you've told the other doctor what happened, but can you tell me, too?'

'Of course I can!' the little girl exclaimed with an expansive gesture. 'Mummy and I were out shopping for some new shoes.'

'Oh, lovely,' Saskia offered, when it appeared the five-year-old was waiting for a reply.

Clearly, it wasn't the response Molly was hoping for.

'Red *patent leather* shoes,' she emphasised after a moment.

'Wow,' Saskia managed, relieved when the little girl nodded with satisfaction.

'And when we got them we called in to see Nana, and she thought they were *bee-yoo-tiful*.'

'Well, of course,' agreed Saskia solemnly. 'But I'd really love it if you could tell me some more about how you hit your head.'

'Oh…' The girl's face fell. Clearly to her the red patent leather shoes were the most important detail of her experience.

Saskia stifled a chuckle.

'I don't really remember. We were walking back, and suddenly there was a really, really loud bang, and then I was on the other side of the pavement and my head was bleeding.'

'Did it hurt?'

'Yes. A *lot*.'

'Can I see?' Saskia stood up and Molly obligingly turned around.

'Of course.'

Tentatively she parted the matted hair and checked the wound. It had evidently been cleaned once, so it was easy to see what was going on.

'Great. And can you remember how you got here, Molly?'

'Mummy brought me in.'

'We were right around the corner,' the mother put in. 'The traffic was heavy, and I knew I could get her here before an ambulance even got out. I didn't even think about head or neck injuries. I know I should have.'

'It's okay,' soothed Saskia. 'I just wanted to see if Molly remembered what had happened and how she felt.'

'I was told the CT scan was fine?'

'It is. Please don't worry. I just wanted to check once more for good measure. Right, Molly, let me go and get my equipment, and then I'm going to give you just a little injection in the back of your head to make sure you don't feel anything—okay?'

'Okay.' Molly nodded cheerfully.

Confident about her patient, Saskia headed out of the bay for a couple of suture kits and some local anaesthetic, glad the little girl didn't seem in any distress, either physically or emotionally.

She was on her way back to the bay when she saw Anouk dashing past the doors at the end of the ward, flanked by two porters pushing a gurney. Relief washed over her. At least her friend was all right. But it didn't look as though they were going to get chance to talk any time soon.

'Right, here we are,' she popped back through the curtain. 'Mum, can you sit here for me? And, Molly, can you lie face down on the bed, looking at your mummy? Good girl.'

Quickly and efficiently she began cleaning the area, and then carefully administered the anaesthetic.

'You might feel a bit of a sharp sting, but then it should feel better. If you can keep as still as you can, sweetheart? Wow, good girl—that was brilliant.'

'Mummy says I'm very brave,' Molly said proudly.

'Mummy is right.'

She distracted the girl for a few moments longer whilst the anaesthetic took hold.

'Okay, this shouldn't hurt, but if you feel any pinching at all you let me know—all right, Molly?'

'All right.'

Working speedily, Saskia began her sutures, twelve in all, and they were made easier by the fact that the five-year-old kept still and focused on her mum, who chatted to her quietly throughout about Nana and the red shoes.

Would she be as calm and collected if it was her child?

She could imagine Malachi being so. It was a nice feeling. But she told herself it was probably just hormones.

'Okay, Molly, we're all done,' she declared as she finished up. 'You were amazing.'

'Good enough for jelly sweets, Mummy?'

'I think maybe you were.' The young woman bent down to kiss her daughter tenderly.

'Right, just rest here while I go and fill in the discharge forms.' Saskia smiled, piling the detritus back into the cardboard bowl and slipping off her gloves.

Just a little longer, to check Molly was okay, and then they could leave. With a final word of congratulation to the brave girl, Saskia slipped out of the bay and back to the desk, to bring the case up on the screen.

Her colleague was on her within moments.

'When you've finished that one, Saskia, there's a nine-year-old in Bay Twelve, complaining of shoulder and back pain. Also caught in the explosion.'

'No problem,' Saskia confirmed.

It looked as if it was going to be a long night.

It was twenty-four hours before the last of the major incident casualties were cleared, either to various departments or home. There were a few stragglers with non-life-threatening injuries still left to be brought in by road, but most of the air ambulances had stopped bringing in critical cases a while ago. The road ambulance arrivals—along with the usual A&E walk-ins—could be dealt with by the new shift.

Her work was done, and Saskia was more relieved than she cared to admit.

Because the pains that had started in her abdomen earlier were still there. Still worrying her.

Her mobile pinged just as she was heading into the locker room to collect her clothes.

Malachi.

The urge to hear his voice suddenly overwhelmed her. Before she could talk herself out of it she swiped the screen and let her phone dial his number.

He picked it up almost instantly. 'Saskia?'

She stopped in the corridor, staring at her phone as her brain sifted through a dozen things to say, whilst her voice couldn't articulate a single one of them.

'Is everything all right, *zvyozdochka*?'

She bit her lip. What was she even doing, calling him?

'Saskia?' he barked into the silent line, almost making her jump into action.

'I'm here.'

'Are you all right?'

'No, I don't think so. I'm not sure.'

'I'm coming in.'

'I… No… Listen, I…' She was stalling.

'I'm coming in,' he repeated. 'Don't leave without me. Is the incident over?'

'It seems to be.'

'Then I'll bring the heli in again. There's so much debris out there the city will still be gridlocked. Besides, it's getting late and the air ambulance pilots will need to get the copters back to base before it goes dark. I'm closer. I can afford to fly that little bit later.'

She should say no. She shouldn't have even called him. They weren't a couple, as he'd pointed out earlier. Or had it been the day before? Her brain faltered. The emergency had gone on so long and time seemed to have merged into itself. She was so tired. Exhausted.

'Okay, I'll head up to the roof now.'

She glanced at the door to the bathroom. *Right after she checked that her worst fears hadn't come true.*

She was just changing her shoes when Anouk rounded the corner, walking straight into her. Without a word she stepped forward and hugged her tightly.

'I was so relieved when I heard you were safe.'

'Why wouldn't I be?' Anouk laughed. 'And never mind me—the hospital is practically buzzing with some gossip that you arrived by private helicopter?'

Saskia thrust her away, her eyes searching Anouk's. 'You haven't heard, then?' she demanded.

'Heard what?'

'That the explosion affected King's Boulevard?'

'That's us.' Anouk frowned.

'Yes. The whole area has been cordoned off until they can determine which buildings are structurally intact and which aren't. We can't go home.'

Anouk didn't answer and Saskia hugged her again. Though whether it was to make her friend feel better or herself, she couldn't quite be sure.

'At least we're both safe.'

'We should book a hotel, then…' Anouk looked dazed. 'I'll call now.'

Guilt jostled around Saskia's chest.

'Not for me.' She placed her hand over Anouk's to still her, even as she reached into her locker for her mobile. 'I'm… I have somewhere to be.'

'Where?'

The guilt swelled. And with it another sharp abdominal pain. It took everything she had not to wince. Not to let Anouk see. Not until she knew what was going on with her body, and not until she'd told Malachi first.

'I… I'm staying with Malachi,' she managed.

'With Malachi?'

Anouk frowned, peering at her a little too closely for Saskia's peace of mind. And then the unmistakable baritone of Sol Gunn, top neurosurgeon and Malachi's brother, came to her rescue.

'Saskia? Are you in here?'

And then he appeared in person, and all Saskia could wonder was whether he knew about her and his brother. If so, how *much* did he know?

But when he rounded the corner fully, his attention seemed distracted.

'Oh, Anouk…'

He paused for a fraction of a second before turning back to her. *Curious.*

'Mal says you need to get going, Saskia. His heli is on the roof and they want it cleared in case another emergency has to come in.'

'I'm going,' Saskia muttered, but Sol had already turned back to her friend, an intense expression clouding his face.

'If you're calling for a hotel, Anouk, you're too late. I heard a couple of guys complaining an hour ago that every hotel in the city is booked out. The cordon is quite extensive—lots of apartment blocks have been evacuated.'

'Great.'

Anouk gritted her teeth and Saskia couldn't bring herself to leave. If their apartment block was in the cordon then Anouk would have nowhere to go. Yet she could hardly invite her back to Malachi's; she didn't even know where she stood with him herself.

'You could find an on-call room,' she suggested hesitantly.

'I'm guessing they'll all be taken, too,' Sol told them. 'They're setting up temporary beds in community centres all around the place.'

'Oh…' Anouk's face fell, and Saskia couldn't help grabbing her friend's hand.

'I could speak to Malachi? See if you can come with us?'

'Or you could just stay with me,' Sol cut in quietly, firmly.

He didn't add to the sentence, but it hung there in the silence. Slowly, so slowly, the reason for the tension between Sol and Anouk dawned on her.

Could it really be…?

'Thanks,' Anouk managed stiffly, 'but I don't think it's a good idea.'

It was just too deliciously ironic to be true. Her and Malachi? Anouk and Sol?

'That's a great idea,' Saskia gushed, before Anouk could shut him down.

When was the last time Anouk had done anything crazy? Why not now?

'I'm sorry—I do have to go,' she muttered, squeezing Anouk's hand again, as if that could convey all the things she couldn't say to her friend in front of Sol.

'I don't understand, Sask?'

She wished, not for the first time, that she'd found a way to tell her friend about the baby. But this wasn't the time.

'It's complicated. I'll explain everything when I can.'

Then Saskia hurried out of the room, before she could say anything more to give herself away.

The cramps were stronger now, along with chest pain. Gripping the wall, Saskia made her way down the corridor and into the bathroom. She needed to know if she was losing the baby.

Slipping into the stall, she closed her eyes and sent a silent plea out into the ether.

No blood. Not even spotting. No sign that she was losing her baby. Thank goodness.

Saskia slumped against the wall with relief. A sob racked her. It was incredible that something she hadn't even thought about, let alone planned, should mean so much to her, and yet it did.

Which was why she needed to go to the maternity wing now, and make sure everything was all right.

Whatever the situation with Malachi, she wasn't going to shut him out of their lives. This was his baby, too, and whether he chose to be a part of it or not would have to be his choice. They were never going to have the kind of deep, passionate love her parents had shared, but that could only be a good thing when she thought about how they had ended up devastating her as a child. She should be pleased that Malachi wanted to be an active part of his child's life.

It was wrong to want to keep him at bay simply because she didn't think she could handle their physical attraction. Which meant that right now he had as much right to know what was happening with this pregnancy as she did.

Sucking in a deep breath, Saskia took her mobile out of her bag and, with shaking fingers, texted his number.

Malachi raced down the stairs to the maternity wing and battled not to let his world fall apart all around him.

How was it that a baby he hadn't even thought he wanted a few weeks ago was now the most important thing in his life?

He snatched open the door to the floor and glanced up and down the corridor, trying to find his bearings. *There.* Room 214… Room 216… He kept moving until he found the room number Saskia had texted him, knocked once and walked inside.

She was there alone, a bottle of water gripped with white-knuckle tightness.

'What's going on?' he demanded without preamble.

'Where's your helicopter?' She shot him a shocked, slightly dazed glance, peering around him as though she half expected it to be in the corridor behind him.

'Dealt with.' He just about swallowed his frustration. 'What's happening with you?'

She didn't look as though she'd heard him.

'You can't leave it on the roof. What if an emergency comes in and an air ambulance needs to land?'

'I didn't leave it on the helipad—it's dealt with. It's safe,' he managed. 'Now, tell me about *you*, Saskia.'

'Oh...she's gone to set up a scan,' Saskia blurted, sending his heart tumbling in a fast, wild freefall which he didn't think would ever end. 'Hence the water.'

Of course.

'Is something wrong with the baby?'

'No...maybe...probably not.' She struggled to speak. 'They think I was just having a panic attack. I had abdominal pains, chest pains, some trembling.'

'You have a stressful career and you just worked a major incident after a three-day shift,' he pointed out, trying to keep any hint of accusation out of his voice.

This wasn't about laying blame. It was about understanding what had happened to Saskia, and potentially to their baby, and why.

'Which is why they want to do the scan. Impact on the developing foetus isn't inevitable, but high anxiety could lead to reduced blood flow to the baby, which could result in low birth weight or premature labour.'

The words pounded down on him.

'Premature labour? That can't happen. So from now on do you need bed rest?' he demanded.

'Not bed rest, exactly,' she countered. 'But they may suggest some activity restrictions.'

A low sound rumbled in his chest. 'I need more than that, *zvyozdochka*. Tell me precisely what restrictions.'

'It's not definite yet,' she hedged.

'Saskia.'

The warning was clear, but still she blinked at him before capitulating.

'Fine. Light exercise is fine, but lifting heavy weights, housework, for the moment they're off limits.'

'Work?' he pushed.

'Let's see what the scan shows,' she countered shakily.

He knew he should let it go and give her some semblance of feeling that she was still in control.

But he couldn't.

'I can't imagine they left that open to interpretation when, as a doctor, you're constantly running around a hospital—a highly stressful environment.'

'Lots of pregnant women work.' She narrowed her eyes at him. 'Some even work in hospitals.'

'And they don't end up here,' he said trying to keep the dark, terrible thoughts at bay. 'Afraid for their baby.'

'We don't know anything yet,' Saskia repeated, but there was no strength to her words. Only thinly veiled fear. 'I can't just take the next five months off for a panic attack.'

He softened his voice, taking her hand. 'This is about the baby. *Our* baby. And your health. If it's about the money, I can cover any expenses.'

'It isn't about the money!' she cried, but she didn't try to pull her hand away. 'This is about letting down the hospital, my patients, my colleagues.'

A savage fury swept through him in that moment, but he couldn't reply. He couldn't even speak.

And then suddenly she shot him a desperate look.

'I don't even know if anything is wrong.'

It was like a fog lifting.

'You feel responsible for them,' he realised abruptly. It was a sensation that he knew only too well, and she didn't need him judging her or condemning her. She needed him to understand and take control.

'I…yes.'

'But this isn't about them. It's about you and it's about our child. And you won't be going through this alone.' Malachi dropped his voice. 'I *will* look after you, *zvyozdochka*.'

She dragged her eyes up to him, searching, imploring. And then she stopped and offered the briefest of nods, her fingers gripping his hand tightly, as though she was never going to let it go.

There was so much more to say. So many ways to reassure her. But at that moment Saskia's consultant returned and, after a brief introduction, led them to an available ultrasound room.

The same one they'd been in for that first scan. It almost felt like fate—if Malachi had ever believed in such things.

But this time the screen was kept turned away from him and Saskia as the checks were carried out, and when Saskia slid her hand back into his all he could do was hold on tightly.

He had no idea what to do with this ball of emotion churning inside him. So he just sat there and stared at the back of the screen, as if he could make everything all right just by sheer force of will.

When the consultant finally glanced up, the faintest smile on her lips, and clicked the sound on so that the baby's rapid constant heartbeat filled the room, it was as if a weight had been lifted.

Still, it felt like an age whilst the rest of the checks were conducted, and he had to sit there, feeling powerless and furious, whilst she prodded Saskia and asked her to move position several times. It felt like another eternity while they took measurements and checked organs.

He'd spent half his life learning to read people, honing the skill to perfection. But right now he couldn't read the consultant's neutral expression, and a part of him didn't even want to. The fact that there wasn't another smile, or any moment of engagement, told him everything.

All he could do was keep Saskia's cold hand nestled in his. The impending news was almost suffocating him, and nightmare scenarios were racing through his mind. He could only imagine the plethora of things that Saskia—a medical professional herself—could be imagining.

'So, the baby looks generally healthy, and it's growing,' the consultant began, showing them a couple of images she'd saved. 'However, there are a couple of areas of concern. The scan shows a potential clubbed foot—but, more concerning, it seems there is a mass on your baby's left foot and another smaller one on the left hand. Your baby's movements seemed to be a little restricted, however, I'd like to do some more rigorous scans before I draw any conclusions—'

'But it's consistent with ABS?' Saskia cut in. 'One professional to another?'

'I'm sorry, Saskia, but it's a working theory, yes.'

Malachi waited for them to elaborate, and when they didn't he spoke.

'ABS?'

'Amniotic Band Syndrome,' Saskia answered dully.

The consultant chimed in quickly. 'But we won't know for sure until we can get some clearer scans.'

'When will that be?' he demanded.

'There's another machine, a better one, but it's in use now. We could try in about half an hour,' she suggested. 'I just need you to keep drinking water, Saskia. That should help, too.'

Saskia grunted in what might have passed as acknowledgement. It only made him feel all the more helpless. There was nothing he could say or do to help right now, and he wasn't used to *not* being the person in the room people looked to in order to solve a problem.

Hell, he didn't know if *anyone* could solve this one.

CHAPTER NINE

'So IT'S DEFINITELY this Amniotic Band Syndrome?' Malachi gritted out, and Saskia turned to face him.

If she was feeling this numb, this out of her own body, then how must Malachi be feeling right now?

'Can you see those weblike lines on the image?' she managed jerkily.

'I'm the only non-doctor in this room,' he said pointedly.

'Right. Sorry. Yes...' her consultant cut in. 'Because it's Saskia, I forgot that you might not be following. So, ABS is caused by thin strands of the amniotic sac which have separated and are wrapping around parts of the baby.'

'But it's a fluid?' he frowned. 'Amniotic fluid. It's meant to *protect* the baby.'

Saskia shook her head, unable to speak. She'd had to pass bad news on to parents and guardians countless times, keeping level-headed in some incredibly high-pressure situations. But this time she was on the other side of the fence. She couldn't even begin to think straight, let alone make her voice form the words to explain.

'Think of it this way,' the consultant interjected gently. 'Two membranes form around the embryo to protect it during gestation, the amnion and the chorion—almost like one balloon being blown up inside another. In between the two is a sticky substance which allows these two membranes to fuse together, usually by week fourteen.'

'But in this case they haven't,' he stated flatly.

'Right—and sections of the amnion have broken away in long, fine strands. These strands can wrap around the foetus, entangling digits, limbs or other parts of the developing baby.'

'We're at seventeen weeks. Why wasn't this spotted earlier?' he demanded, and Saskia could read the fear and frustration in his voice.

It echoed her own.

She reached out her arm stiffly to touch his.

'The strands are so fine that they can be hard to spot on ultrasound, Malachi,' she whispered. 'A diagnosis is usually made by observing the birth defects caused by ABS.'

He turned his head to look at her, and for a moment they didn't feel like two strangers who had made a baby during a one-night stand. They felt like a unit. A team.

'Like these masses on the baby's left hand and foot?'

'Yes,' the consultant confirmed. 'And the club foot we've seen today.'

Malachi turned back to face the woman, away from Saskia. There was no need for Saskia to feel the loss so acutely. Yet she did.

'We…we were intimate,' he bit out at length. 'Last week…'

'No,' the woman shook her head firmly. 'We don't always know what causes chorioamniotic separation, but usually—that is, in about eighty-five percent of cases—it is invasive foetal surgery. Either way, it won't have been sexual intimacy.'

He still looked rigid, as if he wasn't convinced that he wasn't somehow to blame. Saskia wanted to say something but she didn't know what. She didn't know how.

'So what now?' he demanded abruptly.

Something surged through Saskia. She couldn't have said what it was, but it lent her strength suddenly.

'I want surgery.'

'That's what I would advise,' the consultant agreed. 'Though we need to discuss the risks.'

'I know the risks.'

Galvanised, Saskia leaned forward, as though that would somehow better convey her desire.

'But, depending on how tightly those bands are wrapped around my baby's foot and hand, they could end up amputating them in the womb.'

'So they are going to perform the surgery on you *now*?' Malachi growled. 'I realise this is something you can do—operate on babies in the womb—but this is *my* baby. *Our* baby. Talk me through it. I need to understand.'

'There was something else I noted on the scans which we need to discuss,' the consultant said.

Saskia blinked. 'Something else?'

'At one point during the scan your baby moved. It appeared as though part of it moved out of the amniotic cavity.'

'PROM?' She echoed in disbelief, staring at the consultant.

'Right…'

'What is PROM?' he demanded.

Almost robotically, Saskia turned to face Malachi. 'Premature rupture of the membranes. It means that a purely fetoscopic release of the amniotic bands will be impossible.'

'However, we do have the option of surgery in a CO_2-filled uterus,' the consultant added quickly. 'A laparotomy with fetoscopic release of the bands, along with a partial amnionectomy, likely through two uterine ports, with CO_2 as distention.'

'So you'll cut the bands, remove them from the baby's limbs, then what?' she asked.

'We'll cut them away and remove them from your uterus, as well as any amnion.'

'What about Saskia and the baby?' Malachi cut in. 'How do you monitor them to make sure they're both okay?'

'Normal cardiac function for Saskia will be monitored by heart rate, mitral regurgitation and motion of the heart.' The consultant smiled encouragingly. 'The baby's cardiac function will be intermittently monitored by a separate paediatric cardiologist, using an ultrasound probe placed directly into the uterus to produce an image of the baby's heart.'

'And once the surgery is complete?' Saskia asked.

'We'll remove the gas and replace it with warmed saline, remove the ports and suture the uterine openings. Then, once we've returned the uterus to the abdomen, we'll close up.'

'When will I be able to take her home?' Malachi cut in, and the concern in his voice touched her.

'We won't know until we do the scan,' her colleague advised.

'But what are the possibilities?' he pushed.

'It could be anything from a couple of days to bed rest and a hospital stay for the remainder of the pregnancy—we just don't know. But so long as the recovery is smooth you should be discharged within seventy-two hours—although we'll want to do follow-up scans on a weekly basis.'

'Right…' Saskia managed weakly, and her colleague excused herself to confirm the soonest slot for surgery.

She could live with that. She could live with anything so long as it meant that her baby was going to be all right.

'We will get through this.' Malachi pulled her to him as they sat alone in the room. 'Us and our baby.'

She leaned gratefully against his chest, letting the warmth of his body radiate strength into her and breathing in the woodsy scent that was essentially Malachi.

'Thank you,' she whispered.

'For what?'

'For being here. For…caring.'

His hands moved to her shoulders and he drew her away so he could look at her. 'Did you expect anything less, *zvyozdochka*? It is my baby, too.'

'I know,' she acknowledged. 'And I'm sorry if you thought I was trying to exclude you. I suppose I just wanted what…what my parents had, without allowing for the fact that we are different. Our circumstances are different.'

'I can't give you what you want,' he murmured. 'You want a dramatic, passionate marriage like your parents', but…that isn't who I am.'

'I know,' she began, but then the words stopped in her throat.

Did she know that? Really?

She'd thought she'd known. Only the longer she was with Malachi and the more she saw of his kindness, the more she was beginning to question her childhood. Or, at least, the version that was in her head. She talked about their *great love affair* as if that somehow explained their actions, and how it had ultimately impacted on her—the daughter they were meant to have loved.

Yet now—because of Malachi—she was forced to consider what love really looked like. Volatile, passionate, but ultimately destructive, as they had been? Or was Malachi's quiet, strong steadfastness how love should really look?

But for his child, that baby that she was carrying, she reminded herself hastily. *Not for her.* She couldn't afford to forget that distinction.

'It *will* be who you are. One day. When you find the right person,' she told him softly, swallowing hard and forcing an upbeat tone to try and keep the regret out of her voice. 'Clearly that person isn't me, but no matter what you will be welcome in your child's life. I will never stop you being a part of that. We'll work out a system that works for both for us, and for the baby.'

She'd thought it was the right thing to say. The balanced thing. But Malachi stiffened against her, placing his hands at her shoulders and pulling her from him.

'Am I to thank you for your benevolence?'

His voice abraded her skin. She could feel his repressed anger through every hair follicle on her arms and neck. But she still didn't know what she'd said wrong.

'Even now, through all of this, you're trying to square everything away. Tying me up like some kind of loose end.'

'That's not what I'm doing,' she denied.

'Oh, yes, *zvyozdochka*, that's exactly what you're doing,' he seethed. 'You're frightened about handing over the fate of this baby to the surgeons—your colleagues—so you're trying to control everything else instead.'

'No…' She shook her head, but she couldn't deny that he had introduced an element of doubt.

Hadn't Anouk always teased her for being a micromanager? And Andy had been less forgiving, calling her a control freak, and a couple of other less palatable names.

'But I warn you that I won't be boxed away like that,' Malachi continued. 'And if you try you will soon find the terms I am capable of exacting in response.'

'What kind of terms?' she asked, despite herself.

'You don't want to know,' he said ominously.

She ought to feel afraid. Instead she felt something else. *Exhilaration?*

'Actually, I rather think I do.' She lifted her head boldly, her gaze colliding with his and holding it.

The tension stretched between them.

'Not now,' he said abruptly.

But she shook her head. 'Precisely now.'

His black look would have had any number of other people—male and female—cowering, but suddenly Saskia realised that she didn't feel intimidated or afraid when it came to Malachi. She never had.

She'd thought it was only a physical attraction they shared, but the truth was that she'd always felt safe with this man. Secure. Especially now.

The revelation knocked the air from her lungs.

So what did that even mean?

But then there was no time to ponder it, because he was speaking, and it occurred to her that he was doing what she'd asked and telling her what she'd wanted to know.

'Our baby is fragile. Too fragile to be put at any more risk than necessary.'

'I know...' She murmured her agreement.

'And, whilst I understand you love your career as a doctor, there is no way I can believe this high-pressure environment is going to be good for this pregnancy.'

She knew that, too. She'd been thinking about little else since those first pains had started during the hectic rush of the major incident.

'So what are you saying?'

'I'm saying that after the surgery I will be taking you away somewhere so you can rest and you and our baby will be taken care of. I know you love your job—God knows I understand that better than most—but you will not rush back to it and risk yourself or our baby.'

'Taking me where?'

'It will depend how your recovery goes. But if it's smooth then I have a place in Italy. I intend to take you there.'

'Italy?' she echoed weakly.

'It's quiet, and safe, and you can rest there without the worries of everyday life. I will ensure that you have dedicated specialists on hand, and your health and that of our baby will be of paramount importance.'

Vaguely she thought she ought to be objecting. Instead all she could ask was, 'Will you be there, too?'

'I have no intention of being anywhere else,' he gritted out.

Something a little too close to relief trickled through her, but she did her best to conceal it. There was no need for him to find out how dependent upon him she was starting to feel. He was spooked enough at the idea of emotional intimacy with her.

'Okay.'

'And we *will* marry, Saskia. For the baby's sake. I can assure you of that.'

The worst of it was that she had to bite her tongue not to simply agree to that, too. Even if he *was* doing it for the wrong reasons, part of her couldn't help but feel it was the right solution.

At least she would have him in her life. And after the last few days she was beginning to find it harder and harder to envisage a future with her baby and without Malachi closely entwined in it.

'We'll see,' she managed instead, acutely aware that this time it wasn't an outright refusal.

His eyes held hers and, try as she might, she couldn't seem to drag her gaze away. The stayed like that for longer than she could tell—an eternity, perhaps—until they heard the consultant returning and he finally dropped his hands.

She felt the loss acutely.

CHAPTER TEN

THE HELICOPTER TOUCHED down in the grounds of a fourteenth-century *castello*, complete with square tower, just as fresh flakes of snow were falling on the Tuscan mountains, which rose majestically around them. It was as though Malachi himself had commanded it.

The surgery a week ago had been a success, and the baby—a baby girl—appeared to be thriving. The fact that, although she had lost some amniotic fluid during the surgery, the levels had risen again very quickly post-surgery made Saskia feel as though her body was at least now doing what it was supposed to do. Although she hadn't voiced that particular dark thought to anyone—not even Malachi.

The strands which had been entangling the baby had all been cut, and already the swelling in the left foot had begun to reduce—although she would need Z-plasty for the grooves postnatally. The slight clubbing would also be corrected post-birth, with a brace, but to all intents and purposes she now seemed to be healthy and developing well.

And through it all Malachi had barely left her side. He'd made her feel cared for. Supported. It was little wonder that she felt more of a bond with him than ever, even if she knew it was hopeless and not a little foolhardy.

It was why now, as they descended the stairs from the

helicopter, Saskia concentrated on taking in the breath-taking views.

If she hadn't been pregnant she would have been thrilled to be coming here and taking advantage of the skiing on offer, from the lava domes of Amiata to the ski slopes of Abetone. She knew from the few photos she'd seen around Malachi's apartment that he went glacial abseiling and scaling frozen waterfalls in his rare downtime. Now she realised that it must be here that he came to get away from it all.

What did it mean that he'd invited her into this private bolthole of his? Or was she reading too much into it?

She was still mulling it over as Malachi steered her around the helicopter and she finally turned towards the castle itself. It had taken a slow drive to the airfield, his private jet to Italy, and a helicopter ride to get here, but now that she had finally arrived she knew it was worth it.

It stole the very air from her lungs.

The place was magnificent. Stone walls with battlements, sloping bases and arched windows made it impossible for her not to imagine the frescoed walls and coffered ceilings which must surely lie inside. And the building's beauty was matched only by the oaks and cypresses and ilex shrubs which framed it.

'It's a wonder you ever come back to London,' she murmured to him, wondering why it felt so instantly comfortable, familiar to her.

Like a *home*.

It was almost a relief that her words were whipped away, unheard, by the roar of the heli.

Together they made their way across the lawns, glistening white under a thin veil of snow, to the housekeeper, who was waiting at the door.

'I told you to stay inside in the warmth, Imelda,' Malachi admonished, and Saskia was shocked to see the little, rotund older lady, with a faint West Country accent, throwing her arms around him and kissing him soundly on each cheek.

'I stayed at the door, didn't I?' she teased. 'It's so good to have you back, Malachi.' Then she turned with a warm smile. 'You must be Saskia—welcome to the *castello*. We're all just so delighted to meet the future Mrs Gunn.'

Saskia froze, but the woman seemed too caught up in the moment to notice.

'For pity's sake, bring the girl inside—she'll be catching her death. Shall I have hot drinks brought to you? The fires have been lit throughout.'

'Lovely, Imelda, thank you,' Malachi agreed. 'We shall be in the library, I think.'

'You have an English housekeeper?'

'I've known Imelda for almost fifteen years now. I bought this place with my first million, and her late husband was the builder who oversaw much of the renovation work.'

'You didn't do it yourself, then?' she teased.

'I did what I could.' Malachi shrugged. 'But I was still working a lot in the UK back then.'

She waited for him to elaborate further, but he didn't, instead ushering her through long criss-crossing corridors until they stepped through a door into what was clearly the library.

Old leather-bound tomes upon old leather-bound tomes lay behind pretty wrought-iron-framed doors. Wall-to-wall and floor-to-ceiling, save for the gargantuan stone fireplace with its timber mantelshelf which took up a third of one wall, and the two leaded windows, complete with deep sides and cushioned window seats, which nestled into the other.

As they stood in silence, the only noise was the welcoming crackle of the fire as the shadows began to dance around the room. It was only too easy for Saskia to imagine whiling away the rest of her pregnancy here.

He ushered her into the room, taking such tender care of her, before crossing the floor to throw himself into a generous wingback chair, whilst she weighed up the merits of the rest of the seating.

The window seats would afford her a good view, but the wingback chair that matched Malachi's was closer to that inviting fire. So she made her way over and there they sat, in companionable silence, until Imelda brought their drinks, along with some homemade biscuits, still warm from the oven. The older woman fussed over her, ensuring she was comfortable and pain-free, all the while bossing Malachi about and making certain that he was taking care of Saskia.

'She treats you more like a son than an employer,' Saskia said, smiling, when Imelda left the room at last, finally satisfied that her new patient was as comfortable as she could possibly be.

'In many ways she's the mother I never had,' Malachi answered—then stopped sharply, as though he hadn't intended to say anything at all.

'She obviously cares about you a great deal,' she ventured, then waited, hoping that he would say more.

Her heart flip-flopped madly. She knew he had set up the Care to Play charity because she'd met him at the ball, and judging by his close relationship with families like Izzy and Michelle she knew he was more than just financially invested. But Malachi, like his brother, Sol, was such a closed book that those few details were the sum of her knowledge.

It was all Saskia could do not to fall on this new scrap of information as if it was an oasis in the desert and she was a dying woman. But inside she was aching to know more. To understand what made Malachi who he was. To learn what drove him on.

Clearly he didn't intend to elaborate, and she tried not to feel hurt that, even after everything they'd been through with their own little miracle, he still didn't trust her enough to want to open up to her.

It ought to be the wake-up call she needed to remember to keep her guard up where Malachi Gunn was concerned. It was futile to keep wanting—imagining—more with him. In his eyes, their agreement was nothing more than the extension of a business agreement.

She forced herself to take a mouthful of the delicious biscuit. Then another. Anything but give in to the temptation to ask him more about himself and risk him shutting down on her.

But eventually the silence got to her. 'How long are you going to stay?' Saskia spoke at last, when they were alone again.

Really, after Imelda's comments about *the future Mrs Gunn*, there was only one question Saskia wanted to ask, but she feared it would start an argument and she didn't want that. Not when they'd only just arrived.

'I'm here to make sure you and the baby recuperate.'

Not exactly the answer she had been looking for.

'What about work?' she tried instead. 'How will you keep up to date?'

'What makes you think I'll be working?'

'Because you're a workaholic. You'll go crazy being here for too long and not overseeing your business.'

His lips pulled into a crooked smile, as if he was conceding her point. 'I can email…do video conferences.'

'It's beautiful here. I can see why you would enjoy bringing lots of people to see it.'

'Are you fishing, Saskia?' he asked mildly. 'Because I can tell you it isn't one of your more attractive qualities.'

Had she been fishing? She hadn't intended to, but she supposed it was a possibility. Was she here because she was the mother of his baby—someone special—or did he bring many of his 'dates'—for want of a better term—to his private *castello*?

She discreetly released her grip on the arms of her chair, but it was too much to hope Malachi wouldn't notice. His sharp eyes missed nothing. But she was surprised when he answered.

'I don't make it a habit of bringing people here, no. In fact, you are the only person, other than Sol, I have ever brought here. But you shouldn't read too much into that.'

Her heart jolted. She fought to remain passive. To remind herself that it wasn't really about her at all.

'Because I'm pregnant with your child?' she asserted quietly.

He didn't reply but he did incline his head, if only a fraction. She told herself she wasn't disappointed.

'Is that why you brought me here, Malachi? Because of the baby and so that I could rest? Or to further the notion that you had back in the UK that I would marry you?'

He eyed her neutrally, giving nothing away. It caused a thread of irritation to weave its way through her.

'It seems daft to pretend it isn't part of your plan,' she asserted, 'since it was practically the first thing Imelda mentioned when I stepped off that helicopter.'

'I am not *pretending* anything,' he replied, his voice calm. 'I simply don't believe this is the best time to be discussing matters which so…unsettled you last time, Saskia. As you just said yourself, you're supposed to be resting. Stress-free.'

'You've whisked me thousands of miles away, first by private plane and then by helicopter…' She cocked her head to one side. 'And now I'm sitting in a beautiful room, in front of a glorious fire, replete. I hardly think it's the most agitating of circumstances. When do you expect this marriage of ours to take place?'

He looked momentarily irritated, but then smoothed it away quickly. Oddly, the fact that he could master his emotions so easily only peeved her all the more.

'When, Malachi?'

He met her gaze, his eyebrows cocked slightly, as though she was a half-irritating, half-amusing nuisance.

'We will be married by the end of the week.'

Not a suggestion or a possibility, but a statement.

Saskia shuffled in her chair, incensed. 'Is that what you think?'

'You're getting worked up,' he said calmly.

'Do you wonder?' she seethed. 'So, tell me this—what is this *marriage* idea of yours going to look like? How do you suppose it will work?'

'I think this conversation is best left for another day.'

'I don't,' she objected. 'I mean, are you suggesting staying married until the baby is born, or staying married beyond that? If so, then how long? Is it to be a marriage in name only, or are you still suggesting we enjoy certain... shall we say...*benefits*?'

'So many questions...' He clicked his tongue softly. 'Yet you didn't think to ask a single one of them before boarding my plane. Almost as if a part of you wanted to come with me regardless.'

She wrinkled her nose, hating the way he seemed to be able to read into her mind and see her own questions which lay there, jumbled within.

If she'd sought to shame him, she realised she'd misjudged him. He didn't bristle, or take the bait. He merely stretched out his legs all the more, giving the illusion that he didn't have a care in the world.

She felt like launching something at him, but she only had a soft cushion. And, anyway, what good would that do?

'You are not the only one who has spent every waking moment worrying about our baby, *zvyozdochka*.'

His tone was like velvet, but she heard the hard steel beneath it.

'But that isn't what this is about, is it? The simple truth is that you don't find the idea of marriage to me as objectionable as you'd like to make out. Or maybe it's more that you no longer find it objectionable after what you've been through the past week. Tell me why that is.'

Could he hear the sound of her blood rushing around her body? Because to her it was practically deafening. She couldn't tell him that it was because she feared she was falling for him. That his care and loyalty these past few weeks had made her feel more secure than Andy had done in all their years together.

'I never actually said I found it objectionable,' she prevaricated.

'I believe your precise words were "passion is overrated". You were very certain that it shouldn't be a business proposition, and then you proceeded to assert that, "We had a one-night stand. It's over." And that you didn't even want me "like that" any more.'

'Have you got a photographic memory or something?' she demanded sarcastically, in an effort to hide how shaken she felt.

She didn't really expect him to respond. But it seemed that Malachi revelled in catching her off guard.

'Eidetic, if we're being accurate.' He folded his arms across his chest. A move which only served to emphasis the broadness of his shoulders. 'But that's by the by. I'm more interested in how, moments after that bold little statement of yours, you ended up half-naked on my bed whilst I used my mouth to make you scream. I'm sure you remember?'

Oh, yes, she remembered, all right. All too gloriously

vividly. Indeed, it was galling how her mouth threatened to dry up just at the mere memory.

She sent silent thanks for the fact that she was post-op. She might not have had the will to resist him if they'd been standing here under different circumstances.

'We slept together. Again.' She lifted her shoulders. 'But I still don't know what your intentions are for any marriage between us.'

'My *intentions*?' He barked out a sound which might have been a laugh, but she knew wasn't. 'You make it sound so old-fashioned and formal. Like you're still waiting for some romantic declaration of love and commitment which I can't give you. An echo of that profound passion your parents had.'

'And you still scoff at me for that,' she bristled, heat creeping into her tone as she tried to quash the sense of unease which was creeping up on her.

Malachi couldn't know the truth about her parents. She didn't want his sympathy or his pity. She couldn't bear it.

'But just because you never experienced parents who loved one another it doesn't mean you can disparage others who have. And just because you don't believe in it, it doesn't mean it can't exist.'

'You don't know what you're talking about.' His face hardened instantly.

With a thrill, Saskia realised she had somehow got under his skin. She didn't know how, but if this was her one chance then she wasn't about to back down.

She softened her tone until it was almost breezily dismissive. 'I think I know enough.'

'You're wrong.'

'What is there to know?' She made herself shrug. 'You're a tortured man, damaged by his past and a childhood in which he was never loved. It's all terribly clichéd. And now you keep yourself emotionally unavailable and you mock those who might want something more from a relationship.'

'You're walking a very thin line, *zvyozdochka*,' warned Malachi. 'You don't have a clue what you're talking about.'

'Maybe. Maybe not. But whose fault is that?'

'So you think by provoking me I'll tell you what you want to know about me?'

'I think you'll either tell me or you won't. Whether I support you or provoke you won't change anything. I simply decided I didn't want to sit back and let you disparage *my* memories just because you don't understand them.'

'You misunderstand.' His eyes bored into her, practically pinning her to the seat. 'I understand exactly what your memories are. I just don't agree with the way you interpret them.'

'Sorry?'

'You're holding on to this great love affair between your parents and you're searching for the same thing. But you'll never find it because you aren't as selfish and as cruel as they were.'

'My parents were *not* selfish and cruel,' she denied vehemently, because if she was forceful enough then maybe she could make it true. 'They loved each other fiercely.'

'And what about you?' he pushed.

'Of course they loved me.'

He was pushing her dangerously close to the edge, and she felt as though she was clinging on with the tops of her fingers. But she couldn't let him know that. She wouldn't let him see.

'They adored me!' she cried, emotion threatening to clog her throat.

Malachi opened his mouth. Then closed it. His face was shuttered again, and a fresh wave of frustration powered through her.

'So that's it?' she challenged. 'You push so far and then you back away when things start to get hot?'

'I don't think this is a conversation that will get us anywhere,' he replied smoothly. 'Especially not when you're supposed to be recuperating. So, if you've quite finished making up objections, I suggest I show you to your suite, so you can clean up after the flight and rest, even sleep if you wish.'

He stretched out his long, muscular legs and stood with all the grace and power of some glossy big cat in its natural habitat. And equally as lethal.

When he reached out to offer her his hand she briefly considered refusing his help and getting to her feet by herself. But the truth was that between the flight, the operation, and the baby scare, she was feeling far more drained than she'd realised.

Still, she plastered on a bright smile. 'I'm fine.'

Malachi looked unimpressed. 'Your doctor may not have put you on bed rest, but if you don't do what she said in terms of taking it easy, don't think I won't put you in bed myself.'

Saskia swallowed, trying not to focus on the X-rated images which had instantly slipped into her brain at his words, or on the memories of what had happened between them every other time they'd been in the vicinity of a bed.

Malachi had paused, too, as though he was fighting a similar battle.

She followed him through the house, back to the imposing hallway, up the wide, sweeping staircase and along the first-floor corridor, in silence.

Nevertheless, she was sure she didn't imagine that his voice was fractionally hoarser when he spoke again.

'This is your suite.' He stopped outside a set of heavy walnut double doors. 'Dinner will be ready at seven. I'll wait for you in the hallway.'

Saskia was torn between the elegant formality and the fear that it made things too clinical—too detached—between them.

'I'm not entirely sure I'll have anything appropriate to wear. I only brought a small case.' She cast him a vaguely accusatory glare. 'You didn't exactly give me much of a chance to pack.'

'I seriously doubt you had much to choose from, anyway,' he eyed her shrewdly. 'Or do you already have a full maternity wardrobe?'

Her hand flew to her rounded belly on cue. He had a point.

'Fortunately,' he continued easily, 'I had the foresight to have some clothes delivered once I decided we would be coming here. Imelda had them put away in your suite.'

'I don't know whether to feel flattered or insulted.' Her voice was clipped.

'I suggest you just accept it for what it is,' suggested Malachi. 'Rather than overthinking everything you come across.'

Before she could answer he turned away and sauntered up the corridor, hands in pockets. Possibly to his own suite, which was no doubt located as far away from hers as it was possible to get, she decided.

Which was just fine.

CHAPTER ELEVEN

SASKIA STARED AROUND her suite, slightly agog. It had been decades since she'd been part of Hollywood royalty, but she still recalled the beauty of the places she'd lived and the hotels in which she'd stayed.

Malachi's *castello* beat every one of those hands-down.

The first room she'd entered was, she realised after rather a long moment, a living space. Her own private living space. The suite was already generous, but the high ceilings, with their ornate friezes, made it feel positively expansive. Carved wooden shutters framed huge leaded glass windows, and two oversized plush couches sat delicately in the space.

Saskia crossed the room to the next set of double doors, opening them almost tentatively. Another high-ceilinged ornate space lay beyond, only in the middle of this one sat an enormous four-poster bed—arguably as big as her entire bedroom back in her apartment. Underfloor heating discreetly warmed the space, whilst the stunning parquet made her itch to walk across it in her bare feet.

If it hadn't been for her post-op state she might even have twirled around the room like a ballerina. It was such a beautiful, magical space.

She opened a door on what presumably had to be the bathroom, only to find it was a walk-in closet about the size of her kitchen, full of carelessly beautiful clothes that her fingers ached to touch.

Then, finally, she found it. The bathroom. A glorious limestone affair with practically a spa-sized tub for a bath and a waterfall for a shower.

It was enough to make Saskia wish she never had to leave.

Except, she reminded herself fiercely, *for the fact that it belongs to Malachi.*

Wandering in, she found some pins to put her hair up, let her clothes lie where they dropped, and allowed the shower to call to her. It was a revival such as she had never had before. Not just sluicing away the drudge of the journey, but also the crud of the last few weeks.

She washed it all down the long-grid gutter as though it had never existed. Including the last conversation with Malachi, which had seemed to go completely the wrong way. Like a giant step back after all the shuffling forward they had managed together this past week.

It wasn't how she'd wanted it to go. She certainly hadn't wanted to argue…

Saskia had no idea how long she stood there, letting the water pound down over her body, and letting her mind clear of some of its recent obstacles. She only knew that by the time she emerged she felt lighter, happier than she had in a while.

She padded softly through to the bedroom, climbed up onto the high bed and sank back into the downy pillows, intending to stay there for only a few minutes.

She fell into a deep, dreamless sleep within seconds.

It might have helped if she hadn't looked quite so devastating, Malachi thought several hours later, as Saskia walked down the stairs in a figure-hugging maternity dress which showed off the growing bump—*his baby*—perfectly. It also made something thicken and tighten within him.

But, more importantly, she looked well. As though she was recovering more from the operation with every single hour that passed.

It was odd how terrified he'd been this past week. Strange how he hadn't noticed this…this *emotion* which had been building up inside him ever since Saskia had told him that she was pregnant until he'd had to face the fear that she could be about to lose the baby.

That had been the moment he'd realised that he was attached. That he wanted the child—and Saskia—in his life.

Selfish, maybe, since he could never be the kind of man, or husband, she clearly wanted. And this afternoon's conversation should have been a warning. The thing to make him reconsider this ludicrous idea of marriage.

There was no avoiding the fact that Saskia wanted the impossible. She wanted a magical love affair, to be madly in love—and that was the one thing he couldn't offer her.

He didn't even believe in it.

He'd spent the past few hours stalking the *castello* in a grim mood. He had never intended the argument between them to get so heated. He shouldn't have let her get under his skin the way she had. But that was what Saskia had been doing ever since their first encounter at the charity ball all those months ago.

Feisty, and funny, and sexy. He'd been hooked from the start.

Even if he hadn't overheard her telling that silly nurse that she was pregnant, he would have found an excuse to slip back into her life. *Him.* The man who was famous for never getting too close to anyone.

Now he would be tied to Saskia, and the baby she was carrying, for the rest of their lives—and it didn't fill him with horror in any way, even though he knew it should.

But that still didn't mean he was able to spout all the poetry and words of love that she seemed to have decided went hand-in-glove with marriage.

He couldn't make those grand romantic gestures which meant nothing unless you treated the other person with consideration and respect every single day.

No, he couldn't give her the fancy words, but he could offer her loyalty. Commitment. Honour. He would care for their child, and for her, for the rest of his life. He knew from experience that that was far more precious than an intense, passionate fire which would eventually fade and die.

It was only a shame that Saskia didn't see it the same way. Yet. But Malachi was confident that, in time, she would come to appreciate the value in it.

'You look beautiful,' he murmured, holding out his arm as she reached the bottom few steps, and he wondered if he'd ever be able to let go.

Her head snapped up. She eyed him suspiciously, as if looking for a trap, but he simply led her to the dining room, where the table was laid out just for them.

It was time.

It was only when Saskia saw the ring box that she realised this dinner was a proposal. Malachi was going to ask her the question she'd spent months telling herself she *didn't* dream of him asking.

Dimly, she was aware that he was saying the words, but it was as though she was on her own operating table, succumbing to the effects of an anaesthetic: aware of what was going on, but not really present in it any longer.

He was asking her to marry him. And, although almost every fibre of her hungered to say *yes*, the logical part of her brain knew she had to demur.

What choice did she really have?

Her body actually shook with the effort of holding itself

together. Like the harmonic tremors you felt in the ground before a volcano erupted. Only Saskia wasn't about to flare up. Instead she was terrified of breaking down. Especially in front of Malachi.

When he finally finished speaking she forced herself to look up from the ring and into his gaze, and suddenly it was all worse.

So much worse.

She tried to suck a breath into her constricted chest. She'd been here once before, when she'd been ready to accept his proposal—such as it was—only for him to turn around and rescind it.

And it had hurt far more than it had had any right to.

More than her parents' betrayal. More than Andy's betrayal.

Her feeling of rejection had terrified her. Because if he could hurt her that much in a matter of months, what would it be like to marry the man and submit to the illusion that they were more than just co-parents to a baby conceived on a one-night stand?

So Saskia opened her mouth and uttered the only objection she could think of, under the circumstances.

'Why?'

He blinked.

'Why?' he echoed, and the hint of disbelief was almost her undoing.

'Why do you want to marry me, Malachi?'

And she was ashamed that it was less a stalling tactic and more a plea. As if a part of her really believed he would say the words she needed to hear.

'Give me a real reason.'

For a moment he seemed at a loss for words. And then he regrouped.

'This conversation again, *zvyozdochka*?' He managed

to inject as much of a yawn into his voice as possible without actually yawning. 'It is becoming boring.'

'Maybe for you,' she shot back, determined to appear undaunted. 'But since I haven't had a straight answer out of you yet, I can't agree.'

'You're the mother of my unborn baby, Saskia.' His voice was low and even, if a little surprised. 'How much more "real" a reason do you need?'

She didn't know if it was the words or the easy control in Malachi's voice which cut through her most sharply. Surely if he felt anything towards her whatsoever there would be at least a hint of emotion in his words?

'I want…*more*,' she whispered at length.

'More?'

His gaze darkened, his forehead knitting together. She could almost feel the coldness beginning to roll off him.

'Like meaningless declarations of love, perhaps?'

'Why do they have to be meaningless?' Saskia asked, not sure whether she meant it as a plea or an accusation.

'Because they're just words,' he growled. 'They bring nothing to the table.'

'They do for me.'

Before she realised what she was doing she was moving her hand across the table. Stopping it halfway between the two of them. He stared at it for a moment, as if actually trying to work out what she was doing. But he didn't reach his own hand out. Instead he placed his fingers together and dropped his hands to his lap.

'Not if they came from me.'

He shook his head, and the words were so harsh, so threaded with pain, that it almost broke Saskia apart.

'I doubt I even have the capacity for love.'

'I think you do.'

Again he shook his head, and when he spoke, his voice

was so raw and rough she was sure she could feel it actually abrading her.

'No. And even if I did it would be so fractured, so tainted, that it would do more harm to the recipient than anything else.'

'No...'

There had to be more. They hadn't spent the past few weeks getting closer just for nothing. Surely?

'Love from someone like me wouldn't be a gift, *zvyozdochka*. It would be a curse.'

'You make it sound like you're a victim of your past, but the truth is that you're a liar.'

She had no idea where the strength had come from, but Saskia seized it with both hands and let it drag her along. Because it was easier to bear than the pain.

'I'd prefer it if you didn't complicate things further by proposing marriage when all I am to you is a complication.'

'We aren't a couple. We had a one-night stand—uncharacteristic for both of us, but there you have it—and now you're carrying my child. What else would you call it, *zvyozdochka*?'

Saskia opened her mouth to reply, but the words didn't come. Or at least the words that did come sounded distasteful on her tongue, and she couldn't bring herself to utter them.

Malachi had a point. Their baby wasn't planned, and the circumstances weren't enviable, which made it a complication. The difference was that, to her, it was an unexpectedly joyous complication, whilst to Malachi it was apparently on a par with the irritations he experienced in business every day.

His solution was typically practical and logical. But it wasn't emotional. And that was what she wanted it to be more than anything else.

Without warning, all the air seemed to whoosh out of

her. It was all she could do to hold her head up and not deflate right there in front of Malachi.

'We had passion,' she whispered.

His face hardened, the angular lines of his jaw suddenly becoming harsher. Almost cutting.

'That was about sex. Not love.'

'How do you know it isn't both?' She knew she was clutching at hope but she couldn't stop herself. 'If you won't ever give love a chance?'

'I don't believe in it. It's an illusion,' he refuted fiercely. 'Passion comes with a price, and it's always one that's too high. I won't do that to you, *or* our child.'

'Malachi—'

'I told you that from the start,' he cut in, refusing to listen to her.

It was like a howl inside her. Long and low, tugging at her very soul. She'd laid it out there—laid herself out there—and he didn't want her. He never had.

'You're right.' How her voice managed to sound so calm, so neutral, was a small miracle. 'You told me from the start that you couldn't offer me more than your duty. Your responsibility. But I thought there was more to us than that. Or at least I wanted to believe that there was.'

'Because you're carrying around some non-existent romantic notion based on what you want to remember about what your parents had. You compare everything to that. And there's no way anything you find will ever match up. It's impossible.'

'This is what you were saying this afternoon,' she ground out. 'Telling me that my parents didn't care enough when I *remember* how much they loved me.'

'But not enough for them to stick around.'

'They were in a car crash. They couldn't help that.'

'*Zvyozdochka*, they were arguing. I looked into it after that night in my apartment, when you refused to see sense and just marry me. They were having another of their infamous fights which blazed almost as brightly as their so-called great love. They were drunk, and fighting, and people had heard them threatening to harm each other. And then your father apparently ran into a tree on a straight, well-lit stretch of road, with no other cars in sight. Your mother, supposedly unable to bear the pain of his death, took an accidental overdose.'

'Accidental!' she cried, anguished. 'You just said it yourself. They were both *accidents*.'

'No, *zvyozdochka*, they were covered up and sold to the grieving public as accidents. But I think we both know the truth.'

'You're wrong!' She shook her head, but the shaking that had started from her toes and was working its way up her body told her differently.

'I don't think so,' he said quietly. She might have thought even sadly. 'You know exactly what happened and so do I. Yet you've put them on a pedestal and sold it to yourself as some grand love affair, when the truth is that you're using it as some impossible standard you know you can never achieve because it's a way for you to stay emotionally out of reach.'

'That's insane,' she muttered.

Only she had a feeling it made awful, terrible sense. How had she never realised this before? Or had she, on some level?

'You say you want what they had, but you don't, *zvyozdochka*. You're not capable of it because you aren't as selfish as them. You could never do to your child what they did to you. You could never leave our daughter.'

'That makes no sense...' whispered Saskia.

'It does—and you know it does.'

She didn't want to answer. She didn't want to engage with him. But she couldn't help herself.

'I think you're attacking me because it's easier than looking at yourself,' she challenged, not caring that her breathing was shallow and fast, or that she sounded as though she'd run a marathon. 'You're pretending you don't feel something I know you feel.'

'You're mistaken.'

'You and I had an arrangement that was all about practicality. We didn't need to…to sleep together, but we did. Because we *wanted* to. You might tell yourself that you aren't capable of love, but you are.'

He glared at her for a long moment, and Saskia realised she couldn't even breathe.

Until, at last, he spoke. 'Then perhaps I'm just not capable of loving *you*.'

Rejection lodged in her throat, thick and bitter-tasting. Saskia struggled to swallow it down.

'Perhaps not,' she rasped out. 'But I don't think it's that. And I don't think you do, either.'

'All I can offer you is everything I've already promised. I will be the best father anyone could possibly be to this child. And I will be the best provider. I will take of my family the way I have always done. You'll want for nothing—I can promise you that. But I can't promise you love, or happy-ever-afters. I can't pretend this is some great love story. I am who I am, Saskia.'

'You're so much more than you think,' Saskia whispered. 'But if I can't make you see that then perhaps I'm wrong for you.'

'Perhaps you are,' he gritted out, thrusting his chair back abruptly and standing. 'But I will not see our child suffer for our mistakes. We will marry, and we will provide a united front for this child.'

Malachi had no idea what had just happened. Or, more to the point, what he had just allowed to happen.

His head told him that he had done the right thing, but his chest was tight and angry. Full of a churning sense of remorse. Both for what he'd said and the way he'd spoken to her.

But it was for the best, he told himself furiously.

Everything he'd said was the truth. He couldn't be the man she wanted him to be—the kind of man who professed love—he could only be who he was and hope that was enough.

Evidently it wasn't enough for Saskia.

She wanted the words. The flowers. The poetry. All the things he couldn't—*wouldn't?*—give her.

He stalked the grounds of his *castello*, glaring into the darkness to see if perhaps the night sky had fallen in. After all, what other reason could there be for what was going on here?

His head was constantly full of thoughts of Saskia. And it wasn't helped by the idea of her soft, wet body against him, on him, around him. Even at work the meatiest of contracts hadn't been able to distract him from her.

He scowled at the sky even harder—but, no, it was most certainly up where it should be. What was more, it positively twinkled with the prettiest stars, free of urban light pollution, almost as if it were entertained by his uncharacteristic reverie.

It was galling.

He could take off for a night run, go a few rounds in the *castello*'s well-appointed gym, or swim lap after lap until his body ached. But he suspected it would do little to numb his brain from the effect Saskia was having on him.

How was it that she could make him feel powerful and powerless all at the same time?

This wasn't him. This wasn't the untouchable man he'd turned himself into once he'd finally dragged himself and Sol from the bowels of a childhood caring for their junkie mother.

He'd sworn to himself all those years ago that he would never let another person get under his skin like that. Aside from his brother, he'd vowed he would never permit anyone to venture this far into his life. A wife, a family, children. It was never going to be for him. He'd never wanted it.

Yet here Saskia was. Pregnant.

He had no name for this heavy, full feeling which was building in his chest with every passing day, but it didn't seem to be regret. Or resentment.

In someone else he might have thought it was…*joy*. Or happiness. Or even love. But this wasn't someone else—this was him. And he didn't feel those things. He never had. The closest he'd ever come to feeling love was for his kid brother, but it wasn't the kind of unfettered, whole-hearted emotion that normal people seemed to feel.

He wouldn't know how to feel that way if he tried.

With a growl of frustration Malachi spun away from the lake, in which he could suddenly see his own reflection all too clearly, bright in the moonlight. He didn't think he liked what he saw—and stalked back to his room.

He was hauling off his constricting shirt even as he pushed through the door to his suite. Minutes later he was beating a punching bag in the corner of the gym as though he could mete out punishment for his every last frustration and knock his self-doubt into submission. Banish the emotions he hadn't felt since he was an eight-year-old boy, running errands for the local gang just to get enough money to put coins in the electricity meter and a scant bit of food on the table for five-year-old Sol.

He had no idea how long he stayed in the gym. After the boxing he took a long run on the treadmill, imagining in his head that he was actually running through the vineyards outside, which lay all around this stunning valley. Finally he dived into the still waters of the indoor pool and swam one hundred exhausting lengths, then a hundred more, and then another for good measure.

When he finally—*finally*—allowed himself to stop, to breathe, to look up, it was to see Saskia curled up on the window seat of the suite he had given her, a book in her hand.

But she wasn't reading. She was watching him.

He could feel it.

Her eyes caressed his skin as surely as if it had been her hands themselves. How he wished that were the case. He wanted her. He *hungered* for her.

And he did not hunger. Ever.

Yet now it rolled through him like the thunder for which this valley was so well known at this time of year. Raw and uncontrollable.

It was all Malachi could do to keep himself in the water. To turn his back on the woman who affected him in such a primal way. To spin his body in the pool and cut through the water for another hundred lengths.

Because if he hadn't he feared he would have hauled his body out and gone to find her.

CHAPTER TWELVE

'WHAT IS THE matter with you, *bratik*?' Malachi glared balefully across his office to where Sol was helping himself to Malachi's freshly ground coffee and pastries, as he did every time he ventured across town to MIG International's offices.

Malachi told himself he'd returned to the UK because he was needed at work. He knew the truth wasn't anything like that. Still, he comforted himself with the assurance that he'd left Saskia in good hands, with the team of medical experts in Italy.

It wasn't helping him to concentrate.

'What?' Sol cocked an eyebrow, before striding over to flop in a comfortable chair.

'You're full of the joys of spring,' he grumbled.

'And *you're* grouchy and on edge.' Sol eyed him shrewdly. 'More so than usual, that is. Though I wouldn't have thought that was possible.'

'Funny.'

'Thanks.'

'Idiot.' Sol shrugged, inhaling a couple of pastries, whole.

It wasn't that he wasn't happy to see his brother, Malachi decided, it was more that right now he would have preferred to be alone, to throw himself into the work he'd missed whilst he'd been in Italy with Saskia.

Or alone to stew, a cynical voice needled.

The past week had been hell. Like some kind of torture he hadn't known existed. He saw Saskia everywhere he went. He could hear her voice, gently teasing him about all the things he did. Like some kind of haunting such as he had never believed in.

But then, he hadn't believed in a lot of things before Saskia had come along.

This intense, yearning sensation which barrelled around his chest, for one thing. Guilt, probably. Remorse. What else would have been mushrooming inside him for so long now?

He didn't know and he didn't care.

He was so lost in his own thoughts that he answered his brother's next question on autopilot, not really paying attention to what was said until Sol's next statement jarred him.

'You and I have always said that we aren't built for commitment or love...' his brother began slowly. 'That everything *she* put us through destroyed that in us. But what if we're wrong, Mal? What if you and I have *always* been capable of love?'

'This discussion is over,' Malachi ground out.

It was as if his brother was echoing everything that had been going on in Italy, and right now it was the last conversation Malachi wanted to have with anyone. But still he didn't move.

Did his brother know about Saskia?

Did the entire hospital?

Sol shifted, looking oddly uncomfortable.

'There's always been love between you and me,' he said, as though he was repeating someone else's words and wasn't quite sure if he was doing it correctly. 'It may be a different kind of love, but it's love nonetheless.'

'Where did *those* pearls of wisdom come from?' Malachi tried to snort—but, inexplicably, he lacked the scorn that would normally have come so easily.

Sol paused, seeming to consider what to say. 'I don't know,' he concluded at last.

And, despite his own worries, Malachi couldn't help worrying about his kid brother, the way he always had as the big brother. Hadn't he been mentioning Saskia's flat-mate a lot recently…?

'A woman?'

'No…' denied Sol unconvincingly. Then, 'Maybe…'

'Anouk?'

'Are you going to take the proverbial?' He glowered at Malachi, clearly expecting the usual ribbing. But for once Malachi didn't feel like it.

'Maybe another time.'

Sol narrowed his eyes thoughtfully and Malachi pretended to ignore him.

'Yeah, then,' Sol admitted. 'Anouk.'

It was enough to finally get his attention. If Sol, the perennial playboy, could be falling for a woman, it had to say something.

'Something's going on between you?'

'I don't know. Maybe.'

Malachi knew he should back away, but he couldn't. It was too coincidental.

'Serious?'

Sol hesitated. 'Maybe. She's the reason I came here today, at least.'

His brother studied him, cool and perceptive. 'What do you need?' Malachi asked at length.

'You have people who can track stuff down for you, right?'

Malachi inclined his head.

'I want you to track down all you can on this man.' Sol flicked though his phone and found the notepad before spinning it across the desk to him. 'He died thirteen years ago, but he used to live there.'

Wordlessly Malachi read the screen and made a note of the information. He didn't even question it. If Sol needed it that was his business. Besides, if he kept his nose out of his brother's life maybe Sol would return the favour.

'Do you think you can do this without hurting her, Sol?' Malachi heard himself saying the words.

'Sorry?'

'Settling down with Anouk. Do you think you can do that?'

He knew it came across as a challenge, but he hadn't intended it to. All he wanted was to understand. To be sure it wasn't just himself making a mistake.

'I'm not settling down,' Sol denied.

'Then why do you care? I mean, I get that you care about your patients, and the kids at the centre. But I've never known you to care about a woman enough to ask for my help.'

'She's...different.'

Malachi knew his brother was choosing his words carefully. Almost too carefully.

'But that doesn't mean there's anything serious between us.'

'Right...'

Malachi pushed his chair back abruptly and stood up, moving to the window to look out. Not at anything in particular—just as a way to escape the confines of the room, which suddenly felt a little stifling.

Not that it made any difference. Wherever he looked Saskia was back, plaguing his every thought.

Still, it caught him out when Sol suddenly spoke.

'Who is she, Mal?'

Malachi swung around but said nothing. He had no idea what he *could* say. He didn't even know what he thought.

Still, he didn't like the way his brother was watching him a little too shrewdly. As if he knew what was going on.

'I think I prefer the Sol who just beds women and moves on,' Malachi bit out. 'You're acting like a lost puppy—Anouk's lost puppy, to be exact.'

'Sod off,' Sol said casually, before standing up and sauntering over to the sideboard for more pastries. 'I'm no one's puppy.'

'Not usually, no.' Malachi shrugged. 'You're usually fending them off with a stick.'

'What? Puppies?' Sol quipped.

'Puppies, women, little old ladies…' Malachi folded his arms over his chest and shrugged. 'But I've never seen you look at anyone the way I saw you look at that one the night of the gala.'

'Her name's Anouk,' Sol corrected instinctively, realising too late that he'd been baited.

Interesting, Malachi considered.

'And I didn't look at her in any particularly special way.'

Malachi said nothing.

'No clever quip?' Sol demanded, when he clearly couldn't stand the heavy silence any longer.

'I told you—not this time.'

He could hardly batter his kid brother about Anouk when he had left Saskia at his *castello*, four months pregnant, in Imelda's care.

What the hell was he even *doing* here in the UK?

'What's going on, Mal?' Sol asked suddenly.

'Nothing.'

'You're being cagey.'

'Not really,' Mal dismissed casually. Arguably a little too casually. 'No more so than you, anyway.'

'You're kidding, right?' Sol shook his head in disbelief.

'Not particularly.'

'Fine.' Leaning back on the sideboard, Sol eyed his

brother. 'Time to tell me something I don't know, Mal. If you've got the balls for it.'

And just like that they were two kids again, and Sol was pressing him about where he'd been that first time he'd done a job for the Mullen brothers.

It was so random, and yet it felt so appropriate. And before he knew it Mal heard himself reply.

'I always thought a wife, a family, wasn't for us. Not after everything with *her*.'

Sol didn't answer, but Mal knew they both understood he was talking about their mother.

'I always thought I'd done that bit. I'd endured that responsibility. I never wanted to do it again.'

'But now...?' Sol prompted.

'Lately... I don't know.' Malachi swung around from the window almost angrily. 'Forget it. I'm just... Forget I said anything.'

In over two decades they hadn't talked about any of this. About feelings. The Gunn brothers had never bought into the caring/sharing thing. Now Malachi wondered if they'd been wrong to bottle things up.

'Are we capable of it, do you think, Mal?' asked Sol.

He frowned. 'Of what?'

'Of...love.'

It was so out of the blue that Mal couldn't even begin to order his thoughts.

'You *love* Anouk?'

Sol scoffed, but there was an expression in his eyes that had him convinced his brother wasn't just kidding around.

'Don't be stupid,' Sol said. 'I'm not saying that. It's just hypothetical.'

He didn't believe his brother—but that wasn't his main issue.

'Hypothetically, I don't even know if we have that capacity,' Malachi gritted out unexpectedly. 'But maybe the question should be, do we deserve it? More pertinently, does *any* woman deserve to be subjected to our love, *bratik*? Whatever that is.'

Sol stared at him blankly for an age.

'So…you and Saskia?'

'I don't wish to discuss it.' Malachi cut him off harshly.

And then Sol shocked him by placing his hands on Malachi's desk and addressing him urgently.

'But you need to. Right here, right now. Our mother ruined our childhood. It's time we both decided whether we're going to let her ruin our futures, too.'

Saskia knew he was back in Italy the moment she walked through the gym door the next morning. It was something in the air. The way the hairs on her arms lifted as if in anticipation.

She wondered when he'd returned from the UK. And why. The last few nights had been horrendous, tossing and turning and wondering if Malachi was even going to bother coming back.

Her stomach still churned with the idea that he might not. She'd have been trapped with no way out.

So why was it that she didn't feel remotely hemmed-in when Mal was around?

He was the one who had insisted on this sham marriage, on her moving into his apartment, on them forging some kind of relationship, if only for the sake of their unborn baby.

But you didn't have to agree, pointed out a calm, rational voice which sounded altogether too much like her best friend, Anouk.

Shoving it aside, Saskia threw open the door to the gym and marched boldly inside.

She stopped.

Swallowed.

Tried not to stare.

Knowing Malachi was in here all hours, running, swimming, keeping out of her way, had been one thing. The sight of him now, training with a Mu ren Zhuang—all graceful power, his body in complete control of each perfectly landed strike, his bare chest glistening with a sheen of sweat—was enough to steal the breath from her lungs.

He didn't appear to have spotted her, and she knew she should probably alert him to her presence, but all she could do was stand and watch. Mesmerised.

Time passed, but Saskia wasn't even aware of it. Only of the rhythmic, elegant pace of his movements. The hypnotic nature of his training.

And then he placed a plastic water bottle on the top of the training post, kicked the post with one leg to catapult the bottle into the air, then spun around and kicked it with the other foot.

It came thundering through the air towards her, and before she could stop herself Saskia let out a surprised squeak and launched herself sideways.

Malachi was across the room in an instant. 'What are you doing in here?'

'Looking for you,' she retorted, tilting her chin up in defiance at his vaguely accusatory tone. 'You're back, then.'

'Evidence would support that observation,' he returned.

Any other woman might have balked at the dangerous edge to his voice. Saskia decided that she didn't care. Or, at least, what did she have to lose?

'I wouldn't have been surprised if you'd left me here. In the capable hands of Imelda, of course.'

For a moment she thought he wasn't going to answer. So she wasn't prepared when that dark, impenetrable expression eased and he nodded at her.

'Perhaps I was going to. But I thought better of it.'

For a split second she faltered, but then caught herself.

If she didn't take advantage of this moment she would be a fool. Because he could shut her out at any moment and then where would she be?

Her heart thundered.

'Why?' she asked.

'You once asked me to tell you something about myself. Something that wasn't carefully crafted by MIG International's PR machine.'

The roaring in her ears, which had started slowly the moment she'd walked into the gym, became almost deafening. He couldn't be opening up to her—that would be too much to hope for.

'You refused,' she managed instead.

'So now I'm telling you.'

He shrugged, but the dismissive gesture didn't fool her for a moment.

'My parents had a similar sort of ridiculous grand love affair to what your parents had. Passion and drama with a sprinkling of volatility, just like your parents—though it ended rather differently. The first few years of my life were fine. Better than fine. We didn't have much money, but we were a family.'

Her heart was already twisting painfully, folding in on itself even before he'd finished.

'And then my father died. He was a prize fighter, and one night he sustained a head injury. A bleed on the brain.'

'How old were you?' she asked, shocked.

'I was five and Sol was two.'

Her brain began to turn. 'Is that why your brother chose neurosurgery?'

'Maybe.' He lifted his shoulders again. 'Anyway, the same night my mother began her descent into drugs. It was slow at first, but it gathered momentum quickly. By the time I was eight I was caring for her and for my brother full-time.'

'You were a young carer?' she realised, wondering why she hadn't seen it before. How had she been so blind? 'That's why you set up Care to Play?'

And it was why he was insisting on taking responsibility for her and for their baby. It was in Malachi's make-up. It was who he was. The fact that it was *her* carrying his baby had no bearing on it whatsoever. She was nothing special to him. She never would be. She was just the woman who had fallen pregnant with his baby.

It was all finally beginning to make sense.

CHAPTER THIRTEEN

THEY WERE MARRIED a few days later, in the quaint chapel in the grounds of the *castello*. Saskia wore a luxurious cashmere dress of whisper-grey, her hair coiled artfully on her head and a handpicked bouquet of calla lilies in her hands, and her heart beat a tattoo on the inside of her chest.

She recited her vows in front of him, trying not to think too much about the words themselves, or how they related to her. And certainly trying not to listen too closely to the promises Malachi was making, in a voice so deep and clear that it had every hair on her body standing to attention.

What would it feel like to have this man standing in front of her and saying those words because he truly loved her and wanted to be with her? And not just because she was the mother of his unborn child?

She could imagine that if she listened, if she'd imagined those words truly were for her, then she would be swept up in the magic of it. She already very nearly had been.

Malachi had a way of looking at her that made her feel cherished. Wanted. *Loved.* She had to keep reminding herself that it was the baby he felt all those emotions for. Not her.

It wasn't real.

But she wanted it to be. Far more than she had any right to do.

When it was time to kiss the bride she expected some brief peck on the cheek, in line with the way he'd kept away from her these last few weeks. So when he gathered her to him, his hand gently smoothing a stray lock of hair from her face, then pressed his lips to hers in a way which held such unspoken emotion and promise, she was sure she'd crack apart right then and there.

She wanted him with an intensity that threatened to overwhelm her.

She *loved* him.

There was no other word for it. And it hurt beyond reason that he didn't feel the same way. That he would never feel that way.

No wonder she'd been setting herself impossible standards—it had protected her heart. Andy's betrayal hadn't even come close to causing her the pain she felt knowing that she loved the one man who could never love her back.

And after they'd returned to the *castello*, and the meal that Imelda had prepared for them with such love, she was ready when Malachi withdrew some time later, closeting himself in his study to throw himself into work—and keep away from her.

Saskia was sitting in front of the fire in her favourite room in the *castello*. The library. She'd read so many books over the past few weeks and tried out every chair, every window seat, every couch in the room. Suddenly, Malachi strode through the doors, seeming to fill the room with white heat in an instant.

She lowered the book onto her lap carefully and folded her hands, trying not to let them shake with the delicious surprise of it. He had been avoiding her for the last fortnight, holed up in his office, furiously working on some new business deal or other. She was certain that, had it not been for the snowstorms which had battered the region, he would have gone weeks ago, leaving her alone in the *castello* but for the kind and bustling Imelda.

'The doctor has told me that you're doing much better,' he announced, without preamble.

Saskia looked up at him. She'd been begging him for a month now to leave the *castello*, but he'd refused to provide a vehicle and told her the roads were too treacherous for her to go alone. He'd made his concern for her health and that of their baby clear.

Which only made her wonder all the more about what Malachi wanted now.

Was he suggesting that she would be able to return home to the UK? Back to London? Possibly even back to work at the hospital? They would surely welcome her. In all likelihood they'd be short of staff.

'Much better. It seems this rest has been just what I needed. The baby is fine and developing well.'

He dipped his head curtly. 'I thought you might be tired of being cooped up indoors.'

This *was* a surprise.

'I am—as I'm sure I've told you many times,' she agreed. 'Very tired of it.'

'Then make sure you have warm clothes and a decent coat. We're heading out.'

It took her a moment to gather her skittering thoughts. 'Where?'

'You'll see.'

Before she could ask any more questions he spun on his heel and marched straight back out of the library.

For two weeks he had practically ignored her presence here in the *castello*. Did he really think that he could click his fingers now and she would go running?

Well, he could just think again.

She told herself that her racing heart was crossness, not anticipation.

Ten minutes later, the door opened again.

'Since you didn't appear to be moving, I took the liberty of bringing you a thick jumper and your coat. You look warm enough otherwise.'

Saskia stared at him. 'You went into my room? You went through my clothes?'

And her outrage had nothing to do with the fact that in those drawers lurked the laciest scraps of material, which she still didn't even understand why she'd packed.

It was as if a traitorous part of her had imagined a stay in Malachi's *castello* would lead to more...*intimate* pursuits.

'You appeared to need the assistance.' He raised one eyebrow unapologetically. 'Perhaps the doctor was mistaken when he thought you were better.'

She had the vague impression that she was baring her teeth at him. But it was either that or crumple with shame. 'You had no right,' she breathed.

'What kind of a husband would I be if I didn't help the mother of my unborn baby?'

'And here was I thinking that you'd been avoiding me these past couple of weeks—since our wedding that no one seems to know about. Are you hiding me away out of shame?'

Shockingly, Malachi flinched, as if she had scored a direct hit. As though he felt guilty for it.

He regrouped quickly. 'I was trying to be considerate by affording you space.'

'Is that really what you were doing, Malachi?' she asked softly.

And then she seemed to score an even heavier hit as his gaze locked with hers.

His lips pressed into a thin, vaguely appalled line. 'Put your coat on,' he commanded at last. 'We're leaving.'

Then, once again, he exited the room, this time leaving her to scurry behind him.

'Are you serious?'

Saskia stopped at the doors of the *castello*, staring down the steps to the horse-drawn sleigh below. The storms had abated and the late-afternoon winter sun was out, bouncing and shining off the snow. A true wonderland.

'I thought a sleigh ride through the valley might be a nice way for you to get out and get some fresh air.'

'A sleigh ride?'

'Tonight is a celebration and they put on a fireworks display as part of Tuscany's many winter fire festivals.'

A sleigh ride and fireworks? Under other circumstances, it might have even sounded romantic. Still, it would be a glorious way for her to get out. Aside from the brief walks snatched in between blustery snowfalls, she felt as though she'd been cooped up indoors for ever.

But with Malachi?

Pressed up against him in the back of the sleigh, under that blanket she could see covering the back seat? Was that really a good idea?

'With you?'

'That was the idea.' His mouth twitched upwards.

Her head screamed *No!* Yet the thrill that rippled through her body cried *Why not?* And in the end it was her body that won out.

Saskia descended the stone steps as gracefully as she could, pretending it didn't sear right through her when she took his proffered hand and allowed him to help her into the sleigh. She feigned nonchalance when he climbed up behind her, settling down so closely that she was certain the emotions raging inside her were going to cause her entire body to implode with tension.

And then he put his arm around her and drew her into him, and it was like a thousand tiny detonations going off inside her chest.

'So, you told me you've always wanted to visit the Amiata?' he said. 'What do you know about it?'

'I know it's an extinct volcano, and also one of the highest mountains in Tuscany. And I know it has lava domes rather than a volcanic crater.'

'Did you know that its last recorded volcanic activity was between two hundred and three hundred thousand years ago?' he asked, his voice rumbling low around her. 'And that it also puts the *hot* into the hot springs of Tuscany?'

And elsewhere, if she was being honest.

'I did know that, actually. I understand that the water which filters deep down comes into contact with the magma and then trickles its way up through crevices in the Earth's crust.'

It was all she could do to keep her head focussed on the conversation and not the feel of Malachi's body, all heat and steel, against hers.

'Some of it trickles,' he concurred. 'But some of it gushes up at over five hundred litres per second, like the thermal baths at Saturnia.'

'I've always wanted to visit them!' Saskia gasped, unable to stop herself.

'Maybe we can. One day. When you aren't pregnant.'

One day?

Something danced through her at the idea of Malachi thinking into the future, even as logic told her that she was a fool for reading too much into such a throwaway comment.

'So,' she forced a light, even merry note into her voice, 'tell me more about these fire festivals you mentioned before.'

'You've never heard about them?'

'I haven't, as it happens.'

It was as though the moment of openness had created a spark of connection. A strange current seemed to weave around them, even as Saskia berated herself for her foolishness.

'There are fire festivals throughout Tuscany all year round. There are torchlight—or Fiaccolata—festivals, bonfires, fireworks, and candlelight or paper lantern festivals where kids use peashooters to try to set fire to the coloured lanterns.'

'So is that where we're going now?'

'Not tonight,' he laughed, and it should surely worry her that the sound made her whole body heat up, like a shot of the strongest 192-proof Spirytus.

'Rificolona is in September, in Florence,' he explained. 'Tonight is a traditional bonfire festival. A symbolic reminder of an ancient rivalry between two neighbourhoods in the village. There will be stalls, and games, and a small fireworks display and each side competes to have the biggest and best bonfire.'

'And what does the winner receive?'

She felt drawn in already. Something about the passion in Malachi's voice made her realise that this was more than just a festival to him. This was where he loved to be. This was 'home'.

'The reward isn't something you can touch, or take home to display on a mantelshelf.' He smiled. 'It's far more than that. The winning neighbourhood will have the most successful year in terms of health, of happiness, of love.'

'Oh.'

'Last year, the winners were the south side neighbourhood,' Malachi said gruffly. 'The following month two young couples who had each had failed IVF treatment, and who had both given up hope for babies of their own, fell pregnant within a week of each other. A couple of months ago the village welcomed healthy, happy Sofia Lombardi and Marco Alfonsi.'

'Oh,' Saskia managed, her throat suddenly inexplicably thick. Full. 'It sounds…like something worth building the best bonfire for.'

'Yes. I believe it does.'

Perhaps it was the twilight that started to fall around them shortly after their journey began. Maybe it was the pretty swinging lanterns on the sleigh and the soft jingling of the bells. Possibly it was the magic of the horse-drawn ride itself. Whatever it was, Saskia found herself relaxing into the moment, letting her body ease against Malachi's as he told her the names of each mountain in the range, how the nature reserve in the valley was one of over one hundred in the Tuscany area, and which of the buildings made up part of the Medici villas.

He was knowledgeable and witty, sharing anecdotes and unusual facts with her to make the sleigh ride all the more interesting. She couldn't help but wonder what marriage— *real* marriage—to this man might be like. He would certainly make learning fun for any child…

For *their* child.

By the time an hour was over her head was a jumble of conflicting emotions, and she barely realised they were heading back towards the local village, which she had longed to visit every time she'd looked out of her window and down the valley.

The fireworks were starting, and she was just settling back to enjoy them when a scream and a shout went up. Before Saskia knew what was happening, Malachi had withdrawn his arm from around her and was vaulting down off the sleigh. She began to throw the blanket off herself.

'What are you doing?' he demanded.

'Coming with you. If someone has been injured then I'm the best person to be there, don't you think?'

'No, I *don't* think,' he barked. 'Stay where you are! That isn't a request, Saskia. I'll be back in a moment.'

Then he was gone, racing into the melee with all the speed and power of a hundred-metre sprinter.

She hesitated, thought twice, then jumped down and followed him at an altogether slower pace.

The reason for the shout became clear quite quickly. A young boy, wanting to get in on the thrill of the night, had tried to set off his own firework—only for it to go off when he had still been too close.

There was someone running towards the young boy with a bucket of ice, and without thinking Saskia reacted. She grabbed a couple of bottles of water from a nearby food stand and started to run.

'No, wait. Not ice. Um…*non usare il ghiaccio.*' She hurried across the field, aware that Malachi had spun around and was now right beside her, translating in fast, possibly flawless, Italian.

'I told you to wait in the sleigh,' he snapped.

'And I told *you* that if there was a medical emergency then I was better off coming with you,' she replied smoothly. 'But I know you're only concerned, so I'll forgive you trying to boss me around.'

He hauled off his coat and threw it around her shoulders, growling, but somehow it only made her smile, and she felt a warmth seeping through her despite the cold night air.

'Tell them ice can damage tissues and increase the risk of infection. They're better off with cool running water.'

Malachi duly translated, and Saskia wasn't sure if it

was her instructions or merely his presence which had them instantly obeying.

She reached the casualty—a young boy likely around ten years old.

'Can I look?' She smiled gently. *'Posso...guardare?'*

The burn was on his forearm, quite large and already red and swelling, and she threw one bottle of water to Malachi to open whilst she opened the other and began pouring it over his wound. But it was the boy's pale, cold skin and rapid, shallow breathing which concerned her.

'Come ti chiami?'

'Andreas,' a young, worried-looking girl answered. 'His name is Andreas. I am Giulia...*sorella*? Sister?'

'His sister, yes,' Saskia smiled. *'Ciao*, Giulia, I'm here to take care of your brother.'

'Grazie.'

*'E...tuoi...*your parents...are they here?' She cast an apologetic glance at Malachi as she reverted to English, her limited grasp of Italian spent.

He translated quickly, only for Giulia to shake her head and begin speaking in Italian too fast for Saskia even to begin to understand. Then the girl got up and pushed through the crowd.

'There's only their mother. She's working in the town tonight—Giulia is going to try to get hold of her now.'

'Andreas is showing signs of shock,' she murmured to Malachi. 'He really needs to get to hospital. Can you carry him into that house over there? We must keep his wound under running water, but we also need to get him on his back and elevate his legs, to increase blood flow to his head and heart.'

Even as Malachi scooped the boy up, translating her instructions in that calm, firm way of his, Saskia began emptying another bottle of water over the boy's arm, moving his clothing out of the way after ensuring nothing was stuck to the wound.

The owner of the house ran ahead, flicking all the lights on and holding doors open, and a small crowd flanked them, murmuring with concern but apparently happy to follow Saskia's instructions.

Before long the boy was lying on the floor in the bathroom, his arm under the cool flow from a handheld showerhead, his legs elevated by a small upturned laundry basket, his body covered with a blanket.

'How long does he need to stay like this?' asked Malachi.

'I'll check it after ten minutes or so. I could probably use some cling film to cover the burn. Something that will keep it clear of infection but isn't fluffy.'

'So not cotton wool?' He eyed the bag that had been handed to him by the homeowner.

'No—exactly,' Saskia confirmed. 'But if it comes to it we can tip out the cotton balls and use the bag itself. I'd just prefer something off a roll, so I know it's really clean.'

'I'll go and ask what they have. You'll be okay?'

'We'll be fine.' She turned to the little boy. '*Bene*, Andreas?'

He nodded stiffly, already looking a little less clammy.

She sat with him, keeping him under close observation even as the villagers, following her instructions as relayed via Malachi, kept talking to the young lad and soothing him.

It felt like only seconds since he'd left for the supplies she'd suggested, but already he was back, and she had to admit that his improvisation of a fresh roll of freezer bags was well chosen.

'I brought a variety of painkillers, too. I wasn't sure what was best.'

Saskia quickly sifted through them. 'These or these,' she confirmed. 'Not those.'

Malachi relayed the information to the homeowner before turning back to her.

'The ambulance is nearly here. It will take him to the local clinic, eight miles away, so I think it's best you do whatever you think needs doing before we transfer him.'

'Thanks.' Saskia nodded, his trust in her gloriously buoying. 'Can you take this whilst I wrap his arm?'

They worked well together, a surprisingly good team. Malachi seemed intuitive, anticipating what she would need next, and he chatted to the boy to keep him happy about what was going on.

By the time they'd finished, and Andreas had been safely transferred to the ambulance, he looked much more comfortable and Saskia knew she had been accepted by the community.

Then, as she slipped Malachi's coat off her shoulders because he must be cold, she heard their gasps and realised they hadn't known she was pregnant. Suddenly they were the centre of attention again, with everyone rushing to congratulate them—congratulate Malachi.

A thrill ran through Saskia at the way he reacted—as though they were a real couple. So much so that she almost even fooled herself.

For a moment she wondered why she was holding out for some great passion. Why she was pretending she believed in the shining Hollywood example of her parents' great love affair. Especially when she knew the dark, cruel truth.

Maybe Malachi was right. Maybe what they had—chemistry and sexual passion, with a healthy dose of mutual respect—was enough.

Perhaps when they got back to the castle she ought to tell him.

* * *

'Thank you,' she whispered quietly, as he helped her down from the sleigh and walked with her over the grass to the *castello*.

'What? For today?'

'For today…' She tilted her head. 'And for the last few months. I know you've only been trying to help and I haven't made things easier.'

'No, you haven't,' he agreed, but there was no heat to his words. 'Why is that, Saskia?'

'I don't know,' she admitted. 'Perhaps I thought I wanted my child to have more than just two people who married because they thought it was the right thing to do.'

'And there's something wrong with doing the right thing?'

'I don't know. I think I wanted us to know love, and warmth, and *family*. The things the world believes I had. The things you never had. And, more than that, Malachi, I think *I* needed to have that. I wanted more than just a marriage of convenience. I guess I'd had enough of my parents, or Andy, or whoever and I just wanted to have someone who really *wanted* to be with me.'

She stopped, her chest aching as she thought about her parents.

'Actually, scratch that. I want someone who *has* to be with me. Who can't breathe without me. Who can't breathe without our baby. Who doesn't *want* to breathe without us.'

'I told you—that's a movie screen fantasy,' he bit out. 'That doesn't exist.'

'Maybe it doesn't. But, then again, maybe you're wrong and it does exist,' she countered softly, glancing down at her belly as she laid one protective hand over it. 'I think it might do, even if it isn't what I've been pretending to myself it is. Even if what my parents had wasn't it after all.'

* * *

He wasn't sure what he was doing. One moment he was trying to clench his fingers, just so that he didn't give in to the itch to reach for her again. The next he was kissing her.

His hands cupped her face as he practically drank her in, as if she was the most intoxicating thing he'd ever tasted.

Perhaps she was. But he didn't care. He didn't want to stop.

He might have kissed her for hours. Days. Exploring her, reacquainting himself with her and delighting in her. Even when they finally surfaced he found he couldn't let her go, and she sighed a deep shuddery breath, her lips still brushing his cheek.

'What are you doing, Malachi?'

He wasn't sure he even knew. 'You accused me of being controlled, reserved, and you told me you didn't want that.'

'So…' She paused. 'This is you being…impulsive?'

'Yes.'

He dropped another kiss on her shoulder and felt another quiver cascade through her.

'You being reckless?'

'Indeed.'

Another kiss. Another tremor.

'You being…unsuppressed?'

'It *was*,' he growled wryly. And he lamented the loss of the kiss even as his voice vibrated through her. 'Until *you* decided to overanalyse it.'

'I apologise!' Saskia chuckled softly. 'I just—'

'That's enough. Stop talking.' He cut her off, ruthlessly and effectively, his mouth claiming hers. Stamping his authority all over her.

And he found that Saskia didn't seem to mind a bit.

She gave herself up to his touch. She matched it greedy

stroke for greedy stroke. She tasted magnificent, better even than he remembered, and he revelled in every second of it. She slid her arms around his neck and he wasn't sure whether he hauled her closer or whether she pressed herself to him.

Possibly both.

And then he slid one hard, lean thigh between her legs, pressing against her core, making her rock against him. But when she did he found he couldn't get close enough. Her burgeoning bump was in the way.

And judging by the small sound of surprise she made, Saskia had felt it, too.

Instantly, Malachi set her away.

'No, I'm fine—I'm fine,' she protested, moving closer.

'Are you?'

He looked at her with concern until she defused the situation with a laugh.

'I'm not *that* big. It was just unexpected, that's all. I'm not used to it.'

'Really?'

Resisting her attempt to step closer again, he kept his hands on her hips, holding her away.

Suddenly he saw unease lance through her.

'Or is it that you don't find me appealing like this?' she asked.

'Say that again?' he said.

His expression darkened but she didn't know what that meant. Had she been reading him incorrectly all this time? Had he made himself absent these last two weeks not because he didn't want to give in to the attraction they'd once shared, but because he no longer found her attractive?

Saskia hated herself. She didn't consider herself catwalk-model-esque, but nor had she ever needed to be flattered or constantly built up. She had always prided herself on being self-assured—she was who she was, and it was entirely up to other people whether they decided to take it or leave it.

Yet now, suddenly, with Malachi, she found herself wondering how she measured up. What had his past lovers been like? How would her swelling body compare?

'You're not compelled to,' she rambled on, unable to stop herself. But this wasn't her. At least it wasn't who she wanted to be. All needy and timid.

'You can't seriously be asking me that question?'

He sounded…*angry*? Somehow—and Saskia had no idea how—she managed to tilt her head up and look him in the eye, to move away from this mousy stranger who inhabited her body.

'I would rather know.' She was going for confident, but she just sounded sharp.

Malachi cursed. Low, almost under his breath, but she heard it nonetheless.

'Strip,' he commanded.

Had she heard that right?

'Pardon?'

'Strip.'

His voice rasped over her, abrading her from the inside out. In an instant the fire smouldering within her kicked back into life.

'And then I shall demonstrate exactly how beautiful I think you are. Even more so now.'

It was all the reassurance Saskia needed. The hunger in his tone ignited her, like a match to petrol. Without taking another step towards him she locked her gaze with his, the blood pounding through her veins as she slid off her jumper. Taking her time, she began unbuttoning her shirt, and as Malachi inhaled sharply, heat spiralled through her.

A corkscrew of desire headed straight for her core. His eyes gleamed and she allowed it to slide down her shoulders before letting it fall to a puddle at her feet.

But if she'd thought he would fall at her feet, too, she'd been sorely mistaken. The truth hit her as if she'd been doused with a bucket of ice water. His eyes had stopped at her middle. Right where the obvious swell of her abdomen was showing.

And his hard gaze wasn't one of pride or tenderness.

'Malachi—' she began, not knowing what to say.

'You were right,' he cut in harshly. 'This isn't a good idea.'

Pain sliced through her. He was rejecting her—but, more than that, he was rejecting her baby.

Their baby.

Even though she'd known all along what kind of a man Malachi was—a businessman, not a family man—it didn't just hurt. It constricted her heart. As if he'd just thrust his fist inside her chest and was squeezing it.

She couldn't move. Couldn't even breathe. They both stood immobile, staring at each other, and the earth might as well have been splintering apart, fracturing, as a whole chasm opened up between them.

Abruptly, without a word, Malachi turned and strode out of the room.

And the soft closing of the door behind him echoed in Saskia's head, louder and with more finality than the last time he'd walked out on her, back at his penthouse a few months earlier.

Malachi had no idea where he was going. He'd marched around the *castello* before his brain had even registered where his body was taking him.

What the hell had he been thinking?

Somehow she had imprinted on him when he hadn't

been looking. So much for his assertion that marriage to Saskia was the *right and proper* thing to do, given the circumstances.

Deep down, he knew that was if not a lie, then surely only the half of it.

Deep down, he recognised that it wasn't completely honourable, the reason why he wanted Saskia as his bride; the truth was far worse.

Deep down, he understood that Saskia felt it, too.

Which made it all the more dangerous for them to be here in this *castello* in the middle of winter, together.

He couldn't risk staying. He wasn't sure he could trust himself around her.

The only thing he had to give her was his honour, his integrity. He couldn't give her the grand love she wanted but he had promised to protect her.

And their baby.

And so far he had failed at both things.

If anything had happened to his unborn baby because he had given in to this dark, intense...*thing* that twisted inside him, that craved her so desperately, he would never have forgiven himself.

It was a mistake to have married her, and it was a mistake to have brought her here.

She'd told him that ages ago, but he'd thought he knew better.

Turned out he wasn't the man he'd thought he was.

He certainly wasn't the man Saskia—or his baby— deserved.

CHAPTER FOURTEEN

'WHAT HAVE YOU got for me, ladies?' Saskia plastered a smile onto her face, as if that could convince the world that she was feeling happy inside.

Maybe one day she would finally be over Malachi Gunn enough to convince herself of the fact, too.

'Here she is—Moorlands General's little trooper.'

'Well, thank you, Babette,' she forced out, despite knowing perfectly well it hadn't been a compliment.

It never was. And it had been a long enough shift as it was, but Babette's constant sniping hadn't made things any easier. At least she would be out of here in less than an hour. Or should be, anyway.

'What have we got, Maggie?' She turned to the other nurse instead.

'Stella Jones, four years old, nasal foreign body. Previous intervention by parents and local GP, but his attempt to retrieve it only pushed the object further inside.'

'You won't be able to do anything,' Babette commented disparagingly. 'The family have been sent here for local anaesthetic before removal.'

Saskia very nearly bit her tongue—literally.

'I'll take a look anyway.'

'It's a waste of time.'

'Strangely enough, it's my job,' Saskia countered, taking a moment to peruse the notes in peace before heading towards the cubicle.

'Hello, Mrs Jones. I'm Saskia, and you must be...wait... let me guess... Stella.'

Stella cast her a woebegone look whilst her mother practically slumped with relief.

'Stella stuck a bead up her nose a couple of days ago. I tried to get it out, and so did our doctor, but it just won't come down.'

'Stella, would you mind if I had a little look?' Saskia used her softest voice.

Stella wriggled up the bed until her back was wedged into the corner of the wall and shook her head mutinously.

'I'm on her naughty list, too—for bringing her to all these doctors,' the mother offered a weak smile.

'It's a thankless task being a parent, isn't it?' Saskia sympathised, before cranking her smile up a notch and turning back to Stella. 'Has it been hurting a lot, sweetie?'

She was rewarded with a vigorous nod.

The notes said that the object wasn't visible on an anterior rhinoscopy, but she would like to see for herself.

'If I promise I won't try to get it out, would you just let me have a little look? I could pinkie swear?'

The little girl eyed her sceptically for what felt like an age.

'Please let the doctor look, flower,' Mrs Jones cajoled. 'We can't leave it up there—it will make you really ill.'

Stella turned to her mother and shook her head again, but this time it was a little less emphatic. Then she edged across the bed for a cuddle.

Not a bad sign, Saskia considered. It might take a little more careful treading and negotiation, but this might not take as long as she'd initially feared.

'What happened with the GP?' she asked the mother, making no move to approach Stella yet.

'What happened? Well, he looked up her nose and at first he could see the bead, so he tried to get it out with tweezers, but he couldn't. I think he might have pushed it up deeper, because afterwards he wasn't sure he could see it any more, but Stella wouldn't keep still so he couldn't get a proper look.'

'Okay, I see. So—what about this, sweetie?' Saskia kept her back against her seat as she faced the little girl again. 'I'll have a little look—just a look, no trying to get the bead out—and then, if I can see it, maybe Mummy can give you a big kiss and that might help to get the bead out for you.'

'A big kiss?' Stella's mother looked puzzled.

'It's called "the parent's kiss"—basically, it's something a trusted parent or adult can do for a young child, to help simulate the effect of a sneeze or a gentle nose-blow.'

'Will it really work?'

'It might. Especially with it being a small, smooth bead that Stella has put up there. It's certainly worth trying before we move on to anything more invasive. But I have to know if I can even see the object first.'

'Stella, flower, if you let the doctor check your nose, I think I might be able to get you that little puppy toy you liked.'

Stella perked up, so Saskia tried a stage whisper.

'I can definitely tell Mummy that you deserve a puppy toy if you're so brave.'

Within ten minutes, and after a little more cajoling, Saskia had the answer she needed, and now Stella was sitting upright on a chair, her back pressed against the fabric, and her mother was sitting, white-faced, in front of her.

'So, Stella, you're going to open your mouth just a little. Mum, you'll need to use your own mouth to make a seal around your daughter's. You'll press your thumb against the unobstructed nostril and then you'll exhale in a short, sharp puff.'

'Just one?'

'We can repeat the process up to five times, but just one at a time. When you're ready, go ahead.'

'How tightly do I press my thumb on her nostril?'

'Tightly enough to stop the air escaping. The more air that shoots down the obstructed nostril, the more chance it has to dislodge the bead.'

'Oh, I see.' Mrs Jones nodded suddenly. 'Okay. So… I just do it?'

'When you're ready.'

As the mother adjusted her grip on her daughter, Stella squirmed.

Saskia knelt down next to her. 'Don't worry sweetie,' she soothed. 'It's just going to be like a big kiss from Mummy. And the stiller you can stay, the more chance the bead will come out. And I would *love* that, because I don't want to have to try and get it with any of my instruments, and I don't think you want that either, do you?'

Another wild head-shake.

'Good,' encouraged Saskia. 'So, shall we let Mummy have a go at trying to help?'

A tentative nod.

'Clever girl. Okay, be brave and think of that toy puppy. You can look at me, if you like. I do a great Donald Duck impression.'

'Good call, Saskia,' Maggie commented as they finished discharging a much happier Stella. 'Don't you think, Babette?'

Babette sniffed, and Saskia supressed a ripple of ir-ritation. How long would she have to be practising as a doctor before she didn't let Babette get to her? Why did she even care?

'I guess…' Babette shrugged, giving the impression that it was anything but good. 'Hadn't you better be leaving soon, anyway? You don't want to turn up to the gala looking like *that*.'

'What gala?' Saskia regretted the question even as it was leaving her mouth.

'The Valentine's Day gala.' Babette stopped, a gleam instantly chasing the dullness from her expression. 'You don't know what I'm talking about, do you?'

Saskia didn't want to lie. But then, she didn't want to give Babette the upper hand, either.

'I know. I just forgot.' She managed to remain impressively nonchalant. 'I've got a prior engagement.'

'With a tub of ice cream and your pyjamas?' Babette snorted, clearly delighted with the turn of events. 'What could be more important than supporting your husband—the father of your unborn baby—in his biggest charity dinner to date?'

There was no pretending now. Not on either side. Babette was practically purring as she licked the proverbial cream from her whiskers, whilst Saskia felt so winded she was astonished she wasn't on her back on the cold floor of the corridor, staring up at the stark white ceiling.

'Andy has been reminding me about it for months. Making sure I've got everything I need. New dress, sexy heels, gorgeous jewellery…'

The woman was really laying it on thickly now. Saskia bared her teeth and hoped it would pass for a cold smile.

'He really does take care of me—but you know how that feels, don't you, Saskia? Then again…maybe you don't. I *do* hope I haven't caused any offence.'

Saskia had no idea how she managed to open her mouth, let alone speak. She certainly didn't recognise the airy, almost amused voice that came out of it.

'Oh, don't you worry about me, Babette. Now that I'm

out of a toxic relationship and in a much more mature one I don't take offence so easily. It's amazing what a secure partnership does for a person.'

'So secure that you didn't even know about the Valentine's gala the Gunn brothers are holding in order to raise money for their precious charity Careful Playing?' Babette shot back.

But Saskia noticed that the woman didn't sound quite as confident as she had before.

She ramped her smile up a notch. 'Care to Play.'

'Play what?' Babette snapped, now clearly rattled. 'I'm not playing at anything.'

Oh, I think you are.

'Malachi's charity is called Care to Play. It provides a safe centre for young carers to just be kids for a few hours and forget their usual responsibilities. I've volunteered there several times, but Malachi wanted me to ease back until the baby is born.'

That much, at least, was true.

'Maybe he just doesn't want you around,' sneered Babette, having finally dispensed with any attempt at veiling her snipes. 'Have you ever thought that perhaps he doesn't *want* you sticking your nose into other areas of his life, and concern about your pregnancy is just a convenient excuse?'

It was galling how closely her words seemed to mirror all of Saskia's deepest fears. It just proved what a viper the woman was.

But Saskia wasn't about to let her know how acutely her words cut. 'Surely you're not suggesting that Malachi's concern for our baby isn't genuine?' She shook her head, managing to appear genuinely bemused.

'No. I was suggesting—'

'Oh, well, that's a relief,' Saskia cut in swiftly, realising she'd just been handed a way to use Babette's earlier words against her. 'I could only imagine how *offended* he would be if he thought what I just did.'

'What? No...'

But Saskia was already striding down the corridor as fast as she could, head held deliberately high, before Babette could regain her footing and hit her with a typically cutting comeback.

However, the reality was that any sense of victory she was feeling in that moment was fleeting. Any moment now Babette's remarks were going to circle back in her head, echoing all the fears she'd been trying to push aside for what felt like for ever.

Malachi hadn't invited her to the gala tonight. He hadn't even told her about it. His life was so neat, so ordered, with each part of it separate from the others. His work life, his charity, his personal life...

Not one seemed to cross the divide between one and another. Not even her.

Especially not her.

Sadness, and something else she couldn't—*wouldn't?*—put a name to, trickled through her.

They lived together, they were husband and wife, and they were expecting a baby together. Yet in all other areas they might as well be complete strangers.

Saskia didn't know whether that was her fault or Malachi's. She only knew that one of them was going to have to make the first move if they wanted to resolve it.

So why not her?

And why not tonight?

'What the hell do you think you're doing here?'

He gripped her elbow tightly, manoeuvring her off the floor.

It was all Saskia could do to hide her surprise and

school her features into some semblance of a smile as he ushered her firmly through the throng.

'I'm here to support you,' she managed in a low voice, once they were out of the way of the main crowd. 'To support your charity.'

He expelled air slowly through his teeth, making a hissing sound.

'You're not needed, Saskia. Go home.'

'On Valentine's Day? At a ball for couples?'

'You're not needed, Saskia,' he repeated, his teeth gritted.

'But I *want* to be here.'

She would have thought that his expression couldn't darken any further, yet somehow it managed it.

'You have no place here.'

A closeness tightened around her. She tried to fight it.

'I'm your wife…' The whispered plea fell from her lips, but it didn't seem to soften the granite-faced Malachi towards her at all. If anything, he appeared all the more impenetrable.

'So stay in that part of my life. I don't want you in this part.'

She wasn't hearing him right. She couldn't be.

Panic threatened to overtake her.

'You can't pigeonhole your life like that.'

'I can. I do. My business life and my charity work have always been two distinct areas of my life. They don't mix and they don't need to. Why should our crafted marriage be any different?'

'Because…it *is*,' she cried helplessly. 'Because *we're* different. Whatever this was meant to be at the start, it's real now, and we're having a baby together. Or is our baby not real to you any more? Is she not welcome in your life?'

He advanced on her. So close that she couldn't stop herself from backing up, right into the wall behind her. It reminded her of that night back in his apartment at Christmas time. Except this time when he lifted his arms and placed his hands on either side of her head it felt more like a cage than ever.

'Our baby is the *only* real thing about all this,' he said.

His voice was rasping. Much too rough for her to mistake the emotion in it. Not that she was about to.

'And she will always be welcome in my life. *All* areas of my life. And she will be loved more than you can imagine.'

'And yet here I am, the mother of that child, and you don't even want me dipping a toe into the waters of any other part of your life.'

She barely recognised her own voice—it was loaded with something she couldn't quite identify. Or didn't want to.

'You're a master at compartmentalising your life, aren't you?'

She realised her voice was too sharp, too high, but she couldn't stop it. And his expression was so bleak, so haunted, that it scraped inside her. Like a scalpel blade to her chest wall. And when he spoke, in that distant, cold tone, she half expected her skin to freeze and blacken with frostbite.

'You say it like it's a bad thing. Besides, I would have thought that was something you would welcome. After all, it benefits you, too.'

'How does it remotely *benefit* me?' she exploded.

'We aren't a couple, Saskia. We never were. I was your rebound and then you fell pregnant. But I was never the man you were in love with.'

And suddenly everything fell into place.

The simple truth roared through Saskia and she wanted to scream, and laugh, and sob—all at the same time.

He loved her. This beautiful, impossible, impenetrable man loved her—perhaps as much as she loved him.

He just didn't know it yet.

She lifted her hand, tentatively at first, and touched it to his chest, taking heart when he didn't pull away as she'd feared he would.

'You were never just my rebound, Malachi,' she whispered. 'You were always more than that.'

She heard a beat of silence. The moment when he absorbed what she'd said. But she should have known it wouldn't be that easy.

'I don't believe you, *zvyozdochka*.'

Her heart kicked. He'd given himself away with just that one term of endearment, and now her spirit was beginning to soar.

She lifted her hand to cup his cheek. 'It's true. I might not have realised it before, but I know it now. In my entire life I've never done anything like have a one-night stand. I'd only ever been with one man…'

'Whom you loved,' he reminded her grimly. 'You told me as much that first night.'

'I was wrong,'

'You want me to believe that you didn't love him?' He eyed her sceptically.

'I did love him. At the time. Or at least I loved what I thought we had. The fact that he cheated on me—and if we're being honest who knows if Babette was the only one?—means that he was never the man I thought he was. Ergo, I could never have loved him. Not really…'

She faltered, waiting for him to speak. But he didn't. Still, his gaze never left hers. She had no choice but to forge on.

'I think what I was in love with was the *idea* of what we had. But then I met you, and we had that crazy weekend. After that it was all you. You were the one I thought about. You were the one who threw out the questions and *what ifs* in my head. And then I discovered I was pregnant, and

I think that was the excuse I'd been looking for to talk to you again. To see if maybe you'd thought about me, too.'

Silence stretched out between them. All Saskia could hear was ragged breathing. Hers? His? Probably both.

Abruptly Malachi pushed himself off the wall, taking a few steps back. Away from her. She almost reached out to stop him, but knew it would be a mistake.

'But you didn't come to talk to me,' he said. 'You didn't approach me at all. In fact, the first chance you had to see me you ran away from me. You recall that, of course?' He was challenging her. 'You aren't trying to rewrite history?'

'Yes, I recall that. We were in a consultation room. I was at work. You were there for my patient and her family. And… And I had no idea how to tell you that I was pregnant.'

'That's pitiful, *zvyozdochka*.'

'You may be right.' She straightened her shoulders. 'But that doesn't make it any less true.'

His glower deepened. It couldn't be a good sign that he wouldn't even look at her. Instead, his glare was directed at some unseen spot on the wall behind her.

'I was frightened and I was lost. I wasn't sure if I could do it on my own. And then you made it so I didn't have to. When I went in for that emergency scan, when they discovered that our baby was…' She choked on the words, swallowed, then pushed on. 'You were there with me every single step. You made sure I knew we were going through it all together. And I love you for that.'

'You do *not* love me, *zvyozdochka*,' he countered angrily. 'If I am not mistaken, what you feel—what you have described—is gratitude. They are not the same thing.'

She was losing him. She could see it right in front of her eyes and she was wholly powerless to stop it.

Fresh panic bubbled up inside her. 'So now you presume to tell me what I feel?'

'When you're claiming things which cannot possibly be true, then, *yes*. I'm not the kind of man you want, Saskia. Haven't you told me that a thousand times? I do not show my emotions the way you want. I don't speak the words of love you want to hear. I won't give you the poetry and the flowers you seem to think are proof of love. You believe in all of that, yet I do not.'

'And I was wrong!' she exclaimed. 'I got caught up in the hurt of being betrayed and I lost sight of what it means to actually love someone. I thought I needed those big, romantic gestures. It turns out I don't. I just need truth and honesty. I just need *you*, Malachi.'

A storm was raging within him. She saw it blustering over every one of his features. Watched its unobstructed trail. Knew it left devastation in its wake.

'I'm not the right man for you,' he bit out, turning his back on her and moving towards the ballroom. 'I will always be there for our baby, but I don't want you in the other areas of my life. Go home, Saskia. You're free at last.'

'I don't want to be free.'

'And *I* don't want you here.'

As he walked away, swallowed up by the crowd and carried out of her sight, Saskia slumped back against the wall and marvelled at just how badly she'd managed to mess things up.

CHAPTER FIFTEEN

'OKAY, SO ROSIE is a ten-year-old female with a BMI of nineteen. She presented with abdominal pain and a diagnosis of non-complicated gallstone was made. Elective laparoscopic cholecystectomy has been scheduled for today.'

Saskia listened as her colleague ran through the surgery planned for the young patient.

She wouldn't go to the surgery, and knew this briefing was for the benefit of the surgical interns in the room, but she appreciated knowing what her patient was about to face. It gave her a greater depth of understanding, especially when talking to her patients later about post-op care—although of course the surgeon would have run through everything with the family.

'We'll place her supine, in a reverse position, at a thirty-degree angle, making a ten-millimetre incision at the umbilicus and pneumoperitoneum positions...'

Besides, work had always been her saviour when times were rough. She could always trust her job to refocus her brain and show her what really mattered. But this time was different. This time—even though she would never let her patients down or become distracted when it mattered—she couldn't shake Malachi, or the hold he seemed to have over her.

'And inserting two percutaneous atraumatic graspers

into the abdomen via small incisions on the right side and on the mid-clavicular line…'

Her mind wandered to Rosie's parents. For the longest time she'd thought that Kevin, her father, was less concerned about his daughter, leaving her mother to ask the questions and try to understand what was going on with their daughter.

'The cystic duct and artery will be clipped, and the gallbladder extracted through the umbilical porthole…'

Perhaps she should have known better. She'd been a doctor long enough. But when she'd seen him take the surgeon's hand and heard him speak, low and sure, she'd realised that he didn't *need* to say much. He showed who he was, how supportive he was, by his actions, and in the way he didn't try to control the situation, letting his wife ask all the questions she needed whilst he absorbed everything, ready to talk through it with her when they were alone. A constant tower of support for both his wife and daughter.

Much like Malachi had been for her. And for their own baby.

Why had she thought she needed words and promises from him? Instead, he showed her who he was by every action and every deed.

When she'd needed him—when there had been complications with their baby—he had been there instantly. Always. Never leaving her side, and never letting her feel she was alone.

Because he *loved* her.

She'd been waiting and waiting, desperate to hear him say it, angry with herself, and him, when he hadn't. Waiting for beautiful, poetic words of love—more grandiose than anything Andy had ever said to her—which would prove to her that what was between her and Malachi was real.

She'd thought that after Andy's betrayal she'd need Malachi to go bigger and better than anything her ex-fiancé had ever done. Suddenly, she realised her mistake.

She was an idiot.

Because Malachi had done that.

She just hadn't been paying attention.

He had told her he loved her through every little thing he'd done for her. And for their baby. He just didn't know how to say the words.

But she could teach him, now that she understood him better.

Although she couldn't just go to him and tell him. After all the other things she'd said he would never believe her. She needed to prove it to him—to make that gesture she'd yearned for from him. She owed him that much.

Malachi slammed his fist down on the heavy, burr walnut desk.

He couldn't stand it any longer.

Thrusting his chair back from the desk, Malachi stood. He leaned over to activate the intercom to his secretary.

'I need you to arrange the helicopter for me, Geraldine.'

Geraldine's voice came clearly, crisply, through the speaker. 'Of course. Where to, sir?'

'Moorlands General,' he said decisively. 'Now, please.'

'Yes, sir.'

He was just about to terminate the communication when he heard her startled voice.

'Wait…you can't go in there…'

He'd reached for the switch to deactivate the privacy control on the glass wall when the door to his office burst open and Saskia strode boldly in.

'If you're looking for me, I'm right here.'

She placed her bag down and closed the door behind her, but he noticed that she didn't approach his desk. Perhaps not as bold as he'd first thought. The faint tremor in her hands suggested her confidence was a front.

Still, it had momentarily thrown him.

'So you are,' he bit out.

She looked well. Better than well. Her cheeks were red, as though she'd been walking outside in the cold, and her tousled hair made him think she'd recently tugged off one of those warm woolly hats she favoured. But it was the overcoat, pulled tight and cinched over the ever-expanding bump which took most of his attention.

Their baby.

'Well?' she demanded, as the quiet shimmered around the space.

'Sorry?'

'What were you coming to the hospital for?'

He glowered at her for a long moment before answering. 'To see you.'

'Well, it's good that I'm here, then.' Her eyes flashed, a frenetic expression whirling through them. 'I saved you the trouble.'

If he'd had to guess, he might have thought her nervous. Although the Saskia he knew had never been nervous about anything.

That said, she was bouncing around the room in a way he'd never seen her do before.

'Take a seat,' he suggested, fighting to slow his accelerating heartbeat.

'No.' She shook her head. 'Thanks. Are you ready to go?'

'To go where?'

'You'll see.'

And with that she practically danced out of the room, leaving him with little choice but to grab his suit jacket and heavy woollen coat and follow.

He caught up with her just as the lift pinged, ready to

take them down to the lobby. She was bobbing from one side to the other, shifting her weight as though she couldn't bear to be still for even an instant.

'Just slow down, Saskia. I haven't even called the car round to meet us outside.'

'No need.' She bustled them both out of the lift. 'We can walk.'

It was ridiculous, but her barely restrained excitement was infectious. Malachi found himself swept along in it even as he followed her.

'Walk where?'

'I told you—you'll see.'

He wanted to tell her that nothing had changed. That he still couldn't give her all the romance and sentiment she wanted. But he couldn't bring himself to speak; he didn't want to burst this little bubble of hers into which he could already feel himself being drawn.

It might be just an illusion, but it was one in which he wanted to revel—if only for a few more minutes.

And, besides, something had changed.

He'd realised that what he felt for her was—if not love itself—the closest thing he was ever going to get to it. She was like a fire, drawing him in from the cold. Her heat and her laughter had thawed him out when he'd thought he would never feel warm in his life.

It was why he let her lead him through the lobby now, watching her pull her woolly hat down over her curls before glancing over her shoulder to him and preceding him out of the revolving doors.

The streets were slick with rain, and he reached for her arm instinctively, wrapping it around his and ensuring that she didn't slip. And the wide smile she shot him kick-started some new alien sensation inside him.

It was as though she welcomed his care. As though she understood it for what it was.

Even if he wasn't quite sure that *he* did.

'Not far now,' she murmured, and he knew he wasn't imagining the nervous tremor in her tone, despite her overly bright smile.

It was only when they turned into the town hall that the wheels in his head finally began to spin.

'Saskia, what's going on?'

'Shh…nearly there,' she chided with a shaky laugh—but her voice cracked and betrayed her.

Moorlands Register Office.

'Did you know it's a leap year this year?'

Normally he would have known, but this past week had blurred into itself so much that for once he had to stop and think.

'Is it?'

'It is,' she confirmed, her voice pitched higher than usual. 'And even though it might be the wrong month, I… thought I'd take advantage.'

'Advantage?' he echoed numbly.

'You were right all those months ago when you told me I was only holding out for a passionate love like my parents' because deep down I knew it had never really existed. It gave me the excuse I needed to keep people away—just like you do. Only at least you were more honest with yourself about what you were doing.'

'No, I don't think I was,' he refuted. The words were coming out without him intending them to. 'I think *you* were right. I thought I had come to terms with my childhood in a way Sol never had, but all I was doing was keeping it in front of me to…what did you say?…use as a shield.'

'So we've both taught each other something?'

Saskia smiled, and a shard of light pierced through him in an instant.

He'd grown so accustomed to the gloom in his world

that he'd thought it was normal. Fine. But now he'd seen everything bathed in the vibrant colours of Saskia how was he ever to go back to that darkness?

'Why are we here, *zvyozdochka*?' he demanded, perhaps a little more sharply than he'd intended.

But she didn't blink—she just rewarded him with another of her dazzling smiles.

'You taught me that all the words of love and poetry I was holding out for don't bring much to the table after all. You taught me that actions really do speak louder than words, and you showed me how much you love me...*us*,' she corrected, smoothing a hand over her ever-growing abdomen. 'So now it's my turn.'

'This is unnecessary—' he began.

And yet he was doing nothing to move away from her. He certainly wasn't leaving. He was just standing there, breathing her in, trying to hold himself back from the insane need to cover her mouth with his and claim her as his.

His for ever.

'On the contrary, this is *entirely* necessary.' She cut across him. 'This is me proving to you that I don't need grand romantic gestures. I just need the little things that *mean* something.'

'Is that so?'

'It is.'

'And some grand, romantic gesture...?' His mouth twitched, but the gleam in his eyes reassured her.

'Ironic, isn't it?' she said merrily. 'Now, we're already married, so I can't propose. But I *can* organise a renewal of vows. A chance for us to recommit to each other when we both know exactly what we're doing—and why. And a chance for us to do so in front of the two people we care about the most.'

Malachi knew, even before Sol and Anouk stepped

around the corner, that his brother was going to be there. The one person he would have wanted to see him make a commitment to the woman of his dreams. It was as if she knew.

But maybe that was the point. Maybe Saskia really *did* know what he wanted and needed. She understood him, and she accepted him for what he was. And, after all, wasn't that the true measure of love?

'I think, Mrs Gunn,' he managed hoarsely, reaching out to haul her into his arms, bump and all, 'that I love you a little more every single day. And I want you in my life for the rest of time.'

'I'm pretty sure I can manage that,' she whispered, even as his mouth covered hers.

And her arms wrapped around him so tightly he hoped she would never let go.

Baby Gunn was born a mere week premature, with ten perfect toes and nine and a half perfect fingers. Her ankles still bore the scars of the amniotic bands, but Z-plasty would remedy that, just as a few months of night braces would correct the slight clubbing the bands had caused on her tiny chubby legs.

But to Saskia and Malachi their daughter looked beautiful. Their perfect baby, who had truly made their family whole.

* * * * *

MILLS & BOON

Coming next month

A FLING TO STEAL HER HEART
Sue MacKay

Raphael let himself into the house and stopped. Paint fumes hit him. A foreign lightness in the hall made him gape. Wow. What a difference. Should've done it years ago. Except there'd been no motivation before. Izzy had changed everything.

She stood at the bottom of the stairs, dressed in over-large paint-spattered overalls with a roller in one hand and a wide grin on her face. A paint smear streaked across her cheek. Cute. Sexy. 'What do you think?'

I think I want to kiss that spot.

His stomach crunched, his blood hummed.

I think I want to kiss your soft lips and taste you.

Forget humming. There was a torrent in his veins. He was over waiting, being patient, giving her time. He had to do something about his feelings for her.

Dragging his eyes away from the sight that had him in meltdown, he looked around at the white with a hint of grey walls, woodwork, ceiling, and felt his mouth lifting into a smile that grew and grew. 'Amazing. Who'd have believed getting rid of that magenta could make such a difference. This hall is twice the size it was when I went to work this morning.'

'That's a relief.' She placed the roller in the clean tray.

'You were worried I wouldn't like it?' He stepped closer, put his keys and phone on the bottom stair and stood there watching the varying emotions flitting through her beautiful old-wood-coloured eyes.

'Not really.' Her teeth nibbling her lip told him otherwise.

He had to force himself not to reach over and place a finger on her lips to stop her action. 'Why wouldn't I? It was me who bought the paint two years ago.'

Izzy shifted her weight from one foot to the other, then lifted her head enough to lock those eyes on his. 'I worried I've overstepped the mark by doing this without telling you what I was up to.'

Izzy never worried about upsetting him. Carrying on with whatever she thought best was a trademark of their friendship, always had been, and was one of the reasons he adored her. Something was off centre here, and it frustrated him not knowing what that was. 'Relax. I'm more than happy with what you've done. In fact, I'm blown away.' He waved a hand at his new hall. 'This is amazing. It fires me up to get on with doing up the rest of the house.'

He hadn't noticed the tension in her shoulders until they softened, and a smile touched those lips. 'Thank you, Isabella.'

Her eyes widened and she glanced away, came back to lock eyes with him again. The tip of her tongue appeared at the corner of her mouth. 'Phew.'

Raphael could not stop himself. He reached out, placed his hands on her arms and drew her closer. 'Again, thanks. By doing this you've starting turning my house into a home and up until now I hadn't realised how important it is if I'm to continue living here and become ensconced in a London lifestyle, not just working at the hospital every available hour.'

She was shaking under his hands.

His thumbs smoothed circles on her arms. 'Izzy.'

Her breasts rose, stilled, dropped again. 'Rafe.'

Afterwards he didn't remember moving, couldn't recall anything but his mouth on hers at last. Soft. Sweet. Isabella. Strong, tough Izzy. Returning his kiss. Returning his kiss!

Continue reading
A FLING TO STEAL HER HEART
Sue MacKay

Available next month
www.millsandboon.co.uk

COMING SOON!

We really hope you enjoyed reading this book. If you're looking for more romance, be sure to head to the shops when new books are available on

Thursday 20th March

To see which titles are coming soon, please visit

millsandboon.co.uk/nextmonth

LET'S TALK
Romance

For exclusive extracts, competitions
and special offers, find us online:

f facebook.com/millsandboon

🐦 @MillsandBoon

📷 @MillsandBoonUK

Get in touch on 01413 063232

For all the latest titles coming soon, visit
millsandboon.co.uk/nextmonth

JOIN THE
MILLS & BOON
BOOKCLUB

* **FREE** delivery direct to your door

* **EXCLUSIVE** offers every month

* **EXCITING** rewards programme

50% OFF YOUR FIRST PARCEL

Join today at
Millsandboon.co.uk/Bookclub